T0025489

Rumi, known in Iran and Central Asia as Mowlana Jalaloddin Balkhi, was born in 1207 in the province of Balkh, now the border region between Afghanistan and Tajikistan. His family emigrated when he was still a child, shortly before Genghis Khan and his Mongol army arrived in Balkh. They settled permanently in Konya, Central Anatolia, which was formerly part of the Eastern Roman Empire (Rum). Rumi was probably introduced to Sufism originally through his father, Baha Valad, a popular preacher who also taught Sufi piety to a group of disciples. However, the turning-point in Rumi's life came in 1244, when he met in Konya a mysterious wandering Sufi called Shamsoddin of Tabriz. Shams, as he is most often referred to by Rumi, taught him the profoundest levels of Sufism, trans-forming him from a pious religious scholar to an ecstatic mystic. Rumi expressed his new vision of reality in volumes of mystical poetry. His enor-mous collection of lyrical poetry is considered one of the best that has ever been produced, while his poem in rhyming couplets, *The Masnavi*, is so revered as the most consummate expression of Sufi mysticism that it is commonly referred to as 'the Qur'an in Persian'.

When Rumi died, on 17 December 1273, shortly after having completed his work on *The Masnavi*, his passing was deeply mourned by the citizens of Konya, including the Christian and Jewish communities. His disciples formed the Mevlevi Sufi order, which was named after Rumi, whom they referred to as 'Our Lord' (Turkish 'Mevlana'/Persian 'Mowlana'). They are better known in Europe and North America as the Whirling Dervishes, because of the distinctive dance that they now perform as one of their cen-tral rituals. Rumi's death is commemorated annually in Konya, attracting pilgrims from all corners of the globe and every religion. The popularity of his poetry has risen so much in the last couple of decades that the *Christian Science Monitor* identified Rumi as the most published poet in America in 1997.

Jawid Mojaddedi, a native of Afghanistan, is Professor of Religion at Rutgers University. He was a 2014–15 National Endowment for the Arts Literature Translation Fellow and a 2020–1 National Endowment for the Humanities Fellow. Dr Mojaddedi's translation, *The Masnavi: Book One* (Oxford, 2004), was awarded the Lois Roth Prize by the American Institute of Iranian Studies. His other books include *Beyond Dogma: Rumi's Teachings on Friendship with God and Early Sufi Theories* (Oxford, 2012) and *The Biographical Tradition in Sufism* (Richmond, 2001).

OXFORD WORLD'S CLASSICS

*For over 100 years Oxford World's Classics have brought
readers closer to the world's great literature. Now with over 700
titles—from the 4,000-year-old myths of Mesopotamia to the
twentieth century's greatest novels—the series makes available
lesser-known as well as celebrated writing.*

*The pocket-sized hardbacks of the early years contained
introductions by Virginia Woolf, T. S. Eliot, Graham Greene,
and other literary figures which enriched the experience of reading.
Today the series is recognized for its fine scholarship and
reliability in texts that span world literature, drama and poetry,
religion, philosophy, and politics. Each edition includes perceptive
commentary and essential background information to meet the
changing needs of readers.*

OXFORD WORLD'S CLASSICS

JALAL AL-DIN RUMI

The Masnavi

BOOK FIVE

Translated with an Introduction and Notes by
JAWID MOJADDEDI

OXFORD
UNIVERSITY PRESS

OXFORD
UNIVERSITY PRESS

Great Clarendon Street, Oxford, OX2 6DP,
United Kingdom

Oxford University Press is a department of the University of Oxford.
It furthers the University's objective of excellence in research, scholarship,
and education by publishing worldwide. Oxford is a registered trade mark of
Oxford University Press in the UK and in certain other countries

First published as an Oxford World's Classics paperback 2022

Impression: 1

Published in the United States of America by Oxford University Press
198 Madison Avenue, New York, NY 10016, United States of America

British Library Cataloguing in Publication Data

Data available

Library of Congress Control Number: 2022938920

ISBN 978-0-19-285707-1

Printed and bound in the UK by
Clays Ltd, Elcograf S.p.A

for Ladan and Elias

ACKNOWLEDGEMENTS

I SHOULD like to express my gratitude to my immediate family, my friends, and all of the teachers I have studied under. I am indebted to Rutgers University for a sabbatical in Spring 2017 and to the National Endowment for the Humanities for awarding me a fellowship for the academic year 2020–1, during which time most of this translation was completed. I alone am responsible for any flaws.

CONTENTS

Introduction   xiii

Note on the Translation   xxii

Select Bibliography   xxiv

A Chronology of Rumi   xxvii

THE MASNAVI

BOOK FIVE

Prose Introduction   3

Exordium   4

'Take four birds and turn them towards you!'   5

   The Prophet Mohammad's gluttonous guest
     defecates all over his bedding   9

   Outward words and actions reveal inner light   14

   How God makes water clean   15

   How the food of the spirit can nourish the body too   20

   The Angel Gabriel's knowledge from the Preserved
     Tablet and that of ordinary people   22

   Finding the direction for prayer and diving in the sea 22

   'Alas for the slaves of God'   23

   The reason why *'faraji'* was first used for the garment
     of that name   24

   Why Abraham killed the peacock   26

   God's hidden mercy and wrath   28

   The original nature of intellects   30

   The Bedouin whose dog was dying of hunger while
     his bag was full of food   31

   The eye of self-approval   32

   'Those who disbelieve cause you to slip with their gaze.'   33

The peacock which tore out its beautiful feathers 34

How thoughts disturb the purity of the soul 36

In explanation of the Prophet's words: *'There is
no monasticism in Islam'* 37

The lover of God's reward is God Himself 37

'None died without later wishing that they had
died before they actually did.' 38

How intellect and spirit are confined like Harut
and Marut 39

Skills, wealth, and cleverness are like the peacock's
feathers 41

Selfless ones who are safe from their own vices
and virtues 42

Everything other than God is eating and being eaten 45

Why Abraham killed the crow 48

The three types of men one should pity 51

The deer fawn stuck in the donkey stable 52

Shi'ites have to produce someone called 'Abu Bakr' 52

'I saw seven fat cows which seven thin cows ate up.' 57

Why Abraham killed the rooster 58

'We reduced him to the lowest of the lows' . . . *'We make
him regress in creation.'* 59

The existing world and the non-existing world 63

'The companions when you die are your deeds.' 64

'And He is with you' 66

The need to reduce one's preoccupations 66

The door will be opened if you head there 68

Story about the man who claimed to be a Prophet 69

The reason why ordinary people oppose the Friends
of God 71

Evildoers prevent good works 72

A lover recounts all he has done for his beloved 76

'There is no prayer except with presence of heart' 78

Don't compare yourself with your Master! 79

Having sex with a donkey can have fatal consequences 83

God's use of the Master as a mirror for communication 89

Puppies barking in their mother's belly and false claimants 90

The people of Zarwan and their envy of the poor 92

God's bestowal does not require receptivity 96

God's forming of the human body of clay with the help of His Archangels 101

    The mystic recognizes that people are instruments for God 105

The harm of food 109

The folly of wishing the world would last forever 110

The mercy of God, who bestows gifts before they have even been earned 111

Ayaz and the rustic boots and old fleece coat in his closet 115

    Beyond the outward form of the story 118

    Satan and the Jinn 120

    Seeing things as they really are 122

    The union of lover and beloved, who are opposites of each other 124

    'Who do you love more—me or yourself?' 125

    Let's try silence and restraint instead of talking 133

    The ascetic caught by his wife having sex with his maidservant 134

    The repentance of Nasuh, the bathhouse worker who looked like a woman 138

        The mystic's prayer is like God's prayer to Himself 139

    The lion, the fox, and the donkey 147

        The Spiritual Axis Mundi as nurturer 148

        The firewood-seller's donkey who bemoaned its fate 149

The ascetic who relied on God to provide for him   150

A camel claims to have come from the hot baths   152

The call of the enlightened Masters   155

The male prostitute and his client   156

The man who feared for his own life when the
   king was confiscating donkeys   158

The seriousness of breaking a pledge   161

Shaikh Mohammad Sarrazi and his instructions
   directly from God   166

*'If it were not for you, I would not have created
   the heavens.'*   170

The excellence of abstention and hunger   176

A Master reads a greedy disciple's mind   176

The cow who could not relax with confidence
   about food for the next day   177

The ecstatic monk   180

A Muslim invites a Magian to become a Muslim like him   181

The parable about Satan at God's door   183

Free will or predestination?   188

The thief and the chief of police   190

The apple thief and the owner of the orchard   191

'Whatever God wills happens . . . His will is the effective will.' 193

The meaning of *'The ink has dried.'*   194

The dervish who told God to learn how to take care
   of His slaves   196

Majnun's family tell him there are women more
   beautiful than Laili   203

How Johi the prankster got a woman to touch his penis   205

To become a Muslim like you or one like Bayazid?   207

The muezzin with a terrible voice and the grateful
   Non-Muslim   208

If the cat ate the meat, why hasn't it gained its weight?   210

The prince and the ascetic who smashed his pitcher
of wine   212

Ziya Dalq and his brother, the Shaikh al-Islam
of Balkh   214

Dalqak the jester checkmates the Shah in a game
of chess   216

The Prophet Mohammad and Gabriel on
Mount Hira   218

The next realm is real life, if they but knew   221

The guesthouse for thoughts   224

The host's naked wife makes their guest feel unwelcome   224

A father advises his daughter not to let her husband get
her pregnant   228

The pampered Sufi who imagines he can be a warrior   230

Why Eyazi turned from the Lesser Jihad to the Greater Jihad   233

Why a holy warrior threw away his money coin by coin   235

Egypt's king falls in love with Mosul's king's new lover   236

The weakness of the argument of deniers of
the next world   241

God has allotted   247

Shah Mahmud tests Ayaz and his ministers with a pearl   251

Pharaoh's magicians said, '*There's no harm for us.
We are heading to our Lord.*'   253

Explanatory Notes   261

Glossary   281

INTRODUCTION

Book Five of The Masnavi

RUMI'S *Masnavi* is probably the longest mystical poem ever written by a single author from any religious tradition. It consists of about 26,000 verses, divided into six books. The current volume is a translation of the fifth book of *The Masnavi*, and follows Books One, Two, Three, and Four, also published in Oxford World's Classics.

Book Five of *The Masnavi* has possibly become in recent decades the most widely discussed book of the entire poem because of its high number of sexually explicit passages. These passages were notoriously translated into Latin by Reynold A. Nicholson (d. 1945) in the only previous English translation of the entire volume, as was the convention in early twentieth-century Britain for material considered salacious. This censorship has predictably aroused extra curiosity among readers, although most academic commentators have dismissively chosen to avoid discussing such stories seriously. It is important to point out that the original text does not render such material into a different language or try to censor it in any way. Rather, clear and simple language is used to the point of extreme crudeness in the case of genitals and their fluids. This translation strives to be true to the spirit of the original by rendering such passages into similarly simple and explicit English with crudeness as an inevitable consequence.

Readers of Persian literature will know that Rumi is not particularly unusual for including sexual content in a mystical *masnavi* poem, which can be seen even in the English translation of ʿAttar's *Conference of the Birds*.[1] However, as Mahdi Tourage has pointed out in his sophisticated Lacanian analysis of the sexually explicit stories in *The Masnavi*, Rumi does stand apart for his use of crudely graphic detail.[2] While such passages have attracted a disproportionate amount of attention from contemporary readers because of this unusual characteristic, this may have resulted in overlooking the main point Rumi is

---

[1] See e.g. F. Attar, *The Conference of the Birds*, ed. and tr. A. Darbandi and D. Davis (rev. edn, Harmondsworth, 2011), 212–16.

[2] M. Tourage, *Rumi and the Hermeneutics of Eroticism* (Leiden, 2007), 18–25.

trying to convey in this volume, for which the use of crude language
is a useful tool.

Aside from the sexually explicit stories, what stands out in Book
Five is the portrayal of Ayaz as the perfect aspirant and disciple,
whose actions undeservedly attract suspicion and blame from others.
The story is about his secret closet which contained his old rustic
boots and fleece coat as a constant reminder to himself of his modest
origins, and not gold and treasure to the disappointment of those sus-
picious that he was hiding some form of inner corruption with his
secrecy (vv. 1859–). The sexually explicit stories also tend to portray
actual corruption that has been hidden secretly in some way. This is
most obvious in the story of the ascetic who is caught by his wife hav-
ing just had sex with their maidservant because he memorably tries to
hide his secret by standing up to pray—his wife notices the semen
dripping from his penis underneath his long shirt (vv. 2165–2206). In
the story about having sex with a donkey, which is probably the most
talked about of such material, both the slave-girl and her mistress
strive to keep their sexual activity with the animal a secret (vv. 1335–1431).
Moreover, these stories are preceded by the first major story of Book
Five, which is about the gluttonous guest of the Prophet Mohammad
who defecates in his bed and then rushes away to avoid becoming
exposed (vv. 64–288). Immediately before this multi-section story
one finds the exegetical passage that identifies four different birds
with different corruptions of the soul: out of these the duck represents
the guest's greed and the rooster the lustfulness of characters in the
sexually explicit stories (vv. 31–63). All of this is to say that it is more
accurate to see the sexually explicit stories as expansions of this topic
regarding the corruptions of the soul.

One can also see the unusually graphic detail Rumi provides as
functioning to underline the shame involved in such crude behaviour
that motivates the attempts to hide it as a secret, from having sex with
a donkey or committing adultery to defecating in bed as a guest of an
important person. The same theme of hiding secretively such cor-
ruptions of the soul later comes into play in the aforementioned story
about Ayaz and his old rustic boots and fleece coat locked up in
a closet—his rivals' suspicions are based on the assumption that his
secret must be a shameful corruption. Therefore, if the high amount
of sexually explicit content in Book Five is seen in the context of all
of the content in this volume, it can be seen as fitting here because

sexual lust is something that the spiritually inclined prefer to keep secret, especially if they are cultivating a pious reputation.

As an alternative to this more empirical reading, one can approach the sexually explicit material through the lens of Jacques Lacan's psychoanalytical theories, as Tourage has done in his *Rumi and the Hermeneutics of Eroticism* (Leiden, 2007). For instance, he points out that Rumi himself equates the preacher's self-aggrandizing sermon with Johi's penis in his story 'How Johi the prankster got a woman to touch his penis', through the latter's comment: 'No, not her heart, her hand: if it had touched her heart there'd be no doubt' (v. 3338), where 'it' seems to refer deliberately at the same time to both the prankster's penis and the preacher's sermon. Tourage views this as 'an apt comparison since the penis as the male organ signifies the fetishistic literalization of symbols divorced from their inner meaning'.[3]

Mention should also be made of the uniqueness of the prose introduction of Book Five among the volumes of *The Masnavi*. It is well known that Rumi's *Masnavi* has verse introductions to each of its six books, the most famous of which is the 'Song of the Reed' in the first book. It is less widely known that these verse introductions are actually preceded by prose introductions in each volume, probably because they are far less memorable than the poetry. On first sight these prose introductions also show little consistency, alternating for instance in language—Arabic or Persian—and the diverse nature of their content also does not obviously relate to the major themes in the volumes they introduce. Consequently, they have long remained something of a puzzle.[4]

The prose introduction of Book Five stands apart from all the other volumes' prose introductions because it does not even discuss *The Masnavi* itself beyond the first sentence identifying the volume in which it is found, and it is a single, continuous homily that concludes with a Qur'anic verse for which it could be considered an exegesis: '*Let whoever hopes to meet his Lord perform good actions and not associate anything with the worship of his Lord*' (Qur'an, 18: 110). Rumi is referring

---

[3] See further ibid. 116–25. The statement can also be seen as a clever way of highlighting the contrast between the penis and the phallus as viewed through the lens of Lacan's thought.

[4] Carl Ernst has attempted to find consistency in these prose introductions in his article 'A Little Indicates Much: Structure and Meaning in the Prefaces to Rumi's *Mathnawi*, Books I–III', *Mawlana Rumi Review* 5 (2014), 14–25. The prose introduction of Book Five conspicuously stands apart from the ones he considers in this study.

here to a mystical journey to the *haqiqa* 'Reality/Truth/God' by means of the *tariqa* (the Sufi path), a way which is shown by the *shari'a*, which represents here the theory rather than the activity of following the path. In relation to the Qur'anic verse, meeting the Lord would be reaching the *haqiqa*, performing good actions following the *tariqa*, and not associating anything with the worship of the Lord, the *shari'a*. This would mean that *shari'a* does not mean 'law' here, as it invariably does elsewhere, but rather a monotheistic religious belief, for which it is sometimes also used.

What is perhaps most important here is that from the first paragraph Rumi's particular agenda in such an exegesis is to make the point that those who have attained the *haqiqa* should not keep up the theory (*shari'a*) and practice (*tariqa*) that took them there. After all, through a quotation he describes doing so as 'despicable' (*qabih*) and immediately quotes in relation to this the additional saying: '*If the haqiqas appear, the shari'as will become void*'. In the subsequent paragraphs of this prose introduction, he further underlines this point for 'the emancipated ones' who have attained the Truth or have become gold and no longer need the theory and practice of alchemy and the ones who have good health and have no need for medicine's theory and application. This prose introduction is therefore not only radically different from the others in form, but also makes a bold statement that one rarely finds expressed so explicitly and unambiguously. One can see an obvious reason for this in Rumi's devotion to his spiritual master Shams-e Tabrizi, who was widely criticized by his contemporaries for his outlandishly unconventional behaviour, although he had disappeared from Rumi's life a decade earlier. The encouragement to let go of the path and methods that have taken you to your destination expressed here is perhaps surprising since the dominant story in this volume is about Ayaz and his rustic boots and old fleece coat, even though the latter does not encourage anything more than remembering one's modest origins after reaching lofty success. This prose introduction's very unusual nature further suggests that it represents a response to something external to the text itself.

Rumi and Sufism

Rumi has long been recognized within the Sufi tradition as one of the most important Sufis in history. He not only produced the finest Sufi poetry in Persian, but was also the master of disciples who later, under the direction of his son and eventual successor Soltan Valad, named their order after him. Moreover, by virtue of the intense devotion he expressed towards his own master, Shams-e Tabriz, Rumi has become the archetypal Sufi disciple. From that perspective, the unprecedented level of interest in Rumi's poetry over the last couple of decades in North America and Europe does not come as a total surprise. Once his poetry finally began to be rendered into English in an attractive form, which coincided with an increased interest in mysticism among readers, this Sufi saint who expressed his mystical teachings in a more memorable and universally accessible way than any other began to become a household name.

Rumi lived some 300 years after the first writings of Muslim mystics were produced. A distinct mystical path called 'Sufism' became clearly identifiable in the late tenth and early eleventh centuries with the compilation of the manuals and collections of biographies of past Sufi saints. The authors of these works, who were mostly from northeastern Persia, traced the origins of the Sufi tradition back to the Prophet Mohammad, while at the same time acknowledging the existence of comparable forms of mysticism before his mission. They mapped out a mystical path, by which the Sufi ascends towards the ultimate goal of union with God and knowledge of reality. More than two centuries before the time of the eminent Sufi theosopher Ebn `Arabi (d. 1240), Sufis began to describe their experience of annihilation in God and the realization that only God truly exists. The illusion of one's own independent existence had begun to be regarded as the main obstacle to achieving this realization, such that early Sufis like Abu Yazid Bastami (d. 874) are frequently quoted as dismissing the value of the asceticism of some of their contemporaries on the grounds that it merely increased attention to themselves. In this way, most Sufis began to regard love of God as the means of overcoming the root problem of one's own self, rather than piety and asceticism.[5]

The Sufi practice most widely discussed in the early manuals of Sufism is that of listening to music, commonly referred to as 'musical audition' (*sama*). Listening to poetry being sung to music, while immersed in the remembrance of God and unaware of oneself,

---

[5] Translations of representative samples of the key texts of early Sufism are available in M. Sells, *Early Islamic Mysticism* (Mahwah, 1996).

induced ecstasy in worshippers. The discussions in Sufi manuals of spontaneous movements by Sufis in ecstasy while listening to music and the efforts made to distinguish this from ordinary dance, suggest that this practice had already begun to cause a great deal of controversy. Most of the Sufi orders that were later formed developed the practice of surrendering to spontaneous movements while listening to music, but the whirling ceremony of the followers of Rumi, the Mevlevi order, is a unique phenomenon.[6] Although it is traditionally traced back to Rumi's own propensity for spinning around in ecstasy, the elaborate ceremony in the form in which it has become famous today was only established in the seventeenth century.

The nature of the Sufi mystic who has completed the path to enlightenment is one of the most recurrent topics in Sufi writings of the tenth and eleventh centuries, but students of Sufism at the time would tend to associate with several such individuals rather than form an exclusive bond with one master. By the twelfth century, however, the master–disciple relationship became increasingly emphasized, as the first Sufi orders began to be formed. It was also during this century that the relationship between love of God and His manifestation in creation became a focus of interest, especially among Sufis of Persian origin, such as Ahmad Ghazali (d. 1126) and Ruzbehan Baqli (d. 1209). The former's more famous brother was responsible for integrating Sufism with mainstream Sunni Islam, as a practical form of Muslim piety that can provide irrefutable knowledge of religious truths through direct mystical experience.[7]

In this way, by the thirteenth century diverse forms of Sufism had developed and become increasingly popular. Rumi was introduced to Sufism by his father, Baha Valad, who followed a more conservative tradition of Muslim piety, but his life was transformed when he encountered the mystic Shams-e Tabriz. Although many of the followers of the tradition of his father considered Shams to be totally unworthy of Rumi's time and attention, he considered him to be the most complete manifestation of God. Rumi expressed his love and

---

[6] Concerning the contrast between the Mevlevi *sama`* and other forms of Sufi *sama`*, see J. During, 'What is Sufi Music?' in L. Lewisohn, ed., *The Legacy of Medieval Persian Sufism* (London and New York, 1992), 277–87.

[7] The chapter of Mohammad Ghazali's autobiography which describes his experience on the Sufi path is available in translation in N. Calder, J. Mojaddedi, and A. Rippin, eds and trs, *Classical Islam: A Sourcebook of Religious Literature* (London, 2003), 228–32.

utter devotion for his master Shams, with whom he spent only about two years in total, through thousands of ecstatic lyrical poems. Towards the end of his life he presented the fruit of his experience of Sufism in the form of *The Masnavi*, which has been judged by many commentators, both within the Sufi tradition and outside it, to be the greatest mystical poem ever written.

The Masnavi *Form*

Rumi chose a plain, descriptive title for his poem, 'masnavi' being the name of the rhyming couplet verse form. Each half-line, or hemistich, of a *masnavi* poem follows the same metre, in common with other forms of classical Persian poetry. The metre of Rumi's *Masnavi* is the *ramal* metre in apocopated form $(- \breve{\ } - - / - \breve{\ } - - / - \breve{\ } -)$, a highly popular metre which was also used by Attar for his *Conference of the Birds*. What distinguishes the *masnavi* form from other Persian verse forms is the rhyme, which changes in successive couplets according to the pattern *aa bb cc dd* etc. Thus, in contrast to other verse forms, which require a restrictive monorhyme, the *masnavi* form enables poets to compose long works consisting of thousands of verses.

The *masnavi* form satisfied the need felt by Persians to compose narrative and didactic poems, of which there was already before the Islamic period a long and rich tradition. By Rumi's time a number of Sufis had already made use of the *masnavi* form to compose mystical poems, the most celebrated among which are Sana'i's (d. 1138) *Hadiqato'l-haqiqat*, or *Garden of Truth*, and Faridoddin Attar's (d. 1220) *Manteqo't-tayr*, or *Conference of the Birds*.[8] According to tradition, it was the popularity of these works amongst Rumi's disciples that prompted Hosamoddin, Rumi's deputy, to ask him to compose his own mystical *masnavi* for their benefit.

Hosamoddin served as Rumi's scribe in a process of text-production that is traditionally described as being similar to the way in which the Qur'an was produced. However, while the Sufi poet Rumi recited *The Masnavi* orally when he felt inspired to do so, with Hosamoddin always ready to record those recitations in writing for him as well as to assist him in revising and editing the final poem, the illiterate

---

[8] See e.g. Attar, *The Conference of the Birds*.

Prophet Mohammad is said to have recited aloud divine revelation in piecemeal fashion, in exactly the form that God's words were revealed to him through the Archangel Gabriel. Those companions of the Prophet who were present on such occasions would write down the revelations and memorize them, and these written and mental records eventually formed the basis of the compilation of the Qur'an many years after the Prophet's death.

The process of producing *The Masnavi* was probably started in around 1262, although tradition relates that Rumi had already composed the first eighteen couplets by the time Hosamoddin made his request; we are told that he responded by pulling a sheet of paper out of his turban with the first part of the prologue of Book One, the 'Song of the Reed', already written on it. References to their system of production can be found in the text of *The Masnavi* itself (e.g. I, v. 2947). They seem to have worked on *The Masnavi* during the evenings in particular, and in one instance Rumi begs forgiveness for having kept Hosamoddin up for an entire night with it (I, v. 1817). After Hosamoddin had written down Rumi's recitations, they were read back to him to be checked and corrected. The crucial role played by Hosamoddin as Rumi's assistant in this process is highlighted by the fact that Rumi refers to *The Masnavi* on several occasions as 'the Hosam book'.

Rumi's *Masnavi* belongs to the group of works written in this verse form that do not have a frame narrative. In this way, it contrasts with the more cohesively structured *Conference of the Birds*, which is already well known in translation. It is also much longer; the *Conference* is roughly the same length as just one of the six component books of *The Masnavi*. Each of the six books consists of about 4,000 verses and has its own prose introduction and prologue. There are no epilogues.

The component narratives, homilies, commentaries on citations, prayers, and lyrical flights which make up the body of *The Masnavi* are often demarcated by their own rubrics. The text of longer narratives tends to be broken up into sections by further such rubrics, as we have seen. Occasionally the rubrics are positioned inappropriately, such as in the middle of continuous speech, which might be interpreted as a sign that they may have been inserted only after the text had been prepared. Sometimes the rubrics are actually longer than the passage that they represent, especially in Books Five and Six, and serve to explain and contextualize what follows. It is as if, on re-reading the text, further explanation was felt necessary in the form of an expanded heading.

The frequency of breaks in the flow of narratives, which is a distinctive characteristic of *The Masnavi*, reveals that Rumi has earned a reputation as an excellent story-teller despite being primarily concerned with conveying his teachings as effectively as possible to his Sufi disciples. *The Masnavi* leaves the impression that he was brimming with ideas and symbolic images which would overflow when prompted by the subtlest of associations. In this way, free from the constraints of a frame narrative, Rumi has been able to produce a work that is far richer in content than any other example of the mystical *masnavi* genre. That this has been achieved often at the expense of preserving continuity in the narratives seems to corroborate Rumi's opinion on the relative importance of the teachings in his poetry over its aesthetic value.[9] If it were not for the fact that his digressive 'overflowings' are expressed in simple language and with imagery that was immediately accessible to his contemporary readers, they would have constituted an undesirable impediment to understanding the poem. Where this leads Rumi to interweave narratives and to alternate between different speakers and his own commentaries, the text can still be difficult to follow, and, for most contemporary readers, the relevance of citations and allusions to the Qur'an and the traditions of the Prophet will not be immediately obvious without reference to the explanatory notes that have been provided in this edition. None the less, it should be evident, not least from the lengthy sequences of metaphors that Rumi often provides to reinforce a single point, that he has striven to communicate his message as effectively as possible rather than to write obscurely and force the reader to struggle to understand him.

Rumi made painstaking efforts to convey his teachings as clearly and effectively as possible, using simple language, the *masnavi* verse form, entertaining stories, and the most vivid and accessible imagery possible. The aim of the present translation is to render Rumi's *Masnavi* into a relatively simple and attractive form which, with the benefit of metre and rhyme, may enable as many readers as possible to read the whole book with pleasure and to find it rewarding.

---

[9] Rumi expresses his frustration about having to return to the narrative after a break towards the start of Book Two (Rumi, *The Masnavi: Book Two*, tr. J. Mojaddedi (Oxford, 2007), vv. 194–202).

NOTE ON THE TRANSLATION

RUMI put his teachings into the *masnavi* verse form, we are told, in order that his disciples might enjoy reading them more than the prose Sufi manuals he had previously assigned them, with the benefit of metre and rhyme. I have therefore decided to translate Rumi's *Masnavi* into verse in accordance with the aim of the original work. I have chosen to use rhyming iambic pentameters, since this is the closest corresponding form of English verse to the Persian *masnavi* form of rhyming couplets. These are numbered and referred to as verses in the Explanatory Notes and Introduction.

Book Five of *The Masnavi* consists of over 4,200 couplets, the continuity of which is broken up only by section headings. For the sake of clarity, in this translation further breaks have been added to those created by the section headings. In order for the Contents pages to fulfil their function effectively, alternative headings have been employed there, albeit at corresponding points to the major section headings in the text, which refer in many instances to merely the first few subsequent verses rather than representing the section as a whole and occasionally do not represent that section accurately at all.

Although *The Masnavi* is a Persian poem, it contains a substantial amount of Arabic text. This invariably takes the form of citations from Arabic sources and common religious formulae, but the sources for some of these passages are either unknown or oral. Italics have been used to indicate Arabic text, except in the section headings, which are fully italicized. Many Arabic terms and religious formulae have become part of the Persian language, and have therefore not been highlighted in this way. Capitalization has been used when reference is made to God. This includes, in addition to the pronouns and titles commonly used in English, the ninety-nine names of God of the Islamic tradition, as well as certain philosophical terms.

Most of the sources of *The Masnavi* are not widely available in English, if at all, and so references have been provided in the notes only for citations of the Qur'an. Verse numbering varies in the most widely available translations of the Qur'an, some of which do not in fact number individual verses, but since this variation is very slight (a maximum of a few verses) the reader should still be able to find the relevant passages without difficulty. The notes also identify those passages in the translation which represent the sayings and deeds of the Prophet Mohammad (*hadith*) when this is not already self-evident in the text (e.g. by 'the Prophet said'). It should be pointed out that citations in the original *Masnavi* are very often variants of the original sources, including the Qur'an, rather than exact renderings, due to the constraints of the metre that is used. The same applies in this verse translation.

This translation corresponds exactly to the text of the fifth volume of the edition prepared by Mohammad Estelami (6 vols and index, 2nd edn, Tehran, 1990). This is by far the best critical edition that has been prepared, since it offers a complete apparatus criticus, indicating the variant readings in all the early manuscripts more comprehensively and transparently than any other edition. Although R. A. Nicholson's edition of the Persian text is more widely available, due to the fact that it is published in Europe, its shortcomings for today are widely recognized and outweigh the advantage of having his exactly corresponding prose translation and commentary to refer to.

As far as possible, the English equivalents of technical terms have been provided, in preference to giving the original in transliteration and relying on explanatory notes. Where it is provided, the transliteration of names and terms has been simplified to such a degree that no diacritics are used. It is designed simply to help the reader use Persian pronunciation, especially where this would affect the metre and rhyme.

SELECT BIBLIOGRAPHY

General Background

J. T. P. De Bruijn, *Persian Sufi Poetry: An Introduction to the Mystical Use of Classical Poems* (Richmond, 1997).

C. W. Ernst, *The Shambhala Guide to Sufism* (Boston, 1997).

L. Lewisohn, ed., *Classical Persian Sufism: From its Origins to Rumi* (London, 1993).

J. W. Morris, 'Situating Islamic Mysticism: Between Written Traditions and Popular Spirituality', in R. Herrera, ed., *Mystics of the Book: Themes, Topics and Typologies* (New York, 1993), 293–334.

J. Nurbakhsh, *The Path: Sufi Practices* (London, 2002; 2nd printing, with revisions, New York, 2006).

O. Safi, 'On the Path of Love towards the Divine: A Journey with Muslim Mystics', *Sufi*, 78 (2009–10), 24–7.

Reference

Encyclopaedia Iranica, ed. E. Yarshater (New York, 1985–).

Encyclopaedia of Islam, ed. H. A. R. Gibb et al., 12 vols (Leiden, 1960–2003).

J. Nurbakhsh, *Sufi Symbolism*, 16 vols (London and New York, 1980–2003).

On Rumi

W. C. Chittick, ed., *The Sufi Path of Love: The Spiritual Teachings of Rumi* (Albany, NY, 1983).

F. Keshavarz, *Reading Mystical Lyric: The Case of Jalal al-Din Rumi* (Columbia, SC, 1998).

F. D. Lewis, *Rumi, Past and Present, East and West: The Life, Teachings and Poetry of Jalal al-Din Rumi* (Oxford, 2000).

J. Mojaddedi, *Beyond Dogma: Rumi's Teachings on Friendship with God and Early Sufi Theories* (Oxford, 2012).

Rumi, *Mystical Poems of Rumi, 1 and 2*, tr. A. J. Arberry (New York, 1979).

Rumi, *Signs of the Unseen: The Discourses of Jalaluddin Rumi*, tr. W. M. Thackston, Jr (Boston, 1994).

N. Virani, ' "I am the Nightingale of the Merciful": Rumi's Use of the Qur'an and Hadith', *Comparative Studies of South Asia, Africa and the Middle East*, 22/2 (2002), 100–11.

Editions of The Masnavi

Masnavi, ed. M. Estelami, 7 vols (2nd edn, Tehran, 1990). Vols i–vi each contain the editor's commentary in the form of endnotes; vol. vii is the Index.

Masnavi, ed. T. Sobhani (Tehran, 1994).

Masnavi-ye ma'navi, ed. A.-K. Sorush, 2 vols (Tehran, 1996).

The Mathnawi of Jalalu'ddin Rumi, ed. and tr. R. A. Nicholson and E. J. W. Gibb. Memorial, NS, 8 vols (London, 1925–40). This set consists of the Persian text (vols i–iii), a full translation in prose (vols iv–vi), and commentary on Books One to Six (vols vii–viii).

Interpretation of The Masnavi

W. C. Chittick, 'Rumi and *wahdat al-wujud*', in A. Banani, R. Hovannisian, and G. Sabagh, eds, *Poetry and Mysticism in Islam: The Heritage of Rumi* (Cambridge, 1994), 70–111.

H. Dabashi, 'Rumi and the Problems of Theodicy: Moral Imagination and Narrative Discourse in a Story of the *Masnavi*', in A. Banani, R. Hovannisian, and G. Sabagh, eds, *Poetry and Mysticism in Islam: The Heritage of Rumi* (Cambridge, 1994), 112–35.

R. Davis, 'Narrative and Doctrine in the First Story of Rumi's *Mathnawi*', in G. R. Hawting, J. Mojaddedi, and A. Samely, eds, *Studies in Islamic and Middle Eastern Texts and Traditions in Memory of Norman Calder* (Oxford, 2000), 93–104.

A. Karamustafa, 'Speaker, Voice and Audience in the Koran and the *Mathnawi*', *Sufi*, 79 (2010), 36–45.

M. Mills, 'Folk Tradition in the *Masnavi* and the *Masnavi* in Folk Tradition', in A. Banani, R. Hovannisian, and G. Sabagh, eds, *Poetry and Mysticism in Islam: The Heritage of Rumi* (Cambridge, 1994), 136–77.

J. Mojaddedi, 'Rumi', in A. Rippin, ed., *The Blackwell Companion to the Qur'an* (Oxford, 2017), 362–72.

J. Mojaddedi, 'The Ebb and Flow of "the Ocean Inside a Jug": The Structure of Rumi's *Mathnawi* Reconsidered', *Journal of Sufi Studies*, 3/2 (2014), 105–31.

J. R. Perry, '*Monty Python* and the *Mathnawi*: The Parrot in Indian, Persian and English Humor', *Iranian Studies*, 36/1 (2003), 63–73.

J. Renard, *All the King's Falcons: Rumi on Prophets and Revelation* (Albany, NY, 1994).

O. Safi, 'Did the Two Oceans Meet? Historical Connections and Disconnections between Ibn 'Arabi and Rumi', *Journal of Muhyiddin Ibn 'Arabi Society*, 26 (1999), 55–88.

M. Tourage, *Rumi and the Hermeneutics of Eroticism* (Leiden, 2007).

M. Vaziri, *Rumi and Shams' Silent Rebellion* (New York, 2015).

Further Reading in Oxford World's Classics

The Masnavi, Book One, tr. and ed. Jawid Mojaddedi.
The Masnavi, Book Two, tr. and ed. Jawid Mojaddedi.
The Masnavi, Book Three, tr. and ed. Jawid Mojaddedi.
The Masnavi, Book Four, tr. and ed. Jawid Mojaddedi.

A CHRONOLOGY OF RUMI

1207	Rumi's birth in Balkh, north-eastern Persia
c.1216	Rumi's family emigrate from Persia to Anatolia
1219	Alaoddin Kay Qobad ascends Seljuk throne in Anatolia
1220	Death of Faridoddin 'Attar
1221	The Mongol army conquers Balkh
c.1222	Rumi's family settle temporarily in Karaman, Anatolia
1224	Rumi marries Gowhar Khatun
1226	Birth of Soltan Valad, Rumi's son and eventual successor
c.1229	Rumi's family relocate to Konya, Anatolia
1231	Death of Baha Valad, Rumi's father
1232	Borhanoddin Termezi arrives in Konya
c.1233	Rumi begins his studies in Syria
1235	Death of Ebn al-Farez in Egypt
1237	Rumi returns to Konya as leader of Baha Valad's School
	Ghiyasoddin Kay Khosrow II ascends Seljuk throne in Anatolia
1240	Death of Ebn 'Arabi in Damascus
1243	The Mongols extend their empire to Anatolia
1244	Rumi meets Shams-e Tabriz in Konya for the first time
1246	Shams leaves Konya
1247	Shams returns to Konya
c.1247–8	Shams disappears
	Salahoddin the Goldsmith begins tenure as Rumi's deputy
1258	Death of Salahoddin
	Hosamoddin Chalabi begins tenure as Rumi's deputy
	The Mongols conquer Baghdad, the Abbasid capital
1260	The Mongols are defeated in Syria by the Mamluks
c.1262	*The Masnavi* is started
c.1264	*The Masnavi* is resumed after a pause on account of the death of Hosamoddin's wife
1273	(17 December) Death of Rumi in Konya

THE MASNAVI

BOOK FIVE

Prose Introduction

In the name of God, the Merciful and the Compassionate, to Whom we appeal for help and in Whom we trust, Who has the keys of hearts. And may God bless the best of creatures, Mohammad, as well as his family and companions.

This is the fifth of the books of rhyming couplets and mystical explanations, clarifying that the *shari'at** is like a candle which shows the path; unless you obtain the candle the path cannot be travelled. Once you have come to the path, your travelling on it is the *tariqat.** When you reach the destination, that is the *haqiqat.** This is why it has been said: *'If the haqiqahs should appear, the shari'ahs would become void.'** This is the same as when copper becomes gold, or was gold originally—it has no need for the theory of alchemy which is the *shari'at* and neither does it need to rub itself on the philosopher's stone, a process which is the *tariqat*, as it has been said: *'It is despicable to seek a guide after arrival at the goal, and abandoning the guide before arrival at the goal is also blameworthy.'*

In summary, the *shari'at* is like learning the theory of alchemy from a teacher or book, while the *tariqat* is applying the chemicals and rubbing the copper on the philosopher's stone, and the *haqiqat* is the transmutation of copper into gold. Those with knowledge of alchemy celebrate their knowledge of it, saying: 'We know the theory of this.' Those who actually carry out alchemy celebrate applying alchemy, saying: 'We are doing such works.' Those who attain the truth celebrate the truth, saying: 'We have become gold and are free from the theory and application of alchemy. We are God's emancipated ones.' *Each group is celebrating what they themselves have.**

Alternatively, the *shari'at* may be compared with learning the science of medicine, the *tariqat* with restricting one's diet in accordance with the science of medicine or taking remedies, and the *haqiqat* with attaining everlasting good health and being free from the other two. When a man dies to this life, the *shari'at* and the *tariqat* become disconnected from him, and only the *haqiqat* remains. If he possesses the *haqiqat*, he yells: *'Oh, if only my people could know how my Lord has forgiven me!'** But if he does not possess it, he yells: *'Oh, if only I had not been given my record of deeds and remained unaware of my reckoning! Oh, if only my death had been the final decree. My wealth has not availed me; my authority has perished and left me!'** The *shari'at* is the theory, the *tariqat* is the action, the *haqiqat* is reaching God: *'Let whoever hopes to meet his Lord perform good actions and not associate anything with the worship of his Lord.'**

Exordium

Light of the stars, Sultan Hosamoddin,
    Requests I start the fifth book he's so keen.
O Light of God, noble Hosam, to me
    Teacher of teachers of true purity,
If people were not veiled, impure and shallow,
    And if their throats were not so weak and narrow,
I'd have done justice to you through your praise
    And opened my lips to much different ways:
The falcon's shares aren't like the sparrow's shares;   5
    I have to speak simplistically for theirs.
To praise you to the prisoners is a shame—
    Where mystics gather I will praise your name.
It's wrong to speak to worldly men of you—
    Just like love's secret, I'll keep it from view.
Praise will describe and rend the veil to teach—
    The sun, though, is beyond description's reach:
The praiser of the sun is doing self-praise:
    'My eyes see; they're not blinded by its rays.'
But it's self-blame if you should blame the sun—   10
    'My eyes are blind!' you're telling everyone.
Feel pity if you come across one who
    Is envious of the fortunate sun in view.
Can he block it from people's eyes today,
    Or from things that would otherwise decay?
Or can he lessen its unbounded light,
    Or stand up to resist its high-ranked might?
Whoever is the whole world's biggest envier
    Has envy that makes him stay dead forever.

You are beyond what intellects can know,   15
    So their descriptions always fall below.
Although this intellect of mine is weak
    Still it now feels compelled to feebly speak:
Though something can't be captured totally,
    It shouldn't be abandoned easily.
Though one can't drink the whole flood up, one will

Drink water to one's actual limit still.
If you won't let out now the mystery
    Use its shell to give us the power to see!
Words only reach the shell that is external,   20
    But lesser minds think that it is the kernel.
So far below the heavens is our sky,
    But looking from the ground it still seems high.
I keep describing you, so they may yet
    Take the path while they can and flee regret.
You are God's light and you draw souls to Him—
    Most live in darkness of mere doubt and whim.
God's glorification is the precondition
    For this good light to give the blind eyes vision.
The one prepared and striving finds the light,   25
    That one who's not in love with darkest night.
Weak-sighted ones who roam at night will not
    Circle faith's cresset—that is not their lot.
Difficult, subtle points are all in vain
    For those devoid of faith—it is their chain:
While he displays his cleverness, that one
    Can't open up his eyes still to the sun.
He doesn't raise a branch up like a tree.
    He makes holes in the ground like mice. We see
Humans have four destructive qualities—   30
    They're wisdom's gallows, so watch out for these:

*Exegesis of: 'Take four birds and turn them towards you!'**

Wisdom's sun, Abraham, for us today,
    Kill these birds that attack those on their way,
Because each of these four birds, like the crow,
    Plucks the eyes out of wisest men below.
His birds are like those bodily qualities—
    Once slain the soul can soar beyond with ease.
Abraham, to wipe good and bad from here
    Chop off their heads, so foot snares disappear!
You are the whole and all are parts of you,   35
    Open the snares—their feet are all yours too!
You make this world the soul's own nurturing ground,

Behind each army one knight can be found.
Because the body holds four dispositions,
     They have been named the four birds of dissensions.
Bestow eternal life's good luck to people
     By chopping heads of these birds that are evil.
Bring them to life then in a different way
     Such that they cause no harm, unlike today.
These four waylaying inner birds have made   40
     In people's hearts the home where they have stayed—
Since you command the hearts in harmony
     In this age, and you are God's deputy,
Chop off the heads of these four birds, and then
     Make everlasting all your transient men.
The duck, the cock, the peacock, and the crow
     Stand for the soul's four bad traits that we know.
The duck is greed, the cockerel is desire;
     Crows yearn for more, peacocks love ranking higher.
What crows yearn and desire so ardently   45
     Is for the chance to live eternally.
The duck's greed keeps its beak stuck in the ground,
     In land or water. seeking what's around.
Its gullet doesn't rest a moment and
     God's '*Eat!*'* alone is its obeyed command.
Like looters who ransack a house and fill
     Their sack with loot as fast as possible,
Cramming in indiscriminatingly:
     Gold nuggets and chickpeas both, hurriedly.
He crams in things of every kind in case   50
     Another looter comes soon to that place.
Fearful that time's pressed and the chance is small,
     He grabs it all as fast as he can haul.
He doesn't trust in his own ruler's power
     To stop a foe approaching him that hour.
But the believer in his own salvation
     Takes his time raiding with deliberation.
He's safe from loss from foes because he knows
     The power of God's wrath over all his foes;
He's safe from fellow subjects coming there   55
     And wounding him to gain from this affair.

He's seen the just king hold back subjects—none
    Is left alone to harm another one,
So he won't rush, but stays calm over there—
    He knows he's safe from losing his own share.
He has a pure heart, acts with care and patience;
    He is content, unselfish, with forbearance.
Acting with care is the Most Merciful's ray;
    Rushing is Satan's jostling you away
Because he makes one scared of poverty   60
    And slays men's patience's steed wickedly.
Heed the Qu'ran: the devil's evil scheme
    Is threatening poverty in the extreme.*
So you'll take and consume vile things in haste,
    And not be blessed through good acts—what a waste.
The infidel has seven bowels within—
    He grows fat, but his heart and faith grow thin.

The reason for the saying of the Prophet: 'The infidel eats with seven stomachs while the believer eats with one.'

Infidels were the Prophet's guests one time.
    They all came to the mosque at dinner-time:
'We've come expecting hospitality,   65
    O king who welcomes all humanity!
We've come with much need from a far-off place—
    Shower us with your special light and grace.'
That just king who helps all men, strong or weak,
    Turned to his good friends and began to speak:
'Friends, host a guest each so that you divide
    The work between you—you've my traits inside.'
Armies are filled with their king and strike blows
    With their swords due to this at their king's foes.
You slash your sword due to your king's rage now—   70
    If not how could you rage at brothers—how?
The anger of your king reflects on you,
    Making you club your brother as you do:
The king's the soul; his troops are filled with him:
    Soul's water filling streams up to the brim.
If the king's spirit's water should be sweet

The streams fill with sweet water till complete.
Since subjects follow their king's faith alone—
   The sultan of '*he frowned*'* has made this known.
Each of the Prophet's friends then chose one guest,   75
   Among whom was one fatter than the rest.
He was so huge he didn't get selected;
   Like a cup's dregs, he stayed behind, rejected.
The Prophet chose this man spurned by the others.
   His goat herd had then seven milk-filled mothers
That stayed inside his home, so they could be
   Milked there before the meal more readily.
That greedy fat man then stuffed down his throat
   The soup, the bread, and milk from every goat.
The household all grew angry then, each thinking   80
   About the goat's milk they longed to be drinking.
The glutton tapped his drum-like belly when
   He had consumed the share of eighteen men,
Then went up to his bedroom and reclined—
   The angry maid then slammed the door behind.
She even chained the door from the outside,
   Enraged and hurt by that huge man inside.
Then in the early hours that infidel
   Heard nature's call, with stomach pain as well—
He hurried from his bed toward the door,   85
   But found it locked up from the corridor.
That crafty man tried picking it, but he
   Could not unlock the door and thus break free.
In that cramped room he kept on trying this
   with no success, perplexed in hopelessness.
He went to sleep then after his failed scheme,
   And saw a desolate place within his dream.
Since such an empty place was in his mind,
   Asleep he saw just some place of that kind,
Then saw himself there far away from all   90
   And at that moment answered nature's call.
On looking at his bedding once awake
   He saw it shit-filled due to this mistake.
A hundred stresses then filled him inside
   At this embarrassment he could not hide.

'My sleep is worse than being awake, no doubt;
    I eat shit one way, then I shit it out.'
He screamed out, 'Woe is me, oh woe is me!'
    Like infidels in graves, so desperately.
Waiting just for the night to end, so then   95
    He'd hear the room's door open up again
And scamper like an arrow from a bow,
    So no one would see him in there and know.
This story's long but I will make it brief—
    The door was opened; He ran in relief.

Mohammad opens the door of the bedroom for the guest and hides himself, so the latter does not see who opened it and get embarrassed, enabling him to walk out boldly.

Mohammad opened up the door at dawn,
    Giving that lost one access to move on.
He opened it and then began to hide
    To save from shame that stricken person's pride,
So he could boldly walk outside once more   100
    And not see who had opened up the door.
(Either he was blocked out by something there,
    Or God hid him so none would be aware.
'*God's dye*'* can cover up, miraculously
    Veiling the viewer who would normally see,
So he can't see the foe right by his side;
    God's power's many more times multiplied.)
Mohammad saw what happened there that night,
    But God concealed him from that fat guest's sight,
So that a way out would appear from it   105
    And he'd not fall disgraced inside a pit.
But it was destined by God's wisdom's sway
    That he should see himself in such a way.
So many hostile acts will help in fact;
    Destructions, too, can build and keep intact.
The soiled bedclothes through meddling intervention
    Were brought then to the Prophet's close attention:
'Look here at what your guest did. It's so vile!'
    *The Mercy to the Worlds** just gave a smile

And said, 'Bring me a bucket here, and then   110
 With my own hands I'll wash it clean again.'
Each one jumped up to say, 'Don't do that, please,
 For God's sake! Not before your devotees.
We'll clean this shit off—leave it! Please don't start.
 This is work for rough hands, not for the heart.
God said "*By your life!*"* meaning yours alone,
 Made you His deputy upon the throne.
We live in hope of simply serving you—
 If you do it instead, what can we do?'
'I know that, but it's different now,' he said,   115
 'There's a deep reason I'll wash it instead.'
They held back then: 'The Prophet thus decrees.'
 And watched to see revealed the mysteries.
He scrubbed the shit off very carefully,
 Not for show or men's rules, but God's decree.
'You wash this filth!' his heart said, so he'd hear,
 'Deep wisdom lies behind your actions here.'

*The reason for that guest's returning to the Prophet's house at that
moment when the latter was washing with his own hands his defiled
mattress, and his feeling ashamed and rending his clothes and
lamenting for himself and his luck.*

That infidel wretch had a keepsake he
 Noticed he'd lost, and rushed back anxiously.
He said, 'I've left an amulet I kept   120
 Always with me in that room where I slept.'
Though quite embarrassed, he was ruled by greed.
 Greed is a dragon; it's not small. Take heed!
He hurried in Mohammad's house's door
 And saw the Prophet in that room once more
Cleaning the shit off for him on his own,
 As God's hand—evil eyes leave him alone!
He then forgot his amulet and he
 Ripped off his collar so emotionally;
He slapped his own face, then he slammed his head   125
 Against the door and wall until he bled.
Then both his head and nose began to bleed—

That Prince felt pity though he had no need.
He screamed aloud and people gathered there—
    That infidel said, '*People, please beware!*'*
He slammed his head. 'Brainless skull!' he'd protest.
    He beat his breast and screamed 'O lightless breast!'
He then prostrated: 'O all planet Earth,
    Before you shame fills up one of low worth;
You who are whole submit to His decree   130
    While this mere part is lost in tyranny.
You who are whole shake meekly near His might,
    While I, a part, challenge, resist, and fight.
He kept on looking at the heavens too,
    Saying: 'Dear God, I don't dare look at you!'
Once he had trembled more than men can face
    The prophet drew him close in an embrace;
He calmed him down and quietened his cries;
    He gave him gnosis, opening up his eyes.
Unless the cloud weeps how can pastures grow?   135
    Unless the baby cries breast milk won't flow.
A one-day-old knows just how to survive:
    'I'll cry and that kind wet-nurse will arrive.'
The Ultimate Wet-nurse too—don't you see
    Unless you cry His milk won't come for free?
God said, '*Let them weep much!*'* so heed His speech
    Till milk of His grace flows towards your reach.
The sun's deep burning and the rainclouds' weeping
    Are this world's pillars—join them as when weaving!
If not for sunshine's heat and raincloud's tear   140
    Body and accident would not form here.
How would we have four seasons here if not
    For weeping clouds and sunshine that's so hot?
Since tears from clouds combined with sunshine's heat
    Are what maintains this world of ours so sweet,
Make wisdom's sunshine burn, continue keeping
    Your eyes both glistening with the tears you're weeping!
Like babies you need weeping eyes—give up
    This world's bread, for it dries good moisture up!
When body's leafy then the soul shakes all   145
    Its leaves off like a branch does during fall.

A leafy body means the soul's decreased—
    Reduce the body, so the soul's increased!
Now *lend to God** your body's leaves to start
    To make a pasture grow inside your heart.
Loan it, and cut down all your body's food
    To see appear the face *no eye has viewed.**
And when the body empties out its shit
    With musk and lovely pearls the Lord fills it.
It gives its filth to get such purity,   150
    Gaining '*He'll purify you*'* luckily.
The devil scares you, saying: 'Hey, watch out!
    You will be sorry with regret, no doubt:
If you should waste your body now away,
    You'll be regretful and feel much dismay.
Eat this! It's warm and good for your health too.
    Drink that! It's beneficial, healing you.
Considering that the body is your steed
    What's best is that on which it likes to feed.
Don't change your habits. Problems will then start: 155
    A hundred ailments in your brain and heart.'
These are the devil's threats that are so evil.
    He also chants spells hypnotizing people.
He makes out he is Galen just to trick
    And totally deceive your soul that's sick:
'This helps with pain and grief,' he will repeat.
    He did the same to Adam with some wheat.*
He chants spells and makes curious noises too,
    So he can force a feeder bag on you,
As they do when they shoe a horse—you're prone   160
    To then see as a ruby a mere stone.
He grabs you by the ears as if his steed
    And drags you towards coveting and greed.
He puts a horseshoe on your feet, so aching
    Distracts you from the path you should be taking.
His shoe is wavering and feeling doubt:
    'Shall I do this? Shall I do that?' Watch out!
Do what the Prophet chose to do. Refrain
    From deeds of those who're childish or insane.
'*Heaven is ringed by this,*' the Prophet said: 165

'*Hardships*, but they'll make crops thrive more ahead.'
The devil has his spells to cause mistakes,
    Which lure to baskets even toughest snakes.
Though he be flowing water, he will block him;
    Though he be the world's expert, he will mock him.
So join your intellect with a friend's then
    Read and fulfil: '*their work's consulting men*'. *

*The Prophet soothed that Arab guest, calming his agitation,
weeping and lamenting over himself, which he did out of shame,
regret, and the fire of despair.*

This discourse can continue for it's endless.
    That Bedouin was stunned by the king's kindness.
His reasoning left and he then grew insane;   170
    Mohammad's intellect came to restrain:
'Come here!' The man began to stagger then
    To him like one just up from sleep again.
'Come here! Come back now to your wits. Be clear
    For there is much for you to do still here.'
To rouse him he splashed water on his head.
    'God's witness, make me Muslim!' that man said.
'Let me bear witness to your faith. I'm weary
    Of my existence—I'll leave this realm quickly.'
We're in the judge's court and He'll decree   175
    On '*Am I not your lord?*' * for you and me,
For we said 'Yes!' when questioned on this once;
    Our words and actions are our evidence.
Why are we silent at the judge's court?
    Did we not come to witness and report?
Witness, how long will you stay captive here?
    Bear witness now before dawn should appear!
You have been summoned to this place, so you
    Will testify and stop your bad deeds too.
You've sat in this small dock, but you've kept shut   180
    Your lips, with both your hands bound, obstinate.
How will you get out of this court unless
    You testify, as should all witnesses?
It's just a quick task—do it and walk out.

Don't make a small task have to be dragged out.
Whether one moment or a century,
Discharge this trust and then you will be free.

Explaining that ritual prayer, fasting and all external things
are witnesses to the inner light.

This fasting, pilgrimage, jihad, and prayer
Give witness to convictions that you share:
Alms-giving and abandoning jealousy   185
Give witness to your secrets few can see.
And hospitality with lavish food
Declares: 'Guests, we're with you now for the good.'
Gifts, souvenirs, and presents you give, too,
Serve as the proof for 'I am pleased with you.'
What does it mean to strive with wealth and prayers?
'I have a jewel inside me,' it declares.
'My fast and alms-giving are proofs from me
Of piety and generosity.'
Fasting: 'From lawful things he's shown abstention,   190
So with forbidden things he's no connection.'
Alms-giving: 'He gives from his own wealth, so
How could he steal from pious folk we know?'
If tricking others is his work, in short
His proofs will all be voided in God's court.
He is a hunter if he set up bait
For trapping and not sating those who ate.
He is a cat pretending now to fast
And be asleep to catch his prey at last.
He is suspicious with such trickery;   195
He brings shame to those with true piety.
Despite this one's corrupt ways, in the end
God's grace will cleanse him of all that, my friend.
God's mercy shall prevail and He'll bestow
Light on that fraud more brightly than moons glow,
God cleans his effort of impurity;
His mercy cleans him of stupidity,
A cap will cover all his baldness so
The Lord's forgiving kindness is on show.

Water rained from the sky for this solution: 200
    To cleanse impure ones of their own pollution.

How water cleans impurities and how God cleans that
water of impurity. Undoubtedly, Exalted
God is most holy.

Once water turned unclean from having cleaned
    It was then snubbed by senses that had gleaned.
God took it back to goodness's vast sea
    To wash that water's water generously.
The next year it came dragging its hem with it.
    'Where were you?' 'In the sea of those with spirit.
I left here dirty and return now clean
    With robe of honour from where I have been.
Polluted ones, come to me, for my nature 205
    Has gained from that of the Divine Creator.
I will receive all of your ugliness
    And, angel-like, give demons holiness,
When I become polluted I'll return
    To purity's source for another turn.
I'll take off my defiled robe; He'll bestow
    On me another pure robe. This I know.
He acts like this; I do the same—that's why.
    The Lord of the worlds acts to beautify.'
Were it not for our own impurities 210
    How could the water show its qualities?
It steals some sacks of gold from somebody
    Then gives it all to those in penury.
It pours itself on grass that's newly grown,
    Or washes dirty faces that are shown,
Or bears upon its head just like a porter
    The ship that's tossing on the ocean's water.
A million remedies hide in it too
    Since it is from that water that each grew.
Every pearl's soul, every seed's heart, you'll see 215
    Enter the river like a pharmacy.
Orphans on land receive nutrition there,
    Dried up and still ones power to move somewhere.

When it becomes depleted it gets turbid
    The same way we on land become so torpid.

How water prays to God for help after becoming turbid.

It cries from inside, 'O God, come and save me!
    I'm poor now that I've shared all that you gave me.
Over the pure and impure I would pour
    Your wealth, Wealth-giving King, *is there some more?*' *
God tells the cloud: 'Transport it to good places;   220
    You, too, sun—draw it up to higher spaces!'
He takes it on such different routes, till He
    Will finally lead it to the Boundless Sea.
What's really meant by water here, of course,
    Is God's Friends' souls that wash those stains of yours.
When they are darkened by creation's stain
    They head to heaven's purifier again.
They bring back from there the acquired largesse:
    Lessons about His all-encompassingness.
They liberate all from the dry ablution*   225
    And worrying about the prayer's direction.*
They get sick through involvement with the rabble:
    '*Belal, revive us!*'*—they now seek to travel:
Loud and sweet-voiced, Belal, do not forget
    Departure's drum up on the minaret.
The soul soars up; the body stands there, calm.
    That's why when it returns it says: '*Salam!*'*
This parable's a verbal means that's needed,
    So by the masses teachings will be heeded.
None enter flames without protection on,   230
    Save salamanders which do not need one.*
You need the hot baths as a barrier,
    So fire can make your body healthier.
You can't, like Abraham, walk straight inside.*
    They're your apostle: water is your guide.
Only God makes you sated without food;
    The sensual men know that they never could.
Loveliness comes from God here without fail,
    Though sensual men need nature as a veil,

But once their bodies go, like Moses, they   235
    Can see light from their breasts shine anyway.
The water's qualities have testified
    That it is filled up with God's grace inside.

How one's words and actions testify to the light and
consciousness within.

Words and acts tell about the mind to you—
    Infer about what's inside from these two.
Since your mind cannot penetrate inside,
    Inspect the patient's urine from outside.
Actions and words are like the patient's urine—
    They are the evidence physicians look in.
Spiritual healers enter souls through there,   240
    And reach their faith by a route that's so rare.
Not needing acts nor words, they're set apart:
    Beware, they're spies that watch the human heart!
Seek proof in words and deeds from people who
    Join with the ocean not as rivers do:

Explaining that the light within an enlightened person testifies to
that light by itself without words and actions needing to testify.

Vast plains and deserts stretching out of sight
    Are filled up by the realized mystic's light.
God's witness needs no witness—He'll suffice—
    No kindness, hardship or self-sacrifice.
His essence's light has shone out, so he   245
    Is free from ostentation, fortunately.
Don't seek proof from him, such as word and deed.
    The two worlds blossomed through him like a seed.
What's testifying? Making veiled things shown,
    Whether through speech, through acts or new means known—
These show the inner nature of the essence;
    Attributes last, but these fade out in transience.
Gold's mark won't stay on touchstones, but the gold
    Stays valued indisputably when sold:
Fasting, jihad, and prayer have also passed,   250

But souls remain much valued to the last.
The soul showed speech and actions of this nature,
  Rubbing God's order's touchstone: 'O Creator,
Here's proof my faith is sound. There's only doubt
  About the witnesses that have come out.'
The witnesses must all have probity;
  One counts on truthfulness—it's necessary.
To keep their word is for speech witnesses,
  Keeping their pledge is for act witnesses.
False spoken testimony is rejected;   255
  Corrupt act witnesses will be ejected.
Words and deeds shouldn't contradict if you
  Wish yours to be accepted as being true.
'*Your efforts contrast*'*—you're in contradiction,
  Sewing by day, tearing by night in friction.
Tell me who hears conflicting evidence
  Unless being kind through their munificence?
Through word and deed unconscious mind's revealed;
  Each one reveals the secret that's concealed.
Honest testimony will be accepted,   260
  Otherwise it's kept back, confined, rejected.
So long as you contend they'll fight with you:
  Withdraw and wait for them; they're doing that, too.*

How the Prophet offered to his guest the profession of faith to become a Muslim.

This discourse could go on. The Prophet then
  Offered him faith, and he joined Muslim men
With Islam's testimony that is blessed,
  Which breaks apart chains deemed the sturdiest.
The Prophet told him: 'Muslim, I invite
  You to remain here as my guest tonight.'
He said, 'I'd love to be your guest forever,   265
  Wherever I should wander to, wherever.
I am your slave, revived and freed by you,
  At your feast in this world and yonder too.
If some should choose a different feast's spread, then
  Bones will tear up the gullets of those men;

Whoever goes to different ones will see
   The devil share with him a cup for free.
No doubt the devil also takes aside
   Whoever chooses to leave from your side:
If he goes on a journey without you   270
   The devil goes and dines out with him too.
If enviously he mounts a noble horse,
   The devil sits behind him there, of course,
And, if his wife's made pregnant by him, he
   Shares with the devil its paternity.'
(In the Qur'an God says to Satan: '*Share**
   Both wealth and children with them over there!'
The Prophet shed light on this mystically
   In his elusive discourse with Ali.)
'God's Messenger, you've shown well', said that man,   275
   'Your mission like the cloudless bright sun can.
You've done more than two hundred mothers can;
   Jesus's spells could not with that dead man:
My soul's turned, thanks to you, to death's escaper;
   Lazarus revived but still had to die later.'*

This man became the Prophet's guest that night,
   But drank just half his milk, shut his lips tight.
The Prophet urged, 'Drink more, eat cakes with me!'
   He said, 'By God, I'm sated. Honestly!
This isn't affectation, for tonight   280
   I am much fuller than the previous night.'
The Prophet's household were amazed he'd stop:
   'Did the lamp fill up with just one oil drop?
And did the seed for one small bird then sate
   An elephant's huge belly when it ate?'
Women and men with whispers would recount:
   'Elephant-sized, but eats a flea's amount.'
Unbelief's greed and fancies dissipated;
   With a small ant's food, dragons soon were sated.
From unbelieving's beggar's eyes once freed,   285
   Faith's sweetmeats made him strong and without need.
He who would, out of hunger, shake, then found

Like Mary, heaven's fruit fall on the ground.*
The fruit of paradise rushed to his eyes;
    His hell-like belly got a nice surprise.
Mere talk about one's faith makes you content.
    Its essence, though, is bounty's nourishment.

*Explaining that the light which is the food of the soul becomes the
food of the bodies of the Friends of God, so that it becomes friends
with the spirit, for the Prophet even said, 'Satan has
accepted Islam at my hands.'*

Although it is food of the soul and vision
    The body has a share in its division.
The devilish body also used to scoff it   290
    'Satan turned Muslim,' is straight from the Prophet.
How could the devil do that as he said,
    Unless he ate what can revive the dead?
The devil loves this world, both deaf and blind;
    A different love can cut love of that kind.
When it tastes certainty's wine from its cellar
    It then diverts its love that way forever.
O greedy belly, like this turn away!
    Changing your food is now the only way.
Sick-hearted one, turn to the medicine.   295
    A change in nature is the regimen.
Bondsmen of food still stuck in slavery,
    If you can bear being weaned off, you'll be free.
In hunger there is much food—hope for it,
    You timid person, and then hunt for it!
Feed on the light, be like eyes that are seeing!
    Be like the angels, highest human being!
Like angels, make the praise of God your food,
    So, like them, you may flee harm through what's good.
If Gabriel pays the carcass little heed,   300
    He's stronger than the vulture that shows greed.
In this world a fine feast has now been spread,
    Though hidden from the misers who're unfed.
The world might be an orchard that's so nice,
    But mud remains the share for snakes and mice.

How materialists deny the food of the spirit and tremble
longingly for the base kind of food.

His food is mud, in winter or in spring—
    That is for snakes, not for Creation's King.
The woodworm inside wood says foolishly:
    'Who else has such fine sweetmeat just like me?'
The dungworm in the middle of some shit   305
    Knows of no other sweet dessert but it.

Prayer

Show grace and favour, God, who has no peer,
    Since, like an ear-ring, your words pierce each ear.
Drag us now by the ear to that assembly
    Where wine is drunk by everyone who's merry.
Since You have sent a whiff of it, don't seal
    The wine-skin, Lord of faith, we all appeal—
Female and male, both drink from You; Your aid
    Is sought and Your bestowal's not delayed.
You answer even prayers that aren't spoken;   310
    Each moment numerous times You make hearts open.
You have inscribed some letters—rocks have been
    Transformed to wax, through love, once they have seen.
The eyebrow's C, the eye's O, the ear's J—
    With these You've robbed the people's wits away.
Your letters crushed the mind. Keep writing, please,
    Calligrapher with such rare expertise.
You fix imaginal forms too in Non-being
    Each moment fit for every thought and feeling.
You've etched onto imagining's tablet eyes,   315
    Cheeks, beauty marks, and letters people prize.
I will stay drunk and set on Non-existence
    For Its Beloved's truer than existence.
He helped the intellect read such shapes, friend,
    So He could make deliberations end.

Comparison of the Preserved Tablet and every person's
intellectual perceptions from it of their faith, the decree, and their
daily share to the everyday perceptions of the Angel Gabriel
from the Most Mighty Tablet.**

Like angels, wisdom this way gains possession,
    From that same Tablet, of its daily lesson.
See script etched with no fingers in Non Being!
    Its marks make people crazed by what they're seeing.
By fancies everyone is captivated   320
    And digs in hope of gold, intoxicated.
A fancy fills one man with pomp and he
    Heads over to the mountains hurriedly.
A fancy leads another one to take
    The hard path to the sea for a pearl's sake.
Another to the hermitage. Through greed
    Another is inspired to sow his seed.
A fancy makes one waylay he who flees,
    Turns others into salve for injuries.
It makes one summon spirits magically   325
    And someone else count on astrology.
He sees their different acts from the outside
    Spring from the various fancies found inside.
Each one's amazed at how the others act—
    Each has a different taste of things in fact.
If fancies didn't have variety
    How did believers gain plurality?
Since the soul's prayer niche has been made obscure.
    Everyone faces different sides, unsure:

*Comparison between different practices and aspirations
and the difference of opinion among those who seek the
direction for prayer at prayer-time in the dark and
the divers who search on the bottom of the sea.*

Like those who seek the Kaaba and then face   330
    Towards the side they guess leads to that place.
And when the Kaaba's seen at break of day,

It is revealed which people lost their way;
Or like the divers on the ocean's floor,
 Each picking up with haste things for the shore;
In hope of precious pearls or jewels, they throw
 Inside their bags the things they've found below—
Once they rise to the surface of the sea
 Who found a pearl is then known visibly,
And who brought up the tiny pearls as well,   335
 And who brought pebbles up or just a shell.
They will endure at Judgement Day's location
 The well-known, overwhelming tribulation.
Similarly, like moths each group now flies
 Around a candle right before our eyes.
They fix themselves on one flame and then circle
 Around their own particular bright candle,
Hoping for Moses's fire that would turn
 The bush more green although it made it burn.*
Each group has heard of that fire's grace and they 340
 Imagine that each spark acts the same way.
At dawn's break when Eternal Light is seen
 Each candle flame reveals what it had been.
And if good candles burned their wings before
 They now receive from that source eighty more,
But many moths with sealed eyes shall instead
 Stay under the bad candles, filled with dread,
Wings burned, regretful, anguished, breathing sighs,
 Lamenting that vain lust which sealed their eyes:
Their candle tells it, 'I'm burned as you see—   345
 How can I free you from fire's tyranny?'
It weeps and adds, 'My head's consumed, undone—
 How then can I light up another one?'

Exegesis of 'Alas for the slaves of God'*

'Your forms deceived me,' those moths will then state,
 'I saw your actual nature far too late.'
The candle's now snuffed out and wine's run dry
 While the Beloved hides from the weak eye.
Profits have turned to loss and penalty.

We moan to God of blindness bitterly.
The brethren's souls are sound, believing, true,   350
    Surrendering to God, and faithful too.
Everyone's turned his face in their directions
    While the elite turn far beyond dimensions.
A different path is taken by each pigeon,
    But this sort flies beyond each physical region.
Neither domestic birds, nor those that soar,
    Our seed's beyond all seeds and came before.
Our daily bread is ample since our stitching
    The cloak that we wear has transformed to ripping.

The reason why 'faraji'* was first used for the garment of that name

A Sufi tore his cloak while in distress   355
    And then relief came to make him feel less.
He called '*faraji*' that cloak that he'd torn,
    God's Friend's name for it then became well-known.
However, he alone knew its true meaning;
    The dregs-like word is all that reached men's hearing—
God keeps the truth of each name and leaves here
    The dregs-like words that in no way come near.
The ones embracing dregs think mud's for eating;
    The Sufi though will eagerly choose meaning.
He says, 'Dregs have an essence that is pure   360
    That prompts the heart to purity, for sure.
Dregs are hardship; their essence is repose.
    The former's raw, the latter ripe. God knows.
Ease comes with hardship, but you shouldn't fret:
    After death there's a path to more life yet.
If you want peace, son, rend the cloak, then you
    Might rapidly become a pure one too—
Sufis are those who seek such purity,
    Not patched wool-wearers who crave sodomy.
'Sufi' means to the vulgar who are base   365
    Patching clothes and vile sodomy's disgrace.
In hope of purity and a good name

It's good to wear such clothes, but then your aim
Must be its meaning and true principle,
  Not like the fancies-worshippers who're ill.
Your fancy is the club of jealousy:
  It's beauty's palace's security.
It blocks the seeker: 'There's no access here!'
  Every fancy says 'Stop!' when people near,
Except to the wise, sharp-eared one with fervour   370
  From God's help's army as His special favour—
He won't retreat from fancies and he's not
  Blocked thanks to the King's arrow that he's brought.

On this bewildered heart, dear God, bestow
  Some order and give arrows to the bow,
Since, from the hidden cup, you've poured some out
  On soil *from the cup of* the most devout.
On curls and cheeks that mouthful's trace is found—
  That is the reason kings will lick the ground.
Beauty's mouthful is on that ground you kiss   375
  Night and day with your heart's full tenderness.
That soil-mixed mouthful turns mad one like you,
  So think what in its pure form it can do!
Frenzied, men rip their shirts before a clod,
  Since it gained drops of beauty straight from God.
On both the sun and moon there is a mouthful,
  On Saturn too, and on His throne and footstool.*
Mere mouthful or elixir? Please reflect
  On seeing beauty rise from its effect.
Seek seriously its contact, marvellous one: 380
  '*Only the purified can touch this one.*'*
There's some on rubies, pearls, and also gold,
  On wine, desserts, and fruit, if you'd behold,
And on the faces lovely and divine—
  How marvellous must be this special wine!
You stick your tongue in soil to taste a bit—
  Imagine when without soil tasting it!
When that pure mouthful on the Final Day
  Separates through one's death from bodily clay,

You'll bury what's been left behind away   385
   Since severance makes it ugly in that way.
When souls show beauty with no carcasses
   That union's finer than I can express.
When the moon shines without clouds in the way
   Its glory is beyond what words can say.
How lovely is the kitchen with sweet honey—
   All lick their plates though they might have much money.
How lovely is that large stack in faith's field—
   All other stacks are fragments of its yield.
How great that sea of life is with no grief—   390
   The seven seas seem dewdrops on a leaf.
Alast's* cupbearer poured a mouthful on
   This barren, abject soil that we stamp on
And we emerged from that, grew fervent too—
   Pour some more since what we should not we do!
I'd have complained of non-being if permitted
   Or stayed in silence if it's prohibited.
This is the story of the duck of greed—
   Abraham showed it should be killed, not freed.
There's much more in the duck of good and evil,   395
   But I fear missing vital things for people.

Description of the peacock and its nature and the reason why it was killed by Abraham.

The peacock that's two-coloured is to blame:
   It play-acts to show off and earn a name.
It seeks to trap, but has a clueless brain
   That can't tell good and evil, loss and gain.
It will entrap its victims like a snare,
   But of its purpose it's still unaware.
By trapping does it harm or benefit?
   I have spent too much time on pondering it.
Brother, you've lifted up friends, then departed   400
   After all the affection you had started.
Since birth this is what you have done out there:
   You trap them with your love's affection's snare.

From hunting and the airs of self-existence
    Did you gain something worthwhile in that instance?
It's late and your life nearly has run out
    Yet you still earnestly hunt people out,
Catching one, then releasing one confined,
    Hunting again like men of the worst kind.
Releasing that one, seeking with your snare—   405
    This game's for children who are unaware.
Your snare's still empty once the sun has set—
    Shackles and headaches are the most you get.
You hunted then yourself with your own snare,
    Became caged and did not reach your goal there.
Are there trap-owners who will only cage
    Themselves like us, so dumbly, in this age?
Ordinary people's hunting is pig-hunting—
    They're not allowed to eat it; it's just suffering.
Only love is worth hunting, but how can   410
    That be contained in traps by any man?
You should perhaps instead become His prey—
    Enter His trap, abandon yours today.
Love's whispering in your ear: 'Being prey is better
    Than trying to instead be a trap-setter.
Make yourself My fool: be a stupid one;
    Turn to a mote and give up being a sun!
Be homeless and then settle at My door;
    Be moths, don't claim you're candles any more,
So you might taste life's savour finally—   415
    See kingship hidden inside slavery.'
In this world you see things so upside down:
    Bondsmen get called 'king', though they've fallen down:
'Here is a monarch!' now the huge crowd bellows
    To someone tied up, climbing to the gallows.
Like infidels' graves, so ornate outside
    While filled up with God's wrath on the inside.
One's plastered tomb-like, but to no avail—
    They've just put on him self-conceit's thick veil.
With virtues plastered on what's destitute,   420
    Your nature's a wax tree that has no fruit.

*Explaining that everyone knows the mercy of God and everyone
knows the wrath of God, and everyone flees the latter and clings to
the former, but God has hidden wrath in mercy and mercy in wrath.
This is God's scheming and disguising, so people who discern and
see through God's light can be distinguished from those
who see only what is immediately visible.*

One dervish to another: 'Please now share
   What it was like to see God's presence there!'
The other said: 'It's indescribable,
   But for your sake I'll give a parable:
I saw Him and to His left stood a flame
   While to His right a pure stream just the same,
A fire that can burn worlds on His left side
   Like that, a lovely stream on His right side.
One group raised their hands to the fire; another   425
   Appeared so drunk and happy from that Kawsar.
It was a topsy-turvy game they had
   For everybody, whether good or bad:
Those who went to the flames would raise their head
   And come out of the water's side instead.
Those who went to the water suddenly
   Were found inside the fire for all to see;
Those who went to pure water on the right
   Emerged from flames on the left in plain sight;
Those who went to the burning flames instead   430
   Were seen on the right side to raise their head.
Few know the secret of this mystery,
   Hence few approached the fire predictably,
Except those who had then been specially blessed—
   For fire they shunned the water in this test.
Most of them made immediate lust their god,
   So in this they were victims of a fraud.
Troop after troop in haste with greed would flee
   To water and shun fire so heedlessly—
These ones emerged from fires, so you beware   435
   O you who have remained still unaware.
'Stupid fools, I'm not fire,' the fire would scream;
   'I am the blessed fountain and the stream.

You simply were hoodwinked, blind one, back then.
   Enter me, and don't run from sparks again.'
Abraham, there's no spark or smoke in here—
   There's only Nimrod's fraud, so have no fear.*
If you are wise like Abraham, the flame
   Is water to you, moth, so fire's your aim.
The moth's soul can be always heard to bawl: 440
   'I wish I had a million wings, so all
Could burn in that fire that burns mercilessly
   And the outsiders' hearts and eyes not see.
The stupid pity me; they're asinine.
   I pity them through vision that's divine.'
That fire which is the soul of waters too—
   Moths act the opposite to what hearts do:
They see bright light and enter fire; the heart
   Sees fire, then to the light it will depart.
Glorious God plays this game, so He can show   445
   Who is from Abraham's kin here below.
A fire's been given water's form; a fountain
   Now gushes in the fire as on a mountain.
Magicians conjure plates of rice, but then
   The plates look full of worms to other men;
Or scorpions fill a house due to mere sorcery,
   But there is not one scorpion in there actually—
When sorcery can display such things to you
   Imagine what its Maker then can do!
Of course it's fallen every century   450
   Beneath God, woman-like in missionary.
These sorcerers were servants over there
   And, just like sparrows, they'd fall in the snare.
Read the Qur'an on lawful sorcery
   Bringing down *mountain-sized plots** easily.
I am not Pharaoh heading to the Nile—
   Like Abraham, I enter flames and smile:*
I'm *flowing water,** though as fire I seem
   Since water's turned to fire in this strange scheme.
The liberal Prophet truthfully would say: 455
   'Intellect's better than to fast and pray.'
It is an essence, while the other two

Are accidents required of men like you,
So that the mirror shines back radiantly
    Since purity comes in through piety,
But if the mirror at its root is wrong
    Then burnishing that mirror takes too long,
While the fine mirror is like fertile soil
    And needs just minor polishing, not toil.

The differences between intellects in their original created
nature, in contradiction of the Mu'tazilites* who claim:
'In origin all particular intellects were equal, and
any superiority and differences are due to
learning, training, and life experience.'

The intellects are different from each other   460
    In levels from here to the sky, my brother:
One intellect's like the sun's orb, superior,
    One less than Venus and a simple meteor.
One flickers like a lamp about to die,
    The other burns like stars up in the sky,
Such that when clouds drift so that it's in sight
    It will give wisdom that can see God's light.
Particular intellect gives a bad name
    To Universal Intellect, with shame.
The former suffers, hunting in greed's sway,   465
    The latter serves as the True Hunter's prey.
The former's served now, but has lost what's glorious;
    The latter will be raised due to its service.
Like Pharaoh, mere waves make the former fail;
    The latter flees like Sohrab every gaol.*
Checked by the queen in topsy-turvy games,
    It's down to you—don't scheme for selfish aims!
You trust your plots and fancies just like weavers—
    The Self-sufficient one bars all such schemers.
Be clever through good service, then you'll be   470
    A prophet soon in your community.
Be clever till you're rid of your own schemes,
    Till severed from your body as in dreams,
Till you become the lowest slave, for then

Through being less you'll be a lord of men.
But, wolf, don't mix that foxiness that's sly
　With service to become lord. Then you'd lie.
Instead rush like a moth into the flame—
　Don't hoard your service! Gamble in this game!
Quit force, embrace abasement and don't fear!　　　475
　God's Grace goes to abasement, O fakir!
The thirsty one's distress is genuine;
　Pretending you're distressed is like a sin—
When Joseph's brothers wept it was a trick,
　Because they were all envious and sick.*

*Story about that Bedouin whose dog was dying of hunger while his
bag was full of food, and how he lamented over his dog, recited
poetry, and wept and beat his head and face, yet would not
give his dog a scrap of food from his bag.*

A Bedouin wept when his dog was dying;
　'O how I suffer sorrow!' he was crying.
A beggar passing by asked, 'Why these tears?
　What caused this grief? Why sorrow and such fears?'
'I've a good-natured dog,' its owner said,　　　480
　'But look there in the street—he's almost dead.
He'd hunt for me by day, stand guard at night,
　Fierce hunter and thief-fighter with sharp sight.'
'What's wrong? Has he been wounded by a blow?'
　'Severest hunger is what's brought him low.'
The beggar said, 'Patience with trials you face!
　The patient as reward receive God's grace.'
Then he asked, 'O great chief, what's in this sack
　You're holding that looks full? What do you lack?'
'That is my food from last night which I take　　　485
　Along with me for my nutrition's sake.'
'Why don't you give that to the dog instead?'
　'I'm not that generous!' then the Bedouin said.
'Without money a traveller can't get food
　But tears are free, so I've done what I could.'
'Shame on you, pompous fool!' the beggar said,
　'You value more than tears a crust of bread.'

Tears are blood changed through grief, while actual blood
 Spilt pointlessly is worth much less than mud.
The Bedouin made his whole self so base   490
 Like Satan—nothing good left, not one trace.
I am slave to that one you'll never find
 Selling himself except to God, the Kind.
When he should weep rain pours down from the sky;
 When he should moan, 'O lord!' the heavens cry.
I am slave to the copper that you see
 That only breaks itself for alchemy.
Raise broken hands in prayer now, for God's grace
 Races to those who're broken at fast pace.
If you need to escape this narrow pit,   495
 Rush to the fire and stop delaying it.
Observe God's scheming; quit your own, my brothers,
 Because His scheming puts to shame all others.
You'll open up a wondrous hiding-place
 Once your schemes drown in God's without a trace.
Eternal life's the least gain you will see,
 Ascending higher up eternally.

*Explaining that no evil eye is as deadly for a man than the eye of
self-approval, unless his eye has been transformed by
God's Light, so that 'he hears through Me and sees
through Me'* and his self has become effaced.*

Don't notice peacocks' feathers, but their feet
 In case the evil eye gives you defeat,
For that eye makes the mountains tremble too—   500
 Recite: '*They make you stumble*'* for a clue!
That evil gaze made great Mohammad fall
 On the dry road with no rain there at all—
'Why did I fall?' he wondered with more stress,
 'What was the reason? It's not meaningless.'
Until the verse arrived to clarify:
 'Enmity caused it with the evil eye.*
Other men would have been obliterated
 Right then: the evil eye's prey, decimated.
A guard swept you to safety and your fall   505

Served only as a warning sign, that's all.'
Learn from that mountain-like man causing awe—
   Do not expose your leaf! you're less than straw.

Exegesis of 'Those who disbelieve cause you to stumble with their gaze.'*

O Prophet, there are some within that group
   Who with their eyes strike vultures as they swoop—
Their evil gaze can split apart the head
   Of a fierce lion, so it groans in dread.
One casts a death-like glance on camels, then
   Sends after them a slave among his men:
'Go and fetch me some of those camels' fat!'   510
   The slave sees camels on the road, stretched flat,
Each with its head chopped off still lying there,
   Though they used to race horses everywhere.
Through fear of envy and the evil eye
   The stars would change their orbit in the sky.
Water's what makes the water-wheel turn round
   Although when you look water can't be found.
The evil eye's cure is the good eye, friend—
   With one blow it makes that eye's presence end.
It comes from mercy—always that prevails;   515
   The evil eye's from wrath, which always trails.
His Mercy overcomes all wrath, and so
   Each Prophet vanquished his most bitter foe.
And the result of Mercy was the Prophet;
   Nasty foes came from wrath, but he could stop it.
The lust of ducks is less then peacocks' pride,
   A snake next to a dragon multiplied:
The duck lusts after food and sex, but lust
   For power is much worse—knowing is a must:
Status-seekers claim they've divinity—   520
   How can they be forgiven easily?
Adam fell due to lust and greedily eating,
   While Satan fell from pride and status-seeking.
Adam begged quickly for forgiveness first,
   But Satan was too proud to—he stayed cursed.*
The lust for food and sex requires contrition,

But it is not as bad as proud ambition.
Another book would have to be composed
   So hunger for power's root can be exposed.
The Arabs call rebellious horses 'Satan',   525
   Not those that stay in fields where they've been taken.
'Satan' here means rebelling, disobeying—
   This quality deserves our curse and blaming.
One table's spread can feed so many eaters,
   The world's too small though for two power-seekers—
Each cannot bear the other standing there,
   Thus kings kill their own fathers not to share:
'*Kingship is childlessness*'—did you not hear;
   Power-seekers cut family ties through fear:
Such a one is then childless, with no son,   530
   Like fire, not family with anyone—
He burns and ruins all things in his way;
   On gaining naught, he burns himself away.
Become naught, flee from his jaws and don't start
   Seeking mercy from his hard anvil heart!
And don't fear anvils once you've been effaced—
   Learn from absolute poverty's sweet taste.
Divinity, cloak of the Glorious One,
   Becomes a bane to others trying it on.
The crown is His; ours is the belt of service—   535
   Do not exceed the limit of your office.
Your peacock feathers are your bane, beware!
   They make you claim in holiness a share.

*Story about the sage who saw a peacock tearing out its beautiful
feathers with its beak and flinging them down, thereby making its
body ugly and bare. In astonishment he asked, 'Don't you feel
regret?' The peacock answered, 'I do, but life is dearer to me than
feathers and these feathers are the enemies of my life.'*

A peacock one day plucked its feathers out
   Just when a sage was wandering about
In the same field: 'What lovely feathers, yet
   You're pulling them all out without regret!
How does your heart let you tear off your clothes

And fling them on the mud as things one loathes?
Qur'an reciters even use a feather   540
  Of yours as bookmark, which they deeply treasure.
Fans are made from your feathers that are rare
  To circulate for us the healthy air.
You shun what you should have appreciated—
  You don't know God's the one who decorated!
Maybe you do know, yet show this disdain
  To tear embroidery out and stay so plain?'
Many disdains are sins that we could mention;
  They send the slave far from the King's attention.
To show disdain is sometimes sugar-sweet,   545
  But don't be tempted—danger's what you'll meet.
The path of need is the securest way—
  Follow that path and quit disdain today.
So many flapped their wings and showed disdain,
  But in the end it was those people's bane.
Disdain's sweet taste may briefly now delight you,
  But it hides fear and dread that will soon find you.
Though neediness might make you turn thin, soon
  It makes your breast shine brightly like the moon.
Since He brings out the living from the dead   550
  Those who have died were guided well ahead;
And He brings dead ones out from living ones—
  The living self heads to its death, my sons.
Become dead so *the Everlasting One*
  Brings out the living then from you, dead one:
Become December—see soon spring's revival;
  Become night and you'll see the day's arrival.
Don't tear out feathers that you can't replace;
  In grief, good-looking man, don't scratch your face
Which looks just like the radiant morning sun—   555
  It is a big mistake to scratch that one.
Scratching it with your nails is unbelief,
  And causes the moon's face to weep in grief.
Perhaps you can't see your own bright face, friend?
  Come, bring your stubbornness now to an end.

*Explaining that the purity and simplicity of the tranquil soul are
disturbed by thoughts, just as when you write or sketch something on
a mirror and, even after wiping it off afterwards, a mark and
blemish remains there still.*

The face of the calm soul at peace within
    Suffers scratches from thoughts that enter in:
Consider bad thoughts poisonous nails that scratch
    The soul's face each time that such thoughts should hatch.
It's just like sticking a gold spade in shit   560
    To loosen thus a knotted part with it.
Suppose the knot is opened there eventually—
    It's just a tight knot on a purse that's empty.
You have grown old untying knots, my friend—
    So what if some get opened in the end?
The tight knot on our gullets all the while
    Is what decides if we are good or vile.
Solve this big puzzle if you are a man;
    Spend all your energy thus if you can!
You know what's 'essence' and what's 'accident'—   565
    Learn your own meaning. That's more pertinent.
Once you know who you are, flee this and go
    To That One who's beyond what such things show.
'Subject' and 'predicate' steal your attention;
    Blind life is spent on what you hear men mention.
Every proof with no outcome in the end
    Is vain. Reflect upon the outcome, friend!
You've seen each maker only through things made,
    Content with syllogisms men have said.
Philosophers with proofs link bit to bit,   570
    But the elect do just the opposite:
From proofs and veils these mystic greats would flee
    For the Proved One, then bow submissively.
Though, to the former, smoke is proof of fire,
    We love the smokeless fires in realms much higher,
The fire from close to Him especially—
    It's nearer than the smoke that one can see.
If one should flee the soul just for the sake
    Of some imagined smoke, that's a mistake.

In explanation of the Prophet's words: 'There is no
monasticism in Islam'.

Leave plumes, detach your heart from them instead!   575
   Each war requires a foe whom you want dead.
War is impossible without a foe;
   Without lust how can you opt to forgo?
If you don't crave it how can you hold back?
   If there's no foe, no troops need to attack.
Don't be a monk, don't get castrated, friend!
   Lust is what tempts your chastity to end.
One can't forbid lust if no lust is here:
   You cannot fight the dead; this should be clear.
God has said, '*Spend!*'* so first earn to be ready—   580
   One can't spend if one hasn't earned already.
Though absolutely '*Spend!*'* is what He said,
   '*Earn, then spend!*'* is what really should be read.
Since the King said, '*Restrain yourself!*'* likewise
   There must be something from which to turn eyes.
Thus '*Eat!*'* is for the snare of lust and greed,
   While for your modesty: '*Do not exceed!*'*
Without a predicate being used at all
   To have a subject is impossible:
If you have never been enduring pain,   585
   Then no reward will come for you to gain.
More self-restraint will mean more bountiful
   Rewards that give delight to heart and soul.

Explaining that the reward for the work of the lover of
God is God Himself.

He is the lovers' joy and misery;
   He is their payment and their salary.
If something else is still distracting you
   Then it's a trivial thrill, not love that's true.
Love is that flame which, once it blazes up,
   Burns everything but the Beloved up.
Slay other than God with the sword of '*No!*'*   590
   Then see what's left and what that has to show.

The rest will vanish; only God will stay—
    Rejoice, love! You burn polytheism away.
He is both First and Last—there's no division.
    Polytheism comes from cross-eyed vision.
All beauty's His reflection. Wonderful!
    The body does not move but through the soul;
The body in a damaged soul will not
    Turn sweet though put inside a honey pot.
The one who knows this was alive once, and   595
    Took a cup from the Soul's soul with his hand.
One whose eyes haven't seen those cheeks at all
    Believes this smoky vapour is the soul.
Not having seen the most just caliph either,
    He thinks Hajjaj was a fair-minded leader.*
Not seeing Moses's staff change, they see
    A real life in the ropes of sorcery.*
The bird that hasn't drunk pure water will
    Dip its wings in the briny water still.
Things are known by their opposites alone—   600
    Once one feels wounds, then soothing will be known.
That's why you face this world now and not last—
    So you'll enjoy the realm known as '*Alast*'.*
Once you flee here you go up there once more,
    Grateful for the eternal sugar-store.
'There I just sifted dust,' you then will say,
    'From this pure world I tried to keep away.
I wish I came here earlier than now
    So I'd have suffered less in mud somehow!'

*Exegesis of the saying of the Messenger of God: 'None died without
later wishing that they had died before they actually did—if they
were pious, so that they might have reached felicity sooner; if they
were wicked, so that their wickedness might have been less.'*

That's why the Prophet who knew all things said: 605
    'One who dismounts his body once he's dead
Does not feel bad for his death and homecoming
    But for what he'd omitted, each shortcoming.
Whoever dies then wishes he had gone

To his new destination earlier on
So his bad deeds would have been less, or rather,
   If he was good, so he'd have come home faster:
'I have been clueless,' bad men will then say,
   'Increasing my veils with each passing day.
If passing through this world had been more quick,   610
   The veils on me would not have been so thick.'

Don't rip contentment's face so greedily!
   Through pride, don't rip that of humility!
Don't rip generosity's through avarice,
   Nor good prostration's face through wickedness!
The sage said, 'Don't tear plumes that beautify
   Paradise—don't tear what lets you soar high.'
On hearing this advice, it suddenly
   Looked at him, then cried out so mournfully,
Weeping and moaning painfully for so long   615
   That everyone joined in as it felt strong.
Anyone who had asked, 'Why tear them out?'
   Regretted it and didn't wait about
For answers: 'Why did I ask curiously?
   It filled with grief; it was made worse by me.'
Tears dropped down from its face and each within
   Contained a hundred answers folded in.
The soul is moved by weeping that's sincere—
   Even the heavenly throne would shed a tear.
The hearts and intellects come from that realm   620
   Though the celestial light is veiled from them.

*Explaining that the spirit and intellect are confined in clay like
Harut and Marut in the pit of Babylon.**

Harut and Marut, pure ones, tasted it—
   They were confined in the most frightful pit.
The base and lustful world—they're locked within
   This horrible pit on account of sin.
The good and evil both learn sorcery
   From this well-known pair inadvertently,
But first they counsel: each will say, 'Beware

Don't learn from us this sorcery you find rare.
We teach this sorcery for a trial. That's all.   625
   Just for a test—it's not that wonderful.'
Testing requires free will—that is a fact;
   You can't have free will with no power to act.
Desires are like the sleeping dogs you've spied:
   Both good and evil can be found inside—
They stay asleep when there's no power to act,
   Silent like logs in fire, all neatly stacked,
Until a corpse should make them look around—
   Greed's trumpet startles them with its rude sound.
When there's a donkey's carcass in the lane   630
   A hundred dogs will then wake up again.
The dormant lusts that are concealed from view
   Will hurry then to rear their heads up too.
On each dog every hair becomes a tooth
   And they will wag their tails to hide the truth:
Its rear's a trick; anger fills up its head
   Like tinder added to flames seeming dead.
Flame after flame comes from No-Place—your eye
   Will see the flame's smoke rise up in the sky.
A hundred such dogs lurk within us—they   635
   Are hidden from us when there is no prey.
Like hooded falcons with their eyes sealed up,
   Behind veils love for prey still fills them up
Until the hood is lifted and they see
   The prey, then circle mountains instantly.
The sick man's lusts are pacified, for then
   His thoughts are fixed on getting well again—
Once he sees foods like melon, bread, and apple,
   His fear of harm and relish start a battle:
If he has self-restraint, then seeing food   640
   Will help, since in his sick state this does good;
But if he has none, then it's clearly smarter—
   Arrows stay far from men who have no armour.

The answer of the peacock to the one asking it questions.

Once it stopped crying, then the peacock said:

'Begone! You are a slave to looks! Instead
Can't you see that so many awful things
    Come to me from all sides due to my wings?
There are so many hunters everywhere
    Who see my feathers then put down a snare.
So many archers aim from far away   645
    With arrows due to my wings' fine display.
Since I don't have the strength or self-restraint
    To cope with trials and hardship like a saint,
It's better to be ugly now for me
    And in the mountains find security.
These wings are weapons of my pride, my friend—
    A hundred sufferings are what pride will send.'

Explanation of how skills, cleverness, and worldly wealth are, like the peacock's feathers, enemies of the soul.

Skills are the bane of men who're unaware—
    They want the bait and fail to see the snare.
Free will is good for that one who's a seeker   650
    And with '*Fear God!*' is clearly his own leader.
If you lack self-control and piety
    Put down your tools and don't act like you're free.
'My feathers are free will and self-display—
    They seek my end, so I'll tear them away.
The patient man deems feathers worthless, so
    They won't tempt him into wrongdoing's woe,
So feathers won't harm him—he need not tear
    Them out; his shield blocks arrows in the air.
But beautiful feathers are for me a foe,   655
    Since I am prone to self-display, I know.
If self-restraint and patience led me straighter,
    Through free will, my self-battling would be greater.
I'm like a child or drunkard near temptation;
    It's wrong to hold a sword in my low station.
With self-restraint and wisdom, then a sword
    In my hand would win all across the board.
One needs the sun-like wisdom that gives light
    To strike with swords and always get it right.

I lack that radiant wisdom; I'm unfit—   660
    I should just throw my weapons down a pit.
Right now my sword and shield are what I'll throw
    In there, since they'll be weapons for my foe.
Since I lack strength, support, and company,
    My foe will seize my sword and slash at me.
To spite this brazen, unveiled self, I vow
    To scratch on purpose my own face right now,
To thus reduce the beauty that's on show—
    Without my face shown I will meet less woe.
When I do it with this aim there's no sin,   665
    For wounds should cover this fine face's skin.
If my heart's nature was meek modesty
    My handsome face would spread just purity.
I didn't see strength, soundness and past lessons—
    I saw my foe and smashed up all my weapons,
So that my sword would not add to his arms,
    And my own dagger cause me many harms.
As long as my veins throb, I'll choose to flee—
    Fleeing oneself does not come easily.
One who flees someone else can feel secure   670
    Once he gets far from him—he can feel sure—
But my foe is my self and my sad plight
    Is running constantly with no respite!
In India and Khotan no sanctuary
    When your own shadow is your enemy!'

*Description of the selfless ones who have become safe from their own
vices and virtues, which are transient, through the permanence of
God, just like the stars that are annihilated during the day by the
sunshine—the one who is annihilated has no fear of harm or danger.*

One will be, like the Prophet, shadowless
    When one's own selflessness embellishes.
'*Poverty is my pride*'* was this way graced—
    Like candle flames his shadow was effaced:
The candle is aflame then totally;   675
    No shadow of it forms that one can see—
Wax flees from self and shadow into light,

Which, for His sake, the candle brings to sight.
'I poured light to efface you now,' God said,
   Men said, 'To that effacement I then fled'—
These are the necessary, lasting rays,
   Not those of candles that last just for days.
The candle is effaced in fire in full;
   No trace of light or candle's visible.
Through its dispelling darkness it is clear   680
   That wax is what maintains the fire's form here.
The body's candle's not like wax at all,
   For when it weakens there's more light of soul—
With rays that last and aren't for just one night
   The candle of the soul has holy light.

Due to the fact this flame was really light
   It cast no shadow as it burned so bright.
A cloud will cast its shadow on the ground,
   But there's no shadow of the moon around.
Good man, selflessness is like cloudlessness,   685
   Be like the moon's disc in your selflessness—
When clouds are driven over it, we see
   Its light goes; all that's left is memory:
Its light is weakened by the cloud's veil—soon
   The full moon is much less than a new moon.
Clouds make the moon a fleeting memory;
   The body's cloud makes things illusory.
And the moon's beauty? It's His beauty too.
   'Clouds are our enemies,' He said to you.
The moon is free from dust and clouds—it's clear   690
   She has a heavenly orbit far from here.
The cloud is our foe since it always tries
   To hide the lovely moon's face from our eyes.
This veil makes houris look like hags to you
   And the full moon less than a new moon too.
The moon seats us on glory's lap, and she
   Has called our bitter foe her enemy.
The beauty of the cloud comes from the moon,
   But don't err, calling clouds 'the moon' too soon.

The moon's light's shining on the cloud—it seems
    No longer dark, transformed thus by moon beams.
Though it has the moon's colour it is known
    That colour is just on a temporary loan.
Sun and moon are themselves redundant when
    The Source of Light preoccupies all men—
So they know borrowed things are transient
    And tell this world from what is permanent.
Mother, the nurse is only temporary—
    Embrace us in your breast immediately!

'My feathers are the cloud and veil: unclean.   700
    Through God's own beauty they have all turned clean.
I'll tear my feathers out, so I can soon
    Distinguish the moon's beauty from the moon.'
I don't want nurses—better to have mother.
    Like Moses's, my nurse now is none other.
I don't want go-betweens before the moon;
    It causes people's ruin to come soon,
Unless a cloud's effaced while on the way,
    So it can't veil the moon's fine face today.
Being naught itself, it shows her form so clearly   705
    Like Prophets and God's Friends before God really.
A cloud like that won't form a veil, but it
    Rather will tear veils to give benefit,
As when on sunny mornings drops descend
    Without a cloud above at all, my friend.
That was the Prophet's miracle—effacement
    Made clouds transparent to all men's amazement:
Clouds lost their own cloud nature in their view;
    Through patience lovers' bodies do so too.
A body right here, but its bodyness   710
    Transformed without scent's trace and colourless.

'Feathers please others while my brain's much greater,
    Hearing and vision's home, my body's aider.'
To sell one's spirit to trap others is

Unbelief and denial of godliness.
Don't be like sugar cubes for parrots—never!
 Be poison, safe from loss thus altogether.
Don't be a carcass for the dogs, just so
 You get some flattering praise for such a show.
Khezr broke the boat just so that he could spare it, 715
 So the usurper wouldn't confiscate it.*
'*Poverty is my pride*'* so please take heed
 To flee the greedy for *One Without Need.*
Hiding treasures in ruins is to spare
 It from the greedy who won't seek it there.
If you can't tear your feathers off your wings,
 Choose retreat and don't be consumed by things,
For you're both morsel and a morsel-eater,
 Consumer and consumed—take heed, it's clearer!

*Explaining that everything other than God is eating and being
eaten, like the bird that was hunting locusts and so preoccupied with
this that it was unaware of the hungry falcon breathing down its
neck trying to catch it. Now, O hunting and eating human,
do not feel secure against the one who hunts and eats you
even though you can't see Him with your eyes' vision but only
with the vision of the proofs and their contemplation until
your real eyes open, if God wills.*

A little bird was hunting worms one day, 720
 A cat then grabbed it as it passed its way.
Eater and eaten, it was unaware
 While hunting worms its hunter, too, lurked there.
If a thief is pursuing something then
 Police chiefs chase him, as do other men.
His brain's fixed on the door's lock and the loot
 Heedless of the police chief in pursuit—
Absorbed with his own craving, he can't hear
 People pursuing him now drawing near.
Grass feeds on air and water, but is later 725
 Chewed up and fills the stomach of a grazer—
That grass is eating and being eaten too;
 Apart from God, for all the same is true.

'*God feeds you, yet is not fed*'* is well known,
   Neither eater nor food, nor flesh and bone.
An eater who gets eaten cannot be
   Safe from devourers lurking dangerously.
You'll see the eater's not safe once he's dead—
   Go to the court of *that One who's not fed!**
Imaginings each devour another one;   730
   Each thought's devoured too by a different one.
You can't flee from imaginings and you'll see
   That simply sleeping cannot help you flee:
Your sleep's like water; thought is like a bee—
   Once you awake thoughts come back instantly.
Imaginings' bees will buzz right in and they
   Will start to pull you this way then that way.
These are the smallest of devourers really;
   God, the Most Glorious, knows the others clearly.
Flee from the rough devourers now with speed   735
   To Him who said: 'I am your guard'—take heed!
Or to one who has such protection when
   You can't reach fast enough the Guard of men.
Submit to the true master in this land
   And no one else—God guards Himself his hand.
Your intellect's a child and masters you,
   For it is mixed with the veiled ego too.
Join the Whole Intellect of the Creator
   So wisdom comes to you from your bad nature.
Once you place your own hand in His hand, you   740
   Will then escape devourers of men too.
Your hand will join the ones who've pledged good man—
   '*God's hand's above their hands*' says the Qur'an—*
Once you give to the Master your hand, he
   Who has all wisdom one could possibly,
Who is the Prophet of his time, no doubt,
   Such that the Prophet's light through him shines out.
You'll be in Hodaybiyya* as a member
   Of that group who pledged there, if you remember:
You'll be among the ten whose fates were told;*   745
   You'll be transformed as pure as purest gold,
So your association's right, not wrong;

With those we love is where we all belong—
He is with him in this world and the next:
    This is the meaning of the sacred text:
'*A man is with the one he loves—the heart*
    And its desired one won't be kept apart.'*
Don't rest, materialist, near snare and bait—
    Look at all the materialists' sad fate!
You who deem others weak must understand   750
    That far above yours there's a higher hand.
You're weak yet prey upon the weak all day—
    How strange that you're both hunter and the prey!
You have *a barrier both front and behind**
    So you can't see your foe as though you're blind.
Greedy with hunting, you forget you're prone;
    You try to win hearts though you've lost your own.
Don't be less than a bird in seeking bread:
    A sparrow sees *what's back and what's ahead**—
The moment it approaches just one grain   755
    It looks behind and straight ahead again:
'Is there a hunter here, such that I should
    Be careful and abstain now from the food?'
Remember now the wicked people's fates;
    See the death of your neighbours, which awaits.
Without the need for instrument, it's clear
    He can cause death; He's always with you here.
He tortures without weapons—understand
    God deals out justice without use of hand.
The one who asked, 'If God exists, then where?'   760
    Confessed while tortured He existed there.
He who said, 'That's far-fetched and weird!' in fear
    Now sheds tears and cries out, 'You who are near!'
While he now sees that he must flee the snare
    You're trapped due to your feathers, unaware.
I'll pull this wretched snare's nail out; I must
    Make sure not to lose out just due to lust.
I've answered fittingly for your brain's scope.
    Take heed of this: keep searching, don't lose hope!
Sever envy and greed's cord—comprehend   765
    '*A cord of branches on her neck,*'* my friend!

The reason why Abraham killed the crow,* which was a representation of the subjugation of some of the blameworthy and destructive qualities of the disciple.

This topic's endless. I now want to know,
    Abraham, why did you then kill the crow?
What was the point? For a divine command?
    Reveal a little so I understand!
The squawking of that black crow always seeks
    More life in this world, pleading as it speaks,
Like Satan, who had begged the One and Holy
    To grant eternal life for bodies only:
'*Grant me respite till Judgment Day!*'* he said—   770
    If only he'd said: 'I repent!' instead.
Without repentance life is torment. Severance
    From God implies that you are in death's presence.
With God both life and death are sweet; without
    Water of Life is fire none can put out.
It's Satan's curse that in God's presence he
    Asked for life to go on eternally.
To ask God for what's other than Him is
    To seek gain but to lose by doing this,
Long life apart from Him especially—   775
    A loser fox near lion-like royalty
Would ask, 'Prolong my life so I get worse;
    More time for me to lose worth for the curse',
As if he is deserving of it—people
    Like that who seek out curses are plain evil.
Nurturing the soul is what makes life worthwhile;
    The crow's life's eating up shit all the while:
'Give me more life so I can eat more shit!
    Inside I'm evil—keep on giving it!'
If that foul-mouthed one didn't eat shit later   780
    He would beg, 'Save me from my vile crow nature!'

Prayer

You have transmuted clay to gold, and You
    Made Adam, Mankind's father, from clay too—

Your work's transmuting essences, bestowing;
  My work is erring, blundering, and not knowing.
Transform to knowledge my forgetfulness!
  I'm angry—give me patient gentleness!
You who make soil transform to wholesome bread
  And then make life from what's inert and dead.
You who make stunned souls leaders, and O You   785
  Who can make prophets from mere wanderers too,
You make a piece of earth the heavens, You
  Influence through the stars the earth's course too.
One who for Water of Life takes this world here
  Will meet death sooner than the rest, it's clear.
The heaven-gazing inner eye could see
  That every second here there's alchemy:
Your body's cloak is joined up seamlessly—
  Transmuting essences is alchemy.
You were air, fire, or earth from that first day   790
  That you came to exist here in some way.
If you'd remained like that, then how could all
  This loftiness have come to you at all?
It's thanks to the Transmuter and His grace
  Better ones came to take the last one's place;
For millions of existents thus, in turn,
  Their second's better than their previous one.
See it from the Transmuter, not the means—
  You'll stray from Him by seeing go-betweens:
As go-betweens grew, union went from view;   795
  As they decreased, then union's savour grew.
Knowing causes lessens perplexity;
  The latter leads to His proximity.

Why turn away from dying in Him when
  From such death you gained living on again—
What loss came to you from your death like that
  Which makes you cling to life like a mere rat?
Your second's better than your first, so you
  Should seek the Changer and effacement too!
You have seen resurrections by the million   800

From your birth till today you stubborn minion!
Inert, then growing plant-like for a while,
    From that plant state to full life with its trial,
To wisdom then and visions that make clear,
    Further to what's beyond dimensions here.
These footprints reach up to the ocean's shore,
    But once inside the footprints are no more:
Dry stations are designed for cautiousness
    Whether they're cities, forts, or villages,
But stations in the ocean have no floor   805
    Or roof while waves confine you from the shore.
There are no signs at all for such a station.
    No name, address, nor any indication.
Between two stations there the distance is
    More than that from a plant to spirit is.
In prior deaths you saw those lives before,
    So why cling to your body's life some more?
Give up this life, crow—be instead a falcon!
    Gamble away all for God's transmutation!
Give up the old and take the new with glee,   810
    For each new year's worth more than the past three.
If you're not like the palm that gives fresh dates,
    Just pile the old up and forget their states—
Deliver to the blind men now instead
    This rotten, stinking world that's virtually dead.
Someone who's seen the new won't take from you—
    He is God's prey; he's not your captive too.
Wherever one finds those birds that are blind
    They're near you, water of the brackish kind:
Their blindness is increased by drinking you,   815
    For brackish water worsens blindness too.
Thus, worldly men are blind of heart today;
    They drink the brackish water found in clay.
Give briny water! Bury blind ones here,
    Since you lack Water of Life it is clear.
You'll stay and be remembered in this way,
    Unashamed like the black-faced slaves today:
The African's content with blackness—he
    Should be since he was black originally,

But if one had been fair a previous day　820
　　Then turned black, he'd try wiping it away.
When a bird's left behind on low terrain
　　It feels much sorrow and it suffers pain,
But birds that can't fly are quite happy there,
　　Feeding on grain, as if without a care,
For they could never fly originally
　　Unlike the birds that flew instinctively.

The Prophet said: 'Pity three types of men: the great man belonging
to a debased people, the rich man of a poor community, and a
learned man whom the ignorant make a fool of.'

'Take pity on the soul,' the Prophet said
　　'Of those once rich who now are poor instead,
And those brought low who had been venerated,　825
　　And learned men with the uneducated.'
The Prophet said, 'Show pity to these three
　　Even if you're as cold as men can be:
The former leader who is powerless,
　　The one once rich who now is penniless,
And then the scholar whose sad suffering here
　　Among the stupid people is severe.'
Falling from greatness to a nobody
　　Is cutting limbs from bodies tragically:
The freshly chopped off limb so quickly dies　830
　　Even if it should move before your eyes.
Whoever's downed *Alast*'s cup last year will
　　Be still hungover this year and feel ill,
While he, who dog-like loves the kennel here—
　　This base world—can't seek greatness that is dear.
Repentance is what those who sinned will pray—
　　Why should one sigh unless they've lost their way?

*Story about the deer fawn becoming confined in the donkey stable
and how the donkeys attacked that stranger, first with fighting
then with mockery, and how it suffered having to eat straw, which is
not its food. This is a description of the elite servant of God among
the worldly and lustful, for the Messenger of God said,
'Islam appeared as a stranger and will return to being
a stranger—blessed are the strangers!'*

A hunter caught a deer fawn on a hunt
    And put it in a stable, negligent;
Just like a tyrant he kept it confined   835
    With cows and donkeys there, not its own kind.
The fawn ran aimlessly in utter fright.
    He brought straw for the donkeys too that night.
Each cow and donkey ate it with much haste
    As if that straw were sugary in taste.
The fawn would rush this way and then that way,
    Then, worried by the straw, it turned away.
If left behind with those who're different
    One deems that like a deadly punishment.
Solomon said, 'If that hoopoe won't say   840
    A good excuse for its now being away,
I'll kill it or give torment that's so full
    It is a torment that's immeasurable.'
What is that torment? Being caged alone
    With people very different to your own.
Due to the body, pain afflicts Mankind—
    Your spirit's bird's caged with a different kind,
A falcon with the crows surrounding it—
    The crows and owls are always wounding it;
In misery stuck there, it's similar   845
    To a rare Abu Bakr in Sabzevar.*

Story about Mohammad Khwarazmshah, who conquered
the city of Sabzevar, which was entirely Shi'ite. They begged
to be spared, to which he responded: 'I'll grant you safety
when you present to me a man from this city
called "Abu Bakr".'*

Mohammad Alp Ologh Khwarazmshah

Arrived for battle once at Sabzevar.
His forces cornered its defenders and
   As they began to slay those on that land
The latter fell prostrate: 'Will you not give
   The chance to slave for you if we can live?
Whatever tax and tribute you demand
   We'll give without fail on the days you've planned.
O lion-like Shah, we earnestly implore: 850
   Our lives are yours—let us live on some more!'
He said, 'You won't be spared by me again
   Without an "Abu Bakr" among your men—
Bring me an "Abu Bakr" now from this city,
   O deviant ones, if you desire my pity;
Or else I'll mow you down, you wretched folk—
   No tributes or excuses! It's no joke.'
They brought so many sacks of gold instead:
   'Don't seek an "Abu Bakr", please!' they said.
'In Sabzevar how can one have that name?   855
   Finding dry bricks in streams would be the same!'
He turned away from all the gold to say:
   'Infidels, if you can't bring him today
There's no point bringing gifts. I am too old
   To be beguiled by silver and by gold.'
Unless you touch your forehead on the ground
   You can't soar, though your butt sits all around!
They sent men searching everywhere: they'd race
   Seeking out 'Abu Bakr's' near that place.
After three days of rushing all around   860
   A skinny man called Abu Bakr was found.
He had been travelling through, but then felt poorly
   So, almost dead, he stayed to get well fully,
Lying down in a quiet nook—their eyes
   Lit up on seeing him: they said, 'Arise!
The Sultan has demanded you from us,
   To make his mind up not to slaughter us.'
'If I could move myself,' the sick man said,
   'I would have left here long ago instead—
Why stay here in the city of the foe;   865
   I would have reached my friends' town long ago.'

They brought a cart so his complaints would stop
    And lifted Abu Bakr then on the top,
Then took him to the Khwarazmshah at once
    So he could see himself the evidence.

Sabzevar stands for this world—mystics here
    Feel ruined by displacement which is clear.
The Khwarazmshah stands here for God, the Glorious,
    Demanding heart from people who're notorious.
'*He looks not at your forms*,' the Prophet said,   870
    '*So seek the owner of a heart instead*':
God said, 'I watch you through the man with heart,
    Not prayer or alms since they're the lower part.
You thought your own heart could fulfil that too
    And stopped your search for those whose heart is true,
The heart where seven hundred heavens might
    Get covered and stay hidden there from sight—
Don't call your fragments 'hearts', nor claim there are
    People called 'Abu Bakr' from Sabzevar.
The mystic is a six-faced mirror so   875
    God sees through him all six sides one can know;
God only watches through his mediation
    All in the six dimensions from His station:
If God rejects, He does it for him and
    If He accepts, he's why—please understand
Without him God won't give to anyone;
    Of this man's virtues this is only one.
God puts the gift on the palm of his hand—
    From there it reaches others in the land.
His hand's link with the Absolute's great sea: 880
    Perfect, beyond all doubts, uncertainty.
It is a link beyond all words as well;
    One cannot speak about it, so farewell!

If you bring Him a hundred sacks of gold,
    'Bring me an actual heart!' you'll then be told.
'If that heart's pleased with you, then I am too,

But I'm displeased if it's displeased with you:
I don't look at you, but that heart that's whole—
 Bring to my door a gift for that, O soul!'
How does that heart view you? My view's none other—   885
 Heaven's beneath the feet of each one's mother.*
It's mother, father, and the source as well
 Of all creation—tell heart from the shell!
You'll say, 'I've brought a heart to you today.'
 'All towns are full of such hearts,' God will say,
'Bring one that has the *axis mundi* role,
 The true soul of the soul of Adam's soul.'
The Sultan of all hearts awaits that one
 That's filled with light and goodness. Bring that! Run!
You roam around in Sabzevar all day,   890
 But you won't find it searching in this way—
All you are doing is placing on the bier
 A bent and rotten heart to carry here,
Claiming 'I've brought a heart here from afar
 For you—it is the best from Sabzevar.'
He'll say, 'Is this a graveyard that you bring
 A dead heart brazenly for such a king!
Go back, bring one with a king's character;
 Through that comes safety to Being's Sabzevar.'
You could say that heart's hidden, isn't it?   895
 Darkness in this world is light's opposite,
And its dislike since Pre-Eternity
 For sensual Sabzevar's hereditary.
The heart's a falcon and this world's a crow—
 It's hard being trapped with strangers you don't know.
If they act amiably, they just pretend,
 Seeking self-gain through acting like a friend.
Without desire they do it to deceive,
 Reducing good advice you should receive,
Because this carrion-seeking crow is vile   900
 And has a million tricks to use with guile.
If falseness is accepted, he's set free—
 It's changed to seekers' true sincerity
Since those possessing heart, the men of God,
 Shop in the market-place for what is flawed.

Seek them if you are not a soulless person,
    Be the heart's sort, if not foes with the sultan!
But you like those men who will flatter you
    With falseness, not God's Friends whose words are true.
Whoever fits your nature and condition   905
    Seems prophet-like to your corrupted vision.
Abandon lust so fine scent reaches you
    And that scent-seeking organ finds you too—
Lusts have corrupted your own sense of smell:
    Amber and musk seem things that one can't sell.
This discourse has no limit and that fawn
    Is charging in the stable—let's move on!

The remainder of the story about the deer fawn and the donkey-stable.

That lovely fawn endured for several days
    Inside the donkey-stable torture's ways
Like fish on dry land, wriggling desperately,   910
    Or musk mixed with dung inadvertently.
One donkey said, 'This wild one's in a rush
    Believing that it's royalty, so hush!'
Another mocked, 'Through charging it has found
    A pearl it won't sell cheaply in the ground.'
Another: 'It's so dainty I condone
    That it recline now on the royal throne.'
Another donkey fell ill overeating
    And so invited that sweet fawn for feeding:
It shook its head, 'No, let me be tonight.   915
    I'm feeling weak and have no appetite.'
'You're playing hard to get!' the donkey said,
    'Or it's for reputation's sake instead?'
The fawn said to itself, 'That is your food
    Through which your limbs gain strength and you feel good.
I'm more familiar with fine lawns than here,
    Resting in parks where waters all run clear.
Though I now suffer due to destiny,
    How can I ever lose my dignity?
A beggar, but I won't be shameless too.   920

Although my clothes are old my spirit's new.
I've eaten basil, hyacinths, and tulips
   With much disdain shown through my eyes and full lips.'
'Keep bragging then, for we all understand
   It's easy to when in a foreign land.'
'My musk is proof: amber and aloes wood
   Owe debts to it—its perfume is so good.
Only those who can smell will sense this now;
   It's not for donkeys who love shit somehow.
Donkeys like donkey urine's roadside smell—   925
   Why should I give my musk to them as well?'

The Prophet said, '*Islam is marked to be*
   A stranger in this world,' and we can see
Even his followers fled from him though
   Angels share in his essence. Men below
Notice his face looks like their own, but they
   Can't smell that scent in him in any way.
A lion's in a cow's shape in the distance,
   But you don't look more closely in this instance.
If you do, you will quit your body's cow—   930
   That lion ravages it anyhow.
He'll throw that cow out of your head, thus he
   Removes from animal animality.
If cow-like, through him you'll become a lion.
   Content as cow? Then don't seek being a lion.

*Exegesis of 'I saw seven fat cows which seven thin cows ate up.'**
God created those thin cows with the traits of hungry lions,
so they would devour the seven fat ones. Although those
images of the forms of these cows were shown in the
mirror of dreams, perceive the actual meaning!

Once Egypt's ruler dreamt the following
   When his interior eye was opening:
Seven fat cows that looked to be well-fed
   Devoured by seven skinny cows instead.

The skinny cows were lions inwardly   935
　　To eat the fatter cows so easily.
The great man looks like other men outside—
　　A lion who eats men is found inside:
He eats the other man, and helps him gain:
　　Detached, his dregs become pure through this pain:
He spares that man of dregs through pain, so he
　　Can step above the lofty stars you see.
For how long like a vile crow will you cry:
　　'Why kill the rooster, Abraham, say why?'*
He answered you, 'Divine command compelled me.'   940
　　So we can praise it, detail it completely!

*Explaining that the killing of the rooster by Abraham signifies the
suppression and subduing of certain blameworthy and destructive
qualities within the disciple.*

The rooster is so lustful it's addicted,
　　Drunk on that poisonous, vile wine, and conflicted.
Had it not been because of procreation
　　Adam, through shame, would have preferred castration.
Accursed Satan said to God one day:
　　'I want a powerful snare for human prey.'
God showed him silver, gold, and horses then:
　　'Through these you'll easily entice all men.'
Satan said, 'Excellent!' but dropped his head   945
　　And turned as sour as lemons are instead,
Then God gave that downhearted Satan gold
　　And jewels from His mines. Satan was told:
'Take this snare too, accursed one.' He said:
　　'Give me more You who're best at giving aid!'
God gave him greasy sweetmeats that were rare,
　　Exotic drinks and silken robes to wear.
Satan then said, 'I need more help, O Lord,
　　To tie them up with *a palm-fibre cord*,*
So drunken lovers who are brave and strong   950
　　Can manfully break it to prove they belong
With You, and thus stay separate from the rest
　　By means of this snare's cords of lust as test.

O Sultan of the Throne, I want a snare
    That's trickier, to bring them down from there,
And so God brought him wine and harp, then he
    Half-smiled—he was more pleased than previously.
He sent God's power to mislead this: 'Start motion,
    Raise dust up from the depths of tempting's ocean!
Was Moses not one of your servants who   955
    With dust once parted waves all thanks to you?
Water drew back from all sides suddenly;
    Dust shot up from the bottom of the sea.'
Once God showed him a woman's beauty then,
    Since it was more than self-restraint of men,
Satan then snapped his fingers and began
    A jig: 'That's it! As quickly as you can!'
When Satan saw her tempting eyes, both able
    To make men's reason and restraint unstable,
The radiance of that beauty's face that could   960
    Make men's hearts burn like rue and aloes wood,
Cornelian lips, arched brow, and beauty spot,
    God shone there through a veil or so he thought:
Satan saw her light gait, her flirts, and posture
    As God through a thin veil in self-disclosure.

Exegesis of 'We created Man in the best of positions, then we
reduced him to the lowest of the lows'* and exegesis of
'Whomsoever we grant a long life we make him
regress in creation.'*

Beauty to which the angels had bowed down
    Was taken off as Adam was sent down:
'After my being, non-being?' he said that time.
    God answered, 'Living too long was your crime.'
Gabriel said, while dragging by his hair,   965
    'Begone from paradise and from the fair.'
'First glory, now abasement—tell me why?'
    'A gift at first, then judgment,' the reply.
'O Gabriel, wholeheartedly you'd bow,
    So how can you drive me from heaven now?
My robes of honour fall now, as you see,

      Like leaves in autumn falling from the tree.'
That face that is as radiant as the moon
      Ages just like a lizard's back so soon.
That forehead that is beaming soon gets old   970
      And then it looks so hideous and bald.
That proud, tall stature, lethal as a spear,
      Becomes bent-double as old age comes near.
The tulip's red turns to the saffron's yellow.
      Lion-like strength is feeble soon, my fellow.
The one who'd wrestle rivals down will hold
      Onto their arms so he can stand, once old.
These are the signs of pain, and of decay,
      Each bringing messages from death today.

*Exegesis of 'The lowest of the low, except those who believed
and did good things, for they shall have a reward without
remaining indebted.'**

If one's physician is God's Light, however,   975
      Fevers and old age cannot harm one ever.
Weakness there is like drunkards' weakness—he
      Ignites through weakness Rostam's jealousy.
If he dies, his bones soak in savour, learning;
      His atoms float in rays of light and yearning.
Those lacking this are orchards lacking fruit,
      Which autumn will turn over and uproot.
Roses don't last; only the black thorns stay.
      Roses turn flat and yellow just like hay.
O God, what did the orchard once commit   980
      For all its fine robes to be stripped from it?
'It saw itself and that's a poisonous vial—
      Beware, those of you who are now on trial!'
Young beauties who made lovers weep one time
      Repulse the whole world now—what was their crime?
'Their crime was wearing robes that were on loan
      And claiming that those fine robes were their own.
We take them back so you will know for sure
      The stack is ours—its scraps go to the pure;
So each knows that the robe was just on loan,   985

From Being's Sun a single ray alone.
That beauty, power, grace, and virtue too,
  Came here from Beauty's Sun for all to view.
The light of that sun, which is very far,
  Turns back from these walls homewards like a star.
Once it has finally managed to get back
  The walls will lose their light and then look black.
What stunned you in the faces of the fair
  Is the sun's light through coloured glass brought there.
The multicoloured glass displays that light   990
  As being multicoloured to our sight,
But when that lens is not here to view through
  The colourless light then will dazzle you.
Get used to viewing with no lens that light
  So when the lens breaks you won't lose your sight.
For you, book-knowledge easily satisfies—
  Through someone else's lamp you've lit your eyes.
He'll take away the lamp so you can know
  You are a borrower and can't bestow.
If you have tried and given thanks, don't fret—   995
  He'll give a hundredfold back to you yet.
Weep blood now though, if you have not been grateful,
  Because that Beauty's rid of the ungrateful.
He makes the works of the ingrates go missing.
  He leaves the righteous ones' state's worth increasing. *
Goodness is lost to all ungrateful men—
  They will not see a trace of that again.
Gratitude, selflessness, and kind affection—
  All vanish such that there's no recollection.
Ingrates, '*He led their deeds to loss*',* alluding   1000
  To each sought-out goal's flight when they're pursuing.
The grateful, loyal ones are the exception—
  Awaiting them is a most grand reception.
Lost fortune can't give strength now. How could it?
  Future fortune gives special benefit:
Lend now some of your fortune—God said, '*Lend!*' *
  You'll see a hundredfold thus in the end.
Reduce what you consume, for your own gain,
  For Kawsar's pool is what you can attain.

How can the captured prey of fortune flee   1005
    One who pours draughts of true fidelity?
God gladdens them: '*He makes good their condition,*'*
    And He returns to them what they had given:
God says, 'Fate, raiding Turk, give back again
    What you have plundered from those thankful men!'
It does, but they won't take it anyhow,
    Since these men have acquired the soul's wares now:
'We're Sufis and have thrown our cloaks,' they say,
    'We don't take what we gambled once away.
We've seen God's recompense and do not fear.   1010
    Desire and need have left us, it is clear.
We have emerged from filthy, poisonous brine
    To reach Kawsar and all the heavenly wine.
O world, for what you've done with others there—
    Disloyalty, disdain, schemes you prepare—
We in revenge pour back on you. That's right:
    We're martyrs but we have returned to fight,
So you should know that God has servants who
    Are combative and will confront foes too:
They rip the moustache of hypocrisy   1015
    And pitch their tents on forts of victory.'

These martyrs have become combative men;
    These captives have gained victory again.
From Non-existence each raised back his head:
    'Watch us if you're not blind!' these men have said,
To show suns in Non-being beyond compare
    And teach that suns here are mere stars in there.
Existence found in Non-existence—how?
    Things hidden in their opposites somehow?
God said, '*He brings the living from the dead.*'*   1020
    His slaves hope for Non-being now instead:
Doesn't the sower with an empty store
    Put all his hopes on Non-being to bring more,
That from Non-being new crops grow on his land?
    If you have vision you will understand.
You wait for understanding from Non-being

And peace and savour that you're also needing.
Sharing this secret's not permitted here
    Or I'd turn Abkhaz to Baghdad, my dear!*
Thus Non-existence is God's treasury   1025
    From which He brings out gifts continually.
He's the Originator, and in short
    Creates a branch without root or support.

Parable about the Existing World that appears non-existent
and the non-existent world that appears to exist.

God made non-being appear to be, and He
    Made Being seem non-existent similarly.
He hid the sea, but brought the foam to view;
    He hid the wind, but showed the dust to you.
Dust, like a minaret, seems to your eyes
    To move itself up, but how can it rise?
You see the raised dust, not the wind—you just   1030
    Deduce the wind's the mover of the dust.
You see the ocean's foam in constant motion,
    But it can't move at all without the ocean.
Your eyes perceive just foam, the sea you still
    Deduce: Thought's hidden, talk's perceivable.
We deemed negation affirmation wrongly
    With eyes that saw the non-existents only.
How can eyes that emerged in slumber see
    Other than non-existent fantasy?
We got confused because we were astray—   1035
    Truth was obscured, what's false made clear as day.
How did He make the non-existents seen
    And hide Reality from sight so keen?
Well done, O Expert in such sorcery
    Who made the dregs look pure so craftily!
Sorcerers measure moonbeams out to sell
    To traders and earn gold this way so well:
They take cash through this very tricky magic
    And traders pay cash but take home no fabric.
This world's the sorcerer; we're each a trader   1040
    Buying its measured moonbeams, learning later.

Like sorcerers it measures out a cut
    Made out of light from moonbeams, it claims, but
Once it has seized your life's cash, that's no more:
    Your wallet's empty and your fabric store!
You must say '*I take refuge, God, in you!*'*
    And cry, 'Save me from *witches' knots please, too!*'*
Sorcerers blow on knots, so help me please,
    O Saviour, from destruction! Grant release!'
Call also with the tongue of deeds, my people,   1045
    Because the tongue of mere talk is so feeble.

In this world you've three fellow-travellers,
    One loyal and the others treacherous.
The last two are belongings and companions;
    The first one, which is faithful, is good actions.
Wealth will not come with you outside its store;
    Companions reach your grave, not one step more,
And when your final hour comes your companion
    Will say, expressing what his soul would have done:
'I can't come with you any further now;   1050
    I'll linger by your grave though anyhow.'
Deeds are faithful—make them your refuge room
    For they will come with you deep in your tomb.

*Exegesis of the saying of the Prophet: 'You must have companions
to be buried with, they being alive and you being buried with them
when you are dead. If they are noble, they will be generous to you;
if they are base, they will betray you. Those companions are your
deeds, so make them as good as you can.'*

The Prophet said, 'There is no friend for you
    More loyal on this path than deeds you do:
If they are good, then they will stay forever;
    If bad, they'll be snakes in your tomb. Remember!'
Without a teacher from whom you can learn
    How can you do this path's work and thus earn?
Even the paid job that is the most small   1055
    Requires a master's guidance first of all.

Knowledge came first and then the deeds you do
    So they bear fruit eventually for you.
Seek help in gaining skills, O clever man,
    From noble, upright craftsmen if you can.
Seek from the craftsman skills he knows so well,
    O brothers, seek the pearl within the shell!
Be good to all advisers whom you see
    And seek their teaching with humility.
A tanner may have threadbare rags as dress,   1060
    But this won't make his talents any less.
If ironsmiths wear ragged clothes, still they
    Don't lose their reputation in this way.
So strip yourself of pride's clothes and then wear
    Humility's clothes when you're learning there.
Learning a theory is through words men say;
    Learning a skill's through practice every day.
You need a master for your spiritual aim—
    Neither the tongue nor hand can do the same.
Your soul learns from the soul of such a master,   1065
    Not from the theory textbooks or mere chatter.
And though the mystery be inside his heart
    The seeker won't perceive more than a part,
But when He turns this heart to light, that day
    '*Didn't we open up your breast?*'* He'll say.
'We've given you expansion in your breast;
    We put there in your heart what is the best,
Yet you are seeking it from others now—
    When you're the milk's source why seek out a cow?
There's a milk fount in you that's limitless—   1070
    Why seek milk from the cow's urn nonetheless?
O river you've a channel to the sea—
    Why seek pond water? Don't act shamefully!
For *didn't we open up?*'*—did you not get it?
    Why seek it elsewhere still and beg to get it?
Ponder the heart's expansion that's inside you
    So you won't hear God's '*Do you not see?*'* chide you.

Exegesis of 'And He is with you.'*

A basket full of bread is on your head
　Yet you beg door to door for crusts instead.
Look to your own! Be lightheaded no more!　　　1075
　Knock on the heart's door! Why try every door?
You're knee-deep in the stream yet while you're there
　You seek from others water, unaware.
Water's in front, behind and all around,
　But eyes have *barriers front and back** —none's found.
The rider seeks a horse—he's riding one!
　He asks, 'Where can I find a horse, my son?'
'Hey, isn't this a horse beneath you clearly?'
　'So have you seen a horse?' he asks quite weirdly!
Desperate for something clearly in his view,　　　1080
　Unaware of that thing, of himself too.
Desperate for water while inside it: though
　He's deep inside, he can't see currents flow,
Like ocean pearls which ask, 'Where is the sea?'
　They're blocked by their own shell-like fantasy.
Their asking 'Where?' becomes their veil from sight,
　Their cloud that blocks the morning sun's bright light.
Their bad eye is what's blindfolding them all—
　Seeing it lifted just creates a wall.
Their consciousness is now what plugs the ear—　　　1085
　Stay conscious of God if love-crazed, draw near!

Exegesis of the saying of the Prophet: 'Whoever makes his concern just a single concern, God will relieve him of his other concerns. Whoever is distracted by his various concerns—God will not care in which valley He kills him.'

You've split your consciousness in different ways.
　Those idle fancies are worth naught. None stays.
When water's drawn by every bad thorn's root
　From your attention, how can it bear fruit?
Cut off that rotten branch! Water instead
　The good branch, bring it back now from the dead!
Right now they both are green, but see the end

When only one of them bears fruit, my friend!
The orchard's water is for just that one—   1090
   Notice the difference! Farewell, I am done.
Giving water to trees is clearly justice;
   Giving water to thorns is clear injustice.
Justice means putting gifts in proper places,
   Not for all roots that draw them to their spaces.
Injustice means to put in the wrong place—
   It's just a source of misery and disgrace.
Give God's grace to the soul and intellect,
   Not carnal nature, which one should reject.
Load on your body all the grief that's fruitless,   1095
   Not on your heart and soul—that would be clueless:
That's putting loads on Jesus's sweet head
   While donkeys roam load-free in fields instead.
It's wrong to put kohl on your ear, for you
   To give the heart's work to the body too.
If you're of heart, be proud and don't just suffer!
   If body, eat the poison, not the sugar!
Sugar's bad for the body, poison's good—
   It's better not to give the body food:
The body's fuel for hell—you should reduce it;   1100
   If it grows more fuel, then you should uproot it.
You'll be a *firewood carrier* otherwise
   Like Abu Lahab's wife,* whom all despise.
Tell firewood from the Sidra* if you can
   Even though both are green right now, good man!
The Sidra's from the seventh heaven's sphere;
   The firewood is from smoke and flames down here.
Similar in form to senses they may be
   Because one's eyes perceive mistakenly,
But they're not similar to the heart's eye's sight—   1105
   Approach the heart! Strive to, *though it be slight*.
If you lack feet then move yourself a bit
   To see each big and little thing as fit.

On the meaning of the verse 'If you head out on the path, the path
will be opened to you. If you become non-existent,
*you will be made truly Existent.'**

Although Zolaikha shut doors everywhere
    Joseph succeeded still to flee from there.
The door unlocked and then the way out gaped—
    Since Joseph trusted God first, he escaped.
Although the world has no chink one can see,
    Like Joseph we must all try desperately
Until the lock is opened and you view   1110
    The gateway—Placelessness makes space for you.
Clever one, you came to the world one day,
    But can you tell exactly by which way?
You once came from a certain place below—
    Do you recall the path of your trip? No!
So just because you don't recall, don't say
    There is no way out—there's a 'wayless' way:
In dreams you happily travel everywhere,
    But do you know the path that gets you there?
Close your eyes and surrender, then you'll view   1115
    Yourself inside a timeless place anew.
A hundred tempting eyes keep your eyes glued,
    As blindfolds though, since they all just delude.
You stare wide-eyed for love of an admirer,
    Hoping for leadership and to rise higher.
You see in dreams, too, your admirers' faces—
    An evil owl sees only ruined places.
You always hope admirers will come crawling,
    But you have naught to sell them—it's appalling!
If your heart had some spiritual food, you would   1120
    Have been set free from purchasers for good.

Story about the person who claimed to be a Prophet. They
asked him, 'What have you consumed to become so crazy
and to talk absurdly?' He answered, 'Even if I had found
anything to consume I wouldn't have become crazy nor
spoken "absurdly", for whatever good words such men say
to those who are unworthy to hear them results in them
seeming to speak "absurdly", even if they were
divinely commanded in that "absurd" speech.'

'I am a Prophet!' once this person claimed,
    'More excellent than all the Prophets named!'
The people dragged him to their king to say:
    'He claimed: "I am God's Prophet!" Make him pay!'
People surrounded him like locusts there:
    'What trickery! What a deceitful snare!
If you mean that you came from Non-being, we
    Are all then noble Prophets equally.
We came from there, each here a stranger too—   1125
    What, pompous one, is special about you?'
'Did you not come as sleeping children do
    Clueless about the path and stations too,
Then passing them while drunken, drowsily,
    Unaware of this path's topography?
We passed alert and joyful through its stations
    From out beyond this world of limitations,
Having seen stations at their source—we say
    We are like expert guides who know the way.'
They told the king, 'Torture him so such men   1130
    Will never dare to say these things again!'

The king saw he was thin and feeble, so
    He would die easily from just one blow:
'How can one strike or torture him?' he thought,
    'His body is like glass, so I will not.
Instead I'll nicely speak with him and say:
    "Why do you have to boast in this proud way?"
For roughness will not be successful here:

Softness alone lures snakes out and not fear.
He made those gathered round him step away;   1135
    The king was kind; gentleness was his way.
He sat the claimant down and asked him then:
    'Where is your home and refuge?' 'King of men,
Firstly, from *The Abode of Peace* I came
    Travelling down to this *Abode of Blame*,*
With no home nor companion now around—
    Do fish make their homes ever on dry ground?'
The king then asked in jest, 'What did you eat
    For breakfast that you're like this when we meet?
Are you still hungry or did you take something   1140
    To get so drunk and boastful when you're talking?'
'How could I then claim Prophethood?' he said,
    'If I had eaten fresh or dried up bread?
Claiming my Prophethood among this lot
    Is seeking blood from stone, from where there's naught.'
No one seeks from a mountain heart or mind,
    Nor fathoming puzzles of the subtle kind.
The mountain echoes everything you shout;
    It jeers one like the scoffers do, no doubt:
Such men are far from what the Lord has said—   1145
    Don't hope to find life inside something dead!
Bring messages of gold and women and
    They'll happily give up all their wealth and land
On hearing: 'Someone calls you from a distance:
    She is in love with you. Hear her insistence!'
But if you bring God's honey-sweet words here:
    'You who have pledged, approach God now! Come near!
Choose sustenance, not this world of decay!
    Don't die here! There you permanently stay,'
They'll seek your blood and will attempt to kill you   1150
    And not just to defend their faith and virtue.

The reason for the enmity of ordinary people and their distancing of themselves from the Friends of God who call them to God and the Water of Life.

Opting to cling to home and property,
    God's message pains them; that's reality.
A donkey's wound has a rag stuck on it
    And you're removing it now bit by bit.
Due to the pain the donkey will kick out.
    The one who's kept far is most blessed, no doubt,
Especially when the rags are soaking wet
    On numerous wounds. Take heed, avoid regret!
The rag is property, the wound desire;   1155
    The wound is bigger when desire is higher.
Owls only live in ruins: they've not had
    Any news of the cities like Baghdad,
But if a falcon glides near through the air
    It will give news about its king back there—
A hundred foes will mock this royal bird,
    Saying that its reports are all absurd:
'What has the falcon brought us?' they will say,
    'It wants to brag with tales that lead astray.'
Such foes are those who're old and rotten too,   1160
    Or else that breath would make what's old turn new:
It gives new life to the long dead—that's right—
    And wisdom's crown, and it bestows faith's light.
Don't shun the pure bestower of the spirit,
    For he will mount you on a fast steed—spur it!
Don't sever thoughts from the crown-giver who
    Can loosen knots from the heart's depths for you!
Whom shall I tell? Is there one person near
    Seeking the Water of Life who might now hear?
You flee love after once enduring shame—   1165
    What do you know of love besides its name?
Love shows much haughty pride and sheer disdain—
    For love you must endure all these to gain.
Since love is loyal it seeks loyal ones;
    It disregards disloyal companions.

Man is a tree; the covenant* his root—
    You must tend to the root so it bears fruit.
Corrupted covenants are rotten roots—
    They will be cut off from all grace and fruits.
Although the date palm's branches may be green,   1170
    With rotten roots no benefit is seen.
Yet with good roots but no leaves now, we'll see
    A hundred leaves burst forth eventually.
Don't let their knowledge dupe you! Seek the covenant!
    Mere husk is knowledge; kernels are the covenant.

*Explaining that when an evildoer becomes entrenched in his
evildoing and sees the effects of the fortune of the good people,
due to envy he becomes a devil and a preventer of good,
like Satan, because a burnt stack wants all the other
stacks to burn too: 'Have you not seen him who
forbids a worshipper when he wants
to perform the ritual prayer.'**

When you see loyal people doing well
    You're envious like a devil stuck in hell.
Those with weak natures desperately pray long
    That no one else's body should get strong.
If you do not want Satan's jealousy   1175
    Stop all pretensions and seek loyalty.
If you lack loyalty don't speak a word,
    For words are claims for 'I' and 'we' when heard.
If kept in, words enrich the kernel, so
    In silence thus the inner soul will grow.
Words on the tongue spend from the kernel's gains,
    So don't hope a full kernel still remains.
One who speaks little has great thoughts, but when
    Talks shell grows thick the kernel shrinks small then.
And when the skin is thick the kernel's thin,   1180
    But when the kernel's full it has thin skin—
Look at these nuts when they are ripe to know:
    The walnut, almond, and pistachio.
One who rebels becomes like Satan, evil,
    Because he envies fortunes of good people.

When you've been loyal to the covenant
  God will be loyal. He's munificent.
But you have closed your eyes now, haven't you
  Despite '*Remember me and I will you!*'*
Heed '*Keep My Covenant!*' so God replies: 1185
  '*I'll keep your covenant*',* thus bind the ties.
But what is ours, O sad man? I have found
  It's like a dry seed planted in the ground.
The ground will gain no splendour from this seed,
  Nor the ground's owner riches, so take heed!
It just alludes: 'I need this and I know
  From Non-Existence You sent it below.
I ate it and the seed proves my claim's true
  So send us such a bounty, I beg You!
So stop this dry prayer, son, because instead   1190
  The tree needs seeds to be more widely spread!'
If you've no seeds, just prayer, God will decide
  To give a date-palm, saying: '*Well, he tried*',
Like Mary, who had pains but not one seed—
  God made the date-palm fruitful for her need,*
And due to that great lady's loyalty
  God granted wishes to her generously.
God makes those who've been loyal better than
  The other sorts of people here. He can
Make seas and mountains subject to them and   1195
  All the four elements serve their command.
This is a favour and serves as a token,
  So the deniers can tell, though it's not spoken.
The hidden miracles are not perceived;
  Such miracles can't even be conceived—
They are what matter and they last forever,
  Neither cut short and not rescinded ever.

Prayer

Giver of strength and solidarity,
  Rescue people from instability!
Please make the soul, which is now hunched and drooping,   1200
  Be upright in that work it should be doing.

Give patience, fill their scales pan with good traits.
     Free them from that sly one who fabricates!
Free them from envy, Noble One, so they
     Won't turn into cursed demons in that way.
Oh how the masses burn with jealousy
     Over mere transient lusts and property!
Look at how kings lead armies yet they slay
     Their family due to envy's evil sway!
Lovers of dirty harlots also would   1205
     Murder each other for them if they could.
Read *Wis and Ramin, Khosraw and Shirin*—*
     In jealousy how foolish some have been.
The lovers died and their beloveds too,
     So they and their love were worth naught. It's true.
Holy is God who brings non-beings together
     In love and also sets them on each other.
Envies emerge in fake hearts to this day—
     Being compels non-being in this way.
When even such kindhearted co-wives aim   1210
     To ravage one another all the same,
Imagine what the stonyhearted do
     In envy—try comparing from your view.
If the law hadn't spellbound people gently
     All would have ripped their rivals up in envy.
The law tries to deter their worst behaviour;
     It puts the devil in a glass container
Of witnesses, proof, oath, and oath's rejection
     Until the demon goes into detention,
Just like the balance, through which satisfaction   1215
     Of opposites is unified in action.
Know that the law's like scales and measures, saving
     Enemies from their feuds and mutual hating.
If there were no scales how then could one rival
     Escape disputes, suspecting fraud. They're vital.
When such an ugly, faithless carcass can
     Cause enmity and envy in each man,
How must it be for that felicity
     When men and jinn are moved by jealousy?
Demons are envious of decaying things;   1220

They'll never stop their theft and waylayings.
Humans who've cultivated disobedience,
   Through jealousy, themselves have turned to demons.
Read on these devilish men in revelation,
   Their change to demons by God's transformation.*
Know when the devil can't tempt men astray
   He seeks help from those God has changed this way:
'You're on my team now. Help! How much I tried!
   You must help now that we're on the same side.'
Then if they waylay anyone, both kinds   1225
   Of devils celebrate with joy, one finds.
And if one saves his soul and has progressed
   In faith, these envious foes lament, distressed.
They gnash their teeth in envy at those who
   Have gained from teachers wisdom that is true.

*The king asks the claimant to Prophethood, 'That one who is a real
Prophet and is confirmed as such—what has he ever given to
anyone and what will people gain by keeping his company and
serving him other than the advice he tells?'*

The king asked him, 'What is *waḥy* revelation?*
   What's gained by Prophets that's such a sensation?'
The man replied, 'What does he not achieve?
   What fortune's left that he does not receive?'
Although the Prophet's *waḥy* is not a treasure   1230
   It's not less than the bee's by any measure:
When '*God inspired the bee*',* its home thereafter
   Was filled completely with the sweetest halva.
By means of God's *waḥy*'s light, it then transformed
   The world with wax and honey, which it formed.
*We honoured** Man and he soars high—so please
   Don't try to claim his *waḥy*'s less than a bee's!

'*We've given you Kawsar*'*—did you not hear?
   Is that why you stay thirsty when so near?
Perhaps you're Pharaoh and Kawsar to you   1235
   Is filled with blood and vile pollutants too?

Repent, renounce, and totally give up
   Each foe who has no Kawsar in his cup.
Whomever you see flushed with Kawsar, he
   Has Mohammad's nature—keep his company
To be one who *loves for God's sake**, since he
   Gets apples from the Prophet's apple tree!
Whomever you see lacking Kawsar, know
   That man, like death and fever, is a foe,
Be it your father or your mother too,   1240
   For they're the drinkers of your blood. It's true.
Learn now from Abraham the way to act,
   For he renounced his father first in fact.
You'll be one who *hates for God's sake** this way
   And God's love's jealousy won't make you pay.
You will not find the path that leads you there
   Until '*There is just one God*'* you declare.

*Story about the lover who recounted to his beloved the acts
of service and loyalty, the long nights when 'they rise from
their beds',* the lack of food and the parching thirst
during long days, saying: 'I don't know of any other
service besides these, but if there is any, direct me, for
I do whatever you command, even if it is to walk
through fire like Abraham, or fall into the mouth
of a whale like Jonah, or to get killed seventy times
like St George, or to become blind from weeping
like Sho'ayb.* The loyalty and self-sacrifice of
the Prophets is beyond reckoning. Then how
his beloved answers him.*

A lover once recounted all he'd done
   In service to his own beloved one:
'I did this and I did that all for you—   1245
   I took blows from the spears and arrows too.
I lost my wealth, my strength and reputation;
   Due to my love I've faced much tribulation.
No dawn found me asleep or laughing and

No night found me with things I need in hand.'
He detailed all he'd tasted in his sorrow
    Of bitter dregs that he had had to swallow,
Not so she'd feel indebted, but just to
    Show her a hundred times his love was true.
For intellectuals, just a hint will do,   1250
    But how can lovers' thirsts be quenched thus too?
Lovers repeat themselves and still don't falter—
    Can fish be sated by one hint of water?
This lover made complaints about love's suffering
    Repeatedly, but claimed, 'Well, I said nothing.'
Fire was inside him, but he didn't know;
    He wept like candles due to the flame's glow.
'You did all that,' then his beloved said,
    'Open your ears and comprehend instead
The root of love is self-effacing love—   1255
    You fell short: you gave branches of that love.'
The lover asked, 'What is that root precisely'
    'Its root is dying and being naught entirely.
You did it all except the final dying.
    Heed this, alive one, if self-sacrificing!'
That moment he lay down and passed away
    Like smiling roses gambling heads away.
Like an endowment his smile stayed behind
    And like the mystic's unharmed soul and mind.

How can the moonlight ever get unclean   1260
    Although it shines on bad things that are seen?
It goes back to the moon untouched by all:
    To God returns the light of mind and soul.
The moonlight's purity is everlasting
    Though it might shine on an unclean and bad thing:
The light does not acquire bad attributes
    From any unclean, bad thing that pollutes.
The sunlight heard '*Return!*'* and then of course
    It went back hurriedly to its own source.
No stigma stayed from shining on a furnace,   1265
    No hues stayed from the gardens full of roses.

The eye's sight and the seer were both returning—
The plain and desert missed them and stayed yearning.

Once a man asked a mystic scholar, 'If someone weeps aloud
during the ritual prayer and sighs and moans, is the prayer
invalidated by this?' The mystic scholar replied, 'The name of
what is wept is "water from the seeing eyes" so it depends on
what the weeper has seen with them. If he has experienced
longing for God or repentance from sin, his prayer is not ruined,
but rather it is perfected, for the Prophet Mohammad said,
"There is no prayer except with presence of heart." However, if
the person praying has experienced bodily harm or is grieving
separation from a child, his prayer is ruined, because forgetting
about one's body and children is the basis of prayer, as Abraham
showed when he offered his son as a sacrifice in order to perfect
his prayer and when he surrendered his body to Nimrod's
fire. The Prophet Mohammad was commanded to adopt these
ways of acting: "Follow the creed of Abraham"* and "In
Abraham there is a fine example for you."'*

A man once asked a mufti who was there:
    'If someone weeps lamenting during prayer,
I wonder if his prayer is then rejected
    Or is it still thought flawless and accepted?'
'Why is it named "the water from the eye"?
    Consider what he saw that made him cry.
What hidden thing did his eyes see before   1270
    Which made its own two fountains start to pour?
If he then saw the other world, that prayer
    Gains from it splendour that is fine and rare;
If it was due to grief and bodily pain,
    The thread snapped and its spindle! Prayer's in vain.'

*A disciple visited his shaikh (by 'shaikh', which literally means
'old man' I don't mean someone old, but an elder in terms of
gnosis and intellect, even if it is Jesus in the crib or John the
Baptist in infants' school). The disciple saw his shaikh weeping.
He acted in conformity and also wept. Once he had stopped and
had gone out of the room, another disciple who was more familiar
with the state of their shaikh went after him to protect the honour
of his shaikh. He said to the other disciple, 'Brother, I should
have told you: God forbid that you should imagine or say that
the shaikh wept and you also wept, because one has to practise
self-discipline without hypocrisy for thirty years and pass
through bays and oceans full of whales and high mountains full
of lions and tigers for the chance of attaining the weeping of our
shaikh. If you attain it, you will give thanks a great deal
because, as the Prophet Mohammad said, "The earth has
opened up before me."'*

A dervish came before his shaikh one morning;
   The shaikh was weeping then, and loudly moaning.
When the disciple saw his Master cry
   He did, too, water pouring from each eye.
Someone who hears a joke laughs at that time,   1275
   But deaf men also laugh a second time:
The first time is so that he is conforming
   With others there because they are all chortling—
The deaf man laughs like us initially,
   Not sharing our condition actually,
Then afterwards he asks, 'Why laughter, men?'
   And, once he learns why, then he laughs again.
The imitator's like the deaf man here
   Because the joy inside him that shines clear
Is from his master, sent out as one ray,   1280
   Not from inside himself prior to that day.
As bowls of water, glasses filled with light
   Aren't sources, though it seems so at first sight:
When the bowl leaves the river it is clear
   To stubborn fools the water comes from here,

And when the moon sets everyone will know
    The glass's light comes from the moon's bright glow.
He'll laugh like the true dawn with open eyes
    A second time on hearing God's '*Arise!*'*
He'll laugh at his own previous laughter too   1285
    Since copying was all that he would do:
'On long and distant paths that I have taken,
    Thinking I'd found truth's secrets, so mistaken—
In that lost valley how did I rejoice
    In blindness like that?' asks his inner voice.
'What did I falsely see? What was it really?
    My weak perception made me see it feebly.'
The thoughts of novices and those of shaikhs:
    The latter truths, the former merely fakes:
The child thinks of the wet-nurse and milk-drinking,   1290
    Or walnuts, raisins, crying and loud shrieking.
The imitator's a sick child: You'll find
    His arguments and proofs are so refined—
Engrossed in proofs and puzzles as distraction,
    This blocks him from acquiring true perception.
He's used in solving puzzles all his kohl
    Apportioned for developing his soul.
Turn back now from Bukhara, imitator—
    Be self-abased first, valiant hero later,
To then see a Bukhara in your soul,   1295
    Where valiant ones *don't understand** at all.
A courier might be fast on land this hour,
    But when in water his limbs have no power.
He was of those *we carried on the land*;*
    Someone borne on the sea is much more grand.
The King has much to give—run to that King
    You who're now pawn to each imagining!

That simple student out of imitation
    Wept to conform with how he saw that great one:
He wept to copy like the deaf must do   1300
    Since of the actual cause he had no clue.
He then left after weeping heavily;

A senior student followed hurriedly,
    Saying: 'You wept like clouds that have no clue
    Copying what the mystic shaikh would do.
For God's sake, good disciple, think again—
    Though from conformity you seek to gain—
Don't say: "I saw that monarch weep so I
    Wept just like him", for that would be a lie.
Weeping while clueless, guessing, in imitation   1305
    Is different to the weeping of that great one.
Don't you equate the one type with the other
    For they are truly worlds apart, my brother:
His came from thirty years of struggle, friend.
    The intellect can't reach that lofty end
With scores of higher stations still up there—
    Don't think the intellect can reach a share.
His weeping's not from grief or joy—beware!
    The spirit knows *the fountain of the fair.*
His laughter and his weeping both come from   1310
    Beyond all that the intellect can plumb.
Such tears belong to his rare eyes: that's right.
    How should the sightless eye by tears gain sight?
Your sort cannot perceive what this man sees
    By senses, reason, or analogies.'
Night flees when light arrives from far from sight—
    How can night's darkness know about the light?
The gnat flees from the wind—how can the gnat
    Know of the savour winds feel blowing that?
When the Eternal comes it voids the temporal—   1315
    How can the temporal know then the Eternal?
The temporal's stunned by the Eternal's strike—
    The latter naughts it then makes it alike.
You can find many parallels, it's clear.
    I can't be bothered to provide more here.

This *alif lam mim** and *ha mim** both turn
    To Moses's staff when you fully learn.
Though other letters look the same as these
    They have inferior inner qualities.

How can a staff that someone tries out be   1320
    Like that magnificent one? Please tell me!
It's breath's like Jesus's, not any kind,
    Nor breath that's from a sad or happy mind.
This *alif lam** and *ha mim** both came here
    Down from the Lord of Mankind, it is clear.
Can other letters really seem like these?
    If you've a soul don't look with just eyes, please!
Though they're composed of letters similarly
    To writings by the generality,
Mohammad was of flesh and skin, the same   1325
    As others' bodies with regard to frame:
He had flesh, skin, and bones and so did they—
    In composition just the same, you'd say—
But his had miracles by which the rest
    Were vanquished, which reveals how his was best.
With *Ha Mim** of the holy book it's so:
    This is so lofty while the rest are low.
Since life comes from this lofty text at last
    As from the Resurrection's trumpet blast,
It changes to a dragon, parts the sea   1330
    Just like the staff, when God helps generously.
Their form may look like others' at the start,
    But bread discs and the moon are far apart.
The shaikh's tears, laughing, and his speaking too,
    Were not from him, but from God's Essence, *Hu.**
The stupid took the outward form alone
    So subtleties stayed hidden and unknown:
They stayed veiled from objectives naturally;
    Though shown, they couldn't see the subtlety.

Story about the slave-girl who satisfied her sexual lusts
with her mistress's donkey, which the former had taught
how to have sex like a man just as goats and bears can be
taught. She would fit a gourd on the donkey's penis so it
would not exceed a certain length when penetrating her.
The mistress found out about it, but did not see the detail
of the gourd. She sent the slave-girl far away under a
pretext and had sex with the donkey without using the
gourd, and so she died in ignominy. The slave-girl got back
too late and lamented: 'O my dear precious one, you saw
the penis but not the gourd, the male member but not the
other.' 'Every deficient one is cursed' means that every
inner vision and understanding which is deficient is
cursed. After all, those who have deficient external
vision are forgiven by God Himself and not cursed.
Read: 'There is no blame on the blind.'* God
has eliminated the blame, the curse, the
reproach, and the anger.

A slave-girl forced upon herself no less   1335
    Than a male donkey due to lust's excess!
She'd got it used to having sex with her
    The same way that most human males prefer.
A gourd was used for safety in this state
    To limit how much he could penetrate:
She put it on his penis as protection,
    So only half would make the penetration—
If all his penis had then penetrated
    Her womb and guts would have been devastated!
The donkey grew thin and his owner there   1340
    Wondered why he was thinner than a hair.
She showed him to the blacksmith 'What is wrong
    With him that he's grown thinner for so long?'
No sickness could be traced in him: nobody
    Could find the secret of his ailing body
She then investigated seriously
    And her research improved increasingly—

One's efforts must be of a serious kind
    For souls that seek to be the ones that find.
She went to see him, but she noticed there   1345
    The slave-girl was stretched out across a chair.
Through a door crack she saw what they did there
    And that crone truly marveled at the pair—
The donkey was there fucking her somehow
    The way men do, controlled and with know-how!
'How can this be?' she thought in jealousy,
    'I'm due this more as he's my property.'
The donkey was refined and trained so well—
    The table set, the lights turned on as well.

As if she hadn't seen, she knocked and said: 1350
    'Slave-girl, how long will you sweep up?' instead,
To play-act and disguise a little more.
    'Slave-girl, it's me, so open up the door!'
She said naught as she didn't want it known
    She'd learnt the secret to try on her own.
The slave-girl hid the tools that she'd been using
    For the perverse act that she had been doing,
Opened the door and showed a serious face
    As if to say, 'I'm fasting in this place',
With broom in hand as well, as if to say   1355
    'The house was dirty so I swept all day.'
She opened up the door with broom in hand—
    The mistress mumbled, 'Sex coach, who had planned
To put a serious face on in that way,
    Broom in hand—Why's the donkey far from hay
Seemingly interrupted mid-flow too,
    Angry, its penis throbbing, wanting you?'
She mumbled so the slave-girl wouldn't hear
    And treated her as innocent and dear.
She then said, 'Put a veil now on your face   1360
    And take a message to a certain place:
Tell them there this and that, etcetera
    (I've shortened their talk, so it's easier—
You'll grasp the essence of what I do say.)

Once she had sent the veiled one on her way,
Drunken with lust, delight inside her head,
   She shut the door behind her and then said:
'I'll shout my praise now I have privacy;
   I've fled from petty judgements totally!'
Her lust grew wild like goats' lust and she'd melt   1365
   In the sparks of the donkey, which she felt.
Sheer lust like that of goats led her astray—
   Such giddy ones are easily led, aren't they?
Lust makes hearts deaf and blind, so donkeys seem
   Like Josephs, fiery flame like pure light beam.
Drunk on fire, seeking fire, yet in that plight
   So many think they're absolute, pure light
Unless God or His Friends bring them relief,
   Attracting them to turn then a new leaf,
Showing the fiery past imagining   1370
   Is on this path a merely borrowed thing.
Lust makes the ugly look good in your view;
   On this path nothing's worse than lust for you.
It has disgraced so many reputations,
   Made fools of millions of intelligent ones.
Since it makes donkeys look like Josephs here
   Think how it will make Josephs then appear.
Its spell makes dung seem honey to your view—
   What will its tricks make honey seem to you?
Lust comes from eating, so reduce your intake   1375
   Or marry—flee from bad deeds for your own sake!
Overeating will drag to the forbidden;
   Intake must all be spent and won't stay hidden.
Marriage is saying, '*Lord, give strength to me!*' *
   So demons don't bring you calamity.
You want to feast, so marry straight away
   Or else the cat will snatch the food away!
Place on your donkey heavy loads right now
   Before it places loads on you somehow!
You have no clue about fire's harm—step back!   1380
   Don't go near fire when you have such a lack!
Lacking knowledge of fire and pot, some dared—
   Due to the flames no pot nor broth was spared:

Water and know-how must be there already
　　So when it boils the pot will cook correctly.
You don't have blacksmiths' know-how, so don't dare
　　To go near there—flames burn your beard and hair.

That woman dragged the donkey, shut the door,
　　Joyful, but with harsh punishment in store.
She dragged him to a central space and lay　　　　　1385
　　On her back underneath him in the way
She'd seen the slave-girl on her chair before,
　　To satisfy her lustful craving more.
The donkey's penis grew erect and stiffer—
　　It thrust in her and spread a fire within her.
The well-trained donkey pushed in all the way
　　Up to its balls and she died straight away.
The penis in her made her liver tear;
　　Her intestines were also torn in there.
And she said nothing—on the spot she died.　　　　1390
　　The chair fell one side, she the other side.
The room was soaked in blood. What a bad state!
　　The woman fell down dead: *unfortunate fate.* *
A bad death with so much disgrace, O father:
　　She was a donkey's penis's frail martyr!
Heed the Qur'an: '*The torment of disgrace.*'*
　　Don't lose your life through such a fall from grace.
The donkey is the carnal soul: to be
　　Under it is more shameful obviously:
If you die for the carnal soul, be sure　　　　　　1395
　　You're like this woman who was so impure.
He gives our carnal soul the form of donkey
　　Since forms can correspond to natures roughly:
The Resurrection's secret we now see—
　　For God's sake, flee your donkey-body! Flee!
God warned the infidels of burning flame—
　　They said, 'Fire's better than disgrace and shame.'
'But no, that fire's disgrace's root,' God said,
　　Just like the fire that left that mistress dead:
Through lust she bit much more than she could chew,　　1400

Then choked on bad death's morsel and died too.
Eat the correct amount, you greedy lot
   Even of halva and cakes sweet and hot.
God gave a tongue to weighing-scales. Beware!
   Read *Surat Rahman** and take special care.
Don't quit the weighing-scales because of greed!
   Both lust and greed are foes that will mislead.
Greed wants it all and loses it all, so
   Don't worship greed, you, son of so and so!

While walking off, that slave-girl then would say: 1405
   'Mistress, you sent the expert far away,
Wanting to act without the teacher there—
   You'll lose your life in ignorance. Beware!
You stole a knowledge which was incomplete,
   Ashamed to ask me of the risks you'd meet.'
Ropes wouldn't fall on birds' necks if they ate
   From their own harvests and then shunned the bait.
Eat less grain! Don't refill much! When you read
   '*Eat!*'* also make sure to read: '*Don't exceed!*'*
Avoid bait—don't get trapped and die as well.   1410
   Knowledge and true contentment helps. Farewell!

The wise eat from God's bounty here, not grief;
   The ignorant have stayed deprived, in brief.
Eating of grains is finally stopped for all
   The moment when around their throats ropes fall.
How can a bird enjoy grains in the snare—
   Those grains are poison if they're eaten there.
The heedless bird eats them as vulgar men
   Do likewise in the world's big trap, but then
The wise, informed birds keep a healthy distance   1415
   From all grain used as bait with great resistance,
Since grain in traps is of the poisonous kind—
   A bird that seeks grains there is clearly blind.
The hunter chops off heads of foolish ones
   In traps, but leads to parties polished ones:

Sex with a donkey

The former are just good for meat as food;
    The latter's songs and warbles sound so good.

The slave-girl saw through cracks inside the door
    Her mistress under it, dead on the floor.
'Stupid mistress, what did you try to do?   1420
    The teacher would have shown the way to you.
You couldn't see more than just superficially,
    Yet opened up your school to claim your mastery.
The penis was like honey cakes to you—
    How come the gourd escaped your lustful view?
Immersed in lust you simply couldn't see
    The gourd I used for my security.
You saw the surface of the master's craft,
    Claimed mastery with huge boasts and smugly laughed.'
Many pretenders who are unaware   1425
    Of Sufism learned just the wool to wear.*
Impudent ones who didn't act would only
    Learn from the greats how they could chatter boastfully,
Each claiming, staff in hand, 'Behold, I'm Moses!'
    Or, breathing on some fools, 'Behold, I'm Jesus!'
Wait till the day the touchstone makes it clear,
    Demanding the true ways of the sincere!
Ask from the master all that's left to learn
    Or are you blind and too dumb to discern?
You craved all, yet you failed to get your way—   1430
    This stupid flock is just the wolves' own prey.
Hearing the form, you tried interpreting,
    But parrot-like you didn't know a thing.

Comparison of a master's transmission of knowledge to
disciples or a prophet's to his community when they do not
have the capacity for the divine transmission and lack
intimacy with God, to a parrot that has no familiarity
with the form of man to be able to receive transmission of
knowledge from him. God holds the master like a mirror in
front of the disciple, as if he is a parrot, and communicates
knowledge from behind the mirror, saying: 'Do not hurry
it along with your tongue—it is nothing other than divine
communication.'* This is the beginning of an unsolvable
question: when the parrot moves its beak in the mirror's
face you call it an image: it has no volition and power; it is
the reflection of the actual parrot speaking, which is itself
the learner actually. It is not the reflection of the teacher
who is behind the mirror, but the speaking of the parrot is
controlled by that teacher, so this parrot image is a
comparison, not an allegory.

A parrot sees itself when peering at
   A mirror placed in front of it like that.
Behind the mirror stands its hidden teacher—
   That knowing and sweet-tongued one is the speaker.
The parrot thought its image in the mirror
   Was the one talking to him and none other.
It learnt to speak from its own kind this way,   1435
   Clueless about the teacher's cunning play:
He teaches from behind the actual mirror,
   For it won't learn from teachers whose forms differ.
It learnt to talk from that skilled person's teachings,
   But it does not perceive their actual meanings;
It learnt speech from a human bit by bit—
   It can't know more of humans though, can it?
Disciples see themselves like this too, oddly,
   Inside the mirror of God's Friend's own body.
They can't see Universal Intellect   1440
   Behind their mirror, nor do they suspect—
Each one believes a human's speaking there,

Clueless about the mystery, unaware.
Each learns words, but can't know the mystery—
　　They're parrots, not good friends for company.
People learn songs of birds as well by rote,
　　But that's an action of the mouth and throat.
They don't perceive what that bird's trying to say
　　As Solomon did in his special way.
Many have learned the words of Sufis, then　　　　　1445
　　Used them once on the pulpit, but these men
Either gained nothing but the words they say
　　Or God's kind mercy showed them the true way.

*A mystic saw a pregnant dog with puppies barking in its
belly. He was amazed and said: 'The point of the dog's
barking is to keep guard, but barking in the mother's belly
can't be to keep guard. Barking may also be to ask for
company or milk etc., but in this situation it has none of
these uses!' When he regained his composure he prayed to
God: 'No one knows its interpretation but God!'* As reply
he was told that this is an image of the state of those
people who remain veiled and have not had the eyes of
their hearts opened, yet regardless claim inner vision and
deep sayings. Neither strength nor support reaches them,
nor does guidance reach those who listen to them.*

A Sufi on a forty-day retreat
　　Once saw a pregnant dog out in the street,
Then heard the bark of puppies suddenly
　　From that dog's belly where he could not see.
The barking stunned him: 'Can some puppies really
　　Bark loudly from inside their mother's belly?
Have any other ears heard puppies whine　　　　　1450
　　While still inside their mother, or just mine?'
He woke when he was jolted by this vision
　　And with each moment he felt more confusion.
There was no one but God while in retreat
　　To now untie the knot, a major feat:
He said, 'O Lord, because of this big question

I've been held back from *zekr* meditation.
Release my wings, so I can now fly upward
    Inside your *zekr* garden and its orchard!'
A voice replied to him that very moment: 1455
    'This represents the idle men's amusement,
For they remain veiled, yet with closed eyes they
    Discuss things in a vain and pointless way.'
The dog's bark in the womb is so redundant:
    It's not for guarding, neither for a real hunt.
It hasn't seen the wolf to start a fray,
    Nor robbers that it can thus drive away.
The greedy who desire to be the head
    Have little vision, but huge boasts instead:
Desiring buyers and their keen attention   1460
    They prattle nonsense and lack true perception.
They've never seen the moon yet give men signs,
    Corrupting bumpkins with their own designs.
Each does it to gain buyers and high stations;
    Without sight he gives scores of indications.
Only one buyer makes you truly gain,
    But these men's doubts about Him still remain.
To woo a worthless customer these men
    Will lose that One True Customer again.

He is our Buyer: *God has bought,** so rise   1465
    Above concern for other buyers' eyes.
Seek out that Customer who's seeking you,
    Who knows your origin, and your end too.
Don't try to woo each customer you see,
    Don't two-time your beloved faithlessly!
If that one buys, you will not gain one pence—
    He has no wisdom nor intelligence.
He can't buy half a horseshoe, so now why
    Do you show rubies too for him to buy?
Your greed blinds you and it holds back from you;   1470
    The devil makes you like himself, cursed too,
As with Companions of the Elephant*
    And Lot's own people—he's malevolent.

The patient person finds the Purchaser,
 Since he won't sell to every customer.
One who turns from that Buyer throws away
 Good fortune and eternal life that way.
Eternal grief awaits all who are covetous
 As with the Zarwan people who were envious.'

*The story about the people of Zarwan and their envy of the
poor: 'Our father through simpleness used to give away most of
the produce of the orchard to the poor.' He gave a tithe for
grapes, then also when they were turned to raisins or syrup,
and also when he made halva or sherbet with them. He would
also give a tithe for straw, and when he threshed it he would give
a tithe for the unthreshed ears mixed with the straw, then when
he separated wheat from straw he would give another tithe, and
also when he made flour from it another tithe; then he would give
a tithe when he made dough from that, and also another tithe
when he made bread. Unsurprisingly, God placed such a blessing
on that orchard and his crops that, while the other orchard
owners were in need of him, both for fruit and money, he did not
need anything from anyone. His sons saw the repeated payment
of tithes, but did not see the blessing that came from that, like
that unfortunate woman who saw the donkey but not the gourd.**

A righteous, godly man with perfect wisdom   1475
 Who always had foreknowledge of each outcome
Once lived in Zarwan near the Yemen. He
 Was known for kindness and for charity.
His dwelling was the Kaaba for the poor
 Because they'd come to him and feel secure.
Without airs he would give a tithe away
 For whole ears and when wheat was threshed away.
When it was used for flour he gave another,
 And when made into bread once more, my brother.
He'd not omit the tithes for crops he'd grow,   1480
 Giving four times for everything he'd sow.
That generous man would also tend to give

Advice to all his sons on how to live:
'For God's sake, don't you fail now to take heed:
    Never omit the poor's share through your greed.
This way the fruit and crops won't disappear—
    Obedience to our God will keep them here.'

God sent all fruits from the Unseen without
    Hesitancy or calculative doubt.
If you expend where produce comes from, you   1485
    Will make gains—that's the realm for profit too.
The farmer sows most crops in the same field,
    For that's the origin of his last yield:
He sows most back and eats a tiny bit,
    For it grows back and he's not doubting it.
The farmer's busying his hand to sow,
    Since from this soil his corn began to grow.
The cobbler buys with what's left after food
    Both fine grain leather and cow hide that's good:
'These have both been my income's source before—   1490
    They'll bring my livelihood so I'll buy more.'
His income came from these and so of course
    He generously will give back to his source.
Leather and soil are veils—it's understood
    God is the real source of our livelihood.
Sow in the source's soil when you are sowing
    So that a thousand more crops will start growing!
I take it that you sowed in soil you thought
    Would be the means for growth, but it was not?
What will you do if nothing grows in there   1495
    For years, apart from hold your hands in prayer?
You'll beat your head before God then at once—
    Both head and hand prove God gives sustenance.
Thus you'll learn He's the source and people who
    Seek sustenance must also seek Him too.
Seek sustenance from just Him, friend of mine,
    And drunkenness, not from hashish or wine!
Seek wealth from Him too, not from property!
    Seek aid from Him, not from your family!

You'll be without the others in the end,   1500
    So who will you call out to then, my friend?
Call to Him now, forget the rest, so you
    Inherit the real wealth of this world too!
When it's the time of '*someone flees his brother*'*
    And also of '*a son will flee his father*',*
At that time every friend becomes a foe—
    They'd been the idols that kept your reach low,
Since from the Painter you had turned away
    Because your heart was under His art's sway.
If now your friends become foes similarly   1505
    And turn their face from you in enmity,
Take heed and say: 'I've won the prize this way:
    What was tomorrow's has arrived today—
This realm's folk have become my enemy,
    So Resurrection now is shown to me.
Before I flit my time away by spending
    The rest of my life with such men, that's ending—
I had bought faulty goods, but thankfully
    God made me see their flaws immediately:
I would have lost my money otherwise   1510
    And noticed defects too late with my eyes—
With wealth gone and life wasted I'd have bought
    Faulty goods with my life's wealth had He not.
Like selling goods and being paid false gold
    But heading happily home once they were sold—
Thank God the false gold was revealed to me
    Before more of my life passed wastefully.
It would have weighed on my neck then forever,
    A shameful waste of life thus altogether,
But since its falseness was so quickly shown   1515
    I'll quickly side-step it now it is known.'

When your past friend shows enmity to you
    And his spite's scab of envy comes to view,
Don't feel at all bad for his new aversion—
    Don't make yourself a stupid, clueless person!
Rather thank God and pay so all can eat:

Celebrate that you fled his vile deceit
Before becoming old—you've fled it fast
    To seek the Truthful, Lasting Friend at last,
The Lovely Friend who'll always be your friend—   1520
    This cord gets stronger after your life's end.
That Friend can be the Sultan, Lofty Emperor,
    Or one whom He accepts as intercessor.
You've fled the counterfeiter and his crime;
    You've seen his fraud before the end of time.
This world's people's mistreatment now of you
    Is hidden treasure if you only knew:
People are made to mistreat you—their action
    Compels you then to look in that direction.
When life ends, you should know with certainty   1525
    Each will become a stubborn enemy.
You'll be left in the tomb, where you will moan,
    Beseeching God: '*Please don't leave me alone!**
You whose own harshness is to me more loyal
    Than loyal men—their honey's your bestowal.'
Granary-owner, listen to your brain
    And now commit to *God's earth** all your grain
To keep it safe from thieves and pests there too,
    Then with pests kill the demon threatening you!
He threatens you with poverty each day—   1530
    Brave falcon, make that partridge now your prey!
The Mighty Sultan's falcon can't allow
    A partridge to make it its prey somehow!

Their father gave advice–in doing so
    Sowed seeds, but on bad soil none ever grow.
Advisers can keep counselling one for years,
    But counsel also needs attentive ears.
You give advice so kindly like a brother,
    But it goes in one ear then out the other.
A hundred speakers' words have no effect   1535
    On those who will not listen, and reject.
Who better than the Prophets, whose fine speech
    Moved rocks when they used their pure breath to preach—

But what moved rocks and mountains couldn't free
    The wretches from their infidelity.
Such self-conceited hearts have been made known
    In the Qur'an: '*Rather, harder than stone.*'*

*Explaining that God's bestowal and power does not depend on
receptivity the way that human bestowal does, since God's
bestowal is eternal while receptivity is temporal. Bestowal is
God's attribute, while receptivity is the attribute of something
created by God. The eternal cannot depend on the temporal,
otherwise temporality would make no sense.*

A gift from God is the sole remedy;
    It doesn't need your receptivity,
Rather that needs His giving to begin.   1540
    Giving's the kernel; to receive's the skin.
Moses's rod changed to a serpent and
    We know how God transformed to white his hand.*
Thousands of miracles of prophets, friend,
    That even the best brains can't comprehend,
Don't come from causes, but from God's directive—
    Non-entities can't make themselves receptive:
Thus, receptivity's not a condition
    Since they would not exist without God's action.
God has set causes, customs, and our pathways   1545
    For seekers under the azure, as mainstays.
Most things will follow custom carefully,
    But Powerful God breaks that occasionally.
He set up customs that are lovable,
    But breaks such customs with a miracle.
Through causes most things reach us every day,
    But God can easily wipe them all away.
Bound up in causes? Stay within their border,
    But don't imagine you don't need the Causer:
That Causer brings about His every whim;   1550
    He rips up causes—they can't stifle Him.
Mostly He wills through causes anyway
    So that the seeker can pursue the way:

With no cause seen what would he then pursue?
  Thus, on the path he needs a cause in view.
These causes veil our vision actually
  Because His work's not for all eyes to see.
One needs eyes that can see through causes here
  To uproot veils so that they disappear.
They'll see the Causer then in Placelessness   1555
  And learn to trade and earn is meaningless.
All good and evil come here from the Causer;
  Causes and means are nothing though, O brother,
But fantasies on the King's path, no more,
  To let this heedlessness continue more.

*On the start of the creation of the body of Adam with God
directing Gabriel: 'Go and fetch a handful of clay from the
ground!' Or, in another transmitted saying: 'Take
a handful from every corner!'*

When God, the Maker, wanted to make people
  To put them to the test with good and evil,
He ordered Angel Gabriel, 'Straight away
  Go, fetch as pledge a handful of some clay.'
Gabriel devotedly went out to do   1560
  What the *Lord of the Two Worlds* asked him to:
He stretched his hand towards the ground outside,
  But then the ground withdrew, so terrified,
And started to entreat him in this way:
  'For the Unique Creator's sake today
Spare me my life! Please go, take leave of me,
  Withdraw your fast steed's reins considerately!
Leave me, don't throw me in such tribulations
  Of dangerous trials and burdened obligations.
For the sake of the kindness He has shown,   1565
  Sharing the Tablet with your eyes alone,
So you became all of the angels' teacher
  And kept conversing with the Lord as speaker.
Emissary to the Prophets is your role,
  Life of not merely body but of soul—

Greater than Angel Esrafil whose limit
    Is bodily life, while you give life to spirit;
His trumpet's blast makes bodies rise again,
    But your breath nurtures special hearts of men.
The heart's life is the inner soul of bodies,   1570
    So yours is better: hearts rule over bodies.
Angel Michael gives sustenance, but you
    Nourish illumined hearts through what you do.
His gift fills up containers like a treasure,
    But, Gabriel, your gifts are beyond all measure.
Better than wrathful Azrael: it's clearer
    The Prophet said that *mercy's wrath's superior.*
You're monarch of the four who bear God's Throne;
    Due to your wakefulness, you lead alone.
You'll see eight bearers on the Final Day,   1575
    But you will be their leader anyway.'
The ground entreated like this out of fear,
    Guessing the reason Gabriel had come near.
Gabriel felt so ashamed—what it would say
    To him then in entreaty blocked his way:
It had adjured him so much that instead
    He headed back. '*Lord of us slaves,*' he said,
'I didn't take your order lightly—You
    Know better than me what I've listened to:
The ground appealed in that Name, out of fear   1580
    Of which the heavens stop their spin, All-Seer.
On hearing Your Name I felt loss of honour,
    Otherwise snatching clay here is no bother—
You've given such strength to the likes of me
    Angels can rip the skies up easily.'

The sending of the Angel Michael to take a handful of clay from the
ground for the formation of Adam, the blessed body of Mankind's
forefather, God's deputy, the one to whom the angels prostrated
and their teacher.

God ordered Michael: 'Go below today
    And like a lion bring back here some clay.'
When Michael reached the ground he stretched his hand

To snatch some clay from it as he had planned—
The ground shook and began then to retreat;   1585
   It wept tears and then started to entreat:
It made appeals with burning breast so deeply;
   With tears of blood it begged him so sincerely:
'In Kind God's Name, Incomparable, Alone,
   Who made you bearer of His Glorious Throne,
You supervise the whole world's sustenance,
   You serve those thirsting for His Grace at once—
For "Michael" comes from "*kayl*",* thus you became
   Sustenance measurer just like your name—
Save me, set me free, though I am mere mud!   1590
   Witness that I speak while I'm drenched in blood!'
A rich mine of God's Mercy, Michael said:
   'How can I pour salt on those wounds that bled?'
(The devil is the mine of wrath, for he
   Raised shrieks from members of humanity.)
Mercy excels wrath, and for the Creator
   Kindness is dominant in His own nature.
God's servants share His character of course:
   Their waterskins have His stream as their source.
So hear God's Messenger and Guide who led: 1595
   'Men will adopt their kings' faith,' he once said.

Michael went to the Lord of his religion
   Without the actual object of his mission:
'Knower of secrets, Peerless King,' he said,
   'The ground's cries stopped me in my tracks instead.
Tears always meant a lot to you, so I
   Could not ignore its tears when it would cry.
Wailing and sighs as well meant much to you,
   So I could not ignore their claims here too.
You valued teary eyes much previously,   1600
   So how could I ignore them facing me?
Five times the servant gets the invitation:
   "Come to the prayer and make your lamentation!"
Muezzins say, "*Come to the good!*"* That's meant
   For hope against the odds and deep lament.

If you want one to suffer grief today
    You block his heart from entering wailing's way.
Suffering will rain on him without protection
    When there's no desperate cry for intercession.
If you want one released from tribulation   1605
    You lead his soul to paths of supplication.
You said regarding those communities
    Who met your wrath: "Why didn't groups like these
Begin to supplicate then out of fear
    So that their suffering might thus disappear?"
Their hearts just hardened and their sins appeared
    To them as good acts that need not be cleared,
So they did not think they were sinners then—
    How can tears flow from eyes of stubborn men?"*

*The story about Jonah's community is an explanation and evidence
showing that entreaty and lamentation repel affliction sent from
above, and God acts by free will, meaning that entreaty and
magnification are effective with Him, though the philosophers
say that He acts through His inherent nature and as a cause,
not by free will, to make the point that entreaty cannot
alter inherent nature.*

When Jonah's people started suffering   1610
    A flame-filled cloud left heaven, wandering—
It hurled down lightning bolts, rocks burned down here,
    Clouds thundered, people turned pale out of fear.
They all were on their rooftops late one night
    When they could see above what caused such fright.
They rushed down from their roofs and after that
    Outside town without time to bring a hat.
Mothers then even brought their children out
    So they could all shriek loudly and cry out.
From the time of the evening prayer till dawn   1615
    These people's awful suffering carried on.
Their voices went hoarse as they stayed so zealous—
    Mercy came to this group who'd been rebellious.
After their unrestrained sighs and despair
    The cloud then started to retreat from there.

Since Jonah's story's too long to expound
　　Let's go back to the tale about the ground.
Since in God's view entreaty has much worth,
　　More than with others all across the earth,
Take hope and strive hard from now on each day,　　　1620
　　Rise, weeper, and keep smiling, come what may!
The Great King values tears that people cry
　　As much as blood of martyrs when they die.

The sending of Esrafil to the ground in order to take a handful of clay for the formation of Adam's body.

God said to Esrafil, 'Go, fill your hand
　　With clay down there, then come back from that land!'
So Esrafil went down there next and found
　　That he, too, could hear moaning from the ground:
'O angel of the trumpet, from whose breath,
　　Ocean of life, men rise up after death.
Your trumpet's loud blast has the power to　　　1625
　　Raise up from bones men like they're born anew.
With one blast of your trumpet you can say:
　　"Those slain in Kerbala—rise up today!
You who were killed by death's sword raise your head
　　Up from the ground, like branches stretch ahead!"
The world's filled with your grace and powerful breath
　　Through your famed resurrection after death.
Angel of mercy, show us mercy! You
　　Are God's Throne's bearer and bring gifts down too.'
The Throne's the mine of equity and justice,　　　1630
　　Beneath which are four rivers of forgiveness:
Streams of honey and milk forever more,
　　Rivers of wine and water, making four,*
Flow from the Throne to paradise, we know—
　　A little, too, shows up on earth below,
Though these streams are polluted every day
　　By our Unwholesomeness, and our decay.
When just a little from these four arrived
　　On this dark earth, trouble and strife revived;

It aimed to lead base men to seek their source,   1635
   But they became content with it, of course.
He's given milk for babies' nurturing;
   He's turned each mother's breast into a spring.
He's given wine to drive off thoughts and grief;
   He's made grapes fountains that give bold belief.
He's given honey as a remedy;
   He's turned to fountains parts of every bee.
He's given water to each part you're seeing
   Around you, both for drinking and for cleaning.
He's done all this so that you might pursue   1640
   Their source, but these fulfil you, fickle you!

Let's go back to the tale about the earth's soil
   And what she says to charm those causing turmoil:
With a straight face she's giving Esrafil
   All kinds of flattery so it seems real:
'By the truth of that Great One's Holy Essence,
   Don't view as lawful showing me such violence!
I can detect the change that lies ahead
   Because suspicions swarm around my head.
Angel of Mercy, show some now to me—   1645
   The Homa doesn't harm birds needlessly.
O cure and mercy for those suffering pain,
   Act like the pair that came before—refrain!'
He went back to the King, begged to be pardoned
   And told God all about the things that happened:
'You ordered me to fetch clay outwardly,
   But You inspired me not to inwardly:
You said, "Fetch!" to my ears, but nonetheless
   To my mind You forbade hardheartedness.'
'Mercy precedes wrath' and indeed surpasses,   1650
   Lord of good acts whose actions are so marvellous.'

The sending of Azrael, the Angel of Firm Resolve, to fetch a
handful of clay so the body of Adam could be formed quickly.

God quickly said to Azrael: 'Behold

That earth that lets vain fancies take a hold!
Go to that unjust, feeble crone today
   And quickly bring a handful of its clay!'
Azrael, sergeant of divine fate, went
   To earth to fetch clay, since he had been sent.
The earth, as is its way, began to groan,
   Swearing oaths, pleading to be left alone:
'Special youth, bearer of the Throne, O you   1655
   Whom we obey on earth and heaven too,
For the sake of the Merciful One's mercy,
   For that One who was kind to you—leave quickly,
For that King's sake whom people solely worship,
   Who won't reject laments made due to hardship.'
'I can't let spells make me now turn away
   From His commands, which can be clear as day.'
'He has commanded mercy too,' soil said.
   'He ordered both, so choose this. Use your head!'
'That's loose, analogical interpretation—   1660
   Don't hide clear orders with your obfuscation!
Interpret your own thinking in that way,
   Not His command, which is now clear as day!
I do feel sorry hearing your entreaty,
   My heart bleeds seeing salty tears flow freely.
I don't lack pity—I have more than those
   Three previous ones for people suffering blows.
If I should slap an orphan while another
   In kindness hands that orphan some sweet halva,
My slaps are better actually for him;   1665
   If he's beguiled by halva, woe to him!
Your loud cry makes me feel so bad for you,
   .But God is teaching me true kindness too:
Kindness hidden in harshness—this is it:
   A priceless gemstone hidden in some shit.
God's wrath surpasses kindnesses from me;
   Blocking the soul from God harms terribly.
And God's worst wrath beats clemencies, it's said—
   "How good the two worlds' Lord! How good His aid!"
Hidden kindnesses do lie in store—   1670
   Give Him your life and He will give you more.

Dismiss suspicion and wrong-thinking too!
 Now make your head a foot: "*Come!*"* He's told you.
His saying "*Come!*"* gives many exaltations,
 Fair partners, cushions and intoxications.
In sum, I can't dilute that grand command
 Or compromise it. You should understand.'
That wretched ground heard all it had to hear,
 But bad suspicions still plugged up its ear.
That base ground pleaded and prostrated then   1675
 In a new way just like some drunken men.
Azrael said, 'Get up and don't be scared!
 Upon my life, from harm you will be spared.
Don't even think of begging me once more—
 Plead to that Generous, Just King we adore.
I'm slave to His command. I can't ignore
 His orders which raise dust from the sea's floor.
I won't hear talk of good and evil: I
 Just listen to Him who made ear and eye.
My ear is deaf to talk of others here.   1680
 He's dearer than my soul to me, that dear.
The soul came from Him, not the other way.
 He gives a million souls for free each day.
How could I choose the soul ahead of God?
 Why burn a rug due to one flea. That's odd.
I know of no good other than His good;
 I'm *deaf, dumb, blind* to others. Understood?
My ear is deaf to all the ones who moan,
 For I'm a spear held by his hand alone.

Explaining that if you are treated badly by a creature, he in reality
is like an instrument. The mystic is the one who refers things to God
not to the instrument. If he refers it to the instrument in expression,
that's not out of ignorance but for a good purpose, the way that
Bayazid said: 'It has been many years since I spoke to anyone or
heard someone speak to me, though people imagine that I am
talking to them and listening to them, because they do not
see the Greatest Speaker, for they are like His echo to me in
my state.' The intelligent listener does not listen to the echo,
as the saying goes: 'The wall said to the nail: "Why are
you splitting me?" The nail replied: "Look at him
who is hammering me!"'

It's stupid to beg mercy from the spear,   1685
    So beg the King who holds it when you've fear.
How can you beg instead the spear or sword,
    Both captives in the grip of the Great Lord?
He's Azar, I'm the idol; similarly*
    I'm any instrument He makes of me:
If He makes me a pitcher, I'm a pitcher.
    If He makes me a dagger, I'm a dagger.
If He makes me a fountain, I'll give water.
    If He makes me a fire, I'll make things hotter.
If He makes me rain, I'll raise a wheat stack.   1690
    And if an arrow, I'll dart in your back.
And if a snake, I'll poison those who're near.
    If He makes me His friend, I'll serve right here.
*Between His fingers** I am like a pen:
    I'm not lukewarm like some obedient men.

Distracting the old ground with what he'd say,
    Azrael snatched a handful of its clay.
He snatched it like he was a skilled magician,
    The ground distracted like a witless person.
He took the clay to God, obeyed His rule,   1695
    Like taking truant students back to school.
God said, 'By My clear knowledge I now vow
    You'll be those people's executioner now!'

He said, 'O Lord, Your creatures will regard
    Me as the foe when they are hanged. That's hard.
Exalted Lord, will you do this to me
    And let them view me as the enemy?'
God said, 'To them I'll make the causes clear:
    Fever, colic, and madness, or the spear.
I'll turn their whole attention far from you   1700
    To sicknesses and other causes too.'
He said, 'But Lord, there are some servants here
    Who see through causes that You make appear.
Their eyes see through the cause shown in this place;
    They penetrate the veils, thanks to Your grace:
From You they've gained the kohl of Unity:
    They see beyond pain and infirmity:
They don't view fever, colic, or consumption;
    Their hearts don't grant such causes there admission.'

Since all such ailments have a remedy,   1705
    When they're incurable it's God's decree.
Each ailment has a cure. Know this for sure:
    For feeling cold a fleece-lined coat's the cure,
But when God wishes that a man should freeze
    Coldness will pass through countless coats with ease—
God gives him shivers that have no known cure,
    Neither with clothes, nor homes snug and secure.
Physicians turn to fools if He decrees
    And all the cures will lose their potencies.
How can the visionary's perception be   1710
    Veiled by the causes simple idiots see?
The perfect eye can see the root so clearly;
    The squint-eyed man can see the branches merely.

The answer that came from God: 'The one whose vision goes beyond
causes, illnesses, and wounds will see beyond your actions, Azrael,
for you are also a secondary cause, even though you are more
hidden than those other causes. And maybe this is also
not hidden from the sick person: "He is nearer to him
than you, but you do not see."'*

'The one who sees the roots of things', God said,
  'Won't notice you appear in front instead.
You're hidden from the general population,
  But seen as veil by eyes with inspiration,
For if death's hour is sweet to one's perceptions
  His vision's not distorted by possessions.
To him the body's death's not hard to face   1715
  Because they'll leave gaol for a better place,
An open field. They'll leave the world of suffering—
  Nobody weeps for losing what's worth nothing.
If a gaol's watchtower ever is knocked down
  No prisoners will feel bad for it and frown,
Saying, 'Alas, the marble cracked as well
  So now our souls can flee the prison cell.
That lovely marble and that noble stone
  Of the watchtower were lovely and well-known—
Why did one break them, letting prisoners flee?   1720
  For this crime chop his hands immediately!'
No prisoner would say nonsense of this kind
  Unless they'll now be hanged—then they would mind.
Why would a man feel bitter if his treat
  Is fleeing poison for what's sugar sweet?
Freed from the body's turmoil, souls will fly
  On the heart's wings, without legs, and soar high,
Just like a prisoner down a dungeon who
  While dreaming sees a rose garden in view:
'God, don't return me to my body, please—   1725
  I want this rose garden's fine luxuries.'
God says, 'Your prayer is granted. Don't go back.'
  God knows best what is the most fitting track.
How lovely such dreams look to the mind's eyes—
  Without one dying one sees paradise!

Would one then miss one's body one small bit
    Or being awake, chained in a deep, dark pit?
Believer, join the battle ranks—you'll find
    A feast awaits in heaven for your kind.
With hope of soaring high, stand up young man   1730
    Candle-like at the prayer-niche, if you can;
Weep tears all night, in seeking burn away
    Like candles that from top down melt away!
Seal up your mouth to food and drink—instead
    Hurry off to the heavenly table spread!
Fix all your hopes on heaven constantly,
    Dance longing for it like a willow tree!
From heaven fire and water come to you
    Each moment to make daily bread grow too.
Don't be surprised if you're led there this hour;   1735
    Don't think of weakness, but your seeking's power!
Your seeking is what God has placed in you—
    Each search fits well with what it's seeking too.
Strive so your yearning burns more powerfully,
    So that your own imprisoned heart can flee.
People will say, 'Poor so-and-so died then.'
    You'll answer, 'I'm alive, O heedless men!
My body's laid to rest like all that part,
    But eight bright heavens now bloom in my heart.'

When spirit lives among the roses, it   1740
    Will not care that the body lies in shit—
The spirit truly doesn't care about it
    Whether it's in a rose garden or ash pit.
The spirit shouts in yonder world once there:
    '*If only my own people were aware!*' *
But if the spirit weren't to leave the body
    Who'd dwell in heaven's palace then? Nobody.
If spirit won't live when the body's dead
    What then is '*heaven has your daily bread*'? *

*Explaining the harm of sweet and greasy food in this
world and how they block you from the Food from God, as
it is said: 'Hunger is the Food from God with which He
revives the bodies of the true ones', meaning that the Food
from God comes after hunger. The Prophet has also said,
'I pass the night with my Lord and He gives me food
and drink.' God has said, 'They are given
provisions and rejoice.'**

If you side-step these foul scraps as you should,   1745
   You'll then find pastries and most glorious food.
Though you eat many kilos of such pastries
   You will stay light and pure just like the fairies—
They won't give kidney pains and flatulence
   Or torture you with belly aches, not once.
If you eat little here, you're hungry still,
   And you'll belch loudly if you eat your fill.
Eat little and you'll suffer a bad mood
   And aches; feel bloated when you're full with food.
Through *food from God* and His refined nutrition   1750
   You'll sail off like a ship across the ocean.
Be patient and persistent when you fast,
   Ready for God's food to arrive at last.
God, who acts kindly and lifts burdens too,
   Bestows gifts when they're in expectant view:
A sated man won't count the time and wait:
   'Will my food come now or will it be late?'
But someone starving will ask, 'Where is it?'
   After his search, as he's expecting it—
The food won't come unless you are expectant   1755
   From that realm which is totally transcendent.
Wait for it to reach you expectantly
   As for the feast of heaven, valiantly!
All hungry men find food eventually:
   Fortune's sun shines on each one generously.
When an expectant guest eats little food
   The host will bring instead a dish that's good
Unless he's poor or suffers avarice—

Don't doubt Providing God, who's generous!
Lift your head like tall mountains you can view   1760
   So that the sun's first rays fall onto you!
That solid, lofty mountain peak you see
   Waits for the sun to rise, expectantly.

Response to the stupid person who said, 'This world would be lovely
if there were no death and worldly wealth would be lovely if it were
not transient', as well as other similar vain talk.

'The world would be so lovely,' someone said
   'If only we would not all end up dead.'
'If there were no death,' someone else replied,
   'It wouldn't be worth straw that's stacked and tied.
More like an unthreshed and unused old stack
   Left in the field, for which no one turns back.
You're claiming death is life—you are just sowing   1765
   Your seeds in barren soil where they're not growing.
Deceitful reason sees things back to front:
   It claims life's death—you, fool, are ignorant!'

O God, show everything the way it is
   In truth in this realm of deceptiveness!
No one who's died regrets death, though he may
   Regret preparing little for that day.
He's left a pit for a vast open plain
   With fortunes, pleasures, joy in that domain,
Transported there from a house filled with sorrow   1770
   And mourning that was hideous and so narrow.
Not lies, but a great seat of truthfulness,
   Drunk on fine wine and not feigned drunkenness,
From this material fire-temple he's bound
   To that famed Seat of Truth where God is found.
If you've not lived so far enlightenedly
   Only seconds remain—die valiantly!

Concerning what can be hoped for from the Mercy of God,
who bestows bounties before they have been earned:
'He is the one who sends down rain after they have
despaired.'* Many separations produce closeness,
there are many sins that are blessed, and many
joys arrive when punishment is expected
instead 'so that you know that God
changes their bad deeds to good ones'.*

As said in our dear Prophet's own tradition:
    Bodies are told 'Arise!' at Resurrection.
Holy God's order is the trumpet blast: 1775
    'Lift up your heads from those soil graves at last!'
Each soul returns to its own body then
    As consciousness returns each dawn again.
Souls recognize their bodies at dawn too,
    Entering its ruins just like treasures do:
They recognize their bodies and they enter
    The goldsmith's soul won't go in a clothes mender;
The scholar's soul returns in the professor;
    The tyrant's soul goes back to that oppressor.
Divine knowledge bestows this recognition,   1780
    As lambs know their own ewes through intuition.
The foot can tell in darkness its own shoe—
    Of course, my dear, souls find their bodies too.
Dawn's the small resurrection, refuge seeker:
    Analogy reveals which one's superior—
The books of deeds fly left and right that day
    Just as the soul at dawn flies back to clay—
The books of meanness, generosity,
    Corruption, shifting moods, and piety.*
When one awakes at dawn from slumber, then   1785
    The good and evil both return again:
If he had been self-disciplined before,
    The disciplined self will come to the fore,
But if he'd been vile, immature, astray,
    His left hand mourns its black list on that day.*
If he had been devoted, pure, and zealous,

When he awakes he gains a pearl that's precious.
Our sleep and waking testify to you:
    They tell of death and resurrection too.
The lesser resurrection shows the greater;   1790
    The lesser death reveals the death that's major.
These books are unclear and imagined here;
    In the Great Resurrection they'll be clear:
A hidden fancy here with mere hints shown,
    It will grow there to real forms widely known.
The architect's idea for future structures
    Is in him like a seed in soil that nurtures:
When the idea that's inside him comes out
    It's like what seeds in soil will cause to sprout.
Every idea in his head one could mention   1795
    Becomes a form at its own resurrection—
The architect's idea that his mind knows
    Is like the seed in soil that quickly grows.

With these two resurrections I intend
    To teach their moral to believers, friend.
On Resurrection's sunrise all around
    The foul and fair will rise up from the ground.
They'll run to destiny's court to be tried,
    The crucible with real and false inside:
The real coin will go there so joyfully,   1800
    The false coin with extreme anxiety.
And then each moment tests arrive and start;
    Bodies disclose the secrets from the heart,
As when a lamp shows water and its oil
    And when fresh saplings rise up from the soil:
Through onion, leek, and poppy flowers we see
    Winter's secret in spring so vividly.
'*We are devout*,' the verdant say; instead,
    Like violets, others drop their heads in dread,
Eyes boggling due to danger that awaits,   1805
    Weeping like fountains, fearful of their fates;
Their eyes can only wait there open wide,
    Dreading the book of deeds on the left side.*

Their eyes roll left then right to try to see—
   Books don't come on the right side readily.
A book comes to a man that brings distress,
   It's all black, full of sins and wickedness,
Without a single good deed's saving grace,
   Just harm caused to the saints' hearts in its place,
Foulness and sins from top to bottom and   1810
   Mockery of all the mystics in the land,
With all his thefts and fraud, each single lie,
   And Pharaoh-like pretentious claims for 'I'.*
Once that wretch reads his own book he will know
   His onward journey's to the place below.
Like thieves he'll climb the gallows, though that's hard,
   Sins clear to all, forgiveness's way barred,
Those numerous claims and his justification
   Stuffed in his mouth to give him suffocation,
Stolen goods on his person or soon found   1815
   At his home, but excuses not around.
He walks now to the gaol of hell with blame,
   Because thorns cannot ever flee the flame.
Those angels front and back that were unseen
   Now, like police guards, can be clearly seen.
They prod him as they lead him now away:
   'Go to your kennel, dog!' we hear them say.
He drags his feet so much along the street,
   Hoping he can avoid the fate he'll meet,
Then stands expectantly, but makes no sound;   1820
   In hope he tries to turn his face around.
Tears pour down now just like autumnal rains—
   Apart from hope what else of his remains?
He keeps on looking back continually
   To face the Holy Court and its decree.

From radiant realms, God sends down His command:
   'Tell him: "You biggest wastrel in the land,
What do you now expect, you wicked one?
   Why do you look around still, giddy one?
Your book of deeds has reached your hand, you who   1825

Annoy God and still worship Satan too.
Since you have seen your book, why have you turned
  To look back? Look instead at what you've earned!
Why do you tarry pointlessly? What right
  Do you have to seek in the pit some light?
Neither were you obedient outwardly,
  Nor did you then aspire to inwardly.
Neither did you stay up at night to pray,
  Nor did you fast and do without by day.
Neither did you avoid bad things you said,   1830
  Nor did you look behind or up ahead:
What is ahead? Your death and agony.
  What is behind? Your friends' deaths previously.
Neither was there repentance for oppression,
  You who showed wheat for barley in deception.
Your weighing-scales weren't telling the right weight,
  Yet you hope you'll be fairly judged by fate?
Since you leant to the left with all your fraud
  Why should your right hand get your book from God?*
What you earn is a shadow next to you,   1835
  Hunchback, that's why your shadow is hunched too." '
Such harsh words come from that side now to you
  That even would bend sides of mountains too.
The slave says, 'I'm a hundred times worse, Lord,
  Than what you have expounded, every word.
You covered up worse things. You're generous
  Though You've full knowledge of my wickedness.
Putting aside my efforts and exertion,
  Good, evil, unbelief, devout religion,
My supplications made so powerlessly,   1840
  Fancies and whims of mine and men like me,
Being upright or being wicked in its place,
  I always held out hope in Your pure grace
And Your pure kindness to us all regardless
  O Generous One who gives to all regardless.
I turned towards Your generosity
  And I ignored my actions totally;
I turned to hope in You immediately
  For You gave me my being originally:

For free You gave the robe of my existence—   1845
   I've always counted on You from that instance.'

When one recounts one's sins one then will see
   The purest kindness come so generously,
Saying: 'Angels, since that man's heart's own eye
   Kept facing hope bring him to us on high.
As if it matters not, we'll set him free
   And cross out all his sins most generously.
(Someone like God can say he doesn't care
   When he does not gain by being thus unfair.)
We'll light a lovely fire by being kind   1850
   So no sins and no errors stay behind,
A lovely fire from which the smallest flame
   Burns up free will, compulsion, sin, and blame.
We'll set fire to the home of all Mankind,
   Make mystic roses from soil left behind.
We sent the alchemy from the ninth heaven
   Like this *to rectify your every action.* *
What then is Mankind's power and will next to
   The Light of the Eternal Realm that's true?
A piece of flesh is Mankind's speech's source,   1855
   A piece of fat his eyesight's nearest source,
Two bones make up the source of Mankind's hearing,
   The heart, two drops of blood, their source of feeling.
You're just a tiny worm that lives in shit
   Yet in this world you've shown off quite a bit—
You came from sperm, so put conceit behind!
   Ayaz, keep that fleece jacket still in mind!

The story about Ayaz and his maintaining a closet for his old rustic boots and fleece coat and how his peers believed he had buried treasure in that closet because the door was so solid and the lock was so heavy.

Inspired by wisdom, Ayaz would keep hold
   Of his fleece coat and boots, both torn and old.

He'd go inside their closet every day: 1860
   'These are your boots—don't feel grand!' he would say.
'He has a closet,' once the king was told,
   'With silver, a fine jar, and lots of gold.
He won't let anyone come in and he
   Keeps its door locked with high security.'
'How strange! What would that servant want to hide
   From me, his ruler?' their great king replied.
'At midnight, go there!' he told a commander,
   'Open that closet's locked door and then enter!
Whatever you find there will come to you—   1865
   Reveal his secrets to my courtiers too!
Despite honours and kindnesses from me
   Does he hide gold from me objectionably?
Perhaps he shows love, loyalty, and zeal,
   To show wheat then sell barley in a deal?
Anyone with a love-filled life so good
   Shows unbelief if he shuns servanthood.'
At midnight that commander with his men
   Resolved to go there and unlock it, then
Thirty strong, trusted men with torches raised   1870
   Marched to the closet happily and in haste:
'It's the king's order—let's do as we're told:
   We'll raid it and each get a bag of gold!'
One of them said, 'What's gold? He has in there
   Cornelians, rubies, gems beyond compare.'

Privileged to maintain the treasury;
   The king adored him so incredibly—
How can one who is loved that much still value
   The jewels about which greedy men will argue?
The king did not at all suspect him then—   1875
   He was play-acting, testing other men.
He knew that he was free from fraud and faking
   Yet due to this thought his heart started shaking:
'Don't let this be! I don't want him to face
   Suffering nor to now endure disgrace.
He hasn't done this, though he's able to;

I love him—he can do what he wants to.
Whatever he does it is done by me;
   Though veiled from others, he is I, I he.'
He went on, 'It is so unlike his manner—   1880
   This fuss is fuelled by meaningless palaver.
It is impossible for him. Trust me.
   Ayaz is like a bottomless, vast sea.
In it the seven seas are just one drop;
   All being is its waves' crests' foam on top.
All holiness is gained from that great sea;
   Its drops each can perform much alchemy.
He is the king of kings and the king-maker—
   We say "Ayaz" because of envy's danger:
Good eyes are evil eyes because of envy   1885
   When near Ayaz due to his peerless beauty.'

A mouth as vast as the wide sky above me
   Is needed to describe what angels envy!
If I get one mouth like this, that's too small—
   Even a hundred—to describe it all.
I shouldn't say this much about this matter—
   The heart's glass is too fragile and will shatter.
Since my heart's glass is far too fragile, I
   Rend my own cloak as means to pacify.
The first three days of every month, my beauty,   1890
   I must without a doubt become a loony:
Today's the first day, so beware of me—
   It's not for turquoise, but for victory.*
It is the first day of the month each moment
   For hearts to which the King's love gives such torment.
The tale of Mahmud and Ayaz turned messy
   Because this lunatic became so crazy!

*Explaining that what is related is the outward form of the story,
and that the outward form suits those who can absorb only that and
the mirror image of their imagination. However, due to the
transcendent nature of the essence of this story, speech feels ashamed
to reveal it, and due to shame it loses its head, proud beard, and
pen! The intelligent one is satisfied with just a hint.*

My elephant has dreamt of India now;
   This hamlet's wrecked—don't hope for tax somehow!
So how can verse and rhyme still come to me   1895
   With roots of good health ruined totally?
I have more than one madness in love's sadness:
   It's madness upon madness upon madness.
My body melts through that world's indications;
   I view subsistence in annihilations.
Ayaz, my love for you has made me thin—
   I can't narrate more, so now you begin!
I've said so much about your love—you tell
   About mine now! I'm like a tale as well.
You now narrate, not me, you whom men follow!   1900
   I'm Sinai, you are Moses, this the echo.
How can a mountain understand our speech?
   It lacks the knowledge Moses has in reach.
The mountain only knows to its own limit
   The body's only slightly graced by spirit.
The body has the astrolabe's own role:
   It tells you where to find the sun-like soul.
Astronomers who do not have good sight
   Need one who makes the astrolabes just right
To make one for them to provide a clue   1905
   About the sun they seek, but cannot view.
If a soul needs an astrolabe, that one
   Can't know that much about the sky and sun.
You look through the eye's astrolabe, but see
   Only a tiny bit with certainty.
You've seen the world through your eyes' limits only—
   Where is the world? Why feel proud and act boastfully?
Mystics possess a special kohl to see—
   Seek it, turn your eye's stream into a sea!

If reason and my wits had stayed with me   1910
    What is this crazy speech of mine? Tell me!
My brain's lost reason and all consciousness
    So you can't fault me for my craziness—
It's his fault: he stole my intelligence;
    All scholars nearing him lose theirs at once.
You who lead wits and reason far astray,
    Our minds have only you for hope today.
I've not missed reason while you've made me crazy,
    Nor envied beauty while you decorate me,
So is my madness loving you thought good?   1915
    Say: 'Yes!' May God reward you as one should!
Whether he speaks in Arabic or Persian
    Which ears and minds possess its comprehension?
His wine's not right for every mind, that's clear;
    His slavery's earring won't fit every ear.
I've come back like a madman once again—
    Soul, go away and quickly fetch a chain!
If it's not my beloved's tress, I'll just
    Break chains you bring, a hundred if I must!

*The wisdom of reflecting on his old boots and fleece coat, for
'Let Man reflect on what he has been created from.'**

Bring back Ayaz's love's tale now for me,   1920
    For that's a treasure full of mystery!
He would go to that closet every day
    To see his boots and old coat, come what may.
Being intoxicates self with great might,
    Stealing your reason, wiping shame from sight.
From hiding places these intoxications
    Have waylaid millions of past generations:
Azazil turned to Satan tragically:
    'Why now should Adam lord it over me?*
I'm noble, nobly born and I am ready   1925
    For countless virtues to reach me already.
I'm not inferior in good qualities
    To have to serve foes like him on my knees.
I was born from great fire, he from mere clay—

Clay can't compete with fire in any way.
Where was he when I was a major leader
In this world and the glory of the era?'

On 'He created the Jinn from smokeless fire'* and His words about Satan: 'He was of the Jinn and transgressed.'*

Flames blazed within that wretched simpleton;
   He was of fire: *like father's soul, like son.*
But no, it was God's wrath. I've got it wrong   1930
   To give a cause when it does not belong.
The causeless act is causeless totally,
   Fixed from the start of time eternally.
How can a transient thing with imperfection
   Be found in acts of holiest perfection?
What is *the father's soul*? His works, the kernel.
   Its shell's the father whose form is external.
O nut-like one, know love's your friend as well;
   Your soul's love seeks that kernel, breaks the shell.
To that man who was bound to go to hell   1935
   And loved mere forms God gave another shell.
Kernel and inner being both can rule
   Over the fire, but shells are just fire's fuel.
When there's stream water in a wooden pot
   The pot's what feels the flames that are so hot.
Man's inner soul rules over fire, so it,
   As ruler, can't now be destroyed by it.
Grow your soul bigger, not your body—you
   Can then be the fire's king-like ruler too.
You have been adding shell, layer upon layer,   1940
   That's why you're just like shells in smoky air.
The fire has only shells as fuel inside,
   So God's wrath tears off all that shell of pride.
This pride's a product of the shell: it fits
   That wealth and rank are its associates.
What's pride? Heedlessness of the depths inside
   Like heedless ice in sunshine's heat outside:
Once it learns of the sun, then it won't stay
   But rather soften, warm, and melt away.

The body craves on seeing the kernel. Yes,   1945
   It falls in love: *craving brings lowliness.*
When it can't see the kernel it likes skin—
   'Well done content one!' is the gaol it's in.
Might's unbelief here, faith is lowliness;
   A stone becomes a gem by being less:
Boasting 'I' while a stone still is misplaced—
   This is the time to be small and effaced.
Pride seeks more wealth and status constantly,
   But furnaces with dung work properly:
Those first two nurses just increase the shell   1950
   With arrogance, pride, fat, and flesh as well;
They've not looked up to see the kernel's kernel,
   So they imagine that mere shell's the kernel.
Satan was this path's big chief, don't forget,
   Yet he got trapped in status's big net.
Wealth's like a snake, status a dragon—you
   Will find with pure men emeralds for these two:
That emerald makes the snake's eyes jump right out—
   It turns blind and the wayfarer breaks out.
When that chief placed sharp thorns right in the way   1955
   Those pricked said, 'Be cursed, Satan!' every day,
Meaning: 'The pain comes from his perfidy;
   He's the first model of such treachery—
Generation after generation
   Then followed him by serious emulation.'
Whoever sets a bad example so
   People fall blindly later in much woe
Discovers their sins on his neck instead
   Since they're its tail's tip while he is its head.

Adam brought out his coat and old boots though   1960
   And said, 'I am of clay,' so long ago,
Like Ayaz's, those boots were viewed a lot—
   That's why he finally got the praise he got.
Absolute Being's the Craftsman in non-being—
   What can His workshop be then but non-being?
No one would write on previous script would he,

Nor plant on top of old plants a new tree?
  One seeks some paper with no writing on
    And sows on land that nothing's been grown on—
Brother, you be a fresh and unfarmed place   1965
  And whitest paper with no writing's trace,
To then be honoured by '*Nun and the pen*'*
  And God, the Generous, sows seed in you then.
Imagine you've not tasted sweets nor seen
  The well-stocked kitchen where you've often been,
For they intoxicate you such that you
  Forget your old boots, and your fleece coat too.
You'll sigh when you meet death's most tortuous pain,
  Remembering then your boots and coat again.
Until you're drowning in the hideous sea   1970
  From which there is no help or sanctuary,
You won't remember the right rescue boat—
  You won't look at your boots and your fleece coat.
When you're left in the drowning waves of woe
  You'll constantly say '*We've done wrong!*'* and know.
Satan will say, 'He's still naïve. Come chop
  This bird's head—its untimely cry must stop.'
Far be it from Ayaz's path that prayer
  Should be an empty sham for watchers there—
He had been heaven's rooster previously: 1975
  His crowing always started punctually.

On the meaning of the prophetic tradition: 'Show us things as they
are!' And on the meaning of the tradition: 'If the veil were lifted
my certainty would be increased.' And on the poet's verses:
    'When you should look at someone negatively
    You're looking from your own view, narrowly.'
    'The crooked ladder casts a crooked shadow . . .'

Rooster-like preachers, learn from him to crow!
  He crows for God, not money—that's so low.
False dawn can't fool him: he has not been had.
  (The false dawn is the world of good and bad.)
Worldly men's brains are lacking, obviously,
  Since they believed it was dawn actually.

False dawns caused caravans to lose their way:
    They would depart assuming it was day.
May the false dawn not lead men any more—   1980
    It's ruined many caravans before!
You're captive to the false dawn, but don't you
    Consider a false dawn the dawn that's true!
You've no defence from falseness and from evil,
    But why suspect the same from other people?
The wicked are suspicious thus always:
    They see in other men their own flawed ways.
Those wretches who're corrupt and hold suspicions
    Have claimed the prophets are corrupt magicians,
And fabricating leaders who were base   1985
    Suspected Ayaz and his closet space,
Imagining he had a hoard of treasure—
    Don't look at others inside your own mirror!

The king himself knew of his holiness;
    He went along for their sakes nonetheless:
'Open that closet's door at midnight, men!
    He will not have a clue what's happening then.
His secrets will be thus made manifest
    And after I'll treat him how I think best.
I grant you all the gold and jewels in there;   1990
    I want none—I just want to be aware.'
As he said this, his heart began to pound
    For peerless Ayaz. He made no more sound
But thought: 'Does my tongue say this actually?
    What will he do on seeing this from me?
By the truth of his faith, his steadfastness
    Is far too great that he should feel distress
Or angry at my terrible aspersion
    And not work out my actual good intention.'
When wounded men can see the reason why   1995
    They suffer, they sense triumph and won't die.
Interpreters are, like Ayaz, so patient:
    They view the sea of outcomes that are latent,
Like Joseph—what the prisoners' dreams must mean

Is obvious to him—when God's Friend has seen
  The other people's dreams' deep mystery
    How can his own dream's then stay hard to see?
If I stab him a lot, his being one
  With me won't weaken through what I have done:
I stab myself in actuality—   2000
    He knows! I'm truly him and he is me.'

Explaining the union of the lover and the beloved in actuality even
though they are opposites in that neediness is the opposite of being
without need. Similarly a mirror is formless and clear although
being formless is the opposite of form, yet in actuality there is a
union between them, but this needs a long explanation.
A mere hint suffices the wise.

Majnun once fell ill and it was all due
  To grief and separation he went through.
The flame of longing boiled his blood so quickly
  Such that Majnun got very ill with quinsy.
A doctor came to treat him and left saying:
  'There is no way to heal him but by draining:
You must remove his blood now with great care.'
  A skilled phlebotomist was then brought there:
He bandaged Majnun's arm and held his blade—   2005
  The lover then immediately said:
'Quit the blood-letting! You can take your fee.
  If my old body dies, it's meant to be.'
He answered, 'How did my blade manage to
  Do what the jungle's lions couldn't do?
Lions, bears, onagers, and fierce wolves too,
  At night could all be very close to you.'
You won't emit to them a human smell
  When there is too much love in you as well.
The lion, bear, and wolf all know what love is;   2010
  One blind to love is lower than a dog is.
If dogs don't have one vein of love within
  How could the Seven Sleepers' dog begin
To seek hearts? There are many dogs like that
  Even if they're not famous or looked at.

If you've not smelt a heart in your own kind
    You won't smell it in wolves or sheep. You'll find.
Without love there'd be no existence too—
    How should mere bread have joined as part of you?
How did it? Love and appetite achieved it   2015
    Otherwise how could bread reach any spirit?
Love turns to living soul this lifeless bread
    Makes transient lives eternal ones instead.

Majnun said, 'I don't fear knives of physicians—
    My patience is more solid than a mountain's.
I am a tramp—my body's used to blows,
    And lovers always get them, heaven knows.
My being's filled with Layli totally,
    A shell with that pearl's every quality.
I'm scared that if you bleed me now, blood-letter,   2020
    Your lancet entering me might also cut her—
The wise one with illumined heart can see
    We aren't separate, my Layli and me.'

A beloved asked her lover, 'Who do you love more—me or yourself?' He answered, 'I have died to myself and have become living through you. I've become annihilated from self and my own attributes and exist through you. I have forgotten my own knowledge and have become knowledgeable through your knowledge. I have forgotten my own power and have become powerful through your power.'

> *If I love myself, it is you I love;*
> *And if I love you, it's myself I love:*
> *'Whoever has the mirror of certainty*
> *Looks at himself, but it is God he'll see.'*

'Go forth with My attributes to my creatures. Whoever sees you sees Me and whoever sets off towards you sets off towards Me' etc.

To test him a beloved asked her lover
    Over a morning drink, 'Dear, how I wonder
Who is it that you love more—me or you?

O man of sorrow, tell me what is true!'
'I have become effaced in you,' he said,
   'Such that I'm filled with you up to my head.
Nothing's left in my being, my name apart;   2025
   Nothing's left there but you, love of my heart.
I have become effaced in you so fully
   Like vinegar inside a sea of honey.'
It's like a stone that turns into a ruby
   Filled with the sunshine's features most profusely:
The stone's own qualities don't stay, we've found—
   It's filled now with the sunshine's all around.
If it should love itself then after that
   It's love that's for the sun we're looking at;
And if it loves the sun now totally   2030
   It is love of itself assuredly.
Whether the ruby loves itself or whether
   It loves the sun, you must know altogether
There is no difference now between these two—
   Both are the light of sunshine through and through.
Until turned ruby, that stone is its foe
   With two 'I's' still, not one, as you should know;
The stone is dark and blind to day—that's right:
   Darkness is the true opposite of light.
It loves itself? Then it's an infidel;   2035
   It's the sun's biggest blocker then as well.
So then it's not right for the stone to say:
   'I'—it's still dark and subject to decay.
Pharaoh said, '*I am God*', and grew depraved;
   Hallaj said, '*I am God*', and he was saved.*
God's curse is what came down next for the former,
   The latter gained *God's mercy* though, O lover.
That was a stone, this one a jewel so bright—
   Light's lover, while the former hated light.
Hallaj's 'I' was 'He' so stop your meddling—   2040
   That oneness of light isn't like indwelling.*
Strive hard till you reduce your stoniness,
   So then your stone can shine with rubiness.
Be patient when you strive and face vexation—
   See your subsistence post-annihilation.*

Your stoniness will keep becoming less
  And you will gain more lasting rubiness.
Your self-existence will depart—instead
  Intoxication will grow in your head.
Just like an ear, become entirely hearing, 2045
  So you might then acquire a ruby earring!
Dig earth like a well-digger if you've worth—
  Reach water in this body made of earth!
If God's pull comes, the water will gush out
  From earth without the need to dig wells out.
Don't only listen, but strive hard and toil,
  Keep gradually scraping out the new well's soil!
Whoever braved affliction found a treasure;
  Whoever worked hard gained with equal measure.
The Prophet said, 'To bow and to prostrate 2050
  Is knocking on the mystical path's gate—
Whoever swings that door knocker finds out
  For his sake hidden fortune will come out.'

*That amir who made the accusation came with his officers at
midnight to open up Ayaz's closet and saw the fleece coat and old
boots hanging there. They supposed that this was a ploy and decoy,
and so they dug up every suspicious nook, brought excavators and
made holes in the walls. However, they discovered nothing and
became embarrassed and fell into despair. Suspicious men who think
ill of the works of Prophets and Friends of God are like this,
claiming that they were sorcerers and were building themselves up in
pursuit of leadership—after looking closely they feel embarrassed,
but it will not benefit them.*

All those entrusted men came to the door
  Of his locked closet, seeking gold and more.
A few of them unlocked it skillfully
  Using the know-how they'd learnt previously.
It was a complicated lock and hard to open.
  Out of so many locks this one was chosen,
Not to hoard wealth and gold, but just to hide 2055
  The secret from the vulgar, safe inside.
He'd thought, 'Some might think bad things if they see;

Others might say, "You hypocrite!" to me.'
The mystic's secrets of his soul are kept
    Safer than gems from the base and inept.
The fool will deem gold better than the spirit;
    The wise know that they have misunderstood it.

They rushed in fast due to their greed for gold—
    'No, slow down!' by their own brains they were told.
Greed rushes to the mirage pointlessly;   2060
    The brain warns, 'That's not real. Look carefully!'
Greed ruled and deemed gold like the soul, and so
    The brain's yells were all muffled and kept low.
Greed's clamour's volume very much increased;
    Wisdom's prods were all muffled and decreased.
The greedy man falls in delusion's pit
    And hears from wisdom censure after it—
Once his inflated pride has finally burst
    The blaming soul* controls him, not at first.
Until the head bangs on affliction's wall   2065
    Deaf ears can't hear the heart's advice at all.
Greed for nut cake and sugar, which tastes nice,
    Makes children's ears deaf to your good advice,
But once an abscess forms that causes pain
    Their ears then open to advice again.

Those men then opened up the closet's door
    With greed and lust of various kinds in store;
They flooded in the room once it was clear
    Like flies to rotten buttermilk that's near
They fell in there like lovers who'd found luck   2070
    But couldn't drink it and their wings got stuck.
They looked around, saw nothing there of note
    Apart from his torn boots and old fleece coat:
'There can't be nothing here that gives one pleasure—
    The boots are just a decoy for the treasure.
Bring some sharp picks to find what he's concealing,
    Check now behind all of the walls and ceiling!'

That group dug out holes everywhere—they'd keep
   Digging out holes and ditches that were deep.
The holes were shouting out, 'Do you not see,   2075
   You stinkers, I'm an empty cavity?'
Embarrassment then filled those scheming men
   For what they'd thought—they filled the holes again.
Prayers filled their breasts; the bird of these men's greed
   Was left without seed now on which to feed.
The holes left in the wall and door became
   Informers of their wayward, futile aim.
These walls could not be plastered smooth again:
   Ayaz could not be thus denounced by men.
If they went and pretended innocence   2080
   The floors and walls would give much evidence
Against them. They went back from where they came
   To their king very dusty, pale with shame.

*The accusers return from Ayaz's closet to the king with empty bags
and ashamed like those who thought ill of the Prophets once their
innocence and holiness were made manifest, for 'On the day some
faces will be bright and others gloomy',* * and 'You will see those
who lied against God, their faces gloomy.'* *

The king then asked, 'What happened at the closet?
   Your hands are empty—no gold and no wallet?
If you've concealed all of the money's traces
   Why isn't there bright joy now on your faces?'
Although the root of every tree's unseen
   Leaves are *their marks on faces** and they're green.
The branch declares all that the root's been fed,   2085
   Whether candy or poisonous things instead.
And if a root lacks sap to grow leaves, then
   How can its branches have leaves, my good men?
Mud seals the root's tongue, so it can't disclose,
   But its own branch can tell us what it knows.

Those men apologized in desperation—
   Shadows before the moon in full prostration—

For all their rashness, bragging, and conceit,
    Handing the king a sword and winding sheet.
In shame they started biting their own hands   2090
    And pleading, 'O dear monarch of these lands,
If you kill us it's lawful, but if you
    Forgive that would be grace and bounty too.
We've done things that befit us wretchedly—
    O noble king, whatever you decree!
Brightener of hearts, if you forgive our crime
    You would be true to your ways, too, this time.
If you forgive, despair would lessen too,
    Otherwise let us all now die for you!'
'I won't forgive or punish,' he replied,   2095
    'No, that's for Ayaz who'll alone decide . . .'

The king transfers to Ayaz the acceptance of the repentance or
punishing of the accusers who opened the closet, meaning that this
crime was committed against the latter's honour.

'Your crime's aim was his honour and good name;
    You struck the veins of someone none can blame.
Although we are one spirit, outwardly
    There is no gain or loss in this for me.'
It doesn't harm the servant's king when he's
    Accused—it just expands his clemencies.
When He'll make the accused rich like Qarun*
    How much he'll give to innocent men soon!
Don't think the King won't know the things you do—   2100
    His clemency's all that keeps it from view:
What can then intercede so casually
    Before His knowledge but His clemency?
His clemency is that sin's actual source
    Or else awe would have stopped the sin of course.
The blood-price for the murderous self's sin
    Falls on His clemency: it's on the kin.
Our soul got witlessly drunk just on that,
    His clemency—the devil snatched its hat:
If clemency's wine hadn't filled the cup   2105
    How could Satan have then shown Adam up?*

Adam was for the angels previously
    Teacher and coiner of God's currency.
On drinking clemency's wine all the same
    He fell from grace due to cursed Satan's game.
The Kind God's teachings, like nutritious food,
    Made Adam knowledgeable, sharp and shrewd.
That opium of His awesome clemency
    Had led the thief to take his property.
Reason, too, asks His clemency for shelter: 2110
    'Please take my hand for you were my cupbearer!'

The king asks Ayaz, 'Decide either to forgive or punish, for
whichever you choose between justice or mercy will be correct, and
there are advantages in each: there are a thousand mercies within
justice, since: "for you there is life in retribution". The one who*
considers retribution abhorrent only regards this single life of the
murderer and does not look at the millions of lives of innocent people
that will be protected in a fortress due to the fear of punishment.

'Ayaz, judge now these culprits—you are pure
    Through hundreds of abstentions you endure:
If I boil you a hundred times through toiling
    I'll find no dregs in foam caused by your boiling.
Most people fear being tested for the shame—
    All tests fear being applied to you the same.
With knowledge there are oceans that are endless.
    With clemency are mountains that are countless.'
'I know this is your gift,' Ayaz replied,   2115
    'I'm just my boots and coat, your grace aside.'
That's why the Prophet once was heard to say:
    'Whoever knows himself knows God this way.'
The boots: your sperm; the coat: your blood—the rest
    Is His bestowal, friends, and that is best.
He's given you this much so you seek more—
    Don't say: 'There's no more than this much in store.'
The gardener shows some apples so you'll see
    From them his trees' and their crop's quality.
With wheat ears in his hand the sellers show   2120
    Their granary's wheat's worth, so buyers know.

A fine point is explained well by your teacher
  So that you'll tell his knowledge reaches deeper—
'This is all that he knows!' if you should say,
  Like crumbs on beards he'll sweep you far away.

'Ayaz, come and deal justice—in this nation
  You'll lay for a rare justice the foundation.
Those criminals should die deservedly,
  But crave your pardon now and clemency,
To see if mercy dominates or ire,   2125
  Water of Kawsar or the *lahab* fire.'*
Wrath and clemency's branches have been here
  Since that *Alast* to lead men to that sphere.
That's why *Alast* has an unusual nature
  As word: it's both confirmer and negater:
A question that affirms, but equally
  One finds in it the verb for 'not to be'.*
Leave this unfinished and just plough ahead,
  Don't put elite food on the vulgar's spread.
His wrath or grace, the plague or the fine breeze—   2130
  Magnets draw iron, amber straw with ease.
God draws true men to guidance's right way;
  False things draw futile people far astray.
Sweet stomachs draw sweet things—they're similar;
  Acidic stomachs draw up vinegar.
Warm rugs remove the cold when used as seat,
  But cold rugs draw away your body's heat.
When you see a good friend you feel much kindness;
  When you see a vile foe you show much harshness.
'Ayaz, complete this quickly! Expectation   2135
  Can be itself a harsh retaliation.'

*The king tells Ayaz to hurry up: 'Quickly make the judgement call
and don't keep them waiting by saying: "Some days must pass for
our situation to be resolved" for expectation is a red death.'*
Then Ayaz answers the king.*

He said, 'It's your choice, king, what shall be done:

The star becomes effaced next to the sun—
Who then are Venus, Mercury, or a meteor
  To shine in the sun's presence, their superior?
If I had left my boots and fleece alone,
  The seed of blame would not have then been sown:
What was the point of locking up the door
  When enviers had suspicions by the score?
Each put his hand in rivers that flowed by   2140
  Hoping to find a brick there that was dry—
Can a brick in a river stay dry ever?
  Can a fish then defy its water? Never!
They thought that I had shown disloyalty
  Though loyalty feels too small next to me.'

About true loyalty I'd have dictated,
  But for the irksome uninitiated—
Since most seek doubts and problems over here
  We'll talk beyond the surface to be clear.
Break your self and you'll be the kernel only   2145
  And hear at last the lovely kernel's story.
The walnut's sound is made by its hard shell—
  Do oil and kernel make their sounds as well?
They have a sound, but most ears cannot hear—
  That sound is hidden in the mystic's ear.
Were it not for the sweet sound of the kernel
  Who'd listen to the walnut shell's mere rattle?
One bears its rattling to make a connection
  In silence with the kernel's deep dimension.
Be lipless now and earless for a time,   2150
  Then, lip-like, share the drink that is sublime.
You've uttered poetry, prose, and mysteries
  Too long—try to be mute for one day, please!

Story in confirmation of the saying: 'We have tried speech and talk
for such a long time—let's for a little while try self-restraint and silence.'

You've cooked the bitter, salty, and the sour—
  For once try cooking something sweet this hour!

Someone wakes up on Judgement Day to see
    A book in his hand sin-filled totally:
It's header's black like for a funeral,
    Sins in the text and margins till they're full.
All of it sin and badness totally   2155
    Like the foes' realm of infidelity.
A foul and noxious book of that bad kind
    Won't reach the right hand—it heads left you'll find.*
You have your book too from this world. It's planned,
    But will it reach your left or your right hand?
Can you know without trying that a boot
    In the shop fits your left or your right foot?
Know that you're 'left' when you're not right and sound:
    A lion's roar's not like the ape's own sound.
He who gave roses scent and beauty too,   2160
    Has grace that makes each left thing right and true.
He gives each left thing rightness, which is better;
    He gives the salty sea some *running water.*
Though you're left, try being right when He is near
    To witness that His mercy's rule is clear.
If the bad deeds' book's passed from left to right
    Would you consider that to be all right?
How can a book filled with iniquity
    Be fit for the right hand? Please answer me!

*Explanation of a person who talks in one way while his condition is
not appropriate with what he says and claims, similar to the infidels
referred to in 'And if you ask them: "Who created the heavens and
the earth?" They will say, "God."'* How is worship of a stone idol
and sacrifice of life and gold appropriate for a soul which knows
that the creator of the heavens and the earth and all creatures
is God, The Hearing, The Seeing, The Present,
The Observing and The Jealous One, etc.*

There once was an ascetic whose wife would   2165
    Get jealous. His young maid looked very good.
The wife watched him possessively, forbade
    Him from being left alone with that fine maid.

For some time she observed them closely to
    Prevent the chance of trysts between the two,
Until there came God's pre-ordained decree—
    The watchman, reason, then faints helplessly.
When His ordainment should arrive, what's reason?
    The mighty moon can get eclipsed in season.
The wife once at the bathhouse suddenly   2170
    Noticed she'd left her bowl at home, so she
Sent back the maid: 'Go like a bird back there—
    Bring here the silver bowl to rinse my hair!'
On hearing this, the maid revived and thought:
    'This time I'll get the master whom I've sought:
He's all alone at home now so I can.'
    How joyfully back home the young maid ran!
For six years she had longed to be alone
    With him like this: the two now on their own.
She flew inside in such a rush and found   2175
    The master there with no one else around.
Lust now controlled these lovers and these two
    Abandoned caution, left doors open too,
Their bodies writhing as they felt elated,
    Their souls united as they copulated.
The wife remembered all her fears just then:
    'Why did I send that young maid home again?
I've burned my cloth with my own hands! I am
    Letting loose on an ewe the lustful ram.
She rinsed clear quickly both her head and hair   2180
    And held her chador as she scampered there.

The maid had run for love, the wife for fear—
    The difference between them is so clear.
Each moment mystics travel to God's Throne;
    Ascetics move each month one day. It's known
Though the ascetic's day be great and rare
    With *fifty thousand years** it can't compare:
In an adept's life one day lasts as long
    As fifty thousand years. My words aren't wrong.
Intellects are denied this mystery—   2185

If the mind blows up trying, let it be.
Next to love, fear is like a hair: so small.
    All things are sacrificed in love's creed. All.
Love is God's attribute, not fear—God's slave
    Has that along with genitals that crave.
Since you've read '*they love Him*'* in the Qur'an
    Joined with '*He loves them*'* that means that you can
See that love and most passionate love, not fear,
    Are both God's attributes as day is clear.
God's attributes and clay's are obviously   2190
    So different: One Pure, one temporary.
If I describe love non-stop to you, friend,
    Come Judgement Day my words would still not end:
Judgement Day has a date and definition;
    God's attribute has no kind of restriction.
Love has five hundred wings and each extends
    From God's High Throne to where the earth's depth ends.
While the ascetic walks across in fear
    God's lover flies as fast as wind through here.
The fearful can't catch lovers who fly by   2195
    And whose ache makes a carpet of the sky.
Unless God's Light's grace tells them suddenly:
    'From this world and from travel now be free!'
Flee from your own fuss and your scurrying—
    Only the falcon finds paths to the king.
Predestination and free will hold you,
    But God's pull comes from far beyond these two.

The wife reached home and opened the front door.
    They heard it open while still on the floor.
The maid jumped up dishevelled once aware;   2200
    The man stood up to start his daily prayer.
The wife saw that the maid was so dishevelled,
    Confused, beside herself, and very rattled.
She saw her husband standing up in prayer,
    But grew suspicious of commotion there—
She lifted up his shirt tail with good reason
    And saw his balls and penis smeared with semen.

Semen dripped from his penis to the floor,
  His knees and thighs still dirty from before.
She slapped him on the head, 'Vile wretch, you're saying   2205
  That these are testicles of one who's praying?
That these thighs, penis, and this pubic hair
  Are also worthy of doing *zekr* and prayer?'
Be honest, is a book that's full of spite,
  Oppression and wrong-doing fit for the right?*
If you ask infidels, 'Who's the creator
  Of this world and the sky and every creature?'
He'll say, 'God's the Creator from on high,
  To whom all of His creatures testify.'
Do this man's unbelief, sin, and oppression   2210
  Make him fit for such a sincere confession?
And are notorious and corrupt acts fit
  And totally compatible with it?
His actions make his speech a lie, my brother,
  So he is fit now for the dreaded torture.

On the Last Day each hidden thing is shown,
  Each sinner is then by himself made known:
His hands and feet will give clear evidence
  Of his corruption to His Eminence.
The hand will say, 'I stole this and that thing.'   2215
  The lips, 'I was forever questioning.'
The foot, 'I've followed lusts until they're sated.'
  His genitals will say, 'I've fornicated.'
His eyes, 'I've flirted inappropriately.'
  His ears, 'I've kept words of iniquity.'
He's then a lie from head down to his toe
  And his own limbs make sure that we all know,
Just as those prayers that seem fine spectacles
  Are false pretence as shown by testicles.
So act in such a way that yours will say   2220
  Without a tongue, '*I testify*,'* this way.
So your whole body, every limb, will say:
  '*I testify*'* and do so come what may.

It's proof when servants walk behind their master:
　　'He is my master; I fulfil his order.'
If you have blotted your life's book, act fast—
　　Repent for all that you did in the past!
Its root is now, though those days may be over—
　　If it lacks moisture, give contrition's water!
Give Water of Life to your life's root—nourish　　　　2225
　　That tree of your life, watch it bloom and flourish!
Through this, all the past things are made good now
　　And poison turns to sugar too somehow:
God has transformed your evil deeds to good,
　　All are now deemed obedience as they should.
Cling to sincere repentance as your goal—
　　Mister, strive hard with body and with soul!
Heed me about repentance that is true—
　　You once believed it—now believe anew!

*Story explaining the repentance of Nasuh, for just as milk that
flows out of nipples does not wish to return, whoever repents as
sincerely as Nasuh never recalls that sin of theirs with desire, but
rather with each passing moment his loathing increases. This
loathing is proof that he has tasted the delight of acceptance.
That first craving has lost its appeal and this new
delight has taken its place:
Only new love replaces an old one.
Why not seek out a better looking one?
But if his heart desires that sin again, this is a sign that he hadn't
tasted the delight of acceptance and so such a delight did not take
the place of that delight from the sin, and he has not become among
those whom 'we will give ease', * but rather the delight has remained
with him which leads to 'we will give him hardship'. **

There was a man once called Nasuh and he　　　　　　2230
　　Worked washing women's hair, unusually.
His face was like a woman's and he'd hide
　　The fact he really was a man inside.
He kept shampooing them though that was odd,
　　Since he was cunning in deceit and fraud.
He washed their hair for years and none suspected

His secret, so his sex went undetected,
Since both his face and voice were so effete,
  Although his much-aroused lusts were complete.
He wore the chador and the veil, but he   2235
  Was in male youth's prime, lustful as can be.
He would massage and wash princesses' hair
  So he was thrilled that he was working there.
He'd vowed repentance earlier than this—
  His infidel soul broke his promises.
That sinner asked a mystic who passed near:
  'Remember me in your pure prayers, my dear!'
That liberated man knew of his secret,
  But, like God's kind ways, chose not to reveal it,
In his heart secrets, but his lips both sealed,   2240
  Silent with voices in his heart concealed.
The mystics who have downed God's cup have known
  The secrets, but by them they're never shown.
He who's been taught the secrets out of sight
  Was then sealed closed with his own mouth sewn tight.
He just laughed, 'Naughty one, may God grant you
  Repentance for the things you know you do!'

*Explaining that the prayer of the mystic who has reached God and
his petition to God are like the petition of God to Himself, for He
has said: 'I am the hearing, sight, tongue, and hand'* and also:
'You did not throw when you threw, but rather God threw.'**
*The Qur'anic verses, prophetic traditions, and other sayings about
this are numerous. An explanation of the reason God makes it
happen that, while his ear is yanked, the sinner is brought to the
repentance of Nasuh.*

Rising above, that mystic's supplication
  Transformed to good that wretch's situation
Because his prayer is not like any prayer—   2245
  He is effaced; his words are God's. That's rare.
When God asks from Himself and begs this way
  How can He turn that prayer down anyway?
The means came from the Lord's own fabrication
  To free Nasuh from much woe and damnation:

While he was filling up a bowl with water
    A jewel belonging to the king's own daughter
Was lost, one from her earring. All around
    Women were searching so it would be found.
They locked the bathhouse door then suddenly   2250
    And checked the furniture most thoroughly.
It didn't turn up in the furniture
    And they'd not found the jewel's pilferer.
They then searched there with utmost seriousness
    Inside mouths, ears, and every orifice.
They searched in all their crevices as well
    For that pearl that belonged to a fine shell:
'Everyone now get naked,' they were told,
    'Whether you're young or whether you are old!'
The chamberlain searched everyone around   2255
    In turn to make sure that the pearl was found.
In fear, Nasuh went somewhere out of view,
    His cheeks pale, and, from terror, his lips blue.
He saw his death ahead of him and he
    Trembled just like a leaf, so fearfully,
And prayed, 'I've turned back often up to now
    And broken every promise, every vow—
Lord, I've behaved as I am suited to
    And so a black flood has arrived here too.
If my turn to be searched arrives, You know   2260
    How I will suffer then more grief and woe!
A hundred sparks have struck my heart today—
    You can now smell my heart burn when I pray.
May infidels not feel such agony!
    I grab now mercy's coattails—rescue me!
O mother, why did you give birth to me?
    I wish a lion had just eaten me!
O God, do what is fit for Your own role—
    A snake is biting me from every hole!
I clearly have an inert soul and heart   2265
    Or they'd have turned to blood now for a start.
There's little time left now for me to flee—
    Be like the King You are and rescue me!
If you'd conceal me this once, I implore,

I will repent for all I've done before.
Accept repentance from me once again—
   I'll truly strive hard in contrition then.
If I'm at fault again a later day
   Don't ever listen to me when I pray!'
A hundred drops flowed as he wept in dread: 2270
   'I'm in the executioner's hands!' he said.
'I hope no infidel must die like me
   Or unbelievers feel such misery!'
He mourned his own soul as if it were dead
   Since he saw Azrael approach ahead.
'O God!' he cried so often that the wall
   And door of that room joined in with his call.
He was immersed in crying, 'O Lord!' when
   He heard shouts from the searching crowd again . . .

The arrival of Nasuh's turn to be searched and the call: 'We've
searched everyone else. Search Nasuh!' Nasuh's fainting through
fear and the release of his bind after the extremity of it was reached,
as the Prophet would say whenever illness or worry overwhelmed
him: 'Distress, become severe! You will ease off.'

'We've searched the rest. Come here, Nasuh!' they said.   2275
   He fainted, lifeless as if truly dead.
He fell down like a broken wall. His mind
   Had gone—what was inert was left behind.
His wits departed from his body then;
   His soul now joined with God above again:
Once void of his existence in this fashion
   God summoned to Himself Nasuh's soul's falcon.
His ship capsized before it reached its goal,
   But he reached Mercy's coastline through his soul.
His soul joined God when he became unconscious;   2280
   Mercy's wave started surging then, tumultuous.
His soul escaped the body's trap's disgrace
   And happily went to its original place.
His soul, a falcon in the body's fetter,
   Was broken-winged, foot-bound, trapped by the latter—
On losing consciousness with feet unbound

The falcon flew to the best king around.
When Mercy's oceans stir to life anew
    Mere stones can drink the Water of Life too;
A tiny mote grows big and bold instead;   2285
    A dirty rug becomes silk with gold thread;
An ancient corpse will leave the grave; for beauty
    The devil's now the envy of the houri,
The ground turns verdant, lush and bountiful;
    Dry wood sprouts buds and turns so beautiful;
The wolf becomes the lamb's friend; the despairing
    Become now hopeful, positive and daring.

The finding of the pearl and how the chamberlains and handmaids of the Princess asked Nasuh to forgive them.

After that soul-destroying, awful fear
    Came the good news: 'The item lost is here!'
A clamour suddenly rose: 'Fear has passed—   2290
    The single lost pearl has been found at last.
It's been found and we're so exhilarated—
    Give the reward for good news being related!'
The bathhouse filled with clamour, shouts, claps too,
    For sorrow had now disappeared from view.
Nasuh returned now to his wits once more;
    His eyes saw brightness like days by the score.
Everyone now was asking his forgiveness
    And reaching for his hand to shower with kisses:
'Forgive us! We had such bad thoughts tonight   2295
    And once we'd talked we started to back-bite.'
They were suspicious of him most of all
    For he was closest to her of them all:
The princess's shampooer was his role;
    The pair were close—two bodies with one soul.
They'd thought: 'Only Nasuh is capable;
    From the princess he is inseparable.'
She'd wanted first to search him using force.
    Out of respect she let it take its course
So he might place it somewhere clear as day   2300
    And save himself thus during the delay.

They kept on asking him for his forgiveness;
   Requests from them to be excused were countless.
'It was the Grace of God, the Just, instead,
   Otherwise I am worse than what's being said.
Why should you ask a sinner to forgive
   When I'm the biggest sinner who did live?
The bad they've said of me is just a bit
   Of its true total, though you're doubting it.
Others know just a bit of me—they know   2305
   One thousandth of my sins that are so low.
I know and so does He who keeps me covered
   My sins and vile deeds, though you've not discovered.
At first a Satan-like one was my teacher,
   But soon in evil he was my inferior.
God saw this, but He made it all unseen
   To spare me from disgrace if it were seen.
God's Mercy stitched my old fleece waistcoat's holes
   And gave atonement sweeter than pure souls.
He undid all the evil I'd committed;   2310
   He marked as "done" obedience I'd omitted.
He freed me like the cypress and the lily,
   And like good fortune he has spoilt me silly.
Amongst the pure souls' list He wrote my name;
   I fit hell—He gave heaven all the same.
I sighed and then my sigh became a rope—
   That was hung down my well to offer hope:
I grabbed that rope and managed to get out;
   I then became so joyful, fair and stout.
I'd been at the well's bottom, feeling low—   2315
   The world's not big enough for me now though.
All praises be to You, God, Your relief
   Arrived and rescued me from so much grief.
If every hair of mine could speak to You
   They couldn't give the total praise that's due.
I yell to people in this garden, "Oh,
   If only my own people would now know!" '*

*The princess again invites Nasuh to shampoo her after his
repentance had been established and accepted, but he makes an
excuse and turns her down.*

Afterwards someone came to him to say:
   'The Sultan's daughter summons you today.
The ruler's daughter is inviting you—   2320
   Come now to wash her hair without ado!
Her heart wants you alone to wash her hair
   And to massage and scrub her everywhere.'
He said, 'Begone! My hand's out of commission.
   Nasuh's too sick now for this kind of mission.
Find someone else as fast as possible!
   I swear my hand is not available.'
He thought, 'My sin was the excessive kind—
   How can that fear and anguish leave my mind?
I died once and returned from that no less.   2325
   I tasted bitter death and nothingness.
But I repented truly to God—I
   Won't break my vow again until I die.
Only a donkey would go back once more
   To where he had faced horrors once before.'

*Story explaining how someone repents and feels remorse, but forgets
that feeling and tries again what he did before. He falls into eternal
perdition. When his repentance lacks firmness, strength, sweetness,
and acceptability it is like a rootless tree and each day it becomes
more yellow and dry. We take refuge in God from that.*

A bleacher had a donkey that was ill
   With back sores, empty stomach, starving still,
Confined to grassless, stony ground—no hay,
   Nor shelter for this donkey night and day.
Nothing but water there to ease its plight,   2330
   The donkey was stuck there all day and night.
There was a reed marsh and a forest near—
   A lion skilled in hunting without peer
Lived there and once it fought an elephant
   And then got so hurt that it couldn't hunt.

It couldn't hunt due to an injury—
    Other beasts lost their food source suddenly
For they'd eat what that lion left behind:
    Once it was wounded their food, too, declined.
The lion told a fox, 'Go out for me   2335
    And hunt a donkey very rapidly!
If you find one now grazing in the meadow,
    Charm him, fool him, bring him back here, good fellow!
Once I gain strength from donkey flesh, I'll then
    Be able to go hunting prey again.
I'll eat a little, leaving most for you:
    I am the reason you get your food too,
So find for me a donkey or a cow
    And charm it with your spells as you know how.
With your sweet words and charm make it soon lose   2340
    Its mind, then bring it home with a smart ruse.'

Parable about the Spiritual Pole, who is the mystic in union with
God, with regard to his giving to people their nourishment of
forgiveness and mercy to the degree that God inspires him to. Also,
a comparison with the lion, for the other beasts eat portions of his
food and his leftovers in proportion to their nearness to him, not
spatial nearness but nearness in characteristics. The nuances
of this are many. God is the guide.

The Pole's the lion—hunting's the job he does.
    His leftovers are for the rest of us.
Try satisfying him with all your might
    So he gains strength and hunts wild prey in sight.
Men won't get food if he endures some pain:
    The gullet's food arrives due to the brain.
Men's ecstasies are what he's left behind,
    So if your hearts want prey, keep this in mind.
People are bodily limbs—that is their role—   2345
    He's mind and body's under mind's control.
The Pole's wound's bodily, not in spirit, friend.
    The ark was flawed, not Noah, in the end.
The Pole will turn around himself, but he
    Is what the heavens circle ceaselessly.

Help him repair the ark if you become
  His special servant and much gain will come—
Your help is not for him, but you instead:
  '*If you help God, you'll be helped,*'* God has said.
Hunt like the fox and give him all you find   2350
  So you'll gain from him thousands more in kind.
Just like the fox, disciples give their prey;
  Stubborn hyenas hunt the dead all day.
Take dead things to him and they'll come alive:
  Dirt in a garden will make all things thrive.

The fox said to the lion, 'I'll serve you:
  I'll trick and rob it of its mind now too.
My work is charming with tricks anyway—
  It is my job to trick and lead astray.'
It rushed down from the mountain near the river   2355
  To find the poor, thin donkey and deliver
A friendly greeting. That sly fox went near
  The simple, poor beast, when it felt no fear:
'How come you're in this parched land that's so hot
  Among the stones in such a dried-up spot?'
'Whether in heaven or a state that's hateful
  God has decreed my fate, so I am grateful.
I thank God, my Beloved, in all states,
  Good or bad, since there are more awful fates.
Complaining's unbelief when He's decreed.   2360
  Patience, *the key to gifts*, is what we need.
God is the Friend; others are foes. How could
  Complaining of one's friend to foes be good?
If He gives buttermilk, I won't complain
  That it's not honey: there's pain with each gain.'

Story about the donkey of the firewood seller* seeing Arab horses
with provisions in a royal stable and wishing to win the same good
fortune, to teach that one should not wish for anything but
forgiveness, guidance, and God's blessing, for though you
have a hundred kinds of suffering, when you have the savour
of forgiveness everything becomes sweet. Moreover, every
fortune that you wish for before you've ever experienced
it is accompanied by a suffering that you don't see, just as
inside every trap the grain is visible while the snare is
hidden—when you are stuck in one trap you wish:
'If only I had taken the other bait!' imagining
that those grains did not have snares.

A water-carrier's donkey was becoming
    Bent-double like a circle due to suffering.
Heavy loads gave its back sores tragically;
    It longed for its own death so passionately.
What's barley? It did not get straw to fill   2365
    Itself, just blows from iron goads when still.
The royal stable's master once felt sorry
    Because he knew the owner of this donkey.
He greeted him, asked how he was, then he
    Asked why the donkey's back hunched like a C?
'Due to my poverty,' came the reply,
    'This sealed-mouthed beast gets nothing. That is why.'
'Give it to me for a few days and then
    At the king's stable it will thrive again.'
He gave his donkey to him—he was able   2370
    To kindly keep it in the ruler's stable.
The donkey saw there Arab horses, sated
    With food, fat, lovely, and rejuvenated,
Their ground swept, water sprinkled on it too,
    Barley and straw arriving there when due.
The horses were all combed and rubbed down there—
    It raised its muzzle: 'Glorious Lord, up there!
Aren't I your creature, too, though I've a lack,
    A wretched donkey with sores on its back?
Back pain and hunger every night make me   2375
    Wish for my sudden death continually.

Those horses are doing well with food supplied—
   For suffering grief why was I specified?'

The call to work was heard once suddenly—
   The horses had to work with bravery.
They got struck by the enemies outside,
   Whose arrows' barbs pierced them on every side,
The horses got back from the war once able—
   They all collapsed on their backs in the stable.
Their legs were tightly bandaged where they lay,   2380
   The farriers stood there waiting, too, that day.
Scalpels were used to pierce them to take out
   The barbs from their wounds, painfully no doubt.
The watching donkey said, 'O God!' on seeing,
   'I don't mind being poor when I've well-being:
I don't care for that food, nor wounds—it's clear
   Those wishing for well-being quit this world here.'

The fox disapproves of the saying of the donkey:
'I am content with my portion.'

The fox said, 'Lawful work you do for pay
   Is necessary to show you obey:
Nothing's without means in this world, you see.   2385
   That's why to seek your food is necessary.'
'*Seek out God's bounty!*'* is one of God's orders
   Lest someone seize the property of others.
'The door's shut to provisions,' said the Prophet,
   'Young man, and there are several big locks on it.
Our movement, work to earn and our exertion
   Are keys for those locks and to draw the curtain.
The door won't open without keys that fit;
   God won't give food without you seeking it.'

The donkey answers the fox.

'That's just a lack of trust,' the donkey said,   2390
   'He who gave life will also give you bread.

Whoever seeks success, dominion
    Will not lack loaves of bread at all, my son.
Wild animals all feed on what God offers
    And they don't earn, nor do they care for others.
God the Provider gives all daily bread:
    He sets their lot before each. All are fed.
Daily bread comes to all who have true patience;
    Struggles of efforts all stem from impatience.'

The fox answers the donkey.

'That kind of faith is rare,' the fox replied,   2395
    'Few have such massive trust in God inside.
It's ignorant to focus on what's rare:
    The royal path's not for all everywhere.
The Prophet said, "Contentment's hidden treasure"—
    Not all can find what's hidden at their leisure.
Know your own limit and don't you exceed this!
    You won't fall into suffering if you heed this.'

The donkey answers the fox.

'What you claim is the opposite of trust—
    Suffering comes to the spirit from your lust.
Due to contentment no one's perishing;   2400
    By means of lust no one became a king.
Food's not kept back from pigs and dogs, so learn
    That clouds and rain are not things men can earn.
And just as you long for your food each day
    Your food longs for its eater the same way.'

Exposition of the meaning of trust in God by means of the story
about the ascetic who, as a test for his trust in God, left his
hometown and his belongings and went far away from the
thoroughfares others frequented to the foot of a remote and
abandoned mountain. In extreme hunger he slept with a rock as
pillow, saying: 'I have trusted in You to provide the means and my
daily bread by cutting myself off from other means—all in order to
experience the means provided by trust in God.'

A hermit heard Mohammad's famed tradition:
　　'Daily bread comes from God as soul's provision.
It doesn't matter what you wish or do—
　　Your daily bread runs lovingly to you.'
To test this, the ascetic rushed outside　　　　　　2405
　　Through wild plains and slept on a mountainside:
'I'll see if daily bread arrives,' he said,
　　'To strengthen all my views on daily bread.'
A caravan had lost its way near there—
　　They saw him lying still and unaware.
One said, 'How come a naked man's out here
　　In the wild where no town nor roads are near?
Amazing! Is he dead or breathing? He
　　Does not fear wild wolves or his enemy.'
They then came near him and they started touching—　　2410
　　On purpose that man lay still and said nothing.
He didn't even move his head throughout,
　　Nor opened his eyes, eager to find out.
'This weak and hopeless man', the people said,
　　'Has had a stroke because he was unfed.'
They brought some bread and pots of food, so they
　　Could force it down his gullet in some way,
And so that man then clenched his teeth to then
　　Put to the test that promise once again.
They pitied him, 'This man is starving badly　　　　2415
　　And might soon die because of hunger, sadly.'
They rushed to bring a knife to force some gaps
　　Between his clenched teeth for some food perhaps—
They poured some soup inside eventually
　　And pushed in bits of bread most carefully.

'O heart, though you keep cool,' the hermit said,
   'You know the secret, yet stay calm instead!'
'I know and it's deliberate,' it then said,
   'Body and soul by God are both well fed.'
Could there have been a stricter test than this?   2420
   Daily bread heads to patient men with bliss.

The fox answers the donkey and urges the donkey to earn a living.

The fox said, 'Leave these tales of yours for good—
   With *struggles of men with less* earn some food!
God gave you hands, so do some work instead—
   Earn something, help your friends earn daily bread!
Everyone's meant to earn, including you,
   And to help other people earn some too.
Earning's not just one person's burden either:
   We've many jobs, like carpenter and weaver.
The world's maintained by our cooperation;   2425
   All choose to work through fear of deprivation.
Free-loading isn't right—the Prophet's way
   Is to earn your provisions every day.'

The donkey answers the fox: 'Trust in God is the best of ways to earn, for everyone needs trust in God and says, "O God, make this situation of mine turn out right!" and supplication involves trust in God. Trust in God is a means of earning that doesn't need any other means of earning etc.'

The donkey said, 'So far I'm not aware
   Of earning rivalling such trust anywhere:
To praising God there's nothing that comes near
   For drawing daily bread to us down here.'
This argument between the pair dragged on
   Until all questions and replies were done.
The fox then said, 'Know that in His dominion   2430
   There is "Don't harm yourself"* as prohibition.
Patience with arid deserts, stony ground
   Is stupid. God's world's vast. Just look around.
Move your home to the pasture now from here!
   Graze there near a sweet river without fear,

Green pastures just like paradise, a taste
  Of what that's like with grass up to your waist.
Happy the animals who go there too.
  Such tall grass hides the camel from your view.
Flowing fountains are there on every side;   2435
  It's calm and safe for animals inside.'
The donkey, being an ass, did not then say:
  'How come you're now in such an awful way?
Where is the plumpness, pomp, and drunkenness?
  Why is your body thin and in a mess?
If your description of it isn't lies
  Then why can't I see stupor in your eyes?
Those eyes that beg and lack a true, prior vision
  Are caused by neediness and not dominion.
If you've come from the fountain, why're you dry?   2440
  You claim you're musk, but there's no scent. You lie!
Why isn't there on you the smallest sign
  Of what you boast about now and opine?'

Parable of the camel to explain that if you don't see a sign of glory
in someone who tells of good fortune, it is time to suspect
that he is just pretending.

A man once asked a camel, 'Where are you
  Coming from, you whom fortune follows too?'
It said, 'The hot baths that are close to you.'
  He said, 'Your dirty knees show that's not true!'
Stubborn Pharaoh saw Moses's snake,* then
  Begged for respite and mellowed down again.
'He's judgement's lord,' said certain clever men,   2445
  'So he should really have been harsher then.
Whether a snake or dragon marvel, where
  Was his divine wrath and his prideful air?
If he is the supreme lord on his throne
  Why all this flattery for a worm alone?'

As long as your soul lusts for sweets and wine
  Know that your soul's not seen food that's divine:

That vision of God's Light's profound effusion's
    Your severance from the realm of fake delusions.
Since that bird goes to briny water, it   2450
    Has not yet seen sweet water's benefit—
Its faith is imitations of a trace;
    Its soul has never even seen faith's face.
There is great danger for the imitator
    From the accursed devil, that waylayer.
On seeing God's Light, he becomes secure,
    At peace from doubt's annoyances and sure.
Until the sea waves' foam laps on the shore,
    Its source, it keeps on clashing more and more:
That foam's of earth; in water it's exiled   2455
    And while kept separate it becomes so riled.
When his eyes open he can read the plan—
    The devil can't control now such a man.

Although the donkey told the secret, he
    Like copiers, did so just externally.
He had no ship, though he was praising water:
    He ripped his shirt, but he was not a lover.
False hypocrites' excuses are rejected
    Since they're not from the heart, but just affected:
They have the apple's scent, but no real share;   2460
    The scent on him is just to reach you there.
A woman's charge won't break ranks in the fray—
    It only makes her state worse in that way.
You see her lion-like with sword in hand
    In battle, but look at that trembling hand!
Pity the one whose intellect is female
    While his vile self is both aroused and deemed male:
His reason's overwhelmed inevitably—
    He's heading to loss and catastrophe.
Happy the one whose intellect is male,   2465
    His vile self female, vulnerable and frail:
Particular intellects, male and prevailing,
    Seize female carnal souls and leave them flailing.
The female's battle charge looks bold, but she

Shares that poor donkey's asininity.
Animal qualities prevail in them—
   They're drawn to scent and colour in this realm:
A donkey heard of those two in the pasture
   And rational proofs evaded him thereafter
There were no clouds but thirsty men sought rain—   2470
   The hungry self lacked patience to restrain.
Patience is like an iron shield, my friend—
   God wrote there '*Victory comes*' for that's its end.
The imitator's store of evidence
   Comes from his mind, not from experience:
He's musk-smeared, not real musk: he smells of it,
   But in reality he's only shit.
For shit to turn to musk one must graze long,
   Disciple, in that garden for the strong.
Don't eat, like donkeys, hay and barley here—   2475
   Eat Judas Tree flowers like the Khotan deer!
Graze only on fine jasmine, cloves, and rose—
   Go to Khotan's plains with a man who knows!
And get your belly used to herbs to gain
   The knowledge the apostles can obtain.
Quit eating straw and barley and then you
   Can fill your belly with such fine herbs too!
The bodily belly drags to mounds of hay,
   But the heart's belly leads to basil's way.
Eat hay and barley and they'll slaughter you;   2480
   Eat God's Light and then be Qur'an-like too!
You are half-musk and half-dung, so beware!
   Don't raise the dung's share, but the musk's in there!
The imitator may have proofs to show,
   But he has no soul, so how could he know?
When speakers have no soul or greatness now
   How can their speech bear leaves and fruit somehow?
He confidently tells men of the way,
   But shakes within more than a blade of hay.
Although he uses wondrous words to teach   2485
   There is as well a tremor in his speech.

The difference between the call of the perfect shaikh who is united
with God and the talk of the defective ones whose virtues are
acquired and hollow.

Enlightened shaikhs show true paths when they teach
    And they make Light accompany their speech.
Strive to become drunk and enlightened too,
    So His Light joins with all words said by you!
If something's boiled in grape juice, then that flavour
    Will stay with it when it is tasted later,
Whether quince, carrots, walnuts, or an apple—
    You'll find grape juice's taste in any sample.
When knowledge is immersed in Light, no less,   2490
    Men see its Light despite their stubbornness:
Whatever you say will be luminous—
    The sky pours only pure rain over us.
Become sky, cloud—pour rain down here today!
    The drainpipe pours, but not in a pure way:
The drainpipe's water's borrowed patently—
    Water's innate in clouds and in the sea:
The drainpipe stands for thought and contemplation;
    The clouds and sky both stand for revelation.
Rainwater makes a garden bloom with colour;   2495
    The drainpipe starts a quarrel with your neighbour.

The donkey argued with the fox some more,
    An imitator, that fox wiped the floor
With it, for it lacked visionary perceptions—
    The fox's babble gave it palpitations.
The donkey had, through lust for food, grown base
    So it caved in though it knew a strong case.

*The story about that male whore and the question he was asked by a
sodomite while he was buggering him: 'What is that dagger for?'
He said, 'It's so I can tear open the belly of anyone who thinks
bad thoughts about me.' The sodomite satisfied his lusts with
him and then said, 'Thank God that I don't have any bad
thoughts about you!'
My house is not a house; it's a whole region.
My joke is not a joke; it is a teaching.*

A sodomite took a male whore with him
    Back home, then made him bend and buggered him.
That wretch then saw the male whore had a dagger: 2500
    'What's tied around your waist in that strange manner?'
That's there in case a wretched man thinks badly
    To harm me, so I can rip out his belly.'
The sodomite said, 'Thank God that it's true
    That I'd no thought of doing harm to you.'
No manliness, so why bring knives to slit?
    Without heart, helmets have no benefit.
You've been bequeathed the famed sword of Ali,*
    But do you have God's Lion's arm? Show me!
You may know spells of Jesus, but do you,   2505
    Vile man, have Jesus's divine mouth too?
You have just made an ark through a donation,
    But where is one like Noah to be captain?
Like Abraham you smashed some idols, yes,
    But would you jump in fire without distress?*
If you've proof, show by action—when at war
    Transform your wooden sword to Zo'l-feqar!*
What stops you acting to prove you're no faker
    Is actually the vengeance of your Maker.
You've made those who had feard the path turn bold,   2510
    Though more than others you shake and feel cold.
You preach about being patient everywhere,
    But slit the veins of gnats you cannot bear.
Eunuch, standing as if prepared to die
    In front of troops, your penis proves you lie—
With lack of manliness within, you actor,
    Your beard and moustache only lead to laughter.

Repent, shed tears like rain, redeem your beard
　　And moustache from the laughter you had feared.
Through action take the cure for manliness   2515
　　To then be Aries's hot sun, no less.
Leave now your belly, move towards your heart,
　　So God greets you without veil, then don't part.
Step forward and try hard to persevere
　　Then love will pull you closer by your ear.

The fox's trick overwhelms the donkey's wish to remain pure and
*　　with self-restraint, leading it to the lion in the jungle.*

The fox tried his tricks and he persevered—
　　He dragged the simple donkey by the beard.
Where is the khaniqah's musician, son?
　　Let him play drums and sing: 'The ass has gone!'*
A hare can lead a lion down a well,*   2520
　　So foxes can make donkeys graze as well.
Close your ears to the people's spells except
　　Those from the Friend of God, the true adept.
That spell of his beats halva, for it's sweeter—
　　A hundred halvas are his spell's inferior.
Royal jars filled with wine up to the brim,
　　Took their stock from those wine-stained lips on him.
Only the souls remote from the divine
　　Love other wines and not just his lips' wine.
Blind birds can't see sweet water—it's no wonder   2525
　　That they keep circling round the briny water.
Breasts split from spiritual Moses's sheer might,
　　Like Sinai, and blind parrots gain their sight.*
The drum's been banged by Khosraw, Shirin's lover—
　　Sugar's price has plunged lower, it's no wonder.*
Josephs of the Unseen now lead troops near—
　　They're bringing sacks of sugar over here.
Egyptian camels face our way as well—
　　Listen now parrots to their ringing bell!
Our town will fill with sugar in a day—   2530
　　Sugar's low price will plunge more in that way.
Wallow in sugar as the parrots do,

Candy lovers, ignore the bitter few!
Pound sugar cane! This is good work to do.
   Fling your soul to the Sole Beloved too!
No bitter one remains now in our town
   Since Shirin has now seated Khosraw down.
So many sweets, so much wine—it is awesome!
   Shout from the minaret a general welcome!
So sweet will be the vinegar, though old!   2535
   Mere stones will turn to rubies and to gold!
The sun is clapping from the sky above;
   Dust specks are frolicking like those in love.
The garden has made eyes drunk: blossoms now
   Are budding beautifully on every bough.
The eye of fortune's working wondrous magic;
   The soul says 'I'm God' like Mansur, ecstatic.*
If a fox kills a donkey, don't you worry!
   You won't be harmed since you are not a donkey.

*Story about a person who flung himself terrified into a house, with
pale cheeks and lips as blue as indigo, and with hands shaking like
leaves on a tree. The owner of the house asked, 'What's going on?'
He answered, 'Outside they are confiscating donkeys.' The owner
said, 'Congratulations! They are seizing donkeys, but you are not
one. Why are you scared?' He said, 'They are taking them with
   such zeal that they've lost discernment. I fear that today
            they might take me for a donkey.'*

A man took refuge in a house at pace.   2540
   His lips were blue on a pale yellow face.
The house's owner asked, 'Are you okay?
   Your hands shake like an old man's—why today?
What happened? Why do you flee here, dear fellow,
   And how did your complexion turn so yellow?'
'They're seizing donkeys out there now,' he said,
   'To be used by that nasty king instead.'
'My friend, they're taking donkeys—you're not one
   So why are you so worried now? Begone!'
'They are so serious and they seize them quickly—   2545
   They might mistake me also for a donkey:

They are so busy seizing them that they
  Might have lost all discernment in this way.'

When one without discernment is the emperor
  They'll seize the donkey's owner then in error.
Our city's King won't take without perceiving:
  He has discernment; He is Hearing, Seeing.
Be valiant, don't fear donkey seizers here—
  You're not a donkey, Jesus. Do not fear!
Your light fills the fourth heaven—God won't let   2550
  Your own abode be a mere stable yet.
Though in a stable now for something, you
  Are loftier than the stars and heavens too.
The stable-master's not a donkey, is he?
  Not everyone inside is one, you will see.

Why are we hung up on the donkey now?
  Tell of the flowers and rosegarden somehow!
Pomegranate, apple, and the orange trees,
  Wine and so many fair ones who will please,
That sea whose waves are pearls, such pearls that can   2555
  Speak up and see things just like any man,
Or birds that pick fine roses and then lay
  Silver and golden eggs in their own way,
Or falcons nurturing partridges which fly
  Upside down on their backs up in the sky!
The world has hidden ladders one can seek
  And they lead rung by rung to heaven's peak.
Each party has a ladder that is different
  And each path has a heaven that is different—
No one knows of the other's state of heart.   2560
  That realm's expansive without end or start.
One is stunned by the other and he says:
  'Why is he happy? What's here to amaze?'
God's earth's broad and expansive all around;
  Each tree grows from a different patch of ground.
The leaves and branches give thanks and applaud:
  'What a realm! It's expansive and so broad.'

Around the blossom nightingales are gathering:
   'Give us some of the food that you are having!'
Go back now to the fox and pain and hunger   2565
   That lion felt—this talk could stretch much longer.

*The fox takes the donkey to the lion, but the donkey jumps away
from the lion. The fox reproaches the lion: 'The donkey was still far
away. You were too hasty.' The lion makes excuses and begs the fox:
'Go and trick him again!'*

When the fox brought the donkey up the slope
   So it could be killed easily and not cope,
While still far from the lion at some distance
   That lion couldn't wait more in this instance—
It leapt down from a higher point, but lacked
   The strength to catch its prey when it attacked.
The donkey saw it from afar and fled
   To the hill's bottom, panicked, full of dread.
'O king,' the fox said to the lion, 'Why   2570
   Could you not wait for it to come nearby
So that lost one would be so close to you
   That you could easily overpower it too?
Haste is the trap of Satan—in its place
   Patience and planning are the Merciful's Grace.
The donkey saw from far off you'd attack—
   You've shown your weakness now and what you lack.'
'I thought I had my strength,' the lion said,
   'I didn't know I was so weak instead.
My hunger's so extreme in consequence   2575
   I've lost my patience and intelligence.
Could you please once again through cleverness
   Bring back that donkey to me nonetheless?
I'd be indebted. Try hard—you might still
   Succeed in luring it back with your skill.'
The fox said, 'Okay, with God's help to bind
   A seal upon its heart to make it blind
So it forgets the terror it did see—
   This might work due to asininity.
But when I bring it back don't rush out then   2580

And, due to too much haste, lose it again!'
The lion said, 'I've learnt now from before
   My body's weak; I'm injured and so sore.
I won't move till the donkey nears this clearing
   And I'll stay still here as if I am sleeping.'
The fox left, saying: 'King, pray ignorance
   Has veiled the donkey's own intelligence!
It has made vows to its God and Creator
   Not to be duped by any wretched faker—
We'll make it break its vows through trickery;   2585
   We're foes of vows and wisdom's way, aren't we?
The donkey's head's our children's ball; its mind
   Is just a toy for trickery of our kind.'
Reason that Saturn's orbit can affect
   Is lost near Universal Intellect.
Saturn and Mercury have made it knowing;
   Ours is from the Creator who's bestowing.
'*He taught Man*'* is His special signature.
   '*The knowledge is with God*'* we're aiming for.
We have been nurtured by that Radiant Sun—   2590
   That's why we pray: '*My Lord, the Most High One!*'*
'Although the donkey had a bad experience
   Hundreds of them lose to my interference.
That weak-willed one might yet break its own vow,
   And breaking vows' misfortune reach it now.'

*Explaining that breaking a covenant or vow of repentance is the
cause of affliction, or rather it is the cause of transformation as in
the case of 'the companions of the Sabbath'* and 'the companions of
Jesus's table spread'.* He made them apes and swine.* In this
community there is transformation of the heart and at the
Resurrection the body will be given the form of the heart.
We take refuge in God.*

To break a vow or pact means that you'll be
   The victim of its curse eventually.
The Sabbath group broke their vows and this meant
   Hatred, change for the worse and a descent:
God turned them into apes—they'd violated   2595

Their promises to God, it's been related.*
It wasn't a mere bodily transformation
    But transformation of the heart, aware one:
When one's heart is an ape's heart, you should know
    One's earthly body is as well brought low.
If its heart had some worth how could the donkey
    Be brought low for its outward form's sake only?
The famed cave's sleepers' dog* had a good nature—
    Its bodily form did not make it inferior.
The Sabbath group faced outward transformation   2600
    So people clearly saw their degradation.
For breaking vows millions of men we see
    Have turned to swine and asses inwardly.

The fox returns for a second time to that donkey that had fled in order to fool it again.

The fox rushed to the donkey that had fled.
    'One can't be friends with one like you,' it said,
'Ignoble one, what did I ever do
    To be led to a dragon's lair by you?
What caused you to despise my whole existence,
    Stubborn one, but your own appalling essence?'
Like scorpions that bite men's feet even though   2605
    They haven't suffered from them any blow,
Or like the devil, our souls' enemy,
    Though we've not ever harmed him actually.
It's in his nature—our souls' enemy:
    Seeing human demise fills him with glee.
He never quits pursuing all the people.
    How can he flee his nature, which is evil?
Without cause his gross essence constantly
    Draws him to enmity and tyranny.
He beckons you towards a tent—instead   2610
    He wants to hurl you down a well: He'd said:
'There is a pool and fountains in this place.'
    But throws you in a tank head-first at pace.
He flung down Adam to dire situations
    Though he had vision and true inspirations,

And Adam hadn't harmed him previously
   Or done a thing to that foe hurtfully.

'That was due to a charm,' the fox then said,
   'A lion magically was shown instead.
I'm weaker than you—how can I feed there   2615
   If a lion's really there? I wouldn't dare!
Without use of a magic charm back there
   All hungry ones would rush in for a share—
How could that meadow be preserved for us
   If drawing every keen rhinoceros
Or elephant? I wanted to teach you
   Not to be scared if you see such a view
That terrifies, but I forgot to say,
   Immersed in pity for you yesterday.
I'd seen you with no food and very hungry—   2620
   I hurried so you'd find your cure more quickly.
I would have told you of the magic charm
   And that the lion's not real and can't harm.'

The donkey's reply to the fox.

The donkey said, 'Begone, O enemy!
   Your vile face is one I don't want to see.
That God who has made you to be unlucky
   Has made you loathsome, stubborn, and so ugly.
With which face are you coming back this way?
   A rhino's skin is not as thick, I'd say.
You'd sought my blood and did so openly,   2625
   Saying: "Come to the meadow now with me!"
I saw the Angel of Death's own face back then—
   Have you brought here your cleverness again?
Though I'm a donkey, I'm a living being
   With a soul too, so I am not believing.
If a mere child sees what I did behold
   Of terror there, he would at once turn old.
Losing my heart and soul, I rushed in fear
   Headlong far from the mountain to get here.

My legs froze at the moment it occurred—   2630
   Since I'd seen terror unveiled there, you heard
Me cry to God, "I vow God, who is kind,
   Release my legs now please from their tight bind
And I won't heed their tempting talk. I plead
   And promise, God, who helps all those in need."
My God released my legs that moment there
   Due to my sharing my despair and prayer.
That lion would have reached me very quickly
   If He had not—what a fate for a donkey?
The jungle's lion sent you back to me   2635
   Evil sidekick, to use your trickery.
By the pure essence of Eternal God,
   A bad snake's better than a bad friend's fraud.
The bad snakes take a life, but the bad friends
   Will drag one to a fire that never ends.'
Without words hearts take that friend's disposition,
   In ways that are not made clear to your vision.
And when he casts his shadow over you
   That one steals all your moral fibre too.
If your mind has become a drunken dragon,   2640
   The bad friend's emerald, your most feared weapon!
He makes your mind's eye pop out all at once.
   His curses throw you into pestilence.

The fox answers the donkey.

The fox said, 'My drink has no dregs at all,
   But your imaginings certainly aren't small—
You simpleton, it's all just in your head;
   I bring no malice nor make schemes ahead.
Don't view me through the lens of your illusions!
   Why target dearest friends with your suspicions?
Have nice thoughts of your own well-meaning brother,   2645
   Though he may look like he will give you bother!
When such suspicions come out in the open
   A hundred thousand friendships will be broken.
If a compassionate friend should act malicious,
   That tests you, use your brain—don't be suspicious!

Especially me, though I have a bad name—
  It was a charm, not evil you should blame.
And if it was just evil, then that's fate.
  Friends must forgive mistakes, not rush to hate.'

Imaginings, fear, and craving all are major   2650
  Obstacles for the mystical wayfarer.
Imaginings harmed so many men already
  Like Abraham, who was then mountain-steady:
'*This is my Lord!*'* great Abraham once said
  When by imaginings he had been misled.
Those who were experts in interpretation
  Perceived in this way too each constellation.
The world of blinkering imagination
  Pulled that strong mountain up from its foundation.
Such that he said, '*This is my Lord!*'*—how then   2655
  Would geese or donkeys fare compared with men?
Mountain-strong intellects drowned in the sea
  Of such imaginings and mere fantasy.
The flood humiliated mountains—where
  Is safety outside Noah's ark out there?
The faithful split then into seventy-two*
  Due to illusion, which blocks truth from you.
Men with true certainty escape this soon—
  They don't think eyebrows are the crescent moon:
Lacking Omar's light for support, one might   2660
  Allow an eyebrow's hair to block one's sight.*
A million scary ships were badly wrecked
  Due to imagining's massive seas effect.
Pharaoh, philosopher, was one of these,
  The least, and they eclipsed his moon with ease.
No one knows who's the cuckold from the men—
  If one did, he'd know it is not him then.
Your own imaginings now have made you giddy—
  Why focus on another man's already?
I am helpless against my self-conceit—   2665
  Why come to me with yours and take a seat?

With all my heart I seek somebody selfless—
    I'll be the ball for that bat that is precious.
One who's lost ego owns all egos thus—
    Without self-love he's loved by all of us:
A mirror with no image of its own
    Is better—it makes others' faces known.

Story about Shaikh Mohammad Sarrazi of Ghazni.*

Once there was an ascetic based in Ghazni;
    A learned man: Mohammad Sarrazi.
He'd break his fast with vine leaves every night;   2670
    He sought one goal for years with all his might.
The King of Being showed things marvellous
    But he just sought the King's own handsomeness.
Weary of self, he reached a mountain top
    Then said, 'Appear to me or I'll just drop!'
God said, 'It's not yet time for such an honour.
    You won't die if you fall—I want you longer
Alive.' He threw himself down out of love
    But landed in deep water from above.
When that one sick of life saw he'd not died   2675
    He grew shocked and lamented being denied,
For this life seemed like death in his own view
    And everything was topsy-turvy too.
Through unseen routes he begged death in this way:
    '*My life is in my death*'* was what he'd say.
Like life this man embraced death and he was
    Assenting to it for his higher cause.
Like Ali: his sweet basil's sword and knife,
    Narcissus and wild rose were foes of life.*
'Leave for the town the desert where you've been!'   2680
    Said a strange voice beyond seen and unseen.
'You know my secret's details, hair by hair—
    How should I serve in that town over there?'
'Your self-abasement is the work that's better
    You'll then be like Abbas Dabsi, the beggar.*
Take gold from rich men for a while and give
    It to the poor who struggle just to live.

This is the service for a while to do.'
    He said, 'To hear is to obey you too.'
So many questions, answers, and discussion   2685
    Continued then between them in this session
The earth and sky were filled with light—just look
    And you will find it noted in his book.
I have abridged their dialogue, so then
    The mysteries won't be heard by useless men.

After many years the Shaikh comes to Ghazni from the desert and
takes round a basket as instructed from the Unseen,
then distributes what is collected to the poor.
Whoever's heart has glory of Labbayka*
Gets many couriers, letter after letter.
It is like when the windows of a house are open—sunshine
moonbeams, rain, letters, etc. never stop entering.

That fine obedient one went to that place:
    Ghazni, which was illumined by his face.
Some came to greet him happily on that day,
    But he went quickly in a secret way.
All the nobility were decorating   2690
    Their palaces for him, anticipating.
'I've not come to show off,' the Shaikh then said,
    'I've come to beg and get abased instead.
I don't intend to chat, please understand—
    I'm begging door-to-door, basket in hand.
I'm slave to God's command, and His decree
    Deems I should live a life of beggary.
In begging I won't use terms deemed obscure—
    I'll tread the basest beggar's way as cure,
So in abasement I'll get fully drowned   2695
    And hear abuse from everyone around.
God's order's clear and I obey, unfazed:
    He said to crave for *cravers are abased.*
Faith's King told me to crave, so from today
    To hell with being content is what I say.
How can I pose? He wants humility.

I'll not act royal—He wants beggary.
Humility and begging are now precious;
    My begging is like twenty of Abbas's.'*
Basket in hand, the Shaikh went round and said: 2700
    '*Give for God's sake if you're divinely led!*'
Though higher than God's own throne inwardly
    '*For God's sake give!*' was his activity.
The Prophets ply the same trade nonetheless:
    They beg though people near are penniless.
They tell all: '*Lend to God!*'* Contrastingly
    They then say '*Help us God!*' repeatedly.

For him to heaven there were doors galore,
    But still the Shaikh went begging door-to-door,
Since he begged earnestly and for God's sake,   2705
    Not for his belly. It was no mistake.
And if it had been for his gullet's pleasure
    That gullet has so much light none can measure:
For him bread, milk, and honey would be treats
    Better than the fakir's fasts and retreats.
He feeds on light, so don't you say it's bread.
    He plants fine flowers and won't waste them instead.
Just like the flame that feeds off oil and candle,
    From feeding, his light would increase, though ample:
God said for eating bread: '*Not too much, greedy!*'*   2710
    He didn't say for light: '*Be sated easily!*'
Other throats suffer and are tried no less,
    But this man's throat was not prone to excess.
It isn't greed, but a command instead.
    By greed such lofty souls are never led.
If the elixir tells the copper, 'Give me
    Yourself!' Craving is not the cause most clearly,
For God had offered this Shaikh treasures here
    On earth as far as to the seventh sphere,
But he had said, 'Creator, I'm a lover: 2715
    I would be worthless if I sought another:
If I should look at paradise as well
    Or if I serve you due to fear of hell,

Then I would be a pleasure-seeker oddly,
  For these are just to benefit the body.'
Bodies to lovers whom God nourishes
  Aren't worth a bean—in fact they're even less.
The body of the mystic Shaikh became
  Transformed—don't call it 'body'! Not the same!
A lover of God's love seek a reward?   2720
  A trusted Gabriel be a thief? The hoard
Of the wealth of this world was nothing more
  Than straw to Laili's lover, blind and sore—
Gold and mud had the same worth in his view;
  What's gold when one feels life is worthless too?
Wolves, lions, and wild beasts all quickly heard
  Of him and neared as if from the same herd,
For he was purged of animality,
  Love-filled, his flesh now poisonous totally:
To wild beasts wisdom's sugar's poisonous,   2725
  For good is contrary to wickedness.
Wild beasts won't eat the lover's flesh at all.
  Love's known to good and evil ones—to all.
And if they 'eat' by backbiting, instead
  His flesh turns poisonous, leaving them soon dead.
All things besides love are devoured by love:
  The worlds are one grain in the beak of love.
Does a grain ever eat instead the bird?
  Do hay troughs eat the horse? That is absurd!
Serve God, so you might be a lover too;   2730
  Serving's earning: it's action that you do.
A slave yearns for his freedom desperately;
  A lover never wishes to be free.
A slave seeks honours and a big reward;
  A lover's honour's vision of his Lord.
Love is beyond all speech and hearing too—
  Love is an ocean with depths far from view.
Though one can't count the drops inside the sea,
  That ocean makes seas small comparatively.
This discourse could go on and last forever—   2735
  Return to hear of that Shaikh of the era.

On the meaning of 'If it were not for you, I would not have created the heavens.'*

A Shaikh became a wandering beggar there;
　　Love didn't care about his rank—beware!
Love boils the ocean like a cauldron and
　　Love crumbles massive mountains just like sand.
Love splits apart the heavens frequently;
　　Love makes the ground shake also nonchalantly.
Pure love united with Mohammad too:
　　God said for love of him, '*If not for you!*'*
And since in love he was the final goal　　　　　　2740
　　He was unique in his prophetic role:
'If it were not for the sake of pure love
　　Would I have made the heavens up above?
I raised that lofty sphere, so you would know
　　The loftiness of love from down below.
And further benefits come from that sphere:
　　It's like the egg that hatches chicks down here.
I brought the ground low down so you could see
　　That love is based on true humility,
And we gave grass and freshness to bare ground　　2745
　　So you see how ascetics change around.
These solid mountains show the quality
　　Of lovers' states in firmest constancy—
Although the former's just an image, it
　　Is closer to your mind's reach, isn't it?
Anguish is something people will compare
　　With barbs—it's just so you will be aware.
Hearts, too, aren't really stony, but my son
　　We say that as an apt comparison.
If something is beyond conception's limit　　　　　2750
　　Blame your conception's power—don't dismiss it!

The Shaikh goes to the house of a prince to beg with his basket four times in one day due to a prompting from the Unseen. The prince rebukes him for that impudence and he apologizes to the prince.

The Shaikh went begging four times in one day
　　Up to the prince's palace on his way:

Basket in hand, '*Something for God?*' he said,
  '*The soul's Creator seeks a piece of bread.*'
(This statement is absurd and very silly;
  It makes Universal Reason even giddy.)
The prince saw him, 'Impudent one, speak less!
  And don't you smear my name with stinginess!
What thick-skinned front to come in such a way   2755
  To my home and beg four times in one day!
Who's bound to you, Shaikh, over here? I've never
  Seen such a brazen and expectant beggar!
You have made beggars' reputations rot;
  Abbas-like* ugliness is what you've brought:
Abbas-e Dabsi* has your sidekick's role—
  Spare infidels from such an ill-starred soul!'
'I'm bound by God's command,' the Shaikh then said,
  'Be silent and don't boil in rage instead!
Had I seen in me craving for some bread   2760
  I'd have ripped up that belly then instead.
For seven years I've lived off vine leaves due
  To love's fire, which can cook the body too.
From eating fresh and dry leaves, as you've seen,
  This body of mine has been turning green.
While you're behind the human veil that covers,
  Don't look down critically upon God's lovers!'

Clever ones who can split hairs as an art,
  And even learnt astronomy by heart,
With sorcery, magic, and philosophy,   2765
  Though they lacked knowledge of Reality,
Yet have been striving to their highest levels,
  Which helped them to surpass their nearest rivals,
Faced love's withdrawal and exclusivity
  With this sun vanishing from them, you see:
How come the sun just vanished from the sight
  Of those who see the stars both day and night?
So quit this, listen to me and beware!
  View lovers with love's eye now, if you care!
Souls look ahead and there's no time to waste—   2770

They can't apologize now due to haste.
Understand! Don't rely on speech alone!
Don't wound the lovers' breasts—leave them alone!
Their ecstasies are making you suspicious?
Don't quit your vigilance then—keep being cautious!
Compulsory, allowed, impossible:
Select the middle course then, if you will!

The prince cries due to the counsel from the Shaikh and the
reflection of his sincerity, then gives away his treasury after that
boldness. The Shaikh keeps his purity and does not accept it,
saying: 'I can't do anything without a divine prompting.'

The Shaikh said this and then wept loudly there,
Tears rolling down his cheeks, which showed his care.
His being sincere thus touched the prince's mind—   2775
Each moment love cooks marvels, you will find.
Lovers' sincerity moves an inert thing
So moving knowing hearts is not amazing.
Moses's being sincere moved rod and mountain,
What's more it touched too the majestic ocean.*
Mohammad's once moved the moon's beauty and
It stopped the bright sun's movement that was planned.*

Prince and renunciant thus faced each other
And as they both wept they let out a holler.
After they'd wept a while the prince spoke out: 2780
'Arise O worthy man! You can pick out
Whatever you want from my treasury
Though you deserve much more than that from me.
My home is yours. Choose what you like, for you
The two worlds aren't enough. That is my view.'
He said, 'I've not been granted the permission
To pick out something by my own volition.
I cannot overstep or interfere
By my own will like this, if I'm sincere.'
He thus gave his excuse and stepped away   2785
Because the gift was not sincere that day—

It was sincerely free from enmity
　　And rage, but not that Shaikh's sincerity.
'God has commanded me thus,' then he said,
　　'Go like a beggar asking for some bread!'

*The prompting came to the Shaikh from the Unseen: 'In these past
two years you have taken and given on our command, but from now
on you are only to give and not to take. Keep your hand under the
mat, which we have made like the bag of Abu Horayra,* for what is
due to you, and you will find whatever you want there. This is so
that the people of this world should learn that there is something
beyond this world, where, if you take dust in your hand it turns to
gold, and the dead who enter there become alive, the most ill-starred
become the most favoured by the stars, unbelief becomes faith, and
poison becomes antidote. It is not in this world nor outside of it,
neither under nor over, neither joined nor separate, without us
knowing its description. Every moment thousands of impressions and
symbols become manifest: the work of the hand in the form of a
hand, the glance of the eye in the form of an eye, eloquence of the
tongue in the form of a tongue. Neither inside, nor outside, neither
joined, nor separate.' The wise will find a hint sufficient.*

The Shaikh for two years did this and then later
　　An order reached him from God, the Creator:
'You'll give but never beg beyond this hour—
　　From the Unseen We've given you this power:
Whoever asks for something, just like that　　　　　　2790
　　Hand it to him from under this great mat!
Give it from Mercy's treasure with no limit!
　　Dust will now turn to gold in your hand. Give it!
Whatever's asked for, give and don't feel stress—
　　There is no limit to God's huge largesse.
In Our bestowal there is no reduction
　　And no regret about this generous action.
You put your hand beneath the mat to hide
　　The truth thus from the evil eye outside.
From under that mat bring out what they lack—　　　2795
　　Give it to beggars with a broken back!
Give that wage which demands no work to earn it!

Give the fine pearl to anyone who yearns it!
  *God's hand's above their hands** and you should be:
    Like God's hand give provisions liberally!
  Release from their binds those that owe a large debt—
    Like rain, transform to green this world's vast carpet!'

For one more year he worked as he was told,
  Giving the Lord of Judgement's purse's gold:
Dirt turned to gold in his hand. Generous giver,   2800
  Hatem Ta'i* before him was a beggar.

*How the Shaikh knew the thoughts of beggars without them having
to say them, and the amount of loans of debtors likewise, which is a
    sign of 'Depart to My creation with My attributes!'**

If a poor man would not talk, he could read
  His mind and give him something for his need.
He'd give the hunchback what he had in mind,
  No more, no less, exactly the right kind.
They'd ask him then, 'How did you know that he
  Was hoping to receive that secretly?'
'My heart's house now is empty,' he'd advise,
  'Empty of beggars just like paradise;
Nothing but love of God's left in my heart   2805
  And thoughts of union with Him, not to part.
I've swept this house so clear of good and evil
  That it's filled with love of the One God, people—
Anything other than God that I should see
  Reflects from beggars and is not from me.'
If dates appear in water that you see
  They're just reflecting from a nearby tree:
If you see forms in water, they're not there—
  Those are reflections from outside, beware!
To clear the water from the chips on it   2810
  Cleansing the body's a prerequisite,
So no trash stays and no turbidity
  And it reflects one's face reliably.
Your body's full of muddy water—start

To clean that water now, foe of the heart.
You love to pour dirt in the stream through eating
   And sleeping always, though that's self-defeating.

The way to read people's minds.

But once the water's heart is clear at last
   Faces' reflections are then clearly cast.
Unless your inner world's been purified   2815
   Your house is full with evil beasts inside.
Stubbornly stuck in asininity,
   When will you learn of Christ-like souls? Tell me!
If images appear, how will you know
   From where they have arrived to make a show?
Your body fades on self-denial's way
   Until all thoughts inside are swept away.

The slyness of the fox prevails over the donkey's wish to avoid falling into temptation.

The donkey tried debating very long
   With that fox, but its hunger was too strong,
So greed prevailed—its patience had to break: 2820
   Many gullets get cut for love of cake.
That Truth-Supported Messenger has said:
   '*Poverty's almost unbelief*' we've read.
That donkey was the prisoner of hunger:
   'If it's a plot and I die, I'll no longer
Suffer from tortuous hunger anyway—
   If this is life, death's better any day.'
Although the donkey had vowed previously
   It lapsed because of asininity.
Greed makes one blind and stupid—it will make   2825
   The stupid think death's a good choice to take.
For donkeys' souls death isn't easy, is it,
   Because they lack the everlasting spirit?
Lacking this it is wretched totally—
   Boldness before death is stupidity.
(Strive till your soul's eternal—when you die

You'll have provisions on which to rely!)
It has no confidence that the Great Feeder
   Might scatter from the Unseen largesse nearer.
Grace hasn't left it lacking daily bread   2830
   Till now, though it's felt hunger pangs instead.
A hundred other pains take hunger's place
   From indigestion, raising up their face—
Hunger's suffering's better, isn't it?
   It's light and gentle and gives benefit.
Hunger's suffering's purer than such pains
   Especially since it gives you virtuous gains.

Explaining the excellence of abstention and hunger.

Hunger's medicine's sultan, so embrace it!
   Don't look down at it when you have to face it!
Every unsweet thing is made sweet by hunger;   2835
   Without it, all sweet things would be shunned, brother.
One day a man was eating mouldy bread—
   'How can you eat this?' somebody then said.
'When hunger's doubled through abstention's power
   Barley bread tastes like halva then that hour.
I eat just halva after I abstain—
   I fast a lot of course with much to gain.'
Not everyone can truly master hunger
   Because this lower realm is full of fodder.
Hunger's bestowed on God's elite, as then   2840
   It makes them powerful lions among men.
How could such hunger reach each beggar near?
   They give him fodder since there's so much here:
'Eat up for you are worthless!' he is told,
   'You're "bread fowl" not the water fowl that's bold.'

*Story about a Shaikh reading a disciple's mind and learning of his
greed. He counsels him with words and in doing so bestows on him
   by God's command the nourishment of trust in God.*

A Shaikh with his disciple rushed ahead
   Towards a town where there was little bread.

Then fear of hunger gave the latter stress
   Constantly due to his own heedlessness.
The Shaikh could read his mind and was aware: 2845
   'How long will you stay miserable in there?
You are consumed with sorrow over bread,
   Losing all trust and patience from your head.
You're not one of the marvellous elite
   To not have nuts and raisins. You'll soon eat.
Hunger for their great souls is sustenance—
   How could that be for you, you giddy dunce:
Relax, you aren't one of them that you
   Should stay without bread in your kitchen too.
Bowl upon bowl, loaf upon loaf are here   2850
   For regular men needing them. That's clear.
When such a one dies, bread steps up to shout:
   "He killed himself through fear of going without."
After you've gone bread stays—arise and take it!
   You who would kill yourself with grief mistake it.
Trust God and stop your limbs from shaking too!
   Your daily bread is more in love with you
Than you with it. For this it's not come nearer:
   Your total lack of patience, interferer!
If you had patience, it would not now hover,   2855
   But throw itself at you just like a lover.
Why shake with fever fearing hunger when
   One can trust God, then live as sated men?'

Story about a cow that is alone on an island. God fills that big island with plants and basil as fodder for the cow and the cow feeds on it all until nightfall, growing as fat as a mountain crag. When night comes the cow cannot sleep due to misery and fear: 'I've grazed on the whole plain—what will I eat tomorrow?' Due to this misery it becomes as thin as a crescent moon. At daybreak it sees the whole plain greener and lusher than the day before. It eats again and grows fat. Once more at night the same anxiety seizes it. For years it lives like this without developing confidence.

In this world a green island was once known
   Which a sweet-mouthed cow lived on all alone,

Grazing on all the fields till nightfall to
   Be sated and grow quickly stronger too.
'What will I eat tomorrow?' in despair
   It worries at night, wakes thin as a hair.
When morning comes the field turns green in haste,   2860
   Green shoots and sprouts as high as someone's waist.
The cow wakes hungry, so it once again
   Grazes till nightfall on all of the plain.
It thus grows bigger, fattening up like that,
   Its body getting nourishment and fat.
At night due to anxiety and sorrow,
   It grows thin and fears lack of food tomorrow:
'What will I eat at mealtime in the day?'
   For years the cow behaves in the same way,
Never thinking, 'For many years I'd eat   2865
   On this same pasture and I'd never meet
A day when I would not find daily bread—
   Why then this deep anxiety and dread?'
And when night falls that cow grows thin again:
    'My nurturer's gone—how will I cope then?'

This cow's the carnal soul, the field it's in
   Is this world, where through worry it grows thin,
Thinking: 'What will I eat? I am perplexed.
   Where should I seek food during daytime next?'
You've eaten now for years, not gone without—   2870
   Look at the past! In future do not doubt!
Remember the fine food you've eaten here!
   Don't worry 'What's left?' or feel mortal fear!

*The lion makes the donkey its prey, becomes thirsty after its
exertion and goes to the spring to drink water. Before the lion gets
back the fox has eaten the liver, the heart, and the kidneys, which
are the delicacies. The lion looks in vain for the liver and the heart,
then asks the fox, 'Where is the liver and the heart?' The fox
answers, 'If it had had a liver and heart, after experiencing such
suffering on that day and escaping only through a thousand tricks,
how could it have come back to you?' 'If we had listened and
reasoned we would not have become among the denizens of hellfire.'**

The fox took to the lion that fooled donkey.
    The lion ravaged it then very roughly.
Exertion gave thirst to the animals' king
    Who went to drink some water at a spring.
The fox then ate its heart and liver up,
    Not wishing to give a superb chance up,
But when the lion came back from the spring   2875
    It looked for heart and liver—not a thing:
'Where is the liver? Where's the heart gone too?
    No animal can live without these two.'
'If it had had a liver and a heart
    How could it have come back once far apart?
It had seen here the Last Hour's awful day
    And in sheer terror scampered far away.
If it had had a heart or liver then
    How could it have come back to you again?'
It's not a heart if there's no light within;   2880
    It is mere clay when there's no soul within.
Glass vessels that do not have the soul's light
    Are urine vials and 'lamp' here's not right.
The lamp's light is a gift from The Most Glorious.
    Glass and clay are both made by Him; it's obvious.
Vessels are numbered necessarily,
    But all their flames are still in unity:
When light from six lamps mixes you can see
    That such light doesn't have plurality.
Vessels drove Jews to polytheism's error;   2885
    Believers saw the light and sensed much better.
When just the spirit's vessel is in view

That sight sees Seth and Noah then as two.
A stream's a stream when water's flowing in;
  A man is someone with a soul within.
Others are not men, but mere forms instead.
  They have been slain by their own lust for bread.

Story about that monk who went around with a lamp by day in the
  middle of the marketplace because of the ecstasy he felt.

A man would hold a candle and he'd wander
  By day at the bazaar with love and ardour.
A busybody asked him, 'Mister, why   2890
  Do you search every stall that you pass by
And search with that lamp when it isn't dark
  In daylight? Please explain to me this lark.'
'I'm looking for a human who's not dead,
  But living through that Holy Breath,' he said.
'Can such a man be found?' 'This market's full,
  Great sage—surely here men are plentiful?'
'I want one who prevails on this broad street
  Of two lanes, where both rage and lust he'll meet—
Where is he when such rage and lust comes, where?   2895
  I'm searching for this person everywhere.
Where in the world's a man who's real this way
  That I might give my life to him today?'
'You're looking for a certain rarity
  While heedless of both faith and destiny:
You seek the branch, but not the root, you see—
  We are the branch, the root is fate's decree.'

Fate makes revolving heavens lose their way,
  Turns Mercuries to fools too straight away.
The world is made more cramped. Iron and stone   2900
  Become like water through such power alone.
You have resolved to take this path so deeply,
  But you will take step after step naively.
You've seen the millstone turn, but now won't you
  Look at the water in the stream there too?

Have you seen dust rise in the air? You must
   Look for the wind within the rising dust.
Or cauldrons full of thoughts boil fervently?
   Look at the fire beneath it cleverly!
God told Job, 'I have honoured every hair   2905
   Of yours with special patience that is rare—
Don't just regard your patience down below:
   Look at my giving patience, then you'll know.'
How long will you watch water wheels still turning?
   Stick out your head, watch water flow, keep learning!
You often claim, 'I've seen'—When you do see
   You'll be sent many good signs mystically.
You've glanced upon the wave foam's circle motion—
   For true bewilderment look at the ocean!
One who sees foam tells of the mystery—   2910
   For true bewilderment look at the sea!
One who observes foam there makes an intention—
   Seeing seas turns one's heart into an ocean.
One who sees foam is calculating still—
   One who sees the whole sea has no self-will.
One who sees foam will wander by mistake—
   One who has seen the sea is not a fake.

A Muslim invites a Magian to convert to Islam.

A man once told a Magian, 'Unbeliever,
   Become a Muslim, be a true believer!'
'If God wills I'll become one,' he replied,   2915
   'If He gives more grace, faith's intensified.'
'God wants you to believe,' the first man said,
   'So your soul can escape hell's grip ahead,
But your ill-starred self and the horrid devil
   Drag you to unbelief and your fire temple.'
'Well, since the latter pair prevail, I should
   Join with the stronger ones, though they're not good.
I only can side with the stronger option;
   I fall towards the stronger pull's direction.
God wanted for me strong sincerity—   2920
   What value has that wish he didn't see?

The self and Satan both prevailed, you know,
    While His Grace suffered a tremendous blow.
Let's say you build a palace or a mansion
    And fill it with designs that give attraction—
You want it to become a mosque, but see
    Someone transform it to a monastery.
Or you have cloth that's very fine and rare
    To make yourself a shirt that you can wear—
You want a fine shirt, but your enemy   2925
    Makes trousers with that cloth so spitefully.
Dear friend, what can that fine cloth really do
    Other than go with the prevailing view?
You lost, but you can't give the cloth the blame—
    Who's not controlled by those who rule the same?
Against one's will if someone barges in
    Their mansion and brings a big thornbush in,
The mansion's owner is humiliated
    That such an action has been orchestrated—
I'd too be ruined by association   2930
    With someone suffering such humiliation.
Since the self's wish is stronger obviously,
    '*What God wills happens*'* is a mockery.
Though I be the most lowdown infidel
    I wouldn't think such things of God as well:
That someone should, in spite of Him, feel free
    To seek in His own realm authority
And occupy it such that He who made
    The breath can't stop him with the words He's said.
He wishes to repel him and must do,   2935
    The devil though makes him stressed through and through.
Being the devil's slave is so compelling,
    Since he is dominant at every gathering.
This way he'll not avenge me—that would be
    So good, for how could God then rescue me?
The things the devil wishes find fruition—
    So who'll make nice again my own condition?'

The parable of Satan at the door of the Merciful God.

What God wills happens, * *O Lord God!* God is
  The ruler in both Place and Placelessness.
Nobody has the power without His say   2940
  To even change a hair tip in some way.
His is the kingdom, His the command. What's more—
  Satan's the basest dog outside his door.
If a Turk has a dog outside his door
  With its face down there on the threshold floor,
His children pull its tail hard constantly,
  Yet it will stay submissive, abjectly.
But if a stranger passes by, it will
  Attack him like a lion would do still.
'*He's firm with unbelievers,*' * God has said: 2945
  A rose to friends, to foes a thorn instead.
The Turkman gives it broth that is delicious—
  That's why it is a good guard: loyal, vicious.
God brought that base dog, Satan, to existence
  And placed in him so many schemes, for instance.
God feeds him with men's honour, so he'll rob
  That from the good and bad as his own job.
His broth's the honour of your average man
  And that dog Satan eats it when he can.
How can his soul not be devoted fully   2950
  To the decree of His power's door then? Tell me!
Pack after pack, rebellious and loyal
  Like dogs *that spread their paws by thresholds,* * hopeful.
At the cave's doorway to divinity
  They seek, like dogs, commands so viscerally:
God says, 'O devil dog, test them to see
  How they walk on the true itinerary!
Attack, block, watch who's weaker and then see
  Who's stronger also in sincerity!'
How's praying to God going to help you here   2955
  When that proud dog is rushing to get near?
With '*I take refuge!*' you're just shouting, 'Hey,
  Turkman, shout at your dog to clear the way,

So I can come to your tent when it's gone
    And beg for something from you, generous one!'

If this Turk can't stop his own dogs attacking
    This prayer's invalid as the owner's lacking.
'I, too, take refuge from the dog!' he says,
    'I'm helpless in my own home where it stays.
You can't come to my door and I can't go   2960
    Outside through it—we're both stuck, you should know.'
To hell with that Turkman and his guest there—
    One dog has tied the necks up of that pair.
Don't say the true Turk has to shout out here—
    Even lions would vomit blood in fear!
Calling yourself 'Lion of God' to cheers,
    You couldn't cope against a dog for years.
How can this dog hunt for you anyway
    When you have clearly turned to that dog's prey?

*A Sunni believer's response to the determinist believing non-Muslim
and his giving a proof for confirming the free will of God's servant.
The sunnah is a road trodden by the feet of the Prophets and to the
right of that path lies the desert and fatalism, where one does not
believe in one's own power of choice and one denies God's command
and prohibition through an obscure interpretation. Denying the
command and prohibition necessarily denies one paradise, for
paradise is the reward of those who obey God's commands and hell
is the reward for those who oppose the command. I will not say what
else it involves, for the intelligent are satisfied with a hint. To the
left of that path is the desert of free will, where one considers the
will of the created being as overcoming the will of the Creator—
from that arises the corruption that the Magian enumerated.*

The Muslim said, 'Determinists, heed well   2965
    This speech. You've said your piece, now I will tell
My answer—have you seen your own game, player?
    Observe your chess opponent's skill and flair!
You've read out your apology—now hear
    This Sunni's letter! Why not change? Have fear!

You talked on fate as a Necessitarian—
    Hear now its secret in my explanation:
Without a doubt we all possess a will—
    You can't deny what's so perceptible.
Does someone ever tell a stone, "Come you!"   2970
    How can one ask bricks to be loyal too?
No one would tell a man, "Fly in the air!"
    Or someone blind, "Look at me from back there!"
God said, *"There's no objection for the blind."**
    How can God punish them when He's so kind?
You don't tell stones, "You've come too late to me",
    Or ask a stick, "Why are you striking me?"
Would you then tell one subject to compulsion
    Such things, or strike at such a helpless person?
Honour, rebuke, command, and prohibition   2975
    Are for those with the power of choice, O pure one.
There's free will in wrongdoing and oppression—
    By 'self' and 'devil' this is my intention.
Free will is inside you, please understand—
    On seeing Joseph, it then cuts its hand.*
It's in your soul with its own special trigger—
    Joseph's face makes it spread its wings much bigger.
A dog's will's lost when it's asleep, but when
    It sees a bone it wags its tail again.
Horses will neigh on seeing food to eat;   2980
    A cat meows on movement of some meat.
Sight triggers thus the will, as should be known,
    The way sparks jump from fire when breath is blown.
Satan also triggers your will with ease
    As go-between with messages from Vis.
Once he presents the sought one to his victim
    The sleeping will unravels then within him.
In spite of that, the angel comes to offer
    Good things that can raise in your heart a clamour,
Triggering your will to good. These dispositions   2985
    Are both asleep before their expositions:
Angels and devils, both presenters who
    Pump up the veins of free will inside you.
Through inspiration and temptation too,

Your will to do good multiplies in you.
Good man, on finishing your daily prayer
    You greet the angels at each shoulder there:*
"Your inspiration and your instigation
    Triggered my will to pray with true intention."
After sins you send Satan a big curse   2990
    Because it was through him you were perverse.
These opposites present in secret view
    Things hidden in the Unseen's veil to you.'

Remove the veil that's hiding the Unseen
    And you'll see faces of each go-between
And from their words you then can clearly tell
    They were the hidden speakers there as well.
The devil will say, 'Captive of the body,
    I just showed; I did not force anybody!'
'I told you,' then the angel says to follow,   2995
    'That this joy's bound to just increase your sorrow.
Didn't I tell you on a certain day
    That there's a path to heaven in this way?
All lovers of your soul who give souls pleasure,
    We bowed sincerely to your great ancestor.*
At this time we are also serving you
    And we're inviting you to be served too.
That group were enemies of your forefather:
    When told, "*Prostrate!*"* their chief refused the order.
Take theirs and discard ours? Can you not tell   3000
    Our service is the truthful kind as well?
Now look at us and them with a clear view—
    Recognize by our voice and discourse too!'
If you hear secrets from a friend at night
    You'll know it's her when she speaks in dawn's light.
If one night two men bring some news for you
    You'll recognize their speech the next day too.
You hear at night a lion roar, dogs bark,
    But you can't make their forms out in the dark,
But when the noise returns here the next day   3005
    The wise one knows the sound that comes his way.

The gist is this: angel and devil still
    Exist so they'll present things for our will.
A will that can't be seen is inside you
    And me, and it grows when it sees these two.
Teachers discipline children—that is known
    But who would try to discipline a stone?
Would you say to a stone, 'Come the next day
    And if you don't, wretch, I will make you pay!'
Would sensible men strike at bricks or would   3010
    They tell a rock off? Would that do some good?
Fatalism is worse than free will, friend,
    For it denies what senses comprehend.
The latter don't deny their senses though—
    God's acts aren't with the senses that you know.
He who denies the Glorious God's own acts
    Denies the evidence that proves the facts,
Saying, 'There's smoke without fire or that light
    Of candles shines without a wick at night.'
The fatalist sees fire, but still will claim   3015
    It isn't there for his denial's aim.
It burned his clothes—'There is no fire!' he said.
    Like seeing clothes, but saying there's no thread.
The fatalists' claims are just sophistry—
    That's why they're worse than infidelity,
Which claims, 'This world exists, but there's no lord'
    And that to cry out 'O Lord!' is abhorred.
The fatalists will claim that this world's naught;
    The sophistry adherent's in a knot.
The world acknowledges our will, commanding,   3020
    Forbidding, 'Bring this thing, and don't bring that thing!'
He claims none of these actually exist—
    There is no power of choice he will insist.
Animals recognize this sense of will,
    But seeing proof of it is subtle still.
Since our will is perceptible, it's fit
    That burdens for acts should be placed on it.

The inward perception of free will, fatalistic compulsion, anger,
staying patient, being sated, and hunger is with the senses which can
tell yellow from red, big from small, bitter from sweet, musk from
dung and rough from soft—and through the sense of touch, warm
from cold, burning from lukewarm, wet from dry, and touching a
wall as opposed to touching a tree. Therefore, he who denies inner
consciousness denies the senses, or rather even more, for the former is
more apparent than the latter seeing as the senses can be blocked and
stopped from perceiving, but it is not possible to block the way of
experience of consciousness. A hint is enough for the wise.

Inner perception's with the senses, uncle:
    Both of them run in the exact same channel.
'Do!' and 'Don't', both command and prohibition   3025
    Are fine too, as are talk and exposition:
'Shall I do this or that on the next day?'
    This is proof of free will for you, I say.
As for regret you feel for bad deeds still—
    You have been rightly guided by your will.
The whole Qur'an's commanding and forbidding,
    And threats—who'd order stone to do its bidding?
Would any wise man do this anyway,
    To rage at bricks and rocks and then to say:
'I told you to do this, but you instead   3030
    Chose not to, you who're powerless and dead!'
How then can reason order wood and stone
    Or grab a cripple's image when it's known
It's not real, saying: 'Cripple, come and fight
    In war with broken limbs!' This is not right.
How can That One who made the stars and sky
    So stupidly give orders and deny?
You've said it can't be that God's impotent,
    But call Him foolish and incompetent.
Impotence isn't in the free will view;   3035
    Stupidity is worse though of these two.

The real Turk turns to visitors to say:
    'Come without dogs and your long cloaks today,

Then enter safely from the other side,
　　So my dog's mouth stays closed, not open wide—
If you come to its door and choose not to,
　　My dog of course will certainly bite you.'
Go the way slaves should go and do not mind,
　　So his dog will be soft with you and kind!
If you should bring a dog with you, watch out!　　3040
　　It will grow wild in that tent and act out.
If nobody but God possesses will
　　Why do you then rage at the miscreants still?
Why snarl in anger at your enemy?
　　Why deem it his responsibility?
If some roof timber falls on top of you
　　And wounds you very seriously too,
Would you rage at the timber angrily
　　Or hate it like a bitter enemy:
'Why did it break my hand with such a blow?　　3045
　　It has behaved now like a mortal foe.'
When you're absolving grown-ups from all blame
　　Why discipline small children all the same?
You speak about one who has just robbed you:
　　'Arrest him, chop his hands off, jail him too!'
When someone tries to bed your wife you get
　　Intensely angry and will not forget.
If a flood sweeps your property away
　　Will your brain let you hate it from that day?
If wind should blow your turban off, how can　　3050
　　You show it your heart's angry then, good man?
Anger in you proves that your will exists,
　　Refutes excuses of determinists.
And if the rider strikes the camel's back
　　That rider is the one it will attack.
It won't rage at his stick or wish it ill,
　　Which shows the camel, too, has choice and will.
If you should stone a dog, it will attack
　　Similarly and you'll fall on your back.
And if that dog should fetch the stone thrown too,　　3055
　　It's angry with you, but it can't reach you.
Animals' minds can see free will—feel shame

Human, whose mind denies it all the same!
It's clearly dawn, but lust for one last bite
   Means that the faster shuts his eyes to light:
Since all he longs for is to eat some bread,
   He'll claim, 'It's not dawn yet', and turn his head
Away from light: greed hides the sun from eyes—
   That he should turn away is no surprise.

A story explaining the view that people have free will and showing
that predestination and belief in fate do not deny free will.

A thief said to the chief of the police: 3060
   'What I did was just one of God's decrees.'
The chief replied, 'What I am doing, too,
   Is God's decree, dear friend, and just for you.'
If someone steals a radish from a stall,
   Claiming: 'It's God's decree, wise one,' then all
Will see him get punched fiercely in the head
   With: 'This is God's will—put it back instead!'
Since this excuse is not acceptable
   By the greengrocer for a vegetable,
You can't depend now on the same excuse   3065
   When going near a dragon. It's no use.
You risk your wealth, your wife, your life as well,
   With that excuse, vile simpleton, heed well!
Someone could now leave you humiliated
   And then say sorry, but his act was fated.
If you think God's decree's a good excuse
   Then teach us, write a fatwa we can use,
For I've so many things I lust for strongly,
   But fear of God has tied my hands to stop me.
Do me a favour, teach me the excuse!   3070
   Untie my hands and feet so I can choose!
Through your own will you've chosen such a skill,
   Declaring: 'I have thoughts and a free will.'
If not, why did you choose this one skill then
   Among those possible, O chief of men?
When it's the passions' and the self's turn, then
   You have the will of many hundred men,

And if a friend takes something small from you
   The will to fight comes in your soul anew.
When it's the turn for thanks for God's gifts though   3075
   You have no will—you're less than stones men throw.
This will be hell's excuse when you're abused:
   'Please note that when I burn you, it's excused.'
No one thinks this excuses you today
   And it won't keep the punisher away.
This is the way the world works and shows you
   The way the next world will be functioning too.

*Another story in response to the Determinist and confirming free
will and the soundness of command and prohibition, while also
explaining that the Determinist's excuse is not accepted in any creed
or religion nor does it lead to being saved from just desserts for the
deed carried out, just as the Determinist Satan did not find release
through it by saying: 'You made me err!'* A sample indicates
much more.*

A man once climbed another person's tree
   Just like a thief, to take his fruit for free.
The actual owner of the orchard came: 3080
   'What have you done? Before God you've no shame!'
'Well, here in God's own orchard is God's slave
   Eating the dates on its trees, which God gave,
So why blame him for this so stupidly?
   It's the Rich Lord's spread—don't be miserly!'
The owner called a servant, 'Go and fetch
   A rope so I can answer this vile wretch!'
He tied him to a tree then beat his back
   And legs with a big stick in his attack.
'Have shame before God!' then the thief exclaimed,   3085
   'You're killing someone who should not be blamed.'
'God's slave with God's stick', then the owner said,
   'Is beating hard another slave instead:
It is God's stick and His back and His limb;
   I'm just a slave: an instrument for Him.'
He answered, 'I'll ditch fatalism now—
   Free will is from now on what I avow.'

His free will makes all other wills free too:
  He is the rider who raised dust we view.
His free will is what makes ours and His order   3090
  Is backed up by our free choice, its supporter.
Every created thing is capable
  Of ruling over forms that have no will,
Dragging the latter like caught prey back here
  Or dragging someone far off by his ear.
God's craftwork needs no instruments to use
  And can turn someone's free will to his noose.
His will traps men without will everywhere;
  God hunts such men without dog or a snare.
The carpenter has power, too, over wood,   3095
  The artist over portraits, as he should;
The ironmonger's iron knows he rules;
  The builder's ruler over all his tools.
But this case is in fact much rarer still—
  Many wills bow like slaves before His will.
Does your power over inert things deprive
  Them of inertness or do they survive?
Thus, His power over our wills similarly
  Does not deprive us of a will that's free.
Declare that His will is complete yet you   3100
  Can't blame Him for the wrong things that you do—
You've said, 'It's His wish I'm an unbeliever.'
  Well, notice how your will's not absent either!
It's not your unbelief without volition:
  Unwilling unbelief's a contradiction.
Commanding someone who can't is abhorred.
  Anger at this is worse from the Kind Lord.
They beat the ox if it won't take the yoke,
  But not because it can't fly! What a joke!
The ox is not excused for bad behaviour—   3105
  Why should we then excuse the ox's trainer?
You aren't injured—don't now wrap your head
  In bandage! You've free will—feel shame instead!
Strive to get freshness from God's cup—you will
  Become then selfless and without a will.
Then all volition is that wine's completely.

Like drunks you'll be forgiven absolutely:
  If you beat something, wine is beating it.
  If you sweep something, wine is sweeping it.
This drunkard's drunk from God's own cup and so   3110
  He must be just and sound, as you should know.
The sorcerers told Pharaoh, 'Stop! Retreat!
  A drunk has no concern for hands and feet.'*
That One's wine is our hands and feet today
  The outward hand's its worthless shadow play.

The meaning of 'Whatever God wills happens.' That is to say,
'His will is the effective will. Seek His satisfaction. Do not be upset
by others' rejection and anger!' Although the verb is in the past
tense, there is no past or future in God's actions, for there is no
morning or evening for God.*

'*Whatever God wills happens*'*—thus the message
  Is not: 'Be lazy here!' within this passage.
It urges to be serious and sincere:
  'Prepare to be of service over here!'
If someone says, 'Whatever you wish to',   3115
  Then you can do what you desire to do:
You are permitted to be lax and slacken
  Because whatever you desire will happen.
But when you're told, '*What God wills comes to be*'*
  Your fate is His decree eternally.
Why don't you hover near Him like a servant
  To pray with zeal and fully be observant?
If you are told, 'What the vizier seeks out
  And all his wishes must be carried out',
Would you rush faster than all other men   3120
  So he could show his kindness to you then,
Or flee from the vizier and his home too?
  The latter won't draw his help now to you.
This saying's turned you lazy—your perception
  And thoughts are upside down with that selection.
What if they say: 'This sire decrees'—what's this?
  It means: 'Don't sit with others, but be his:
Stick near this lord, for his is the decree:

He saves the friend's life, slays the enemy.
What he should wish for you will see today.   3125
  Choose service to him and don't go astray!'
It doesn't mean: 'Since he rules, don't go near
  In case you're put to shame, which you should fear!'
The true interpretation's what makes you
  Ardent, hopeful, fast, and respectful too.
And if it makes you lax, that situation:
  Is altering and not interpretation.
It's meant to make men ardent everywhere,
  To hold in two arms those who feel despair.
Ask the Qur'an its meaning or that man   3130
  Who's set fire to desire for the Qur'an,
To be its sacrifice and thus accept it,
  To take the role of essence of his spirit—
One either smells the roses with one's nose
  Or that oil that's absorbed the scent of rose.

*Similarly the Prophet said, 'The pen has dried', which means the
ink has dried after it has written: 'Obedience and disobedience are
not equal, neither honesty and theft.' The ink has dried. Thanks
and the ingratitude of unbelief are not equal. The ink has dried.
'God does not let the reward of the righteous be lost.'**

'The ink has dried' has this intention too,
  To trigger the important work from you.
The pen wrote that all actions will elicit
  Effects and consequences too, which fit it:
The ink has dried: live wrongly and you'll suffer;   3135
  If you bring goodness though, you're bound to prosper.
Bring cruelty and lose luck: *the ink has dried.*
  Bring justice, then eat fruit: *the ink has dried.*
When thieves steal, hands are lost: *the ink has dried.*
  When they drink wine they're drunk: *the ink has dried.*
Do you think God would come now possibly
  Like one dismissed from prior authority,
To say, 'This matter's not in my purview—
  Don't come to me to moan like you used to!'
Rather it means, '*The ink has dried*', so justice   3140

Is not the same in my view as injustice.
I've made distinct what's good and what is evil,
   As well as bad and worse, for all you people.
If you're more disciplined than other men
   God's grace will know and make it count more then
Than that bit you excel by—you will see
   The mote become a mountain generously.
If a king makes no serious distinction
   Between the good and seekers of oppression,
The one who trembles, fearing his rejection,   3145
   And he who eyes his fortune for dissension,
Considering them the same without a difference,
   Then he is not a real king in this instance.
If you increase your efforts just one bit,
   God's weighing scales will carefully measure it.
Before the other kings you work all night,
   But they can't tell what's falseness and what's light.
And if a slanderer should speak ill of you,
   That nullifies your years of service too,
But to *the Hearing and the Seeing* King   3150
   The slanderer's words will not mean anything.
He makes the slanderers feel despair—if they
   Approach us with advice they wish to say
To speak ill of the King in front of us:
   '*The ink has dried*: don't show Him faithfulness!'
How can '*the ink has dried*' mean actually
   That loyalty now equals treachery?
Give treachery for treachery: '*It's dried.*'
   Give loyalty for loyalty: '*It's dried.*'
There's pardon, but where's glorious hope that you,   3155
   Through piety, might yet be made pure too?
A thief who's pardoned saves his life, but how
   Can he become a treasury minister now?
Come, righteous one, each crown and banner must
   Have first developed out of actual trust,
So if the sultan's son betrays instead
   The sultan will arrange to chop his head.
But if an Indian slave shows loyalty
   '*Long may he live!*' says the authority.

What of a slave? A loyal dog at the door　　　　　　3160
　　Will make its owner happier than before—
He'll kiss its mouth—and much victorious grace
　　He'd give if he'd a lion in its place.
Even a thief who should one day do service,
　　His truthfulness uprooting then his falseness,
Like Fozayl, once one of the highwaymen,*
　　Repenting though much faster than ten men.
The sorcerers showed Pharaoh* in that instance
　　Similarly their faithfulness and patience—
They lost their hands and feet—high price they paid—　　3165
　　Those worshipping for years would not have stayed
The course—you've served for half a century
　　So when will you acquire sincerity?

Story about the dervish who saw in Herat the well-dressed slaves of the Amid of Khorasan, on Arab horses, wearing gold-embroidered cloaks and bejewelled caps etc. He asked, 'Which princes or kings are they?' He was told, 'They are not princes; these are the slaves of the Amid of Khorasan.' He looked up towards the sky and said, 'O God, learn how to take care of slaves from the Amid!' (Over there they call the chief accountant 'Amid'.)

Once in Herat a man who was outspoken
　　Noticed a nobleman's slave in the open
Riding with satin clothes and gold belts too.
　　He turned towards the sky, and prayed: 'O You,
God, why don't you learn from their master too
　　How to maintain slaves better than you do?
God, learn how to maintain them properly　　　　　　3170
　　From this chief who's a royal appointee!'
He lacked food, destitute and naked too,
　　Trembling due to the winter's cold. He who
Was brazen as he'd lost his consciousness,
　　And had grown rude due to his laziness.
Relying on God's numerous gifts, he thought:
　　'The mystic is God's close friend, is he not?'
The king's friends can show boldness of this sort,
　　But don't you show it when you lack support!

God gives waists, better than such belts; instead   3175
　Of giving crowns God gives your actual head.

The king once blamed those slaves' lord and had bound
　His hands and feet, then brought his slaves around
And tortured them before he said, 'Show me
　Your master's hidden gold immediately!
Tell me his secret, base ones, all of you,
　Or I'll cut off your tongues and your throats too!'
He tortured them for one whole month—all night
　And day the rack, pain, torment: what a plight!
He started cutting them, but not one slave   3180
　Would tell his secret—he's the one they'll save.
The dervish heard a voice in his dream say:
　'First learn to be a slave, then come this way!'
You who've ripped Joseph's shirt should then know too,
　It's your own fault if that wolf now kills you.*
Wear all year round what you weave here yourself.
　Eat all year round what you sow here yourself.
These constant sufferings are all your own reaping:
　'*The ink has dried*' has this specific meaning.
My principle won't shun the righteous ones: 3185
　Good ones to good ones, bad ones to bad ones.
Work hard because King Solomon is living—
　While you remain a devil, his sword's winning.
When you become an angel there's no fear
　Of Solomon and his sword, as it's clear
He rules the devils not the angels and
　Strife is not in the heavens, but on land.
Abandon fatalism for it's empty,
　So you may know the mystery of the mystery:
Quit fatalism of a lazy mind   3190
　To learn about a very dearer kind.

Abandon being loved—be of the lovers,
　You who think you are better than the others.
You who're more silent than the night, why bother

Looking for customers for words you utter?
Although they nod their heads in front of you,
   You're wasting time to please them as you do.
Why do you say to me now, 'Don't be jealous!'
   How can someone who loses naught be envious?
Shameless one, teaching those who have no worth   3195
   Is drawing patterns on a clod of earth.
Teach yourself love and insight, for that made
   A pattern on *a huge rock* that won't fade.
Your soul's your pupil who is loyal. When
   The others fade where will you seek them then?
In order to make others great and knowing
   You're making yourself empty and appalling.
The time your heart joins Eden here eventually
   Then speak up and don't fear becoming empty—
The order '*Be!*'* came to that one to say: 3200
   'This ocean won't diminish—speak away!'
'*Be silent!*'* means don't waste on jest your water
   Because the orchard's dry-lipped. That's the order.
This discourse could go on and on, my friend—
   Quit this dry discourse and look to the end!
Am I now jealous that they stand before you?
   They're mocking—they're not lovers who adore you!
Observe lovers beyond God's bounty's veil
   Who shout for you continually and wail.
So be the lover of those who're unseen!   3205
   Don't cherish those who last mere days, though seen.
They've used you up with falseness and attraction.
   For years you haven't got from them a fraction.
Why wearily traverse the vulgar way
   When it cannot fulfil you anyway?
When you are well all are your friends, but when
   In pain and grief, who but God loves you then?
And when your teeth are hurting and your eyes,
   Who will reach out? The One who answers cries.
Remember then that sickness and take note—   3210
   Like Ayaz, take heed from an old fleece coat.
The fleece coat which Ayaz held in his hand
   Is your own pain, if you can understand.

The infidel determinist again answers the Sunni who invited him to
Islam and to abandon his belief in determinism. The debate becomes
prolonged on both sides, for only real love which has no self-interest
in it can solve it: 'And that is God's Grace, which He bestows on
whom He wishes.'*

The fatalist began to answer next.
    This made the first debater feel perplexed,
But if I tell you all of this debate
    Starting my discourse will then have to wait.
We have more vital things to say to you
    Through which your understanding gains a clue.
I've said a little of their argument: 3215
    In a small part the whole is evident.
There will be till the world ends such debates
    Between the two views and their advocates.
If one could not defend against the other
    That view would have completely vanished, brother.
Not finding a good answer for their question,
    They would have fled the way of their destruction.
Pursuing their own path was destined thus:
    The Nurturing God gives proofs to them, like us,
So they'll not listen to the other view   3220
    And thus stay blocked from their good fortune too,
So all those seventy-two sects should stay
    In the world till the *Resurrection Day.**
The realm of darkness and of absence here
    Requires the earth as shadow. Thus, it's clear
Till Resurrection seventy-two are staying,
    With constant chatter while they're innovating.
The precious value of the treasury
    Is clear from locks on it for all to see.
The destination's greatness, trusted men,   3225
    Is clear from all its twists and highwaymen.
The Kaaba's greatness and the crowds' converging
    Is shown by the vast desert's Bedouin's robbing.
Corrupt creeds' paths have very narrow passes,
    Barriers and robbers who steal from the masses.
This path has turned into the other's foe—

The imitator's mixed up and can't know:
He sees sincerity in either way
    And each group pleased with his own path today.
If they've no answer, they'll stick stubbornly   3230
    To the same view for all eternity,
Saying: 'Our greats knew all the answers here,
    Although right now for us they aren't clear.'

Love is the only muzzle for distractions—
    What else has stopped such whispers from their actions?
Seek out a fair beloved—be a lover,
    Hunt water-fowl from one stream to another!
How will you get it from the person who
    Steals yours—your water and your knowledge too?
Beyond intelligibles here, through this love   3235
    You'll find intelligible things from above.
Beyond this intellect God has some others
    Directing heavenly causes for us, brothers:
You earn a living with this one; with that one
    The heavenly sphere turns to your rug to squat on.
He'll give you even more if you should gamble
    Your intellect for love of the Eternal.
Some women gambled intellects away
    And rushed to Joseph's love's pavilion's way.*
Life's cupbearer then stole their power of reason—   3240
    With wisdom they became full from that season.
The source of countless Josephs is God's beauty—
    If you're not less than women serve It truly!
Soul, love alone can cut short disputations
    For it will rescue you in conversations:
Love stupefies their eloquence, which lacks
    The courage to confront it with attacks—
It fears that if it answers back at all
    Out of its mouth a precious pearl might fall.
It seals its mouth to good and evil so   3245
    No pearl will fall out of its mouth below.
The Prophet's own companions gave this message:
    'The Prophet would read a Qur'anic passage

And, at the time of scattering generously
  The pearls, he wanted presence, gravity.
It's like a bird is perched upon your head
  And your soul trembles through a sense of dread
That it might leave, so you can't move or sway
  In case that lovely bird should fly away—
You don't breathe out, you stifle your cough too,   3250
  So your Homa won't soar away from you.
If someone says to you sweet words or bitter,
  To say, 'Hush, please!' you touch lips with your finger.
Bewilderment's that bird: it's silenced you,
  Closing the lid, boiling you inside too.

*How the king asked Ayaz, 'Are you telling the feeling of grief and
joy to an old boot and a fleece coat, which are inanimate?' to get
Ayaz to speak.*

'Ayaz what are these marks on your boots here
  Like lovers' on the idol they revere?
You've made your boots a faith in the same way
  Majnun had done with Layli's face one day.
You've tied your love to two things that are old   3255
  And hung them in a closet too, I'm told.
How long will you say fresh words to that pair
  And breathe the secret to inert things there?'

Ayaz, you draw your words out lengthily
  Like Arabs on campsites nostalgically.*
Which Asaf do your boots remind of now?*
  It seems your fleece is Joseph's shirt somehow?
Like Christians who confess to priests who hear
  All of their sins and hatred of that year,
So that the priest forgives, since his forgiveness   3260
  In their eyes is the same as God's forgiveness.
The priest is not aware of sin and pardon,
  But love's bewitching with its strong conviction—
Love can make Josephs with imagination,
  Excel Harut and Marut as magician.

They show a form evoking him and after
   Attraction to the form gets you to chatter:
You'll tell the form a million secrets then
   The way one tells his best friend among men.
No form or shape is there, yet it produces   3265
   A hundred *'Am I not?'s* a hundred *'Yes!'s*,*
Like a heartbroken mother who has cried
   Next to the grave of her child who has died:
She now tells secrets, deeply passionate—
   She sees as living what's inanimate.
She deems the soil as living, with an ear
   And eye although it's just soil that is here.
Each lump of that grave's soil has consciousness
   And ears to hear when she's impassioned thus.
She thinks the soil is listening actually—   3270
   Now look what a magician love can be!
On that fresh grave she has let her head drop
   With massive tears that flow and never stop.
During his life she'd never placed so near
   Her face to her son's face, though he was dear.
After a few days' mourning has soon passed
   The fire of her love dies and does not last.
(Love for the dead does not last—save your love
   For that Alive One who leads souls above.)
The graveside makes her sleep eventually: 3275
   A lifeless thing made her act similarly,
For love has taken its spell and moved on—
   Ash is all that is left once flames have gone.

In a mere brick the Elder can still view
   All you see in a mirror facing you.
The Elder is your love, not white beard hair—
   He gives a hand to thousands in despair.
Love will create forms during separation,
   The Formless One will rise up, though, in union:
'I'm consciousness and drunkenness's source: 3280
   My beauty's what you see in forms, of course.
Now I have drawn the veils off finally—

Beauty's seen with no intermediary:
Since you've been so engaged with My reflection,
　Gained strength thus for My Essence's inspection,
When My attraction pulls from this side, then
　The priest's no longer seen by Christian men.'
Instead now they seek pardon in his place
　Beyond that veil, directly from God's grace.
When a spring gushes from a rock it's clear　　　3285
　Within the spring the rock will disappear:
No one will call it 'rock' now since that essence
　Flowed from the rock and overwhelmed its presence.
Comparable to bowls are forms this side—
　They're made sublime by what God pours inside.

Majnun's relatives said, 'Layli's beauty is limited. It's not so great.
There are many more lovely than her in our town. We'll show you
one or two of them. Take your choice and release yourself and us!'
Majnun answers them.

The stupid said to Majnun once, 'Your Layli
　Is fair, but not exceptionally lovely.
There are a million radiant sweethearts here
　In our town who are lovelier and it's clear.'
'The form's the flagon; beauty is the wine.　　　3290
　Through her form, God gives me wine that's so fine.
He gave you from the flagon vinegar,
　So you'd not get pulled by your ears to her.'
Glorious God's hand gives honey and gives poison
　From the same pot according to the person.
You see the vessel, but that wine will not
　Show its face to such an unwholesome lot.
Mystic taste's *women who look modestly*,*
　Showing the spouses signs exclusively.
The women who look modestly * are wine,　　　3295
　Their vessels veil like tents, dear friend of mine.
The sea is tent-like: ducks can live therein
　But it means death for crows if they dive in.
Venom supports the snakes, but then again
　To all the others it means death and pain.

Every bounty's and every trial's form, brother,
    Is hell to one and heaven to another.
Therefore each single body that *you see*
    Has food and poison in it *you don't see.**
Our body's like a pot and it contains   3300
    Both nourishment and what brings inner pains.
The bowl's seen, blessings hidden—one partaking
    Will know exactly what it is he's tasting.
Joseph's form was just like a lovely goblet—
    His father drank a hundred fine wines from it.
It was just poison for his brothers though
    Since it just made their spite and rage both grow.
Zolaikha that time got drunk on it too,
    Through a rare opium from love, which she drew:
From Joseph she received a nourishment,   3305
    As Jacob did, but hers was different.
Different drinks although the flagon's one,
    So no doubt's left about Unseen Wine. None.
The jar's from this world, wine from the Unseen
    The jar is visible; its wine's not seen,
Hidden within from the uninitiated,
    Yet crystal clear to the initiated.
O God, our eyes have got drunk now we're merry.
    Forgive us, but our burden is so heavy.
O Hidden One, You've filled the East and West,   3310
    Yet You're above the light from East and West,
A secret who reveals our secrets too,
    The force that causes streams to gush is You.
Your essence hidden, Your gifts are perceived.
    You're water; we're the millstone that received,
Or You're the wind and we're dust that is blown:
    The wind is hidden, but the dust is shown.
You are the spring; like orchards we are green—
    He's hidden yet His gifts are clearly seen.
If we are hands and feet, You are the soul—   3315
    The hand's own movement's in the soul's control.
You are like intellect; we're tongues—reflect
    On how tongues gain their speech from intellect.
You are like joy; we're laughter that is best—

It's the result of joy that's truly blest.
'*I testify!*'* says every move we make
For the Eternal, Glorious One's sake.
The millstone says, '*I testify!*'* when moved
So that the stream's existence can be proved.
You are beyond speech and conception—please   3320
Put me to shame with all my similes!
The slave can't hold back from your fair depiction;
'May my soul be your carpet!' is its mission,
Just like that shepherd* who said, 'God, come here
Before your shepherd lover! You're so dear.
So I can find fleas in your shirt and kill them,
Then stitch your boots together, kiss your coat hem.'
No one could equal him in love and passion,
Though he fell short when praising in that fashion.
His love had pitched its tent up in the sky;   3325
The soul became his tent's guard dog on high.
When love of God's sea surged, it struck his heart,
But only struck your ear—how far apart!*

Story about the male prankster Johi wearing a chador, sitting among the women during a preacher's sermon and moving around. A woman discovers that it's a man and screams.

There was once a well-spoken preacher, who
Had women gathered near him, and men too.
Johi, a man, dressed as a woman there
In purdah so the rest stayed unaware.
Someone then asked the preacher: 'Pubic hairs—
Do they invalidate my daily prayers?'
The preacher said: 'If pubic hairs are long   3330
Then, yes, for prayers your growing them is wrong—
So that your prayers can be now deemed approved
Shave them or with a cream have them removed!'
The questioner asked, 'How long must pubic hairs
Have grown before invalidating prayers?'
He said, 'The length of one small barley grain—
If they've grown that much, shave them off again!'

Johi, in purdah, asked a woman near:
  'Sister, please check my pubic hairs right here.
For God's sake reach down with your hand to see   3335
  If they're too long already, helpfully.'
She reached into his trousers as he'd planned
  Then felt his penis rub against her hand.
The woman screamed aloud in shock and dread—
  'My speech has touched her heart!' the preacher said.
'No, not her heart, her hand!' Johi yelled out,
  'If it had touched her heart there'd be no doubt.'
Pharaoh's magicians' hearts were touched by God
  Then saw as one Moses's hand and rod.*
Snatch walking sticks from old men and you'll see   3340
  Them suffer more than that group previously:
Their cry '*There's no harm*'* reached the heavens, ringing,
  'Chop off our limbs. The soul is freed from suffering.
We've learnt we're not the body; we endure
  Through God beyond the body. We are sure.'
The one who knows his essence is so lucky—
  He's built a palace in eternity's sanctuary.
Children will cry for nuts and raisins, but
  Wise men know they are trivial things to cut.
Body is nuts and raisins to the heart;   3345
  A child can't learn men's knowledge—tell apart:
The one who's veiled is just a child, still small,
  While actual men possess no doubts at all.
If testicles and beards make men of you,
  Billy goats have long beards and much hair too.
That kind of goat is a bad leader—he
  Leads others to the butcher rapidly.
He's combed his beard and thought, 'I am ahead!'
  Ahead only for grief and falling dead!
Choose this path and abandon now the beard!   3350
  Leave ego and the troubled thoughts you'd feared,
So you'll become for lovers rose scent too,
  The guide inside the rose-garden who's true.
What is the rose scent? It's the breath of wisdom,
  The guide that leads to the eternal kingdom.

*Shah Mahmud tells Ayaz once more, 'Clearly explain your boots
and fleece coat so your fellow servants can gain advice from
the teachings of that since 'religion is counsel' according
to the Prophet.*

'Ayaz, tell me the secret! What is this?
　Before such boots you're showing neediness?
My other servants then might learn from you
　The secret of the boots and fleece cloak too.
Slavery now has gained light from you and　　　　3355
　Light rises to the heavens from low land.
Slavery's now the envy of the free
　For you have given life to slavery.
The ones who in life's ups and downs believe
　Make infidels regret their lack and grieve.

*Story about an infidel in the time of Bayazid who was told,
'Become a Muslim!' and his answer to them.*

In Bayazid's time once a Muslim told
　A non-believer to 'come to the fold':
'Why not become a Muslim now like me
　To gain salvation and great majesty?'
He answered, 'If this faith that you profess　　　　3360
　Is Bayazid's, the whole world's shaikh no less,
I wouldn't cope with its heat: I don't dare
　As that is much more than my soul can bear.
Though I'm not sure about faith, still I can
　Say I avow the faith of that pure man.
I've faith his is the highest of them all,
　So glorious and fine it can enthrall.
And I believe in his faith secretly
　Although a seal shuts my mouth totally.
But if it's your faith that you have in mind,　　　　3365
　I have no wish for weak faith of that kind.
People who are inclined, once they have seen
　Belief like your belief, feel much less keen:
They see a name that has no meaning oddly,
　Like calling deserts "safe escapes" absurdly.

On seeing your faith, if the truth be told,
　　His keenness to profess belief turns cold.'

Story about the muezzin with a horrible voice who gave the call to
prayer in the region of Non-Muslims and to whom one of their
members gave a gift.

Once a muezzin whose voice wasn't pretty
　　Would give the call in a Non-Muslim city.
'Don't say the call to prayer,' they begged, 'It's frightening   3370
　　As this will lead to enmity and fighting!'
Not heeding them, he disregarded prudence
　　And gave the call in that non-Muslim province.
Men feared a civil war across this land.
　　Then a Non-Muslim came with robe in hand,
Halva and candle also, suddenly,
　　As if a friend, as happy as can be,
Asking, 'Where's that muezzin? Let me know—
　　The one whose prayer call makes my pleasure grow.'
'What pleasure from that ugly voice we hated?'   3375
　　'His voice reached our church,' then the man related,
'I have a daughter who is fair and charming—
　　She wanted to convert, which was alarming.
The passionate fervour wouldn't leave her head.
　　Non-Muslims gave her counsel, but instead
In her heart grew love of Islam's belief—
　　I was the aloes wood, my censer grief:
I suffered so much pain and agony
　　Because she was being drawn there constantly.
I knew of no solution. I'd despair   3380
　　Till that muezzin made the call to prayer:
My daughter said, "That sound's detestable—
　　What am I hearing that's so terrible?
In my whole life I've never heard a sound
　　So ugly in this church when I've been round."
Her sister said, "That is the call to prayer:
　　It is a Muslim practice, so beware!"
She doubted her and asked another near:

That person said, "She is correct, my dear."
Her face turned pale once she found out it's true   3385
   And she got turned off turning Muslim too.
Rescued from torment and anxiety,
   Last night I slept without fear, peacefully.
This is the joy his voice gave me. I've brought
   Him gifts in thanks—where is the man I've sought?'
On spotting him, 'Accept this gift!' he said,
   'Since you've saved and protected me from dread.
The kind act you have carried out for me
   Has made me your own slave eternally.
If I had wealth and property, I would   3390
   Fill your mouth up with gold now—it's that good.'

Your faith is falseness and hypocrisy—
   Like that prayer call it waylays terribly.
In admiration of great Bayazid
   And his true faith, my soul regrets indeed,
You're like that one who had sex with a donkey:*
   She said, 'Ah, what a peerless stallion fucks me!
If this is sex, the champions are the donkeys;
   Our husbands' thrusts are shit inside our pussies!'
Bayazid gave all that true faith would need—   3395
   Bravo to that unique lion, Bayazid!
A drop of his faith enters in the sea
   And that sea drowns in it incredibly.
A tiny spark lights in a jungle and
   The jungle gets consumed by it: burned land.
A king or army has a fantasy
   And it destroys that wartime enemy.
A star shone through Mohammad's face and made
   The Jews and Magians' essences both fade.*
Those who gained faith entered security;   3400
   Others' denial would grow increasingly.
Their previous unbelief did not stay here—
   It sowed new Muslimness or a new fear.
This is a superficial rendering.
   Motes can't compare to his faith, for that thing,

The mote's a wretched body, miserable.
  It's not the *sun that's indivisible.*
My mentioning motes has a concealed aim too—
  You're mere foam, and the ocean's far from you.
If the Shaikh's faith's bright sun should once display   3405
  From the East of his soul its faith, they say
All men below would gain a treasure and
  Above they'd gain a verdant, heavenly land.
He has a soul of luminous light and he
  Has his own earthly body equally—
I wonder if he's this or that? Tell, uncle,
  For I am stuck deciphering this puzzle!
If he's this, brother, what's that? Which is right?
  The seven heavens are filled with his light.
If he's the soul, what is the body, friend?   3410
  I wonder which one he is in the end?

Story about the woman who told her husband, 'The cat ate the
meat.' The husband put the cat on the weighing scales and saw
that the cat weighed half a mann unit of weight. He said,
  'Wife, the meat weighed at least half a mann. If this
    amount of weight is the meat's, where is the cat?
      If it is the cat, where is the meat?'

There was a wife once of a household head
  Who was deceptive, vile, and stole instead.
He'd bring things and she'd use them up so quickly.
  The man had to keep silent, so unlucky.
That man brought meat once for a guest to savour,
  Which he'd acquired through much demanding labour.
His wife ate it with wine so greedily.
  Her spouse came; she rebuffed deceitfully:
He said, 'Our guest's here. Where's the meat right now?   3415
  We must serve a good meal to him somehow.'
'The cat ate it, so head back to the store
  And buy some meat again if they have more!'
He told a servant, 'Bring the balance here
  To weigh the cat, which should make matters clear!'
The cat weighed only half a *mann*. He said:

'Deceitful woman, that cat's not been fed
With meat I bought—if you're right, then how can
  The cat right now itself weigh half a *mann*?
If this weight is the cat's, where is the meat?   3420
  If it's the meat, how is the cat complete?'

If Bayazid's the body, what's the soul?
  If he's the soul, what is this man's form's role?
It's so perplexing friend—it's not for you
  Or me to understand. We have no clue.
He is both, yet for crops the seed's the key—
  Leaves are derivative and secondary.
Wisdom has brought these opposites together:
  The thigh meat with the neck meat now, O butcher!
The soul can't cope without the body, but   3425
  The soulless body's cold, inanimate.
Your body's seen, your soul is out of view:
  Causes in this world are set by these two.
By throwing soil you won't break someone's head,
  By splashing water neither—but instead
If you mix soil and water you will see
  It will then break the man's head easily.
Once it breaks, water goes back to its source
  And soil to soil eventually of course.
God's wisdom through our human unions is   3430
  To show both neediness and stubbornness.
But there are other marriages as well
  Which no ear hears and no eye sees to tell.*
If the ear hears how can it stay an ear?
  How can it hear more talking still down here?
If ice and snow were to perceive the sun
  They'd give up frozenness, their course now run—
They'd turn to water with no ripples in it;
  David-like air would make some chainmail with it.
Water's the cure for every tree's survival,   3435
  Each benefiting from its flow's arrival,
But frozen ice stays inside its own body
  And it tells every tree it sees: '*Don't touch me!*'

Its body has no friends because of this;
     Its share is naught but selfish avarice.
It's not a waste though—livers will revive—
     Though it won't herald verdure that will thrive.

'You are a star, Ayaz. All constellations
     Aren't worthy of its passage. Aspirations
You have mean you don't rate their loyalty,   3440
     And how should yours rate others' purity?'

Story about the prince who told his slave to fetch wine. The slave
went and headed back with a jugful. On the way an ascetic told him
to act righteously and threw a stone to break the jug. The prince
heard about this and resolved to chastise the ascetic. (This was in
the epoch of Jesus's religion when wine had still not been forbidden,
but the ascetic was showing disgust and preventing enjoyment.)

There was a joyful prince who loved wine. He
     Was all hard-pressed and drunk men's sanctuary,
Considerate, kind to the poor, and fair,
     Gold-giving, ocean-hearted, jewel so rare,
Commander of the faithful, monarch too,
     Knower of secrets, sentry, friend who's true.
He lived in Jesus's time and harmed none,
     Gentle and so adored by everyone.
Another prince came as a guest and he   3445
     Lived in a joyful manner, similarly.
They needed wine to feel good and wine then
     Was lawful and permitted for all men.
Then short of wine, the prince called, 'Slave, please go
     Have our jug filled by that one whom you know:
That monk with special wine, so our souls then
     Can be relieved of every stress again.'
One gulp from that monk's jug can do more than
     A thousand vats of regular wine can.
There's something hidden in that wine that's special;   3450
     It's like the cloaks that can make people regal—
Don't judge the cloak that's tattered. Truth be told

They've simply smeared some black stuff over gold—
The evil eye makes it seem bad to you:
  That ruby looks smoke-tarnished in your view.
Since when are treasures found so easily?
  They're found in ruins where most men can't see.
Adam's treasure was likewise out of view:
  His body was that cursed one's blindfold too.
He viewed that bodily clay as weak, not strong: 3455
  'My clay blocks you!' the soul said all along.

The slave took two jugs and ran happily
  And quickly to the monk's own monastery.
He paid with gold for gold-like wine: he'd brought
  A stone and a fine jewel is what he got:
A wine that rushes to the king's head, then
  Puts on the Saqi the gold crown of men.
Once fervour and commotion spreads around
  Slaves and kings altogether gather round—
Bones disappear with only souls remaining,   3460
  Throne and bench equal in this state we're sharing.
When sober they're like oil and water oddly
  Once drunk they are like soul inside the body.
They turn *halim*-like:* nothing separate;
  All differences are thus submerged in it.
The slave was bringing that wine through the town
  To the home of the prince of good renown
When an ascetic faced him suddenly,
  One suffering a dry mind in agony:
In the heart's fires his body burned away;   3465
  His house removed all but God from the way.
The merciless, gruesome trials that he'd been handed
  Meant that for countless times he had been branded.
In every hour his heart would strive to fight,
  Busy with power struggles day and night.
He'd suffered greatly for more than a year;
  His patience left him that night, as is clear.
He asked, 'What's in the jar?' The slave said, 'Wine.'
  He asked, 'Who is the owner, friend of mine?'

'The glorious prince,' the slave said straight away.   3470
    He said, 'Is then the seeker's work this way:
Seeker of God and drinking to feel bliss
    Satan's wine—from its power lost consciousness?
Even without wine your wits are so feeble
    That others' wits must help to keep them stable—
What will they be like when you're drunk, no less,
    You who've been trapped like birds by drunkenness?'

Story about Ziya Dalq, who was very tall while his brother the
Shaikh al-Islam Taj of Balkh was extremely short—the latter
insulted his brother Ziya: once Ziya came to his brother's lecture,
where all the notables of Balkh were present and he paid his respects
before walking in. The Shaikh al-Islam only half-rose from his seat
unusually. Ziya then said, 'Yes, you are of course so tall you can
afford to show less of your height!'

Ziya Dalq, an inspired man, had a brother
    Who was a high-ranked preacher like no other:
Balkh's 'Taj Shaikh al-Islam' was his position,   3475
    And he was small and short just like a chicken,
Though learned, talented, and manly too,
    But Ziya was the sharper of the two.
The former short, Ziya was very tall.
    Shaikh al-Islam was proud, showed airs to all,
And felt ashamed of his own brother Ziya,
    Although he was a rightly-guided preacher.
Ziya came when his brother held a session,
    The classroom filled with pure men of position.
The Shaikh al-Islam then in his proud way   3480
    Stood up for his own brother just half-way—
'Since you're so tall, my brother,' Ziya said,
    'Show a bit more and gain rewards instead!'

Then the ascetic said, 'Where'd your brain go
    To drink wine? You are knowledge's own foe.
Your face is fair, so why put on dark make-up
    That isn't something Africans need take up.

Lost one, when did light ever enter you
    That you sought darkness and to lose wits too?
Seeking shadows in daytime is all right,   3485
    But you seek shadows on a cloudy night!
If a drink's lawful for the vulgar, it
    Is still banned for God's seekers, isn't it?
The lover's wine is their hearts' blood; their eyes
    Stay focused on the path to the goal's prize.
On such a path through very scary climes
    Wisdom, the guide, would get veiled countless times.
If you throw dust on your guide's eyes, you'll see
    The caravan get lost most dangerously.
Barley bread harms and is forbidden too   3490
    For carnal souls—give yours bran bread and you
Keep God's path's enemy abased! You must control it:
    The thief deserves the gallows, not the pulpit.
The thief's hands must be chopped off legally—
    If you can't do that, bind them carefully.
If you don't you'll be bound—make no mistake:
    If you don't break his legs, then yours will break.
Why give the foe some wine and sugar cane?
    Damn it! Let it stay bitter once again.'

Then the ascetic threw a stone its way   3495
    And smashed the jug. The slave then ran away
Back to the prince: 'Where is the wine?' he said.
    He told him what had happened, why he'd fled.

The angry prince goes to chastise the ascetic.

The prince leapt up with fiery rage and said:
    'Show me his house, so I can pound his head
With a big club that I have kept in store
    For such an ignorant son of a whore!
What does he know about enjoining right?
    Just like a cur he's seeking fame tonight,
So by this falseness he'll gain a position   3500
    And make himself known for some kind of mission.
He has no other talent, but this one,

Namely acting falsely to everyone.
If he's insane and wants to trouble me
    An ox's penis is the remedy,
So Satan leaves his head and what he's done—
    Without being whipped would donkeys ever run?'
With club in hand the prince rushed to the site;
    Half-drunk, he reached his target late that night.
Enraged, he sought to murder that ascetic,   3505
    Who hid beneath wool, fearing something tragic:
Hiding under rope-makers' wool, he'd hear
    The things the prince would say once he drew near.
Only a mirror with a hard face can
    Tell someone to his face: 'You're ugly, man!'
A steel face like a mirror's would tell you:
    'Look at your ugly face that's in clear view!'

Story about Dalqak's checkmating the Sayyed Shah of Termez.

The Shah played chess with Dalqak, his court jester,
    Who mated him—the Shah raged in a temper:
Dalqak said, 'Checkmate!' The proud Shah instead   3510
    Threw all the chess pieces then at his head:
'Take that, wretch, for your checkmate!' Dalqak stayed
    Most calm: 'Have mercy, please!' is what he said.
The Shah told him to play again. Not bold,
    Dalqak shook like one naked in the cold.
The Shah got mated in that second game:
    When the time to say 'Checkmate!' finally came
Dalqak leapt to a corner that was near,
    Threw linen on himself due to his fear.
Under some pillows and six throws he lay   3515
    Hiding from the Shah's anger on that day.
The Shah said, 'What is this? What have you done?'
    He said, 'Distinguished Shah, checkmate! I've won.
How can one tell the truth and then not hide
    When you're enraged and filled with fire inside?
You're mated, but I'm, too, by the Shah's blows—
    I'll say "Checkmate!" beneath sheets, so he knows.'

The prince's uproar spread outside as he
  Kicked at the door and grabbed things violently.
People rushed out from all around to say: 3520
  'Forgive, superior one! Accept today!
His brain had dried up, and his wisdom now
  Was less than that we find in kids somehow.
Dotage has made worse his renunciation
  Which didn't lead to any revelation.
He's seen trials, but no treasures from his Lord:
  He has toiled hard, but not seen a reward.
Either the jewel was not there in his labour
  Or recompense's hour will come much later.
Or his toil was like the deniers' kind,   3525
  Or the reward for it just lags behind.
It's pain and bad luck for him that he'll tarry
  All on his own now in a blood-filled valley.
His eyes hurt and he sits there in a nook
  Crestfallen with a very bitter look.
Without an eye doctor to play that role,
  Or knowledge to discover some good kohl,
He strives with guesswork and opinions merely—
  Until that works, it's just 'perhaps' or 'maybe'.
His journey to the Loved One's a long trip   3530
  Since he does not seek Him, but leadership.
Now he reproaches God and is heard muttering:
  'I've worked out that my lot in life is suffering.'
And then he argues with his luck, 'All fly,
  But I have had my wings both severed—why?'

Whoever's trapped in senses such as smell,
  Though world-denying, he's repressed as well.
Until he exits that most cramped cell's door
  How can his soul feel joy, his heart grow more?
One never gives ascetics a sharp blade   3535
  While in retreat before their breakthrough's made,
Since they'd tear their own stomachs for relief
  From anguish, disappointment, pain, and grief.

How the Prophet Mohammad threw himself down from Mount
Hira* due to the hard challenge of Gabriel's appearing to him so
late, and Gabriel's appeasing him by saying: 'Don't cast yourself
down from the many fortunes that await you!'

Mohammad when he felt apart and weak
    Would want to jump off a high mountain peak
Till Gabriel would say: 'Don't do that! You'll see
    Much fortune coming through the order '*Be!*'*
Although Mohammad would at first refrain
    Severance would leave him feeling weak again—
He'd feel prepared to jump off for relief   3540
    Headfirst from that tall mountain due to grief,
Then Gabriel would return to say, 'Don't fling
    Yourself from there! You are a peerless king.'
It carried on until the veil was lifted
    And from within he gained the jewel that's gifted.
Since people kill themselves from trials, compare it:
    This is the source of all trials—who could bear it?
Men are amazed by life-risking attackers*
    But we're all sacrificing in our manners.
Happy the man who sacrificed the body   3545
    All for the sake of something that is worthy.
All can self-sacrifice and in that way
    Spend their whole life, before being killed one day,
Killed in the East or West where neither yearner
    Nor the thing that is yearned for last much longer.
The fortunate man's devoted to being skilled
    In this—more lives are gained through being killed.
Love, lover, and Beloved will keep living—
    In both worlds they're renowned and they are prospering.
Pity the lustful, O munificent ones!   3550
    Their state is of repetitive destructions.

The crowd said, 'Prince, forgive him and refrain!
    Consider his misfortune and his pain,
So God will then forgive your sins like his
    And add a pardon for your blemishes.

You've broken many jugs while you were heedless
    And set your heart on gaining full forgiveness—
Forgive so you can be forgiven too!
    Fate calculates what it deals out to you.'

The prince answers those neighbours of the ascetic interceding for
him: 'Why was he so impudent? Why did he break my jug of wine?
I will not accept intercession in this matter, as I have sworn to give
him what he deserves.'

'Who is he to throw stones?' the prince then said,   3555
    'To break my jug and not feel any dread?
Even fierce lions, if they should come near,
    They do with caution since I'm one they fear.
Why did he hurt my slave's heart and embarrass
    Me, too, before my guest back at the palace?
He spilled drinks better than our blood and he
    Has fled, like women, somewhere sneakily.
How will he save his life? If he should fly
    High up the way a bird soars in the sky,
I'd fire an arrow of my wrath and tear   3560
    His useless wings apart without a care.
If he heads to the big rocks when he flees
    I'll drag him out of those big rocks with ease,
Then start to beat his body as a warning
    To every scoundrel of what will be coming.
He showed to all of us hypocrisy—
    I'll give him and his kind their due. Watch me!'
Bloodthirsty anger overwhelmed him then.
    Fire spilled from his mouth scaring other men.

For a second time the interceding neighbours kiss the hands
and feet of the prince and appeal.

The intercessors, due to this commotion,   3565
    Kissed both his hands and feet to then petition:
'Spite doesn't suit you, prince, although that wine
    Has all been lost. Without it you're still fine.

The wine acquires its value from your goodness;
  Water's pureness wishes it had your pureness.
Act like a king—forgive him, merciful one,
  O noble one, son of a noble one!
All wines are slaves to your fine form and face;
  All drunks are envious of you in this place.
You have no need for red wine's rosiness—   3570
  Leave that, for you're the actual rosiness.
Your Venus-like cheek's brighter than the sun;
  Rosiness near your colour feels outdone.
Wine bubbling in the jar invisibly
  Bubbles through yearning for your face to see.
You're the whole ocean—why desire some dew?
  You are all being—why seek non-being too?
Bright moon, why do you want the dust below?
  The moon seems yellow next to your bright glow.
"*We've honoured*"* has now placed its crown on you;   3575
  From your breast hangs the chain of "*We gave you*".*
You're lovely and the source of loveliness.
  Why feel towards mere wine such neediness?
The essence: Man. This world: the accident,
  Like branch and rung while he's the goal in front.
Wisdom and reason are your slaves, so why
  Sell yourself cheaply when your value's high?
All creatures must serve you—how should an essence
  Seek help from accidents? That would be nonsense.
You're seeking knowledge still from books, alas!   3580
  You seek sweet taste from halva still, alas!
Wisdom's sea's hidden in a drop of dew,
  A vast world in a tiny body too.
What's music, wine, or sex for you tonight
  To seek from them some gain and some delight?
So should the sun seek loans from motes today?
  Should Venus seek wine from a jar of clay?
Your soul's beyond descriptions; all the same
  You're trapped here, the eclipsed sun—what a shame!'

The prince answers them again.

He said, 'I'm wine's companion. You're in error.   3585
   I'm not content with one taste of this pleasure.
I want a wine that makes me swing and sway
   Like jasmine flowers, this way then that way.
Released from fear and hope, I then may follow
   By swaying all around just like a willow:
Like willow branches swaying left and right
   Which, due to wind, are dancing now in sight.
One who conforms to such wine's joyousness—
   How can he be content then with just this?'
Prophets left such joys since they were immersed   3590
   In the divine joy, which they rated first.
Their souls had seen the others' gaiety,
   But that just seemed to them frivolity—
Why would one choose befriending a dead rival
   When one's been near an actual living idol?

Exegesis of 'The next realm is real life, if they but knew.' The gate,
wall, and area of that world and its waters, pitchers, fruits, and
trees are all alive and they speak and hear. Referring to that, the
Prophet Mohammad said, 'They call something a carcass because of
its being dead, not because of its bad smell and filthiness.'*

Each atom of the other world is living:
   They all can understand and they're conversing.
In this world great ones have no peace—its fodder
   Is only fit for cattle to eat, brother.
Someone who has a rosegarden would not   3595
   Drink wine in furnace rooms with what he's got.
Pure spirit's home is '*Elliyin*';* the fit
   For the mere worm is homes built inside shit.
Those drunk on God have the pure, cleansing cup;
   The blind birds drink the briny water up.
Just those who'd not seen Omar's fair rule trust
   That bloodthirsty Hajjaj's rule was just.*
Small girls are given lifeless dolls for play
   Since they've not played with live things in that way.

A wooden sword is better for a toddler   3600
    Until they gain more strength when they grow taller.
Christians are satisfied with portraits shown
    In monasteries, although they're lifeless stone—
Since we see golden eras from such men
    Mere shadows cannot satisfy us then.
One of his forms is sitting here, the other
    Is like the lofty moon in that realm, brother.
One mouth tells fine points here to someone near
    The other talks with God Who holds him dear.
His outer ear receives speech normally;   3605
    His inner ear hears secrets of God's '*Be!*'*
His outer eye sees human forms down here;
    His inner eye's stunned through '*his eyes don't veer*'.*
In the prayer row his outer feet are standing;
    Above the heavens inner feet are circling.
Count every part of him like this: each one
    Is in time while beyond's a mystic one.
The former lasts till death comes finally,
    The other is part of eternity.
'*Governor of two states*': one of his titles,   3610
    Another is '*Imam of the two qiblas*'.*
He doesn't need seclusion or withdrawal;
    No darkening cloud hangs over him at all.
This man's retreat is the sun's orb—how can
    The night, that stranger, veil him then, good man?
Sickness and caution gone, crisis diverted,
    His unbelief's faith. Unbelief's been thwarted.
He's at the front, like 'A', through steadfastness;
    He's lost his attributes, with which he'd dress.
He's separate now from his own wishes and   3615
    His soul's gone to Him who makes it expand.
Naked in front of that Unique King there
    Who gives it holy attributes to wear.
It wears a robe of that King's qualities.
    It flies from pit to palace now with ease—
When dregs become pure that is what you witness:
    They rise from the bowl's bottom to the surface.
At the bowl's base bad luck made his soul stay,

Mixed with terrestrial parts of him in clay;
Its mean companion tied its wings both up,   3620
   Or else it would at once have soared straight up.
When the rebuke came, telling it: '*Go down!*'*
   Like Harut they then hung it upside down.
Harut of heaven's angels previously
   Was hung like this due to rebuke, you see:
Hung upside down for straying from the head,
   Claiming headship and going alone instead.
A basket filled with water had the notion
   Of self-sufficiency, then left the ocean;
Not one drop was left in it naturally—   3625
   The ocean called it back compassionately:
A favour without cause, nor for work done,
   That's from the ocean—a blessed hour for one.
By all means gather on the shore, although
   The people there are pale—God might bestow
Through His kind grace some jewellery anyway
   And give your pale face colour in this way.

The best complexion is one pale and sallow
   Since it's from hope of meeting God tomorrow.
Bright, beaming cheeks in contrast are so ruddy   3630
   Because the soul is so content already.
Hope makes one thin, pale with humility—
   This person's ailment isn't bodily.
Even Galen, on seeing a pale face,
   Would then expect a sickness he can trace.
When you have also fixed hope on God's light
   Mohammad's words: '*His self's abased*' are right.
Light with no shade is lofty and so lovely—
   You're still embroiled if your own light is patchy.
Naked lovers all want the naked body—   3635
   Clothes can stay on for impotent men only.
The food is for those fasting; for the fly
   The trivet's like the soup as it darts by.

The king appeals to Ayaz again: 'Explain your action and solve the
puzzle for the deniers and the blamers, for it is not considerate to
leave them in confusion.'

This speech is limitless, beyond all measure:
    'Ayaz, tell me about your states! A treasure
Brought from the mine of newness? How can you
    Be satisfied with states you're here used to?
Relate to us those fine states and conditions—
    To hell with our states and talk of dimensions!'
'Though inward states can't be related truly   3640
    I'll tell about the outward state now fully:
Death's bitterness was altered by God's grace
    To be like candy for my soul to face,
And if that sugar's dust could reach the sea
    Its bitterness would turn sweet totally.
A million states reached me just like this one
    Then went back to the Unseen, O true one!
Each day states different than the previous day—
    Like flowing rivers they each pass away.
Each day's thought is a different kind; through thought   3645
    Each single day a new effect is brought.'

Comparison of the human being to a guesthouse and different
thoughts to different guests. The mystic, content with those thoughts
of sorrow or joy, is like a hospitable person who is kind to strangers,
like Abraham, for Abraham's door was always open to receive
guests with generosity, for unbeliever and believer, the trustworthy
and the treacherous alike, and he showed a fresh face to all guests.

The body is a guesthouse and each morning
    A new guest comes into the guesthouse, running.
Don't say that they are burdensome somehow
    Or they'll go back to Non-existence now.
Whatever comes to you from yonder realm
    They're all your guests—be a good host to them!

A man came at a bad time as a guest;
   The host housed him and gave him what was best.
He laid a feast on for him generously.   3650
   A party was being held then locally.
Secretly to his wife the host then said:
   'Tonight, wife, make two beds, not just one bed:
Roll out a mattress by the entrance door
   And on the other side roll out one more.'
His wife said, 'Glad to serve, you know. To hear
   Is to obey, light of my eyes, sweet dear!'
She made the beds and then she left there promptly
   To go to the big circumcision party.
Her husband stayed there with the guest to eat—   3655
   He served him every kind of lavish treat.
Till midnight this pair talked about the past,
   The good and bad, until that hour had passed.
The guest got sleepy and could not chat more—
   He went towards the mattress by the door.
The husband thought it too rude to make clear:
   'Your bed is on the other side, right here—
For you we've rolled a mattress out already
   On that side, so you'll sleep just like a baby.'
The plan that he'd made with his wife before   3660
   Was ruined as the guest slept by the door.
It rained so heavily that night the crowds
   Were stunned by the huge thickness of the clouds.
The wife arrived home thinking that her partner
   Was by the door, their guest in the far corner.
Naked, she slipped beneath the blanket there
   And kissed with lust the guest, still unaware:
'Big man, this is what I had feared,' she said,
   'And now it's happened just as I did dread.
The rain and mud have stranded here our guest,   3665
   So he'll remain a burden and a pest,
For how can he leave in the mud and rain?
   A burden on your head, he will remain.'

The guest got up from bed immediately:
  'Stop woman, I have boots. Mud won't stop me!
Don't worry! I will leave immediately.
  May one's soul never get filled up with glee,
So it can reach its actual home much earlier:
  Rejoicing waylays every single traveler.'
The wife regretted saying things unfeeling   3670
  Once that distinguished guest said he was leaving:
She said, 'Don't get upset, O princely guest
  Because of my well-meaning little jest!'
Her begging didn't work: he went away
  And left them feeling bad he didn't stay.
That couple mourned by wearing blue thereafter;
  They viewed him as a candle without holder—
He went off and the desert, through his light,
  Was spared of total darkness late at night.
The husband made his home a guesthouse also,   3675
  Ashamed of what occurred and filled with sorrow.
The image of the guest would mystically
  Say through a hidden route continually:
'I am Khezr's friend: I'd have bestowed for free
  Much treasure, but that's not your destiny.'

Comparison of everyday thoughts that come to one's mind with new
guests who from the start of the day arrive at the house and behave
in a bad-tempered and demanding way with the master of the house.
The virtue of being hospitable and putting up with the guest's airs.

Each moment, like an honoured guest, a thought
  Enters your breast, and every day they're brought.
O soul, deem each a person and no less,
  For thought's what gives a person worthiness.
If a sad thought waylays the joy you're feeling,   3680
  It's readying for joy you'll soon be seeing,
Sweeping the house of all else with much force
  So new joy comes from goodness's own source.
From the heart's branch it shakes off yellow leaves
  So it will grow from now on fresh green leaves.
And it uproots the root of old joys so

New savour from beyond instead might grow.
Grief pulls up rotten roots to show to you
   The other root they've covered up from view.
Whatever grief spills from the heart it then   3685
   Brings something better in its place again.
For those with certainty especially:
   'Grief is the slave of those with certainty.'

The clouds and lightning frown once in a while
   So vines won't get burned by the sun's hot smile.
Good and bad luck can be guests in your heart
   Like stars that enter one house then depart.
When it comes to your heart's house, you should be
   Like its ascendant: sweet in harmony,
So when it joins the moon it will then sing   3690
   Your praises warmly to the heart's own king.
For a full seven years Job showed contentment
   And patience with 'God's guest' despite the torment,
So, when that stern-faced one would go back, it
   Would praise him there before God, as was fit:
'Job never frowned at me,' that guest would say,
   'Due to love, though to kill what's loved's my way.'
Before God's knowledge, out of loyalty
   And shame, he stayed sweet facing agony.
When a new thought comes in your breast, then meet it   3695
   With smiles and laughter when it's time to greet it,
And say: '*Creator, save me from its badness*
   And don't prevent me gaining from its goodness!
Enable me to give what I see praise
   Yet not feel sorry when each one decays!'
Watch over that sour-faced thought and instead
   View it as sugar sweet inside your head!
Although the cloud seems sour-faced, it brings you
   Rose gardens and ends barrenness here too.
Consider the sad thought a cloud—refrain   3700
   From looking sourly at what's sour again!
The pearl might be held in its hand today—
   Strive so it is content on going away!

Even if there's no pearl and it's not wealthy
    You will acquire a habit that is healthy,
And will a later time gain benefit,
    Some day when you are least expecting it.
The thought that blocks your happiness is planned:
    It's from the Maker's wisdom and command.
Young man, don't call it wretched, for it may   3705
    Yet be a star that brings good luck your way!
Deem it the root, not a mere branch, so you
    May always reach your goal in what you do:
If you deem it a branch and as malignant
    Your eyes will hold out for the root, expectant:
Waiting expectantly's a waste of breath—
    Living like that keeps you always in death.
Deem it the root and hold it close, to be
    Delivered from death by expectancy.

The Sultan Mahmud praises Ayaz.

'Ayaz, so humble, with sincerity—   3710
    Yours is more than the mountain and the sea.
When lust should come to you, you still don't stumble:
    Your mountain-strong intelligence won't crumble.
Neither in spite and anger's time do you
    Lose some forbearance as most others do.'
Penis and beard don't give one manliness,
    Or else the crown's for donkeys' penises!
Based on the way God speaks in the Qur'an
    How can a body signify a 'man'?
What value have the souls of animals?   3715
    Take a look when you pass the butchers' stalls:
So many heads are placed on tripe like that,
    All worth less than a tail with all its fat.
Only whoremongers, due to stiff erections,
    Let reason be a mouse and lusts all lions.

A father advises his daughter to prevent her husband from getting her pregnant.

A noble man once had a daughter who
    Was radiant-faced and silver-breasted too.
He found a husband once she was mature
    But that man wasn't good enough for sure.
If you don't cut it when it's ripe you'll see   3720
    Your melon will be far too watery:
Out of necessity he gave his daughter,
    For fear of sinful acts, to one below her:
'Guard yourself from your husband!' he had said,
    'So you do not get pregnant, though you've wed
The beggar as a sad necessity—
    One can't count on a stranger's loyalty.
Abandoning all, he might leave suddenly
    And his child stay as an iniquity.'
The daughter said, 'Father, I will obey.   3725
    I value all the good advice you say.'
Every couple of days the father would
    Tell her to take precautions that she should.
The daughter still got pregnant suddenly—
    They were both young, so unsurprisingly—
She hid it and her father wasn't told
    Until the baby had reached six months old.
Once it became quite obvious, her father
    Asked, 'What is this? I warned you not to falter.
All my advice was wasted breath since it   3730
    Has not been beneficial one small bit.'
'How could I guard myself,' she then cried out,
    'Couples are fire and cotton, there's no doubt.
From flames can cotton ever take precaution?
    Or have you seen a fire behave with caution?'
'I warned you not to go near him, not to
    Let that man's semen enter inside you,
That when he climaxes, without delay
    You really need to pull yourself away.'
'How could I guess when he'd ejaculate?   3735
    That is too hard for one to estimate.'

He said, 'The moment his eyes should dilate
    That means he's going to ejaculate.'
She said, 'By the time his dilated, mine
    Turned blind, O father—I could see no sign!'
Not every intellect stays steadfast, friends,
    When anger, lust, or violence descends.

*Description of the faintheartedness and weakness of a Sufi brought
up in comfort, who has never struggled and has never experienced
    the pain and burning of love, having become deluded by the
prostrating and hand-kissing of the common folk and their looking
    at him with veneration and pointing at him to say, 'This is the
    Sufi.' He has become deluded and sick through imaginings like
    that teacher whom the children told that he was ill.* Falsely
    imagining 'I am a warrior and a hero', he has gone on raids
    with soldiers, and said, 'I'll show my outward skills too. I am
    unrivalled in the Greater Jihad, so how can the Lesser Jihad
be difficult for me?'* He has seen the false image of a lion and has
    done feats of bravery and become intoxicated with that bravery,
    heading to the jungle to find a lion. The lion mystically says,
    'Now you will find out, and again you will find out.'**

A Sufi joined an army readily.
    The battle's clamour rose up suddenly.
With wounded men and baggage he stayed back   3740
    While horsemen rode ahead for the attack:
The heavy, earthbound ones stayed, while instead
    The *foremost of the foremost** rode ahead.
After victorious combat they returned
    With spoils of war and profits they had earned.
They gave the Sufi something: 'Here's your pay!'
    Refusing it, he just threw it away.
They asked him, 'Why so angry and uptight?'
    He said, 'I was denied the chance to fight.'
He wasn't pleased with their kind gesture, for   3745
    He hadn't drawn a dagger in the war.
They then told him, 'Here is a prisoner
    Whom we've brought back—kill him if you prefer!
Chop off his head and be a warrior too!'

The Sufi felt encouraged; his joy grew.
Water's best for ablution, but you can
    Use sand instead if you have none, good man.*
The Sufi led the tied-up prisoner
    Past all the tents, to play the warrior.
He stayed then with the captive for so long   3750
    The others said, 'He's been some time. What's wrong?
A tied-up infidel is ready now
    To be killed, so why take time anyhow?'
One of them went to find out: there he found
    The prisoner over him while on the ground
Like a male lion on a lioness:
    The captive on the Sufi's back no less!
With hands tied he was biting furiously
    The Sufi warrior's throat, and he could see
While he was biting in ways that were vicious   3755
    The Sufi sprawled beneath was now unconscious.
The infidel, with hands bound, like a cat
    Had cut his throat without a knife like that:
With his own teeth he had half-killed the Sufi
    Whose bleeding throat had made his beard all bloody.
At the hands of your hands-bound carnal soul
    You play the base and witless Sufi's role.
You whose path can't ascend a little hill,
    A million mountains lie before you still.
You're scared stiff of this little ridge's slope,   3760
    So, at the mountain's peak, how will you cope?

The warrior killed the infidel then quickly
    With a sword, zealously and with no pity.
They poured rose water on the Sufi's head
    To wake him up as he lay there half-dead.
He saw the group once he woke up and they
    Asked him, 'What happened to you there today?
What was the problem, our dear friend? Please share
    How you became unconsciousness over there?
Did you become like that, sprawled on the ground   3765
    Due to a half-killed captive with hands bound?'

'When I stretched to chop off that captive's head
  He looked at me in an odd way,' he said.
'He opened his eyes till they were enormous,
  Then rolled them scarily—I fell unconscious.
That rolling of his eyes seemed like an army;
  Words can't describe how much this would alarm me—
To sum it up, the way they rolled around
  Made me lose all my wits and hit the ground.'

*The warriors advised him, 'With such little courage and heart that
you faint at the rolling of the eyes by an infidel captive whose hands
are bound, such that the dagger falls from your hand, be wary and
stay in the khaniqah's kitchen rather than go to the battle, so you
will avoid being embarrassed!'*

The group said, 'Don't approach the battle now   3770
  With a weak stomach like yours anyhow!
Since you got so drunk through that captive's eyes
  Your ship was wrecked, it would be no surprise
If you then fail with rampant lions instead
  Whose swords treat like a ball the foe's chopped head.
How can you swim in blood when you still lack
  A man's experience of how to attack?
The sound of chopping necks drowns out the sound
  Of washers slamming heavy clothes around.
The headless bodies jerk still in their struggles   3775
  While chopped heads float on blood just like big bubbles.
Trampled by legs of horses one can see
  Hundreds of fighters die immediately.
Someone who flees a mouse can't draw a sword
  In battle lines against a murderous horde.
It's war, not supping broth, so please don't think
  You need just roll your sleeves to have a drink.
Don't sup soup—find a sword to use today!
  We need an iron Hamza in this fray.*
It's not for the fainthearted one to kill—   3780
  A fake man flees unreal illusions still.
The man's work's not for women, so beware—
  Women belong at home—you'd best stay there!'

Story about Eyazi, who took part in seventy holy wars bare-chested
in the hope of becoming martyred. Once he lost hope in that
happening, he turned from the Lesser Jihad to the Greater Jihad,*
choosing seclusion. Suddenly he heard the sound of holy warriors
and his self inside him pulled its chain to go and fight, but he grew
suspicious of his self and its desiring this.

'I came to battle naked,' said Eyazi,
   'Ninety times to get wounded very quickly.
I went towards the arrows in the air
   So one would pierce me, and I didn't care.
None but the fortunate martyr will get struck
   By arrows in a vital part. Such luck!
No body part's stayed woundless, but I live   3785
   Though arrows made them much more like a sieve.
The arrows didn't strike a vital part
   Due to luck, not through shrewdness on my part:
Since being martyred wasn't meant to be
   I started a retreat immediately—
The Greater Jihad's what I undertook:
   My body thinned due to its hardships—look!
I'd hear the drums of warriors start their banging
   Each time the warriors' army would start marching.
My self would shout from deep within—I'd hear   3790
   It in the early morning with my ear:
"It's time for holy wars, so stand upright
   And busy yourself now in the great fight!"
"O wretched, faithless self," I answered back,
   "How far you are from yearning to attack!
Speak truthfully that it's a trick today!
   I know the carnal soul does not obey.
If you don't tell the truth then I will hit you
   And force on you more discipline and tests too."
The self cried out at this immediately   3795
   Without a mouth, but still deceitfully:
"You kill me here each day, as you know well,
   Torturing me like I'm an infidel.
No one knows my condition under you:
   You kill me with no sleep and no food too.

One blow in war enables me to flee
    Your body and show off my bravery."
"O wretched soul, you hypocrite!" I said,
    "You lived as one and as one you'll be dead:
A show-off in both worlds, so ostentatious;   3800
    In both worlds you were also clearly pointless.
I vowed not to leave my retreat while I
    Still have a living body, till I die,
Because what it does while in this seclusion
    Is not for any person's eye's attention:
In this retreat, its movement and its stillness
    Are only for God's sake—He's the sole witness.'

This is the Greater Jihad, that the lesser,*
    Both for a Rostam or Ali-like warrior,
Not for the one whose wits will flee his body   3805
    When a mere mouse's tail moves very slowly—
That one must stay, like women, far from here,
    The battlefield with weapons like the spear.
Both are called 'Sufi', though it's understood:
    One's killed by needles, one eats swords as food.
The former's just the surface of a Sufi
    And gives a bad name to those who are truly.
Possessively, God etched their forms this way
    Upon the human body's house of clay,
So such forms would move magically about,   3810
    But Moses's rod still stay veiled throughout—
The rod's truth eats the former easily,
    Though Pharaoh's eyes have too much dust to see.*

Another Sufi twenty times would go
    To battles to receive blow after blow,
Fighting with Muslims infidels, but he
    Would not retreat with them so readily—
He bandaged his own wound and was soon back
    Fighting the foes with a renewed attack,
So that one cheap blow wouldn't kill his body,   3815

But in the battle he'd be struck by forty:
For him to die with one blow would be awful,
That his soul should leave easily one so truthful.

*Story about that holy warrior who every day would take out a
dirham coin from a purse of silver and throw it separately into a
ditch in order to battle his carnal soul's greed and desire. His carnal
soul tempted him by saying, 'Since you are throwing them into the
ditch, throw them all at once so that I can be relieved, for despair is
one of two reliefs.' He said, 'I won't give you this relief either.'*

A man had forty dirhams in possession
　　Each night he'd throw one of them in the ocean,
So it would give his carnal soul more stress,
　　The agony drawn out by this process.
He would advance with Muslims to attack,
　　But at retreat's hour he would not rush back—
He'd get another wound and wrap that too;　　　3820
　　Arrows and spears by him were split in two.
Once all strength left him he'd fall finally
　　On *Truth's Seat** due to his sincerity.
Sincerity's to give up life, so heed:
　　'*Excel the others!*' Read: '*Those true indeed.*'*
All of this death is not just outwardly—
　　Body's a tail for spirit if you see:
Blood has been spilled by many a raw one
　　Just outwardly while his soul has lived on—
Its tool broke, but the brigand was still living;　　　3825
　　The soul lives on although its steed is bleeding.
The horse was killed before they made the journey
　　And he became thus raw, disturbed, and ugly.
If martyrs are made every time men bleed
　　Dead infidels would match Abu Sa'eed.*
So many trusted martyred souls are moving
　　Around the world the same way as the living.
The brigand's soul died, but his sword will stay
　　Held in another killer's hands today:
The sword's the same although the man is new,　　　3830
　　But its appearance still perplexes you.

When the soul is transformed the body's sword
    Stays under the control of the Kind Lord.
A real man is the one who feeds on suffering;
    Others are empty like the dust, worth nothing.

*An informer describes a girl and shows a portrait of her on paper to
the Caliph of Egypt, who falls in love with her and sends a
commander with a huge army to Mosul where they wreak much
destruction and slaughter many for the sake of his aim.*

Egypt's Caliph was told by an informer:
    'Mosul's king married a young houri stunner:
He has a gorgeous maid now by his side
    Who can't be matched though one search far and wide.
Beyond all words, her beauty has no limit—   3835
    Here is some paper with her portrait on it.'
That Kaiqobad-like monarch* saw the portrait,
    Grew mesmerized and even dropped his goblet.
He sent to Mosul a fine leader then
    With a huge army of so many men:
'If he won't give up that fair one to you
    Destroy his palace and his whole court too!
If he complies, leave him alone and take her,
    So I can finally lie down and embrace her!'
So off to Mosul went the famed commander   3840
    With numerous men and many a drum and banner.
The thousands were like locusts swarming wheat,
    Heading to give that city's men defeat.
He used a mangonel on every side
    As big as Mount Qaf for the war he plied.
Arrows and rocks would wound so many fighting
    And swords flashed through the dust like bolts of lightning.
They kept on spilling blood for a whole week.
    Stone towers, like soft wax, became so weak.
Mosul's king saw the war's atrocity   3845
    Then sent an envoy there immediately
To ask, 'Why spill believers' blood so badly?
    There's so much killing—this war's toll's huge sadly.
If you desire possession of this city

It can be yours without the bloodshed's cruelty.
I'll simply leave and you can take possession
    And never be avenged for your oppression.
And if your wish is riches, jewels, and gold
    That's easier than the city to be sold.'

The ruler of Mosul sacrifices that maid to the Caliph so that the
bloodshed of Muslims would not continue.

Their envoy met the army's great commander   3850
    And then received the portrait from the latter:
'Look at this paper! We want her,' he said,
    'Give her or I'll take over now as head!'
The envoy went back to his king—his order:
    'Don't overrate form. Take her to the border!
In true faith's time I'm no idolater—
    She suits much more that idol-worshipper.'
The envoy took her to him hurriedly
    And he then fell in love immediately.
Love is a sea, the heavens foam on it—   3855
    Zolaikha's love for Joseph showed us it:
Love's passion makes the heavens turn above;
    The heavens would be lifeless without love:
How should inert things die in plants, good men?
    And plants self-sacrifice for spirit? Then
How should the spirit for that Breath which made
    Mary get pregnant with no human aid?*
Each wouldn't move like ice—how could they fly
    Like locusts when they need what's not nearby?
Atoms are lovers of perfection and   3860
    They all rush up as saplings rise from land—
Their rush says '*Glory to God!*' and their role's
    To cleanse the bodies for the sake of souls.

The army chief deemed a mere pit the road:
    He thought that barren soil was good and sowed.
The dreamer saw an image, copulated
    With her in sleep and then ejaculated—

But when he woke up he became aware
   The plaything from dreams was no longer there:
'I came for nothing—O alas!' he said,   3865
   'A shame I fell for that flirtatious maid.'
This army chief was just the body's champion,
   Not manly, sowing seeds in land so barren.
His love's steed tore its bridle and let fly:
   He yelled, 'I'm not concerned that I might die!
Why should I care about the Caliph now?
   Love makes my life and death the same somehow.'
Don't sow with heat and ardour in this manner—
   Instead seek the advice of a true master!
What's reason and advice when love's flood's growth   3870
   Extends its talons to destroy them both?
'*In front a barrier, and one more behind*'*—
   Besotted minds don't see front or behind.
The torrent's come to kill him with its spell
   And thus a fox can throw lions down a well:*
Inside it a false image tricks the eye,
   So it brings down a lion of massive size.
Don't let men near the women out of caution,
   For man and woman are like sparks and cotton.
Such fire's quenched by God's water, nothing less: 3875
   Joseph stayed chaste thus, facing wickedness,
Stepping back like a lion from Zolaikha
   Despite her cypress-like, attractive figure.

They went from Mosul and camped at a spot
   Near woods and meadows—he was feeling hot
From love's fire that was blazing now so high
   He could no longer tell earth from the sky.
Inside his tent he reached out for that sweet one—
   Where was fear of the Caliph or his reason?
When lust should beat drums in the valley, then   3880
   Your reason's like a flimsy radish, men.
A hundred Caliphs seemed less than a fly
   Right at that moment to his flame-filled eye.
Once he had pulled his trousers off and lay

Between this woman's legs, then straight away
His penis started pressing her arse firmly,
  But then commotion rose among the army—
He jumped up naked and went to the horde
  Holding in his hand a fierce, fiery sword.
He saw a wild black lion now attack   3885
  The army's centre without holding back.
Like demons all the horses now grew manic,
  Stables and tents in chaos due to panic.
That lion jumped from distance frighteningly
  High in the air like billows of the sea.
The army chief was fearless now and valiant,
  Nearing the lion, like a drunk, so violent:
With his big sword he calmly sliced its head
  And rushed back to the fair maid in his bed.
Once he appeared again to her, his member   3890
  Was still erect the way she could remember:
He'd fought a lion yet this man could keep
  His penis still erect and not asleep.
That lovely, fair-faced idol instantly
  Was mesmerized by his virility.
She lustfully had sex with him and they
  Were two souls joined as one in a strong way.
And through the union of these souls together
  From the Unseen there soon would come another:
Through being born it comes forth without question   3895
  As long as nothing waylays its conception.
Whenever two should join so they can mate
  A third is born, whether it's love or hate.
Such forms are born, though in the Unseen realm—
  When you go there you will see all of them.
They're your relationships' own progeny—
  Don't celebrate each partner hastily!
Be wary, wait until the time it's due—
  Know that '*the offspring shall all join*'* is true,
For they are born from acts and causes, so   3900
  Each has its form and speech, which you should know.
Their cries arrive from lovely reaches: 'You
  Who did forget us—come without ado!

Men's and women's souls are kept waiting—why?
  Walk much more quickly to arrive on high!'
On that false dawn the captain went astray,
  Falling in milk like flies who've lost their way.

The army chief regrets the sin he committed and makes the maid swear not to tell the Caliph what happened.

For a few days the chief stayed in this way,
  But then regretted their big sin that day.
He made her swear, 'O fair face like the sun,   3905
  Don't give the Caliph hints of what we've done!'
The Caliph got drunk when he saw this woman:
  A bowl fell off his roof all of a sudden.
She was to him more pretty than he'd heard:
  Seeing is more than hearing someone's word.
Description forms a picture in the mind;
  Appearance is for eyes not ears, you'll find.
A man asked a great speaker, 'Make it clearer
  What truth and falsehood are, respected speaker!'
He grabbed his ear: 'This is false actually.   3910
  The eye is truth and it gains certainty.
The former's false compared next to the latter;
  Most sayings are this way, friend, for that matter.'
A bat might screen itself from that bright sun,
  But not from the idea of the sun,
And that idea alone will scare it too,
  Driving it to the darkness out of view:
The thought of light alone gives it such fright
  So it prefers the darkness of the night.
It's due to the idea of your foe   3915
  That you stick close to the good friends you know.
Moses, your revelation shone down there
  On Sinai, but too much for it to bear.*
Don't be deluded and imagine you
  Can through the image reach the real thing too.
Men don't fear warfare's image on its own:
  '*Before war there's no bravery*', it's known.
Based on an image of what an attack is

The weak try, like Rostam, to make advances.
Rostam's mere portrait on a bathhouse wall 　　　3920
　　Is their view of a comrade in a brawl.
When hearsay's seen for real what will they do?
　　An actual Rostam would feel bound then too.
Strive so it moves from ear to eye for you
　　So what was false before becomes now true.
Your ears will join your eyes and they will be
　　Each turned into a jewel incredibly.
Then your whole body will become a mirror,
　　All eye and that jewel in your breast. Thereafter
Your ear will raise imaginings and they 　　　3925
　　Will serve as go-betweens on union's way.
Strive to make these imaginings grow soon
　　So go-betweens can be guides for Majnun.

The foolish Caliph was for a while smitten
　　And grew infatuated with that woman.
Nowhere from East to West do empires last—
　　They're like a lightning flash which soon has passed.
You whose heart sleeps—the kingdom that won't last
　　Is merely like a dream: it soon has passed.
What do you want with all its pomp and glory? 　　　3930
　　It grabs your throat like executioners. Hurry,
Even in this world there is a safe spot—
　　Don't heed the hypocrites who claim there's not!

*The proof of the deniers of the next world and an explanation
of its weakness, since their arguments amount to: 'We do not see
any other world.'*

The proof of the deniers: 'If there really
　　Were something else, we would have seen already.'
If children can't see reason totally
　　Should it be something rational men should flee?
If rational men can't see some sides of love
　　Still there's no waning in love's moon above.
Joseph's brothers did not see handsomeness 　　　3935

In him, but Jacob's eyes saw nothing less.*
The rod was wood in Moses's own eyes—
    The Unseen eye saw a wild snake surprise.*
Outward and inward eyes engaged in battle;
    The heart's eye won and showed proof that could settle.
Moses's hand was just that in his sight,
    To the Unseen's eye though it was pure light.*
This discourse cannot here reach termination.
    To one deprived, it's mere imagination:
Gullet and balls are his realities,   3940
    So don't share the Beloved's mysteries!
We see as trivial throats and testicles
    So the soul shows us gorgeous spectacles.
To testicles and gullet, lovers say:
    '*To you your faith, to me mine*'* come what may.
Ahmad,* don't argue with denial—abort it!
    Talking with infidels is just not worth it.

The Caliph comes to that pretty maid's side in order to have sex.

The Caliph wanted to have sex and so
    He went towards the maid to let her know.
Remembering her gave him a stiff erection;   3945
    He longed to hump that cause of love's expansion.
Once he lay down between her legs, by fate
    His pleasure's opening quickly slammed its gate:
A mouse's scratching reached his ears and then
    His penis grew limp and lust fled again.
He thought a snake had made the noise, one that
    Was moving rapidly beneath a mat.

The maid starts to laugh at the weakness of the Caliph's lust and the strength of the Captain's lust, and the Caliph understands her laughter.

The woman laughed when it turned limp and she
    In utter shock laughed uncontrollably.
She then recalled the Captain's manliness: 3950
    He'd killed a lion, stayed firm nonetheless!

The woman's laughter went on endlessly;
    She couldn't close her lips incredibly:
She laughed so hard as if she'd got high on it;
    Her laughter blocked all thought of loss or profit.
Any new thought made her laugh even more
    As when a floodgate opens up the door.
Crying, laughter, sadness, and joy—of course
    Each of them has an independent source:
Each is a treasury—keys are in the hand   3955
    Of that One Opener, brother—understand!
That laughter wouldn't stop as she wished badly.
    The Caliph therefore grew more harsh and angry.
He drew his sword from its sheath then, demanding:
    Tell me your laughter's secret! Why this laughing?
The laughter's made my heart suspicious—tell me
    The truth! You can't by other means placate me,
If you try to deceive me with a lie
    Or bring a cheap excuse—I'll know, for I
Have deep inside my heart a special light,   3960
    So you must tell me what is true tonight!
There is a bright moon in each king's heart, though
    Forgetting's cloud may cover it below:
There is a lamp inside the heart, O lover,
    Though lust and rage can spoil it like a cover.
I have clairvoyance in my heart now, so
    If you don't tell the truth I seek to know
I'll chop your neck off with this sword—say it!
    Making excuses has no benefit.
If you tell me the truth, I'll set you free—   3965
    I swear to God you will live happily.'
Seven Qur'ans he then brought there together
    And swore to God he wouldn't break this ever.

The maid discloses the secret to the Caliph in fear of the sword's
blow and due to being bound to the Caliph who said: 'Tell me the
truth about the cause of this laughter or I will kill you!'

Since she had no choice she disclosed then all:
    The manliness of that Rostam of Zal.

She shared facts with the Caliph one by one:
　　The bride chamber where it had all begun,
The lion's killing and his coming back
　　With penis hard still after his attack
Like rhino horns, and then the shameful weakness   3970
　　Of a mouse causing his soft, drooping penis.

God reveals secrets, making them all known—
　　Don't sow bad seeds for they'll be seen once grown:
Water, clouds, fire, and the hot sun will raise
　　The secrets from the soil through nature's ways.
The new spring comes, succeeding the fall too—
　　It's proof that Resurrection's claim is true.
All of the secrets will in spring be shown;
　　Whatever soil's consumed will then be known:
It comes out from its mouth and lips to all,   3975
　　So that its thoughts and path are visible.
Every tree's roots and food, which are concealed,
　　Eventually on the treetop are revealed.
Each grief that brings pain to your heart reached there
　　Through wine you drank, but you are unaware
From which wine that pain has arrived in you
　　Out of all of the wines you've drunk, aren't you?
The hangover's the blossom of a seed—
　　One who knows is a visionary indeed.
Blossom and branch don't look like seeds, but then   3980
　　Sperm doesn't look like bodies of grown men:
Material doesn't look like product now—
　　How can the seeds resemble trees somehow?
Man's sperm is made by bread, and yet they differ:
　　Men come from sperm, although they aren't similar.
Jinn are from fire, but don't resemble that;*
　　Clouds are from vapour, but don't look like that.
Though Gabriel's breath made Jesus, one can't claim
　　That in their form the two are just the same.
Man's made of clay, but doesn't look that way;   3985
　　Grapes don't resemble their own vines, do they?
How can theft look like gallows to one's eyes,

Obedience like eternal paradise?
Sources aren't like their products—that is why
    Pain's source can be hard to identify.
There always is a cause for punishment,
    For how could God hurt one who's innocent.
The source and what leads to it actually
    Caused it, though there's no similarity.
Your pain comes from a lapse—heed this with trust!   3990
    And its affliction is due to your lust.
Though you can't work out which sin, hurriedly
    Seek God's forgiveness with humility.
Prostrate, repeating: 'God, my suffering is
    Not more than what I'm due for trespasses.
Free from injustice, You're magnificent—
    How could you hurt a soul that's innocent?
Though I don't know with accuracy which sin,
    Sin must have been what made this pain begin.
Since you concealed the cause from my reflection   3995
    This means you'll save my sin from eyes' detection.
Though I deserve to have my sins now shown,
    Punishing me would make them too well known.'

*When the monarch learns of the treachery he resolves to conceal it
and forgive her, then give her to his captain. He knows that this
trouble is what he deserves and is due to his intention and unjust
treatment of the ruler of Mosul, for 'Whoever does evil, it falls
back on him',* and 'Your Lord is watching.'* The monarch fears
that if he should seek revenge instead, that vengeance would fall
back on his own head the same way that the injustice and lust
already had.*

The monarch came to his wits, begged forgiveness,
    Recalling his past sins and obstinateness:
'What I have done to others has now earned
    My soul a punishment. That's what I've learned.
I sought another's spouse out of ambition
    And fell inside a pit from retribution:
I'd knocked on someone else's door, so he   4000
    Knocked back on my door so deservedly.

Seeking to have sex with another's wife
   Is actually pimping out your own dear wife:
Suffering the same is what that earns, you see—
   A bad deed earns the same back equally.
You've instigated and drawn also to
   Yourself the same: you are a cuckold too!

The king thought, 'I, by force, took that king's maid
   Then she was seized from me too, so I've paid.
My treachery made my trusted friend and servant   4005
   Treacherous also—my own act was no different.
It's no occasion for revenge from me—
   I did this to myself: naivety!
If I avenge the maid and my commander
   This new sin will come back to haunt me after,
Just as what happened was for my own crime—
   I've tried her and won't do it one more time.
Mosul's king's grief has broken my neck—how
   Should I attack this other person now?
God's let us know the recompense that's due: 4010
   "*If you repeat, we will repeat it too.*"*
Since adding any more is pointless now
   Patience and mercy are appropriate now.
"*Lord, we've transgressed!*":* we lapsed and it's on us.
   Your mercy's huge—have mercy now on us!
I have forgiven, so please pardon me
   The new sin and the errors previously!'
He told her, 'Slave girl, don't you give away
   To others what I have just heard you say!
I'll pair you with that champion once again—   4015
   By God don't tell this tale to other men,
So he won't be far too ashamed to face me.
   He did one bad thing; his good deeds are many.
I've tested him before so often too:
   I've put in his care those more fair than you
And found that I could trust him totally.
   For bad things I've done, this was God's decree.'

He summoned the commander to his side
    And cooled the vengeful anger deep inside,
Then gave him an excuse convincingly: 4020
    'I've turned off this new slave-girl suddenly.
The mother of my child now boils with anger
    Stemming from jealousy that I acquired her—
I owe her: she deserves much more from me
    Than to be treated now so terribly.
She's feeling jealous and this makes her suffer;
    The slave-girl's presence makes her feel so bitter.
I want to give the slave-girl to another
    And you, my friend, more than the rest deserve her.
You risked your life to bring her here, so to   4025
    Choose someone else would be unfair to you.'
He later married her to his commander,
    Crushing in this way both his lust and anger.

Explaining that 'we allotted' means that He gives one the lust
and strength of donkeys and another the wisdom and
strength of Prophets and angels.
Turning away from lust shows excellence:
Doing this showed the Prophets' eminence.
The fruit of seeds that were lust-free when sown
Only at Resurrection will be known.*

That king lacked donkeys' kind of machoness,
    But not the Prophets' kind of manliness.
It's manly and resembling a true Prophet
    To quit your lust and rage and never covet.
The donkeys' manliness can be left out.
    God called him 'Great Commander Sir' without.
To have God look at me though I be dead   4030
    Beats being alive but far from Him instead.
Tell manliness's kernel from its shell;
    Instead of paradise lust leads to hell.
The Prophet said, '*Hardship's surrounding heaven
While hell's surrounded by your lust and passion.*'

O Ayaz, you fierce lion and demon-slayer,
    True wisdom's manliness in you is greater.
Many great men could not see what for you,
    The real man, was so easily in view.
You felt the pleasure of obeying me   4035
    And gave your life for its sake loyally.
Listen to this next tale on the delight
    When you obey me, seen through mystic light!

The king at a meeting in his court puts a pearl in the hand of the
vizier, asking: 'How much is it worth?' The vizier says a very high
price and the king tells him, 'Crush it!' The vizier says, 'How
could I break it?' and so forth.

One day the king rushed to his court and found
    All of his closest courtiers gathered round.
He took a radiant pearl out and then quickly
    Placed it on the vizier's hand and asked, 'Tell me
What is this pearl's worth, if the truth be told?'
    'More than a hundred donkey loads of gold.'
He ordered, 'Crush it!' 'How can I when I   4040
    Want all your treasuries' net worth to stay high?
How could I let a pearl that's priceless be
    Wasted like that by doing your decree?'
The king said, 'Bravo! Here's a robe of honour',
    And took the pearl back to give to another.
The generous king gave that vizier all clothing
    And robes that he had previously been using.
He then engaged them all in conversations
    About old puzzles and new situations,
Placed that pearl in the chamberlain's hand, then   4045
    'What is this fine pearl worth?' he asked again.
'It is worth half a kingdom in my view.
    May God protect it well from damage too!'
The king said, 'Crush it!' 'King, with your sword blazing,
    To crush this radiant pearl would be heartbreaking.
Not just its value, look at it shine bright—
    It's brighter than the sunniest day's light.
How should my hand break that? How should I be

An enemy of the king's treasury?'
The king gave him a robe too, raised his pay,   4050
  Then praised his wisdom with the things he'd say.
The king who did this testing at his palace
  Next gave it to the Minister of Justice.
He asked the same thing he had done before
  And he bestowed a sought out robe once more.
It seemed the king was raising each one's pay,
  But really he was leading off the way.
Fifty-odd ministers spoke the same way
  As the vizier from earlier in the day.
Though the world's based on copying, all the same,   4055
  Once tested, imitation's put to shame.

*The pearl passing from hand to hand finally comes to Ayaz's hand,
showing his wisdom and refusal to imitate them or become beguiled
by the king's giving them riches and robes of honour, increasing their
salaries and praising their intellects. One should not consider the
imitator a Muslim, as it is very rare for the imitator to hold
strongly to his conviction and come through the trials soundly, for
he does not have the firm resolve of mystics, except those whom
God keeps pure. This is because The Truth is One and Its
opposite may look similar, but is really very misleading. Since the
imitator does not recognize the opposite, he cannot really have
come to know God. However, despite his not knowing Him,
God looks after the likes of him with His grace, so that ignorance
of his does not harm him.*

The king then turned to Ayaz, 'Now I ask you
  To tell me what's this radiant pearl's true value?'
Ayaz then answered, 'More than I can say.'
  The king said, 'Crush it to bits straight away!'
He crushed it with some rocks that he'd brought there
  As that seemed the best course for one aware.
Because of his auspicious star's concurrence
  Rare wisdom helped him in this strange occurrence,
Or maybe that pure one'd dreamt of this case   4060
  And therefore brought two big rocks to this place,

Like Joseph at the bottom of the well,
  To whom God showed the outcome none could tell.*

Success and failure are seen equally
  By those whom God has told of victory.
For one who's joined to God forever, why
  Should combat and defeat still terrify?
Losing a knight and bishop is so trivial
  When one knows that check-mate will be successful:
If someone takes your knight, that is no shame   4065
  Since it is not required to win the game.
A man can't love a horse like his own kin,
  His love for it is to advance and win.
Don't suffer pain just for a mere form's sake!
  Seize the deep meaning free from form's vile ache!
Ascetics worry for their final fate
  When Judgement Day arrives and it's too late.
Mystics have grown wise over their beginnings
  And so they don't feel stress about their endings.
That fear and hope was felt by mystics too,   4070
  But knowledge of the past consumed those two:
Knowing that he has sowed beans previously,
  The mystic knows what will grow finally.
A mystic, he's fled fear and hope's emotion—
  God's sword has sliced in two all the commotion.
He did have fear and hope from God before—
  Fear faded, hope came clearly to the fore.

Once Ayaz crushed that pearl as ordered to
  The ministers raised a hullabalo
'What utter lack of feeling! We can tell   4075
  Whoever crushed it is an infidel.'
That whole group through sheer ignorance had broken
  The pearl of the command the king had spoken:
That costly pearl, the fruit of love's affection—
  Why was that veiled from those men's minds' perception?

How the ministers reproached Ayaz, saying: 'Why did he crush it?'
and Ayaz's answer to them.

Ayaz said, 'Noble men, is the king's order
   More precious or the pearl you worry over?
The ruler's order or that pearl—which one
   Is better in your view? Speak everyone!
Drawn to the pearl and not the king today,   4080
   Your prayer niche faces ghouls, not the true way.
I won't turn back from our king my own face
   Towards a stone like polytheists—disgrace!'
Any soul choosing coloured stones before
   A king lacks jewels in its inner store.
Turn away from the rosy plaything, brother!
   Make reason stunned in Him who gives all colour!
Come to the stream, slam your jug on a stone!
   Ditch scents and colours for That One alone!
If on faith's path you aren't a waylayer too   4085
   Don't worship them the way that women do!

The nobles cast their heads down all at once,
   Seeking forgiveness for their negligence.
From each one's heart there rose a massive sigh
   Like smoke that's rising upwards to the sky.
The king then told his whipper: 'They are base
   So take them far from this distinguished place!
How can base ones deserve it? Their mistake
   Was shunning my command for a stone's sake.
By this corrupt sort my wish was ignored   4090
   Due to a coloured stone, which they adored.'

The king intends to kill the ministers and Ayaz intercedes for them
before the royal throne, saying: 'To forgive is better.'

That loving Ayaz then all of a sudden
   Sprang forwards to the throne of that great sultan,
Prostrated, cleared his throat, then begged and praised:
   'O king, by whom the heavens are amazed,

The heavens gain from you auspiciousness.
    You're chivalry of all the chivalrous:
The generous acts that all the rest have done
    Are all effaced before you, generous one.
O fine one, whom the red rose saw before   4095
    And then, in shame, tore off the shirt it wore.
Forgiveness is content with your own pardon
    And, through your pardon, fox defeats the lion.
What can support a person who is heedless
    Of your command apart from your forgiveness?
Their disrespect and heedlessness are due
    To your pardon—forgiving's mine is you.
Negligence comes from brazenness, while reverence
    Is all that can cure sick eyes in this instance.
The heedlessness and disrespect they've learned   4100
    In flames of reverence will get quickly burned.'

Awe of God gives one wisdom's wakefulness
    And rids the heart of lax forgetfulness.
No one will sleep while they're under attack
    In case their cloak is swiped behind their back—
When fear of losing cloaks does this, how then
    Can one sleep when one's throat's at risk again?
'*Don't punish us if we forget!*' * is telling:
    It shows that negligence is somehow sinning.
It means he wasn't totally respectful   4105
    Or else he'd not have lost by being neglectful.
Though negligence was fully necessary
    And not avoidable, his choice was free,
For he was lax in acts of reverence
    And from this came wrongdoing, negligence.
He's like a drunk who sins then makes the claim:
    'I'd lost my wits so I'm excused from blame',
But he is told, 'You caused it; it's on you:
    You lost your will power with the things you'd do.
Your wits did not leave on their own, nor too   4110
    Your will power—they were ordered both by you.'
If drunkenness came outside your control

It would be from the Saqi of the soul—
  He would have backed you and he would have said:
    'I am the slave of God's true drunk' instead.
All of forgiveness one finds in this sphere
  Is one mote of Yours, from which all appear.
They're singing praise of Your forgiveness: '*People,*
  Beware that This One truly has no equal.'
Grant them their lives! Don't banish them, for they   4115
  Desire fulfiller, want you—let them stay!
Be merciful on those who've seen your face—
  How can they bear an exile from your place?
You talk of separation—you can do
  What you wish, but not that I beg of you!
A million bitter, six-fold deaths hurt less
  Than exile from Your face in terms of stress.
Keep exile's bitterness from men and women!
  Sinners appeal to You for help, so listen!
Death's sweet in hope of union with You, yes,   4120
  While worse than fire is exile's bitterness.
Among the flames the infidel will say:
  'What pain would I have if He'd looked my way?'
Because that glance can make all pains taste sweet,
  The blood-price for magicians' hands and feet:

Exegesis of the words of Pharaoh's magicians when they were
*punished: 'There's no harm for us. We are heading to our Lord.'**

The heavens heard, '*There's no harm*'* and at that
  They turned into a ball just for that bat.
'God's grace prevails above the wrath of others.
  So Pharaoh's punishment can't harm us sorcerers:
If you should learn our secret, O deceiver,   4125
  You'd free us from the pain, blindhearted leader.
Beware, come to this side and hear one say:
  "*Would that my people knew!*"* for once today!
God's bounty's given us a leadership
  Different to your own transient pharaohship.
Look up at the grand, living realm a while,
  You who are stunned by Egypt and the Nile!

Abandon now this dirty cloak and you
   Can drown that Nile in the pure soul's Nile too!
Beware, O Pharaoh, and let go of Egypt: 4130
   Scores of Egypts are in the spirit's Egypt.
You say, "*I am lord*"* to your subjects though
   What this word means is something you don't know.
How can "lords" tremble at what they control
   Or "I" be slave to body and to soul?
We are the real "I", free from that false "I"—
   The latter suffers grief as days pass by.
That "I" meant bad luck for you, while ours meant
   For us good fortune that was heaven-sent.'
If you had not had this mean 'I' then would   4135
   Good fortune have arrived which is so good?
In thanks for fleeing temporality
   Upon the gallows we advise for free:
The gallows are your journey's *Boraq*,* and
   Your realm's delusory. Won't you understand?
This is our life—in death's form it's concealed;
   Yours: death which in the husk of life is sealed.
Light seems a fire, and fire light—here's confusion.
   That's why it's called '*the world of mere illusion*.'
Beware, don't rush! Become naught first, and then   4140
   On setting rise up from the East again!
The heart was stunned by the 'Eternal I,'
   But this 'I' is a frigid, shameful 'I'.
Through that I without self, souls feel so glad
   They've left this world's 'I' as if something bad.
They flee this 'I', become an 'I' that's true—
   Bravo to that 'I'! It blocks suffering too.
As it flees, selfhood races after it
   Once it sees it has no self left in it:
If you seek it, it won't seek you just yet—   4145
   It seeks you when you die though, so don't fret!
You are alive—corpse-washers can't wash you.
   You still seek—what you seek can't now seek you.
If intellect could solve such mysteries
   Razi would have the mystic's expertise.*
He was *one who did not taste it to know*;

His intellect's confusion would just grow.
This 'I' can't be unveiled by contemplation—
　　It's just unveiled through self-annihilation.
Intellects fall in their failed quest for it　　4150
　　In incarnation and commingling's pit.*
Ayaz, through nearness you have passed away
　　Just like a star in sunlight of the day,
Like semen you're transmuted bodily,
　　Not duped by incarnation's heresy.

Forgive, You in whose coffer is forgiveness,
　　Whose mercy is the foremost in its kindness.
Yet who am I to say "Forgive!" and plea
　　To You, the Sultan of the order '*Be!*'*
Who am I to exist when You're around,　　4155
　　You in Whose 'I' all I's of ours are found?

Ayaz sees himself as a wrongdoer while intervening and begs
forgiveness for this—he sees himself as doing wrong by begging
forgiveness. This self-abasement comes from recognition of the
majesty of the king, for the Prophet has said, 'I know God better
than you and fear him more than you.' God said, 'Only God's
servants with knowledge really fear Him.'

'How can I make the angry merciful?'
　　Ayaz said, 'Or teach being affable
I now deserve a million slaps, it's true
　　If I'm subjected to those slaps by you.
What can I say before you? Am I free
　　To now remind of generosity?
What is not known to you? Nothing at all.
　　Where can I find a thing you don't recall?
You who are free from ignorance, whose knowledge　　4160
　　Forgetfulness can't hide things from or damage,
You deemed a nobody a somebody:
　　With light you've made him sun-like totally.
Please listen, since you made me somebody,
　　When I beg you for generosity!

Since you removed me from the form that held me
    That intercession was your doing really.
And since this home's been emptied of its "I"
    Nothing that's here belongs to me. That's why.
You made my prayer like water that flows by—   4165
    Please now accept it and give a reply!
You brought about this prayer in the first instance,
    And finally you're the hope for its acceptance.
Forgive for my sake, please, each single thing
    So I can boast about the whole world's king.
I was so smug and pain-filled totally—
    The king made me pain-filled men's remedy.
I was a hell with evil and with dread—
    Grace's hand made me Kawsar-like instead.
Hell burned away with vengeance many men—   4170
    I made them all grow quickly back again.'

What's Kawsar's work? It's letting all burned men
    Grow fully back and be enriched again.
Drop by drop it declares munificence:
    'What hell's consumed I will restore at once.'
Hell is just like the cold that is autumnal,
    O rosegarden, while Kawsar's spring is vernal.
Hell is like death and the grave's soil that fills it—
    Kawsar is like the blast of the last trumpet.
O you whose bodies burned in hell, God rather   4175
    With His deep kindness pulls you to His Kawsar.
Eternal God, since Your Great Mercy told it:
    '*I made them so that through Me they might profit.*'*
'*Not that I profit from them*'* is Your kindness
    Through which deficient ones can realize wholeness.
Forgive these body-worshippers now! Pardoning
    Is better coming from the Sea of Pardoning
Pardon from creatures is like floods and streams.
    Towards the ocean race the horseman teams.
Each night from shredded hearts requests for pardons   4180
    Come heading for You, King, just like the pigeons.
You make them fly away at dawn's first light,

Imprisoning them in bodies till the night,
And then, at night, flapping their wings they fly
  With love for palace rooftops from the sky,
So they can snap the thread that joins them to
  The body, then reach fortune-giving You.
Flapping wings in the air and safe from falling
  Back headlong, saying: '*To Him we're returning.*'*
The call '*Come!*'* comes from That One's generous way,   4185
  Beyond which grief and strong desire won't stay.
'You suffered much in exile on the earth,
  O noble ones, so you'd then know My worth.
Stretch your legs in My tree's shade and quit stress,
  Then here enjoy some lovely drunkenness.
Legs weary from the path of all the faithful,
  Those cared for now by houris who're eternal.
The houris are both kind and flirting, saying:
  These Sufis have returned from their wayfaring.
Sufis as pure as the sun's light, who had   4190
  Fallen on earth and dirt that was so bad.
Both pure and unaffected, they return
  As sunlight heads back to its orb in turn.

'This group of sinners, sir,' Ayaz now says
  'Have all regretted their mistaken ways:
They've realized their faults and sins committed
  Though by the king's dice they had been defeated.
They turn their face to you with sighs today,
  O you whose kindness clears for them the way—
Give soiled ones access to your cleansing places   4195
  And the Euphrates of Your pardon's graces,
So they can wash longstanding sin away
  Then line up with the purest ones to pray,
Among those ranks that can't be counted up,
  Immersed in the light of "*We're those lined up.*"'*

When all this discourse reached such a description
  The pen broke and the paper ripped—can someone

Measure with just a saucer the vast sea,
    And can lambs carry lions easily?
If you are veiled, stop being veiled so you   4200
    Can see the Marvellous King then in plain view.
That drunk group smashed Your goblet, but those who
    Are drunk on You can still be pardoned too.
Their drunkenness on wealth and luck in fact
    Came from Your wine, You who're sweet in each act.
They're drunk on Your own picking them for favour—
    Forgive those drunk on You please, O Forgiver.
A hundred vats of wine still can't compare
    With being addressed by You—such joy is rare.
You made me drunk, so don't now punish me   4205
    Because the law does not think drunks should be!
Inflict it when I sober up, for I
    Will never sober up until I die!
Whoever's drunk, Bestower, from Your cup
    Is free from punishment and sobering up,
Forever drunk from self-annihilation;
    None come back once effaced in Your elation.
Your grace says, 'Go, you who have wagered now
    Yourself in My love's yoghurt drink somehow:
You've fallen in my yoghurt like a gnat—   4210
    Not drunk, you are the wine itself like that.'
Gnat, vultures will get drunk on you when you
    Ride on that honey's sea the way you do.
Mountains are mere motes when they're drunk on you;
    You hold the point, the compass, and line too.
You make upheaval others fear shake, scared;
    Each precious pearl is cheap when it's compared.
If God gave me five hundred mouths I would,
    O soul and world, describe you as I should.
Knower of secrets, I've one mouth and that   4215
    Near you, from shame, becomes crushed fully flat.
I'm not more crushed than Non-existence and
    These people come from Its mouth to this land:
From the Unseen a million forms in place
    Wait to spring forth with goodness and with grace.
From begging You, now spinning fills my head,

O You before whose kindness I am dead.
All our desire comes from Your own direction:
   Wayfarers travel due to God's attraction.
Does dust rise up without wind forcing motion?   4220
   Can ships set sail at all without an ocean?
None near the Water of Life die—that water
   Is just dregs though compared with Your pure water.
The Water of Life is the prayer direction
   For those who love life—gardens bloom from that one.
Those who drink death live through His love and they
   Don't want the Water of Life's draught today:
When Your love's water gave its hand, from then
   Water of Life was worthless to these men.
Each soul's revived by that same Water of Life   4225
   But You're the Water of the Water of Life.
Death's resurrection You gave every moment
   So I could see Your kindness is so potent.
Dying became like sleep to me, since I
   Am sure of Resurrection when I die.
If all the seas become mirages too
   You'll drag them back by their ears. They're from You—
Reason trembles at death while love is fearless;
   Rocks aren't scared of rain like mud that's porous.

This is the fifth book of *The Masnavi*.   4230
   It's like the stars that now shine over me.
Not all can navigate well from a star—
   The boatman though can read them from afar.
Others just gaze at them, so unaware
   That signs of fortune can be read up there.
At night become acquainted till the morning
   With such sublime stars that are devil-burning!
Each blocks the evil-thinking devil there
   By pouring oil from their fort through the air,
So, for the devil, stars are like a scorpion—   4235
   To Jupiter though they're a *close companion*.
And while the devil's shot by Sagittarius
   Water for crops and fruit comes from Aquarius.

Though Pisces wrecks the ship that is astray,
  For friends it makes ships Taurus-like today.
Though, Leo-like, the sun rips into night,
  Rubies gain robes of honour from its light.
Beings have raised up from Non-being their head,
  Poison for some, for others sweets instead.
Become loved, wipe your bad traits clean away   4240
  So you'll eat sweets from poison jars today:
Omar met no harm from the poison given
  Since sweets were cures for his discerning vision.

EXPLANATORY NOTES

PROSE INTRODUCTION
[written in Arabic, numbered by page and line]

P.3 l6 *shari'at*: the Persian vocalization of the word for shariah, now used in English. It is left in transliteration to match the other two rhyming terms used with it, and also because it does not seem to mean 'law' in this context, but religious belief in general, whereas the English use of shariah is invariably for law.

P.3 l6 *tariqat*: the Sufi path followed by aspiring Sufi mystics under the instruction of their Master.

P.3 l9 *haqiqat*: The Truth, representing the end of the Sufi path (*tariqa*).

P.3 l9–10 *'If the haqiqahs should appear, the shari'ahs would become void'*: the terms *haqiqah* and *shari'ah* here are the Arabic equivalents of *haqiqat* and *shari'at* used above.

P.3 l23–24 *Each group is celebrating what they themselves have*: Qur'an 18: 110.

P.3 l30–31 *'Oh, if only my people . . . forgiven me!'*: Qur'an 36: 26–7.

P.3 l32–34 *'Oh, if only I had not been given . . . and left me!'*: Qur'an 69: 25–9.

P.3 l36–37 *'Let whoever hopes to meet . . . the worship of his Lord'*: Qur'an 18: 110.

TEXT
[numbered by verse, or couplet]

31 Heading *'Take four birds and turn them towards you!'*: Qur'an 2: 260, where it represents the start of God's instruction to Abraham after he asks God to be shown how He gives life to the dead. (He is to slaughter the birds and put their parts on hills where God will revive them so they fly back to him.)

47 *'Eat!'*: Qur'an 5: 88, where God tells Mankind to eat the clean and lawful things He has provided.

61 *Because he makes one scared . . . in the extreme*: a reference to Qur'an 2: 268, where it is stated that Satan threatens men that he will make them poor.

74 *'he frowned'*: Qur'an 80: 1, the first verse of a chapter so entitled, which tells how Prophet Mohammad frowned and turned away from a blind man who had asked him a question. He did this because the blind man interrupted his attempts to convert one of the notables of Mecca to Islam.

102 *'God's dye'*: Qur'an 2: 138, where believers are described as receiving the colour given by God. It is therefore often understood as a kind of inner baptism.

109 *The Mercy to the Worlds*: Qur'an 21: 107, a verse understood to refer to the Prophet Mohammad with this description.

113 *"By your life!"*: Qur'an 15: 72, where it is understood as God's use of this
expression in reference to Mohammad as an oath to emphasize the truth
of what is being related.

127 *'People, please beware!'*: possibly intended as a version of Qur'an 5: 41 or
5: 92, where the same command is given in relation to obeying the
Prophet Mohammad.

138 *'Let them weep much!'*: Qur'an 9: 82, where it is said in relation to the
enemies of the Prophet Mohammad who pretended to be on his side and
are referred to there as 'hypocrites'.

147 *lend to God*: Qur'an 73: 20, where it is part of instructions to believers
whom God knows are unable to perform the nightly vigils that the
Prophet Mohammad and a small group of his devoted followers perform.
The idea of 'lending to God' is clearly strange and has needed to be inter-
preted extensively, with one suggestion being donations to charities.

148 *no eye has viewed*: from a Sacred Tradition of the Prophet Mohammad in
which God speaks and describes the greatness of the rewards for His
worshippers in this way.

150 *'He'll purify you'*: Qur'an 33: 33, where it stated that God will purify the
family of the Prophet Mohammad.

158 *He did the same to Adam with some wheat*: a reference to Qur'an 7: 23,
where Adam and Eve eat from the forbidden tree.

168 *'in work consult, good men!'*: Qur'an 42: 36, where it describes the behaviour
of the righteous believers.

175 *'Am I not your lord?'*: Qur'an 7: 172. See 'Alast' in the Glossary.

219 *is there some more?*: Qur'an 50: 30, where hell asks God this question after
being asked if it is full with the damned.

225 *They liberate all from the dry ablution*: a reference to the provision for
performing ablution when no water is available, using sand.

225 *And worrying about the prayer's direction*: a reference to the fact Muslims
face the direction towards the Kaaba in Mecca when they pray.

226 *'Belal, revive us!'*: from a saying of the Prophet Mohammad, when he
addressed his Abyssinian disciple Belal, who is best known as being the
first muezzin of the Muslims because of his beautiful voice.

228 *the body stands there, calm . . . 'Salam!'*: this couplet uses symbolic
allusions to the Muslim ritual prayer, specifically the position of standing
with which it begins and the greetings with which it ends.

230 *None enter flames . . . Save salamanders*: an allusion to the belief from
ancient times that salamanders are immune to fire.

232 *You can't, like Abraham, walk straight inside*: this refers to the popular
story that Nimrod had Abraham thrown into a massive bonfire. Abraham
was miraculously protected by God, who turned the fire into a comfortable
rose-garden for his sake.

257 *'Your efforts contrast'*: Qur'an 92: 4, where people's contrasting behaviours are judged.

261 *Withdraw and wait . . . they're doing that, too*: Qur'an 32: 30, where it represents instructions to the Prophet Mohammad in relation to his opponents.

273 *In the Qur'an God says to Satan: 'Share*: Qur'an 17: 64, where it represents part of God's instructions to Satan about how to try to mislead faithless men.

276 *Lazarus revived, but still had to die later*: a reference to Jesus's miracle of reviving Lazarus four days after he had died. Lazarus is not mentioned in the Qur'an, but his story is transmitted in exegetical traditions about miracles of Jesus mentioned in the Qur'an, including raising the dead.

286 *Like Mary, heaven's fruit fall on the ground*: an allusion to Qur'an 19: 25 where Mary is miraculously instructed to shake the trunk of a tree for its fruit to fall down for her to eat.

318 Heading   *The Preserved Tablet . . . The Most Mighty Tablet*: these titles both refer to the same Tablet. See 'The Tablet' in the Glossary.

339 *Moses's fire that would turn . . . burn*: a reference to Qur'an 28: 29–30, where Moses's encounter with the burning bush is related.

347 *'Alas for the slaves of God'*: Qur'an 36: 30, in lament for human failings to recognize Prophets.

355 Heading   *'faraji'*: the meaning of *'faraji'* is open, referring to the cloak being torn open.

378 *His throne and footstool*: references to God's throne and footstool in heaven according to Islamic theology.

380 *'Only the purified can touch this one'*: Qur'an 56: 79, where it refers to the Qur'an itself.

391 *Alast's*: Qur'an 7: 172. See 'Alast' in the Glossary.

438 *Abraham, there's no spark . . . Nimrod's fraud*: see note to v. 232.

452 *mountain-sized plots*: based on Qur'an 14: 46, which refers to plots by the enemies of the Prophet Mohammad against him.

453 *Like Abraham, I enter flames and smile*: see note to v. 232.

454 *flowing water*: Qur'an 67: 30, where it alludes to God's unrivalled power to produce flowing water from the ground.

460 Heading   *Mu'tazilites*: the Mu'tazilites were a highly influential rationalist Islamic theological group, who were favoured by the Caliph Ma'mun in the early tenth century, but went out of favour in later decades in the face of opposition from more scripturalist theological schools.

467 *Like Pharaoh . . . like Sohrab every gaol*: this verse alludes in its first hemistich to the story about the fate of Pharaoh after the parting of the waves for Moses and his followers, and in the second hemistich to Sohrab, son of Rostam, the main hero of the *Shahnama* (the Persian national epic by Ferdowsi).

477 *When Joseph's brothers . . . envious and sick*: a reference to the story about Joseph and his brothers, which the 12th chapter of the Qur'an, entitled 'Joseph', is taken up with.

499 Heading   *'he hears through Me and sees through Me'*: taken from possibly the most well-known Sacred Tradition, or saying of the Prophet in which he presents a message from God in his own words, which is cited most frequently in Sufi literature. God affirms that his worshippers continue to draw close to Him through extra acts of devotion until they eventually see and hear through Him, and thus subsist through Him.

500 *'They make you stumble'*: Qur'an 68: 51, where the enmity of the disbelievers in the Prophet Mohammad is described through what they would do to him.

503 *Until the verse arrived . . . evil eye*: the verse in question is the previously quoted 68: 51, which clarified that the cause of the Prophet's fall was the look of one of his enemies at him with the wish that he should stumble.

507 Heading   *'Those who disbelieve . . . with their gaze'*: Qur'an 68: 51. See note to v. 500.

521–2 *Adam's fall . . . cursed*: a reference to Qur'an 7: 23, where Adam and Eve eat from the forbidden tree, for which they were banished from heaven.

580 *'Spend!'*: Qur'an 2: 267, where God tells believers to spend of the good things produced on earth that they have earned from God.

581 *'Spend!' . . . 'Earn, then spend!'*: Qur'an 2: 267. See note to v. 580.

582 *'Restrain yourself!'*: Qur'an 3: 200, where believers are instructed to do this in order to be successful.

583 *'Eat!'*: Qur'an 5: 88, where God tells believers to eat of the good and lawful things provided by Him.

583 *'Do not exceed!'*: Qur'an 7: 31, where God tells Mankind not to be extravagant in eating and drinking.

590 *the sword of 'No!'*: the Arabic term *laa* with which the Muslim testimony of faith ('No God but God') begins.

597 *He thinks Hajjaj was a fair-minded leader*: al-Hajjaj ebn Yusof (d. 714) was a governor of the Hejaz for the Umayyads who is remembered in later tradition as being particularly oppressive.

598 *Moses's staff . . . sorcery*: a reference to the Qur'anic story (20: 65–72) about the help given by God to Moses, so that he could meet the challenge of Pharaoh to perform a miracle greater than the sorcery of his magicians. By magic they make their rods move about, while through God's help the transformation of Moses's rod into a snake is more astonishing.

601 *'Alast'* : Qur'an 7: 172. See note to v. 391.

621 Heading   *Harut and Marut in the pit of Babylon*: see 'Harut and Marut' in the Glossary.

650 *'Fear God!'*: Qur'an 3/102 among many cases of using this expression.

674 *'Poverty is my pride'*: a saying of the Prophet Mohammad that is pithy and poetic in Arabic.

715 *Khezr broke the boat . . . confiscate it*: a reference to the Qur'anic story (18: 65–82) about Khezr and Moses. One of Khezr's seemingly illogical and unjust actions was to stove a hole in a boat belonging to a poor man.

716 *'Poverty is my pride'*: see note to v. 674.

727, 729 *'God feeds you, yet is not fed'*: Qur'an 6: 14, where God is described to explain why He alone should be worshipped.

741 *'God's hand's above their hands'*: Qur'an 48: 10, in a passage where taking an oath with the Prophet is said to be the same as taking an oath with God, so the Prophet's hand represents God's hand.

744 *You'll be in Hodaybiyya . . . who pledged there*: the Treaty of Hodaybiyya is said to have been agreed shortly before Muslims took over Mecca. The Prophet Mohammad and his followers headed to Mecca to perform the pilgrimage and then agreed a peace treaty that recognized their religious rights, hence it was a major turning-point.

745 *the ten whose fates were told*: this group of 'ten blessed ones' are major companions of the Prophet Mohammad who were guaranteed heaven according to tradition.

748 *'A man is with . . . kept apart'*: a saying of the Prophet Mohammad.

752 *a barrier both front and behind*: Qur'an 36: 9, where it refers to the way those destined never to believe are blocked by God Himself.

754 *what's back and what's ahead*: Qur'an 36: 9. See note to v. 752.

765 *'A cord of branches on her neck'*: Qur'an 111: 5, in reference to the wife of Abu Lahab (lit. 'Father of Flame'), an uncle of the Prophet who was his mortal enemy. He and his wife are condemned in the 111th chapter of the Qur'an, which has also been named '*Lahab*'.

766 Heading *The reason why Abraham killed the crow*: this is related to the story about Abraham and the four birds, one of which was a crow, which begins with v. 31.

770 *'Grant me respite till Judgement Day!'*: a variant of Qur'an 7: 13, where it represents part of Satan's appeal to God after being banished from heaven.

845 *To a rare Abu Bakr in Sabzevar*: Abu Bakr was the first political successor of the Prophet Mohammad, who is revered by Sunnites but is considered to have been an illegitimate usurper by Shi'ites—therefore one does not find anyone named 'Abu Bakr' among their communities, such as the one in Sabzevar referred to in the story that follows.

846 Heading *Mohammad Khwarazmshah who conquered the city of Sabzevar*: a reference to the siege of Sabzevar in 1186 by Mohammad Khwarazmshah.

885 *Heaven's beneath the feet of each one's mother*: a famous saying of the Prophet Mohammad.

933 Heading   *'I saw seven fat cows which seven thin cows ate up'*: Qur'an 12: 43, where it represents the first part of the dream of the Egyptian ruler, which was eventually interpreted by the Prophet Joseph.

939 *'Why kill the rooster, Abraham say why?'*: related to the story about Abraham and the four birds, one of which was a crow, which begins with v. 31.

949 *a palm-fibre cord*: Qur'an 111: 5. See note to v. 765.

963 Heading   *'We created Man in the best . . . the lowest of the lows'*: Qur'an 95: 4–5, where it is part of a statement explaining that humans had been debased after originally being created in the highest form.

963 Heading   *'Whomsoever we grant a long life we make him regress in creation'*: Qur'an 36: 68, where it is traditionally understood as a demonstration of the power of God to both create and diminish.

975 Heading   *except those who believed . . . without remaining indebted*: Qur'an 95: 6, the verse that follows the verses quoted in the previous heading and qualifies them.

997 *He makes the works of infidels . . . increasing*: Qur'an 47: 1–2.

1000 *'He led their deeds to loss'*: see note to v. 997.

1003 *'Lend!'*: Qur'an 73: 20. See note to v. 147.

1006 *'He makes good their condition'*: see note to v. 997.

1020 *'He brings the living from the dead'*: Qur'an 30: 19, where signs of God's divinity are presented.

1024 *Or I'd turn Abkhaz to Baghdad, my dear!*: Abkhaz was a remote and obscure place compared with Baghdad, the much-celebrated capital of the Muslim world.

1043 *say 'I take refuge . . . witches' knots please, too!*: Qur'an 113: 1–4, one of the shortest chapters of the Qur'an, which takes the form of a prayer for protection.

1067 *'Didn't we open up your breast?'*: Qur'an 94: 1, where the Prophet Mohammad is being addressed by God.

1072 *didn't we open up?*: Qur'an 94: 1. See note to v. 1067.

1073 *'Do you not see?'*: Qur'an 51: 21, where the question is asked about seeing the signs of God on earth.

1074 *'And He is with you'*: Qur'an 57: 4, in a verse presenting God's omnipotence and omnipresence.

1077 *barriers front and back*: Qur'an 36: 9. See note to v. 752.

1101 *You'll be a firewood carrier . . . Abu Lahab's wife*: Qur'an 111: 4, which is understood to be a description of a couple from the Prophet Mohammad's tribe who were his mortal enemies.

1102 *Tell firewood from the Sidra*: the Sidra is a tree believed to mark the utmost reach of the seventh heaven, as stated in Qur'an 53: 14.

1107 Heading   *'If you head out on the path . . . made truly Existent'*: these two verses come from one of Rumi's own quatrains (No. 742, ed. Foruzanfar).

1137 *The Abode of Peace . . . Abode of Blame*: Rumi is using these rhyming expressions in Arabic here to refer to heaven and earth, respectively.

1168 *The covenant*: see 'Alast' in the Glossary.

1173 Heading   *'Have you not seen . . . ritual prayer'*: Qur'an 96: 9–10, where it describes reprehensible behaviour that will be punished.

1184 *'Remember me and I will you!'*: Qur'an 2: 152, where God is the speaker to Mankind.

1185 *'Keep My Covenant!'. . . . 'I'll keep your covenant'*: Qur'an 2: 140, where Jews are addressed by God about their covenant with Him.

1192 *Like Mary . . . date-palm fruitful for her need*: an allusion to Qur'an 19: 25 from *Surat Maryam*, which describes the miraculous birth of Jesus.

1206 *Wis and Ramin, Khosraw and Shirin*: two of the most famous medieval Persian romances, written by Gorgani (d. *c.*1058) and Nezami (d. 1209), respectively.

1222 *Read on these devilish men . . . by God's transformation*: this seems to refer to Qur'an. 112, which refers to 'demons of Mankind' as being the enemies of the Prophets established by God.

1228 *What is wahy revelation?*: *wahy* is the term used in Islamic theology for the highest form of revelation received by Prophets, such as the Qur'an.

1231 *'God inspired the bee'*: Qur'an 16: 68, where the verb from the term for *wahy* prophetic revelation is used for divine inspiration given to the bee.

1233 *We honoured*: Qur'an 17: 70, where it is stated that God has honoured and favoured human beings above all creatures.

1234 *'We've given you Kawsar'*: Qur'an 108: 1, the origin of the name Kawsar (see Glossary), which can be translated literally as 'abundance'. Here Mankind is told that God has bestowed on it 'Kawsar', so they should appreciate this and pray to Him.

1238 *'He loves for God's sake'*: from a saying of the Prophet Mohammad.

1242 *hates for God's sake*: see note to v. 1238.

1243 *'There is just one God'*: this is the first part of the Muslim testimony of faith or *shahada*.

1244 Heading   *'they rise from their beds'*: Qur'an 32: 16, where it forms part of a description of the pious devotees of God, who would even get up at night to pray to Him.

1244 Heading   *Sho'ayb*: a prophet mentioned in the Qur'an (e.g. 11: 84–95), who was sent to the vanquished community of the Midianites, and has been identified with the biblical Jethro.

1264 *'Return!'*: Qur'an 89: 28.

1267 Heading   *"Follow the creed of Abraham"*: Qur'an 16: 123, where the Prophet Mohammad is instructed to follow Abraham's creed.

1267 Heading   *"In Abraham there is a fine example for you"*: Qur'an 60: 4,
where the example of Abraham is recommended to believers in general.

1284 *'Arise!'*: Qur'an 74: 2, where the Prophet Mohammad is told to arise and
warn others about God's judgement to come.

1295 *don't understand*: Qur'an 7: 179, where it is part of the description of the
denizens of hell.

1297 *we carried on the land*: Qur'an 17: 70, where it is listed as one of the
favours Mankind has received from God.

1318 *alif lam mim and ha mim*: examples of the so-called 'mysterious letters'
with which several surahs of the Qur'an begin, such as Surahs 2, 3, 29,
32, 40, and 42.

1322 *alif lam and ha mim:* see note to v. 1318.

1328 *Ha Mim*: see note to v. 1318.

1332 *Hu*: the term used for God's Essence, literally meaning 'He'.

1335 Heading   *'There is no blame on the blind'*: Qur'an 24: 61 and 48: 71, a state-
ment that is repeated in the Qur'an.

1377 *'Lord, give strength to me!'*: an abbreviated version of the invocation *'There
is no strength or power except through God'*, which is recommended in many
of the sayings of Prophet Mohammad, especially when one is faced with
extreme difficulties.

1391 *unfortunate fate*: Qur'an 52: 30, where it is an expression used to refer to
poets when the Prophet Mohammad was accused of being a soothsayer
or poet.

1393 *'The torment of disgrace'*: Qur'an 10: 98, where it refers to the punishment
of disbelievers.

1402 *Read Surat Rahman*: Qur'an 55: 8–9 is intended here, where the Qur'an
specifically instructs not to cheat with weighing-scales. ('Rahman' is the
name of Surah 55.)

1409 *'Eat!' . . . 'Don't exceed!'*: Qur'an 7: 31, where they are part of instructions
given to humanity.

1425 *Of Sufism learned just the wool to wear*: the term 'Sufism' comes from the
wearing of wool by early ascetics and mystics, maintained today by the
use of woollen cloaks.

1432 Heading   *'Do not hurry it . . . communication'*: a combination of two
non-consecutive verses of the Qur'an, 75: 16 and 53: 4.

1447 Heading   *'No one knows its interpretation but God!'*: Qur'an 3: 7, where
the Qur'an discusses itself.

1465 *God has bought*: Qur'an 9: 111, where it is said that God has bought the
believers of lives with heaven, in return for their complete devotion to
Him, even if that means being killed while fighting for His cause.

1471 *Companions of the Elephant*: an allusion to the Qur'anic story (105: 3) in
which God sends birds to throw down stones at a huge army attacking the

Prophet Mohammad's tribe and intent on destroying the Kaaba. This defeat of the army from South Arabia, which even boasted an elephant, is traditionally believed to have taken place shortly before Mohammad's birth in the very same year, and thus serves as a sign that God provided help to pave the way for His prophet's future success.

1475 Heading   *that unfortunate woman who saw the donkey but not the gourd*: a cross-reference to the story which begins with v. 1335 in this volume.

1502 *'someone flees his brother' . . . 'a son will flee his father'*: Qur'an 80: 34, as part of the description of the Last Day.

1526 *Please don't leave me alone!*: Qur'an 21: 89, where it is part of Zechariah's prayer to God.

1528 *God's earth*: Qur'an 4: 97, where the vastness of God's earth is emphasized.

1538 *'Rather, harder than stone'*: Qur'an 2: 74, where it describes the deniers of the miraculous signs of God.

1541 *Moses's rod changed . . . God transformed to white his hand*: allusions to Moses's rod, for which see the note to v. 598 above, and to the miraculous transformation of Moses's hand mentioned in the Qur'an (20: 22, 28: 132).

1589 *For "Michael" comes from "kayl"*: the name Michael is not originally Arabic, so the etymology is claimed here for the play on words. *Kayl* means 'measuring'.

1602 *"Come to the good!"*: part of the Muslim call to prayer sung by the muezzins.

1606–9 *You said . . . stubborn men?*: this seems to allude to Qur'an 6: 43: 'If only they had shown humility when calamity came from Us! Rather, instead their hearts were hardened and Satan made their ugly deeds seem beautiful to them.'

1631 *Streams of honey and milk . . . running water*: the four streams in paradise mentioned in Qur'an 47: 15.

1672 *"Come!"*: the Qur'an several times tells the reader 'Come!', albeit using different verb forms from those given here.

1687 *He's Azar, I'm the idol; similarly*: based on an occurrence in Qur'an 6: 74, in the Muslim tradition Abraham's father's name is Azar.

1692 *Between His fingers*: alluding to a saying of the Prophet Mohammad about the hearts of all men being held 'between two fingers of the Merciful God'.

1712 Heading   *"He is nearer to him than you, but you do not see"*: Qur'an 56: 85, where God is understood as the speaker.

1742 *'If only my own people were aware!'*: Qur'an 36: 26, where it is uttered by a prophet in reference to his disbelieving community and the knowledge of the honour and pardon he had received from God.

1744 *'heaven has your daily bread'*: Qur'an 51: 22.

1745 Heading   *'They are given provisions and rejoice'*: Qur'an 3: 169–70, where it describes martyrs as not really being dead, but instead taken care of by God.

1774 Heading   *'He is the one who sends down rain after they have despaired'*:
Qur'an 42: 28, where God's favours to the faithful are recounted.

1774 Heading   *'so that you know that God changes their bad deeds to good ones'*:
Qur'an 25: 70, where it describes those who are repentant for their sins.

1784 *The books of meanness . . . piety*: a reference to the Muslim belief in the
giving of books of deeds after death in the process of judgement. See
Qur'an 69: 19.

1787 *His left hand mourns its black list on that day*: see note to v. 1784. The left
hand is believed to receive the book listing bad deeds, while the right
hand receives the book listing good deeds.

1806 *Dreading the book of deeds on the left side*: see note to v. 1787.

1811 *And Pharaoh-like pretentious claims for 'I'*: a reference to Qur'an 79: 24,
where Pharaoh says 'I am your most exalted lord!'

1834 *Why should your right hand get your book from God?*: see note to v. 1787.

1853 *to rectify your every action*: Qur'an 33: 71, where believers are told that
God will forgive their sins and rectify their actions.

1891 *It's not for turquoise, but for victory*: in Persian 'turquoise' and 'victory' are
very similar words.

1920 Heading   *'Let Man reflect on what he has been created from'*: Qur'an 86:
5, where God's power is illustrated through a reminder of how humans
are created.

1924 *'Why now should Adam lord it over me?'*: a reference to Qur'an 2: 34 ,
where the angels bow down to Adam, but Satan refuses.

1929 Heading   *'He created the Jinn from smokeless fire'*: Qur'an 55: 15,
where God's kindnesses are recounted to those who might deny them.

1929 Heading   *'He was of the Jinn and transgressed'*: Qur'an 18: 50, where
Satan is described in this way in reference to his refusal to bow to Adam.

1966 *'Nun and the pen'*: Qur'an 68: 1, the beginning of the Surah of The Pen.

1972 *'We've done wrong!'*: Qur'an 7: 23, where Adam and Eve admit sinning
after eating from the forbidden tree.

2037 *Pharaoh said, 'I am God' . . . was saved*: Rumi here contrasts Pharaoh with
the Sufi al-Hallaj. The former claimed divinity according to the Qur'an
(see note to v. 1811), while the latter is considered by Sufis as the vehicle
for the theopathic utterance, *'I am The Truth.'*

2040 *Hallaj's 'I' . . . isn't like indwelling*: 'indwelling' here is the translation for
the theological term *holul*, often translated as incarnation and associated
by Muslim theologians with the Christian view of Jesus's divinity. Hallaj
was accused of this belief about himself by theologians because of his
theopathic utterance, *'I am The Truth.'*

2042 *See your subsistence post-annihilation*: in Sufi stations of the path, subsist-
ence through God (*baqa bellah*) is considered a superior station that
comes after annihilation in God (*fana fellah*).

2064 *The blaming soul*: in Sufi theory 'the self-blaming soul' or *nafs-e lawwame* is an early stage of the soul once the seeker is no longer controlled by his self and is struggling against the latter.

2082 Heading   *'On the day some faces will be bright and others gloomy'*: Qur'an 3: 106, where it refers to Judgement Day.

2082 Heading   *'You will see those who lied against God, their faces gloomy'*: Qur'an 39: 60, where it describes people resurrected on Judgement Day.

2084 *their marks on faces*: Qur'an 48: 29, where such marks are said to be the effect of prostration in prayer.

2099 *Qarun*: Qarun is the figure named Korah in the Bible, who led a rebellion against Moses. Qur'an 28: 76 mentions the wealth given to him and 28: 81 the devastating punishment he received, being swallowed up by the earth.

2105 *How could Satan have then shown Adam up?*: see note to v. 158.

2111 Heading   *"for you there is life in retribution"*: Qur'an 2: 179, where it refers to the security that is gained by punishing murderers.

2125 *Water of Kawsar or the lahab fire*: for Kawsar, see the Glossary. For *lahab* see note to v. 1101.

2128 *A question that affirms . . . the verb for 'not to be'*: *Alast* comes from the verb used in Qur'an 7: 172, *alasto* (lit. Am I not?), a question that seeks affirmation.

2136 Heading   *a red death*: this Arabic expression does not have a single, universally accepted definition, but its use here clearly indicates a slow and agonizing death.

2156 *A foul and noxious book . . . heads left you'll find*: see note to v. 1787.

2161 *running water*: Qur'an 67: 30, where it is part of a question to deniers of God about the source for water.

2165 Heading   *'And if you ask them: "Who created . . . "God."'*: Qur'an 31: 25, where it is the disbelievers who are asked and would even answer in this way.

2183 *fifty thousand years*: Qur'an 70: 4, where the day of ascent for angels and the Holy Spirit is described as being fifty thousand years in length, emphasizing its sublimeness.

2188 *'they love Him' . . . 'He loves them'*: Qur'an 5: 54, a verse frequently cited in discussions of the possibility of a relationship of love between God and Man.

2207 *a book that's full of spite . . . fit for the right?*: see note to v. 1787.

2220–1 *'I testify' . . . 'I testify'*: *ashhado*, the term used here, is the first word of the Muslim testimony of faith or *shahadah*.

2230 Heading   *'we will give ease'*: Qur'an 92: 7, where it refers to those who are generous and believers in God.

2230 Heading   *'we will give him hardship'*: Qur'an 92: 10, where it refers to those who are stingy and deniers of God.

2244 Heading   *'I am the hearing, sight, tongue, and hand'*: see note to v. 499.

2244 Heading   *'You did not throw when you threw, but rather God threw'*:
Qur'an 8: 17, in a passage describing the Prophet Mohammad's actions in
battle as being in reality God's actions. This is one of the most frequently
cited Qur'anic verses in Sufi discussions of annihilation in God.

2318 *If only my own people would now know!*: Qur'an 36: 26. See note to v. 1742.

2349 *'If you help God, you'll be helped'*: Qur'an 47: 7, where believers are
told this.

2362 Heading   *the donkey of the firewood seller*: despite the wording of the
heading, in the subsequent poetry the owner of the donkey is a water-
carrier instead.

2386 *'Seek out God's bounty!'*: Qur'an 62: 10, where believers are told to do this
after prayers.

2430 *"Don't harm yourself"*: Qur'an 2: 195, among a list of general command-
ments to Muslims.

2444 *Stubborn Pharaoh saw Moses's snake*: Qur'an 20: 65–72. See note to v. 598.

2504 *the famed sword of Ali*: this refers to 'Zo'l-feqar', the legendary sword of
Ali, the Prophet Mohammad's cousin and son-in-law.

2507 *Like Abraham . . . jump in fire without distress?*: this refers to the popular
story that Nimrod had Abraham thrown into a massive bonfire. Abraham
was miraculously protected by God, who turned the fire into a comfortable
rose-garden for his sake.

2508 *Transform your wooden sword to Zo'l-feqar*: see note to v. 2504.

2519 *Where is the khaniqah's musician, son? . . . and sing: 'The ass has gone!'*:
a reference to a story in *The Masnavi: Book Two* (vv. 517–).

2520 *A hare can lead a lion down a well*: a reference to a story in *The Masnavi:
Book One* (vv. 904–).

2526 *Breasts split from spiritual Moses's sheer might . . . Like Sinai*: an allusion to
Qur'an 7: 143, where Moses asks God to reveal Himself, and, in response,
God reveals Himself to a mountain, flattening it. On witnessing this,
Moses himself collapses and faints.

2527 *The drum's been banged by Khosraw . . . it's no wonder*: *Khosraw and Shirin*
is a romance by Nezami Ganjavi (d. 1209) about Khosraw II (r. 590–628
CE), a Sasanian king, and an Armenian princess called Shirin, which
means 'sweet', hence the reference to sugar.

2538 *The soul says 'I'm God' like Mansur, ecstatic*: See 'Hallaj' in the Glossary.

2589 *'He taught Man'*: Qur'an 96: 5, from the Surah traditionally believed to
have been the first one revealed.

2589 *'The knowledge is with God'*: Qur'an 67: 26, where the Prophet states this
and explains that his own role is as a warner only.

2590 *'My Lord, the Most High One!'*: these are the names by which God is
addressed when the Muslim is in the position of prostration during prayer.

2593 Heading *'the companions of the Sabbath'*: Qur'an 2: 65, where it says that those who broke the sabbath were turned into apes in disgrace.

2593 Heading *'the companions of Jesus's table spread'*: Qur'an 5: 114, where God answers Jesus's prayer for a table spread for everyone and also warns that anyone who denies Him subsequently will suffer an unprecedented torment.

2593 Heading *He made them apes and swine*: Qur'an 2: 65, where it says that those who broke the sabbath were turned into apes in disgrace.

2595 *God turned them into apes . . . it's been related*: see previous note.

2599 *The famed cave's sleepers' dog*: see 'Seven Sleepers in the Cave and their Dog' in the Glossary.

2652 *'This is my Lord!'*: Qur'an 6: 76–8, where this represents Abraham's premature declarations of faith in a star, the moon, and the sun, respectively, before he finally discovers that God is the only eternal object worthy of worship.

2655 *'This is my Lord!'*: Qur'an 6: 76–8. See note to v. 2652.

2658 *'The faithful split then into seventy-two'*: there are a group of sayings of the Prophet Mohammad that foretell the division of Muslims into seventy-two factions.

2660 *Lacking Omar's light . . . an eyebrow's hair to block one's sight*: a cross-reference to a story in *The Masnavi: Book Two*, vv. 119–21.

2669 *Shaikh Mohammad Sarrazi of Ghazni*: a Sufi from Ghazni in what is now Afghanistan, who is also mentioned in Rumi's discourses, the *Fihe ma fih*, as well as in Rumi's father's book, *Ma'aref*.

2677 *'My life is in my death'*: part of a famous poem by al-Hallaj (see 'Hallaj' in the Glossary), which is also a cross-reference to a longer version in *The Masnavi: Book One*, vv. 3949–51.

2679 *Like Ali, his sweet basil's . . . of his life*: a cross-reference to the story about Ali ebn Taleb (see 'Ali' in the Glossary) and his embrace of his own death found in *The Masnavi: Book One*, especially 3959, which mentions both basil and narcissus.

2682 *You'll then be like Abbas Dabsi, the beggar*: this seems to be a reference to a beggar known for extreme wretchedness, who was also referred to by Rumi's predecessor Attar in his poem, the *Asrarname*.

2688 Heading *Labbayka*: the first word of a prayer repeated by Muslims while performing the pilgrimage to Mecca; the equivalent of 'Here I am for You'.

2699 *My begging is like twenty of Abbas's*: see note to v. 2682.

2703 *'Lend to God!'*: Qur'an 73: 20. See note to v. 147.

2710 *'Not too much, greedy!'*: Qur'an 7: 31, where believers are instructed to eat and drink in moderation, not excessively and wastefully.

2736 Heading *'If it were not for you, I would not have created the heavens'*: a sacred tradition attributed to the Prophet Mohammad, where God is the speaker and is referring to Mohammad.

2739 *'If not for you!'*: see note to v. 2736 Heading.

2757–8 *Abbas-like ugliness . . . Abbas-e Dabsi*: see note to v. 2682.

2777 *Moses's . . . rod and mountain . . . the majestic ocean*: references to the Qur'anic miracles of Moses.

2778 *Mohammad's once moved the moon's beauty . . . movement that was planned*: references to the miracles of the Prophet Mohammad.

2788 *the bag of Abu Horayra*: Abu Horayra was a companion of the Prophet Mohammad who is said to have lived in great poverty, but had a food bag that always kept him well-fed.

2797 *God's hand's above their hands*: Qur'an 48: 10. See further the note to v. 741.

2800 *Hatem Ta'i*: the subject of many stories about his generosity, he is believed to have lived in the 6th century CE, and had died before the mission of the Prophet Mohammad.

2801 Heading   *'Depart to My creation with My attributes!'*: a part of God's address to the Sufi Bayazid Bastami during his mystical ascension.

2872 Heading   *'If we had listened and reasoned . . . denizens of hellfire'*: Qur'an 67: 10, where the disbelievers who find themselves in hell say this.

2931 *'What God wills happens'*: Qur'an 7: 121.

2939 *What God wills happens*: Qur'an 7: 121.

2945 *'He's firm with unbelievers'*: Qur'an 48: 29, where the Prophet Mohammad is described in this way.

2951 *that spread their paws by thresholds*: Qur'an 18: 18, where the dog of the Seven Sleepers in the Cave (see the Glossary) is described.

2972 *"There's no objection for the blind"*: a statement repeated in the Qur'an. See note to v. 1335 Heading.

2977 *On seeing Joseph, it then cuts its hand*: an allusion to Qur'an 12: 30–1, which describes Egyptian women cutting their own hands by mistake after being mesmerized by Joseph's handsomeness.

2988 *on finishing your daily prayer . . . each shoulder there*: a reference to the way the daily prayer is closed by greeting angels over each shoulder.

2997 *We bowed sincerely to your great ancestor*: see note to v. 1924.

2999 *"Prostrate!"*: Qur'an 2: 34. See note to v. 2997.

3079 Heading   *'You made me err!'*: Qur'an 15: 39, where this is said by Satan to God.

3111 *The sorcerers told Pharaoh . . . hands and feet*: a reference to the story about Moses's sorcerers and Moses with his miraculous rod. See further note to v. 598.

3113 Heading   *'Whatever God wills happens'*: Qur'an 7: 121. In the original Arabic the verb is in the past tense, hence the comment about the past.

3113 *'Whatever God wills happens'*: Qur'an 7: 121.

3117 *'What God wills comes to be'*: Qur'an 7: 121.

3133 Heading   *'God does not let the reward of the righteous be lost'*: Qur'an
11: 115, where believers are told to be patient in the knowledge that
God won't let their reward be lost.

3163 *Like Fozayl, once one of the highwaymen*: this refers to the early frontier
ascetic Fozayl ebn Iyaz (d. 803), who is said to have been a highwayman
before his conversion.

3164 *The sorcerers showed Pharaoh*: a reference to the story about Moses's
sorcerers and Moses with his miraculous rod. See further note to v. 598.

3182 *You who've ripped Joseph's shirt . . . wolf now kills you*: a reference to the
brothers of Joseph making it appear to their father Jacob that a wolf had
killed Joseph.

3200 *'Be!'*: Qur'an 36: 82. The divine fiat; the way in which God is repeatedly
described as granting created things existence, before which they are
described as non-existents in a storehouse.

3201 *'Be silent!'*: Qur'an 7: 204, where God instructs to be silent and listen
when the Qur'an is recited.

3212 Heading   *'And that is God's Grace, which He bestows on whom He
wishes'*: Qur'an 57: 21, where it describes the bounty God will give to
those who devote themselves to Him enthusiastically.

3221 *So those seventy-two sects . . . till the Resurrection Day*: see note to v. 2658
regarding 'seventy-two sects' and 'The Resurrection' in the Glossary.

3239 *Some women gambled intellects away . . . Joseph's love's pavilion's way*: an
allusion to Qur'an 12: 30–1, which describes Egyptian women cutting their
own hands by mistake after being mesmerized by Joseph's handsomeness.

3257 *Like Arabs on campsites nostalgically*: the first section of an Arabic *qasida*
poem is typically nostalgia for a campsite the poet has departed from.

3258 *Which Asaf do your boots remind of now?*: a reference to Asaf ebn Barkhiya
who represents a Friend of God at the time of Solayman in Sufi theoso-
phy. He was the minister of Solomon identified by exegetes as the
individual who miraculously transports Sheba's throne in the Qur'anic
narrative (27: 38–40).

3265 *A hundred 'Am I not?'s a hundred 'Yes!'s*: Qur'an 7: 172. See note to v. 391.

3294 *women who look modestly*: Qur'an 55: 56, where the modesty of devout
women is praised.

3295 *The women who look modestly*: see note to v. 3294.

3299 *you see . . . you don't see*: Qur'an 69: 38–9, as part of an oath regarding the
authenticity of the Qur'an as revelation from an apostle and not the work
of a poet.

3318 *'I testify!'*: see note to v. 1243.

3319 *'I testify!'*: see note to v. 1243.

3322–6 *Just like that shepherd . . . how far apart*: a cross-reference to the 'Moses
and the Shepherd' story found in *The Masnavi: Book Two*, vv. 1724–1800.

3339 *Pharaoh's magicians' hearts . . . hand and rod*: Qur'an 20: 65–72. See note to v. 598.

3341 *'There's no harm'*: Qur'an 26: 50, where it represents the magicians' response to Pharaoh's threats after they acquired faith in God.

3393 *You're like that one who had sex with a donkey*: a cross-reference to the story earlier in this volume (vv. 1335–1408).

3399 *A star shone through Mohammad's face . . . both fade*: this verse poetically describes the coming of Mohammad as outshining the previous religious groups.

3431 *Which no ear hears and no eye sees*: this description is found in a saying of the Prophet Mohammad about what the righteous can expect to receive as reward.

3462 *They turn halim-like*: Rumi refers here to a porridge-like mixture of meat and wheat most commonly called *'halim'*, although he uses the alternative name *'harisa'*. The point is that after a lot of effort blending the very contrasting ingredients they do not appear as separate parts.

3537 Heading   *Mount Hira*: it is while meditating in a cave on Mount Hira that the Prophet Mohammad meets the Angel Gabriel and receives the first revelation of the Qur'an, according to traditional biographies.

3539 *'Be!'*: Qur'an 36: 82. See note to v. 3200.

3544 *life-risking attackers*: this appears to be a reference to the fearless *fedai*s of the medieval Nizari Ismaili community, known for their 'suicide missions'.

3575 *"We have honoured"*: Qur'an 17: 70. See note to v. 1233.

3575 *"We gave you"*: Qur'an 108: 1. See note to v. 1234.

3593 Heading   *'The next realm is real life, if they but knew'*: Qur'an 29: 64, where the fickleness of people's faith is discussed.

3596 *Pure spirit's home is 'Elliyin'*: the *Elliyin* is the highest sphere of heaven in Islamic cosmology. The term is derived from Qur'an 83: 18.

3598 *That bloodthirsty Hajjaj's rule is just*: for Hajjaj, see note to v. 597.

3605 *'Be!'*: Qur'an 36: 82. See note to v. 3200.

3606 *'his eyes don't veer'*: Qur'an 53: 17, where it is understood as referring to the Prophet Mohammad's focus during his ascension.

3610 *'Imam of the two qiblas'*: the term *'qibla'* means the direction one faces for prayer, namely towards the Kaaba in Mecca for Muslims. The point being reinforced in this verse is the mystic's presence in this world and beyond simultaneously.

3621 *'Go down!'*: Qur'an 2: 36, where Adam and Eve are told this after having eaten from the forbidden tree.

3739 Heading   *like that teacher whom the children told that he was ill*: a cross-reference to a story in *The Masnavi: Book Three*, vv. 1523–.

3739 Heading   *I am unrivalled in the Greater Jihad . . . for me?*: the 'Greater Jihad' is the struggle against one's self, while the 'Lesser Jihad' is holy war, according to a well-known saying of the Prophet Mohammad.

3739 Heading   *'Now you will find out, and again you will find out'*: Qur'an 102: 3–4, where it refers to finding out about the afterlife when one dies.

3741 *foremost of the foremost*: alludes to Qur'an 56: 10, where it refers to the foremost in paradise.

3748 *Water's best for ablution . . . good man*: a reference to the concession in Islamic law that allows Muslims to use sand to ritually clean themselves before prayer if water is not available. In this case, killing a prisoner is the substitute for war combat.

3779 *We need an iron Hamza in this fray*: Hamza is the subject of a popular biographical tradition exemplifying bravery which is traditionally understood to have stemmed from the biography of the Prophet Mohammad's paternal uncle Hamza ebn Abd al-Mottaleb.

3782 Heading   *he turned from the Lesser Jihad to the Greater Jihad*: see note to v. 3739 Heading.

3804 *This is the Greater Jihad, that the lesser*: see note to v. 3739 Heading.

3810–11 *But Moses's rod still stay . . . dust to see*: see note to v. 1541.

3821 *Truth's Seat*: Qur'an 54: 55, where it indicates where the righteous will sit in paradise.

3822 *'Those true indeed'*: Qur'an 33: 23, where it describes those who have kept their pledge to God.

3827 *Dead infidels would match Abu Sa'eed*: the 'Abu Sa'eed' being referred to here is probably the much celebrated Sufi Master from Khorasan, Abu Sa'eed ebn Abe l-Khair (d. 1049).

3836 *That Kaiqobad-like monarch*: Kaiqobad I (r. 1220–37) was the Konya-born monarch of the Seljuq empire when it was at its peak.

3858 *that Breath which made Mary get pregnant with no human aid?*: a reference to the Qur'anic (21: 91, 66: 12) version of Mary's immaculate conception, which involves the Angel Gabriel blowing the Holy Spirit into her.

3871 *'In front a barrier, and one more behind'*: Qur'an 36: 9. See note to v. 752.

3872 *And thus a fox can throw lions down a well*: this seems to be a cross-reference to a well-known story in *The Masnavi: Book One* (vv. 904–), although in that story a hare is in the place of the fox mentioned here.

3899 *'the offspring shall all join'*: Qur'an 52: 21, where it is stated that the righteous will be joined with their offspring in paradise.

3916 *Moses, your revelation . . . for it to bear*: see note to v. 2526.

3935 *Joseph's brothers did not . . . Jacob's eyes saw nothing less*: a reference to the story of Joseph and his brothers' plot against him that had distressed his loving father Jacob.

3936 *The rod was wood in Moses's own eyes . . . a wild snake surprise*: an allusion to the miraculous transformation of Moses's rod into a snake, for which see the note to v. 598.

3938 *Moses's hand . . . it was pure light*: an allusion to the miraculous transformation of Moses's hand mentioned in the Qur'an (20: 22, 28: 132).

3942 *'To you your faith, to me mine'*: Qur'an 109: 6, where it is an emphatic statement of differentiation for believers from unbelievers.

3943 *Ahmad*: Ahmad is an alternative name for the Prophet Mohammad.

3983 *Jinn are from fire, but don't resemble that*: the Jinn (see the Glossary) are said to have been made from fire, according to the Qur'an (55: 15).

3997 Heading   *'Whoever does evil, it falls back on him'*: Qur'an 41: 46.

3997 Heading   *'Your Lord is watching'*: Qur'an 89: 14.

4010 *"If you repeat, we will repeat it too"*: Qur'an 17: 8, where it refers to repeating sins and repeating the punishment for them.

4012 *"Lord, we've transgressed!"*: Qur'an 7: 23. See note to v. 1972.

4027 Heading   *'we allotted'*: Qur'an 43: 32, where it refers to the allotting of livelihood and rank in this world as coming from God.

4061 *Like Joseph at the bottom of the well . . . none could tell*: a reference to the prophetic dream in the Qur'anic story about Joseph, which the twelfth Surah of the Qur'an is almost entirely taken up with.

4104 *'Don't punish us if we forget!'*: Qur'an 2: 286, where it represents a prayer from believers to God.

4123 Heading   *'There's no harm for us. We are heading to our Lord'*: Qur'an 26: 50. See note to v. 3341.

4123 *'There's no harm'*: Qur'an 26: 50. See note to v. 3341.

4126 *"Would that my people knew!"*: Qur'an 36: 26. See note to v. 1742.

4131 *"I am lord"*: Qur'an 76: 24, where Pharaoh is said to have claimed this title.

4137 *Boraq*: This is the name of the Prophet Muhammad's fabulous winged steed for his night journey from Mecca to Jerusalem.

4147 *Razi . . . expertise*: This refers to Fakhr al-Din Razi (d. 1210), a polymath known especially for his intellectual prowess in rationalist philosophy and scholastic theology.

4150 *In incarnation and commingling's pit*: Incarnation and commingling here are translations for the technical terms *holul* and *ettehad* in Arabic and Persian. They represent the entry of God into a human being and union with God through a kind of fusion rather than self-annihilation and have been considered erroneous by most Sufi theoreticians. Hallaj (see Glossary) was accuses of incarnationism.

4154 *the order 'Be!'*: see note to v. 3200 above.

4176–7 *'I made them so that through Me . . . Not that I profit from them'*: part of a Sacred Tradition from the Prophet Mohammad in which God is the speaker.

4184 *'To Him we're returning'*: Qur'an 2: 156, where it represents what the patient devotees of God say in the face of calamity. It has become the most popular verse of the Qur'an to use in relation to death.

4185 *'Come!'*: see note to v. 1672.

4197 *"We're those lined up"*: Qur'an 37: 165, where the Angels say they are lined up for the ritual prayer.

GLOSSARY

Alast the Qur'anic 'Covenant of Alast' (7: 172) is when mankind testified that God is the Lord by saying 'Yes!' in response to His question 'Am I not (*alasto*) your Lord?' This is understood to have taken place when mankind was pure spirit in the presence of God, before entering the world.

Ali Ali ebn Abi Taleb, cousin and son-in-law of Prophet. He is presented in Sufi literature as the first Sufi Friend of God, on account of being the disciple of the Prophet Mohammad. In Sunni Islam he is revered as the fourth Rightly-guided Caliph, while in Shi'i Islam he is the first Imam, or religious and political successor of the Prophet.

Ayaz identified as a Malik Ayaz in popular tradition, he appears in Persian literature as the exemplary slave, who rises to the rank of a noble under his master, Shah Mahmud of Ghazni (see **Mahmud**), because of his total and uncompromising dedication.

Azrael the Angel of Death, who appears in many stories to signal to individuals the imminence of their death. This is represented memorably in one of the shorter stories in Book One of *The Masnavi* (see Bk 1, vv. 960–74).

Bayazid Abu Yazid al-Bastami (d. 874), an eminent Sufi from what is now north central Iran. He is a highly popular figure in Persian Sufi literature, in particular because of the many bold and controversial statements he is reported to have made, such as 'Glory be to me! How magnificent my rank is.'

Bukhara city in Central Asia near Rumi's birthplace, which was a major cultural capital during Rumi's lifetime.

Esrafil the angel who, according to Muslim eschatology, signals Judgement Day at the end of time with a blast of a trumpet.

Galen Greek physician and authority on medicine of the 2nd century CE, whose works came to symbolize Greek medicine and ethics in the medieval Middle East.

Hallaj Mansur ebn Hosayn al-Hallaj (d. 922), a controversial Arabic-speaking Sufi of Persian origin whose death on the gallows is believed to have been a major turning point in the history of Sufism. He is famous for his alleged utterance 'I am the Truth', the most notorious of the theopathic utterances made by Sufis. Rumi's predecessor Faridoddin Attar, in whose eyes Hallaj was the most important Sufi of the past, writes that this utterance was the reason for his execution, but this is not supported by the sources stemming from the time of the events (see further 'Hallaj' in *Encyclopaedia Iranica*). Rumi on a number of occasions justifies Hallaj's utterance, arguing that it expresses greater humility than saying 'I am the slave of God', as one's own existence is not even acknowledged (the 'I' in 'I am the Truth' is God).

Harut and Marut a pair of fallen angels referred to in the Qur'an (2: 102). According to the exegetical tradition, they looked down on Man for his sinful nature, but when put to the test on earth themselves, they became prone to lust and tried to seduce a beautiful woman; that woman became Venus, while Harut and Marut were imprisoned in a well in Babylon forever as punishment.

Homa a mythical bird comparable with the phoenix, but particularly associated with soaring at the highest levels of the heavens and bestowing kingship.

Houri Houris are the beautiful female companions of righteous men in paradise.

Jinn supernatural creatures living in a parallel universe to humans and sometimes interacting, according to pre-Islamic Arabian tradition and also in later Islamic tradition.

Joseph the handsome son of Jacob in scriptural traditions, including the Qur'an, where the entirety of the 12th Surah is dedicated to his biography. See also **Zolaikha**.

Kawsar the heavenly fount of divine grace mentioned in Qur'an 108: 1.

Laili the object of **Majnun**'s excessive love. Laili (or Laila) and Majnun are the archetypal pair of lovers in the Arabo-Persian literary tradition.

Mahmud Shah Mahmud of Ghazni (d. 1030), the master of the legendary slave **Ayaz**.

Majnun (lit. the madman), the name given to Qays, the lover of Laili after he fell madly in love with her.

Michael the Archangel Michael mentioned in Qur'an 2: 98, who is attributed with providing sustenance to Mankind.

Mount Qaf see **Qaf**.

Omar Omar ebn al-Khattaab, the second successor of the Prophet as caliph, and one of the four Rightly-guided Caliphs. Although his career as caliph was highly successful militarily, he is none the less portrayed as a pious ruler who lived simply and ruled compassionately, even introducing a moratorium on the corporal punishment for theft during a famine.

Qaf in medieval Islamic cosmology, Qaf represents a range of mountains that surround the world and mark the border with the spiritual realm.

The Resurrection this refers to the end of time when the dead are resurrected and the truth is revealed. Rumi uses this Qur'anic image frequently to represent the experience of mystical enlightenment, through which reality can be witnessed in this life.

Rostam the heroic Persian king whose feats are recounted in the *Shahnama* (Book of Kings), the Persian national epic by Ferdowsi.

Saqi the cup-bearer. In Sufi poetry the Saqi can also represent the Sufi master or God.

Seven Sleepers in the Cave and their dog seven companions who, together with their dog, are described in the Qur'an (18: 9–26) as hiding in a cave during the reign of the tyrant Decius, and praying to God for protection. They slept there for some 309 years before waking up and returning to the outside world, though it seemed to them like a single night. Their experience is referred to in the Qur'an as a demonstration to sceptics of God's power both to protect his faithful servants and to resurrect men on Judgement Day. In the earlier Christian version of this Qur'anic story, they are known as the Seven Sleepers of Ephesus.

The Tablet in Muslim theology, the Preserved Tablet is where all knowledge is recorded and the source of all revelation, of which the Qur'an is one part.

Water of Life the Water of Life is a miraculous stream or fountain which grants eternal life. It is found usually in darkness and with the help of Khezr.

Zekr (lit. remembrance), the remembrance of God by means of the repetition of His names or short religious formulae about Him. This repetition, which is the heart of Sufi practice in all its diverse schools, can be performed silently, under one's breath, or loudly in an assembly. Sufis are instructed to give total and uncompromising attention to God during *zekr*, losing awareness even of themselves performing the repetition.

Zolaikha the wife of Joseph's owner Aziz (or Potiphar in the biblical tradition) when he was sold as a slave. Her intense love for Joseph, which leads her to try to seduce him (Qur'an 12: 21–35) is celebrated in Sufi literature.